Losing Kate

Kylie Kaden was raised in Queensland and spent holidays camping with her parents and two brothers at the Sunshine Coast, where much of *Losing Kate* is set. She now lives in Brisbane with her husband and three young sons. *Losing Kate* is her first novel.

Find out more at www.kyliekaden.com.au

Losing Kate

KYLIE KADEN

BANTAM
SYDNEY AUCKLAND TORONTO NEW YORK LONDON

This is a work of fiction. Names, characters, places and incidents either are the product of the author's imagination or are used fictitiously. Any resemblance to actual persons, living or dead, events, or locales is entirely coincidental.

A Bantam book
Published by Random House Australia Pty Ltd
Level 3, 100 Pacific Highway, North Sydney NSW 2060
www.randomhouse.com.au

First published by Bantam in 2013

Copyright © Kylie Kaden 2013

The moral right of the author has been asserted.

All rights reserved. No part of this book may be reproduced or transmitted by any person or entity, including internet search engines or retailers, in any form or by any means, electronic or mechanical, including photocopying (except under the statutory exceptions provisions of the Australian *Copyright Act 1968*), recording, scanning or by any information storage and retrieval system without the prior written permission of Random House Australia.

Addresses for companies within the Random House Group can be found at www.randomhouse.com.au/offices

National Library of Australia
Cataloguing-in-Publication entry

Kaden, Kylie, author.
Losing Kate/Kylie Kaden.

ISBN 978 0 85798 340 4 (paperback)

A823.4

Cover design by Blacksheep Design
Cover image © Elisabeth Ansley/Trevillion Images
Internal design by Midland Typesetters, Australia
Typeset in Bembo, 12.5/17 pt and FG Petra by Midland Typesetters, Australia
Printed in Australia by Griffin Press, an accredited ISO AS/NZS 14001:2004 Environmental Management System printer

Random House Australia uses papers that are natural, renewable and recyclable products and made from wood grown in sustainable forests. The logging and manufacturing processes are expected to conform to the environmental regulations of the country of origin.

To Mum, for believing I could.

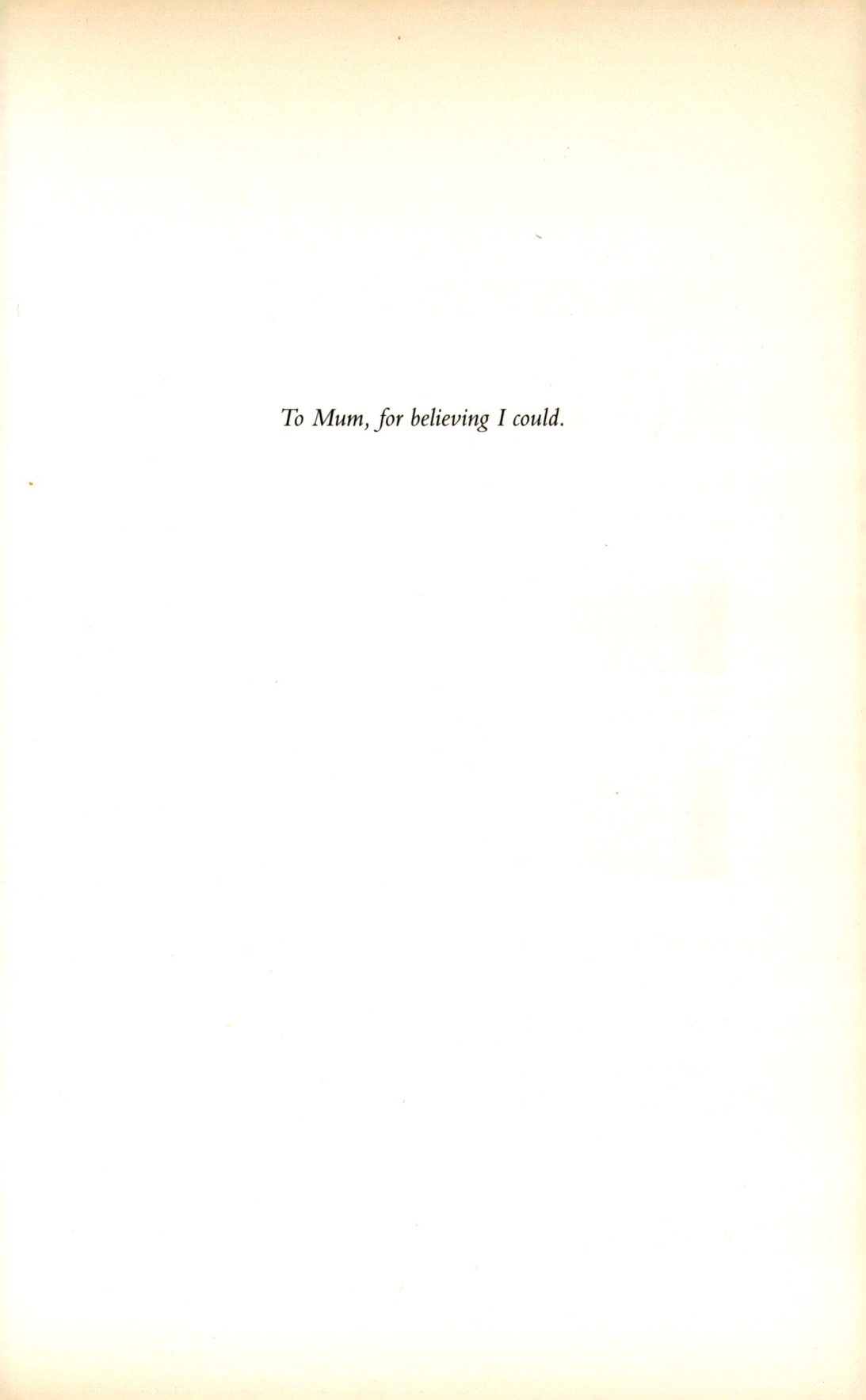

Author's Note

实 is the Kanji symbol for truth.

CHAPTER 1
You. Again.

His neck gives him away. I've seen enough of that neck over the years. I've stared at it from the bench seat in the car, from the row behind his in Double Biology. It is thick and strong, with twin dark freckles to one side. Now here it is again, in my back yard. I know it by the pattern of hair where it kinks on his nape. I know it by the twist in my gut. I've developed tunnel vision as I monitor his position in the crowd, throat tight with the chance he'll turn and look my way. I just want this all to end, but I'm trapped.

Jack is back.

It's auction day. Prospective buyers huddle under the old gum tree like sheep. The serious few have plastic paddles and nervous eyes and I wonder which of them might become my new neighbour. The street buzzes with cars and signage. My neighbour Meg says I should embrace the spectacle; she's brought popcorn from her place, her sticky brood of boys in tow. So I've pulled chairs out to my back landing. I dare say

I'd even started to enjoy the shenanigans unfolding on the block behind mine, until I saw Jack's neck.

When I first bought this place, something about the easement — that stretch of ant-nest-ridden nutgrass leading to the vacant lot out back — irked me. I'd often sit out here at wine-o'clock, my eyes reaching across the grassy expanse, and wonder who'd take it on. A developer with a design for a brick box? A crazy Moroccan lady who'd teach me how to chew tobacco and paint? The blankness of it niggled. But that's all about to change. The auctioneer, sweating in his suit, delivers his obligatory spiel on the special conditions of auctions, warning the sale is unconditional. He asks for opening bids. 'Make no mistake, ladies and gentlemen, this land will be sold today!' The crowd falls silent as the bidding commences.

Two ladies offer bids in big chunks, and I almost forget about Jack's neck. As the auction continues, I can't help but watch the way he moves, how he holds himself. I think about abandoning my cover, escaping inside my cottage, but fear cripples me and I stay slumped safely behind my verandah post. I grow small beneath its shield. My throat tightens. Then he turns and I can see his profile, his chiselled cheeks.

Jack breaks from the scrum of serious punters, chasing an absconding child. He crouches in front of a boy in a baseball cap, who is busy pushing a ball through the fence to Meg's dog. I reel inside, as I see the man he's become. He is broader now. His calves are tanned and taut, fading into khaki cargoes that tug tight across his arse. Dark wavy hair, longish and scruffy, cradles sunglasses nesting on his head. He has not frozen in time; just stopped existing to me.

Meg nudges me, pausing in her quest to shovel orange goop into her toddler's face. 'Hottie at three o'clock. I'm rooting for him. Can't have my best friend celibate for life,' she whispers.

'You breeders can't help yourselves,' I say. Meg is always trying to recruit me into the couple club – which has close ties to the smug-mum club. 'Besides, he's not even bidding.' I give no indication that I know him. He'll be gone in a bit, and I can leave that story untold. With that hope in my mind, I glance his way. That's when our eyes collide.

He double-takes. 'Frankie?' I see him mouth across the crowd.

My cover's blown. I hear each beat of my heart pulsing through my ears. I climb out of the deckchair. This is madness. He left town. But it *is* him. Meg raises her eyebrows as he approaches and I hear her say, 'You *know* him?'

'Jack?' I reply in mock surprise, holding my hand up to cut the jagged sun. 'You're back in Brisbane?' I walk out to the adjoining fence, just as I hear the auctioneer bellowing.

Jack nods. 'Figured it was time.' His eyes scan my face. I'm guessing it's more weathered than the last time he saw it. He looks over to my back landing where Meg is telling off her kids who are scurrying around throwing popcorn at my dog.

'What? This your place?' he asks, eyes wide.

'Yep – bought it a few months back.' Unfortunately it looks much the same as it did then. But I love every rustic inch of it. 'I've just had it re-stumped and levelled, so it's looking a bit worse for wear – a few cracks to bog yet.'

He winces. '*You* live *here*?'

I feel compelled to defend it as if it's a scruffy child. 'It's no palace but it's not that bad.'

He shakes his head and tries half a smile. 'No, it's not that, it's . . .' After a moment, his face brightens and seems to relax. 'It's just weird, you being here.'

No shit, Sherlock. I could say the same thing. I didn't escape like you.

Meg's son bounces behind us doing a cheeky-monkey impression – loudly. The auctioneer scowls in his direction, and Meg attempts to gag him.

'And they're all yours?' Jack asks, gesturing to Meg's brood.

'No, no, they're from next door. It's just me here. Me and Bear, the mutt.' I realise Meg and I probably look like a nice little lesbian couple.

Jack huffs, nodding his head. Then he just seems to gaze at me, eyes narrowing in disbelief. It rattles me. The two of us – colliding in a sea of faces.

'Look at you, Francesca Hudson, all grown up.' His eyes linger and heat flushes my cheeks. I guess I'm supposed to be an adult. I'm pushing thirty. My chestnut plait is shot with natural highlights, but I feel no different on the inside. I feel just as I did at twelve, listening to Jack's mixed tapes on my battered old Walkman as I rode behind him. I can still hear the chink of spokey-dokeys bleeding through the beat.

'Hope I'm not distracting you from bidding,' I laugh.

He scratches his head. 'Er, not me, no.'

I relax a notch. 'Phew, now *that* would be freaky,' I scoff, and a snort-laugh escapes. I lean in close. 'Besides, the block is a swamp every time it rains . . .'

'Is that right?' A dimple appears on his cheek. Then he's side-tracked again, looking around the crowd, at the little boy now on hands and knees with his ball at the fence, and it gives me a chance to suss him out. His clothes are different – brand names, ironed. His hair is longer, with an actual style. He's better groomed now, not a trace of the greasy forehead and nineties' chambray shirts, but he is still the Jack I knew. I'm reminded of the grungy beat of 'Smells Like Teen Spirit', and with it the memory of late nights lazing on his dusty basement floor, chasing thoughts around our minds, making plans to change the world. Us against them all.

His attention returns. 'So, how have you *been*?' He swallows hard, fidgets needlessly with his shirt collar.

What do I say after thirteen years, after everything that took him away?

The megaphone blares. 'Going. Going. Gone! Sold! To the lady in black!' The crowd claps half-heartedly, and breaks away. A blonde in a linen shirt and black leggings approaches the sales desk. The winning bidder is immaculately groomed, coordinated, fit – my polar opposite. I look at the chocolate stains on my tracky dacks. I'm not sure we're going to have much in common, Gym-Barbie and me, but the place is sold at least, and there's no crazy Moroccan lady in sight. I'm a tad disappointed.

Meg waves to get my attention, gestures with her thumb that she's heading home, and gathers up her gang. She reminds me of a mother chimp at Taronga Zoo, monkeys climbing off every limb.

'Are you here gauging the market then?' I ask Jack, returning my attention to my *Class of 2000* reunion for two.

His lips tighten, his grey eyes thin. 'Not exactly . . .'

Behind his shoulder, I see the winning bidder hovering near the officials, staring out at the crowd.

Jack turns to scan the crowd too.

That's when the lady in black smiles and waves. *At Jack.*

My jaw drops.

He *knows* her?

And that's when the baseball-cap-wearing boy spots him, and races over.

'Daddy!' his little knee-high voice chirps. 'I found doggee. He *lickded* me.'

Daddy?

'There you are!' Gym-Barbie arrives with gritted teeth, part perturbed, part relieved. Her arms fold over Jack and he returns her hug. 'I was looking for you.'

'I was keeping Oli out of your way.'

I want to run, but I am stuck – like a fly – in their magic moment.

'It's great, Sara,' Jack says to her. 'We got it!'

'I can't believe it!' Her face is flushed. All the restrained emotion of the bidding spills over. 'And for less than we thought!'

About now, she notices my awkward existence, behind the chain-wire fence that separates our two properties. She composes herself, gives me the once-over as I stand next to my crooked cottage. 'I see Jack's already got friendly with the neighbours. He doesn't waste much time.'

I look at Jack, but his eyes skip away like he'd rather look at anything but me. *Why won't he introduce me?*

It unnerves me – he just stands there, saying nothing. *What's his problem?* Any chance he's had to say 'Sara meet Frankie. Frankie meet Sara' is lost. It marches out with the crowd.

Sara's eyes ping-pong between us and she loops a toned arm around Jack's waist. Blonde she might be, but she isn't stupid. She probably thinks all this unspoken tension comes down to some heated one-night fling. *If only it were that simple.*

'Er, I'm Frankie,' I mutter, extending my hand before things get any worse. 'And yes, I live at 83A. In the shack.' She takes my hand, as I remember to breathe. Her skin feels soft in mine, and I'm suddenly aware of the crusted paint under my nails, the splatters on my clothes – a sample of every Bunnings' paint colour on my weatherboard walls is on me somewhere.

'Well, looks like we'll be neighbours then. I'm Sara. Nice to meet you.' Her face doesn't match her words, as she stands wedged between Jack and me. I get the feeling she's wishing auctions had a cooling-off period. All I can think is: *what the hell just happened?* Sara keeps talking, her excitement returning.

'We've already picked the house to be moved here once it settles.' She chats on. And on. About plans. About relocations. About their last subdivision and how much money they made.

'So, you're a builder, Jack?' I ask when I can finally get a word in, still bamboozled, still piecing it all together, wondering why she can't know we know each other.

'Nah. Renovating is just a weekend thing,' he says. 'I manage a restaurant – Duck Duck Pig on the river? Might have heard of it?'

I nod, try to hide my ignorance. My cuisine usually comes from cardboard boxes or the local Thai takeaway, but he doesn't need to know that. 'I work on the south side, so I'm not really in the know about that kinda thing.'

'Where do you work?' Jack asks and his brow wrinkles with the question.

'I'm a case worker at the hospital.'

He gives me the all-too-familiar pity nod. *Yes, Jack, I am a do-gooder. Cue the violins.* My mind reaches back to the last conversation we had about our futures. On a beach half a lifetime ago. On the day we would never forget.

'Sara works in health – well, kind of,' Jack says, adjusting his sunglasses. 'She's a pharmaceutical rep.'

Does that make her a drug dealer? Maybe she can stick me with some extra-strength Zantac samples to get me through this circus.

'Not exactly the same thing, hon,' she laughs, touching his shoulder. She's taking every opportunity to drape some part of herself over him. 'So how long have you lived here, Frankie?'

'Six months or so.' I survey my worker's cottage – the flaky paint, the rusty roof – and turn back to her. 'Don't worry, it's a work in progress – hence the paint.' I touch my face and feel dried flakes of 'Winter White'. Between the paint and the chocolate stains, I can just imagine her impression of me – that I'm as poorly maintained as my house. Sara's gaze flits away.

'Oh, they're ready for me over there. I better go sign my life away!' She gestures to Jack. 'Are you coming?'

Jack tries to pull the boy away from my dog. 'Yep, just a sec,' he calls to Sara, whose face has turned to cement.

She crosses her arms.

'I'll bring Oli over in a minute. You go. Let him play for a sec,' Jack continues when she looks unconvinced. 'He'll just be in your way.'

That seems to satisfy her, and she trails off.

Jack hesitates and looks at the lawn, as if the answer to

our predicament is written in the blades of grass. 'How's this gonna work, Fray?' He still hits things head on, and it still unnerves me. I prefer to hide in shadows. I like my shadows.

How *is* this going to work? *Guess I can always move, sell up . . .*

'It's weird, Jack.'

He nods, his gaze lingers, and I know he knows what I mean. 'It should only be six months tops. We'll bring in the new house, do it up, then sell it off. Hopefully for a profit.'

So that's the length of my sentence. He is in my life again, till Christmas at least, whether I like it or not. I think of the reason he left my life with no goodbye. I remember the media circus, the cops. It was half a lifetime ago, but every small detail of that harrowing night at the beach is etched in my mind.

What he did.

What *we* did.

And now my accomplice is living in my backyard.

CHAPTER 2
The Beginning of the End

Cooloola National Park, South East Queensland
11 pm, 18 November 2000

As the headlights approach, I slow my rapid breaths and think it through. A deserted beach. A missing girl. A fed-up boyfriend. If she doesn't turn up soon, Jack is in deep shit.

'It's the ranger!' Dan calls, pointing to the beach, pulling me back to reality. The boys spring to action, race to the sandy flat, two sweeps of light beaming on their pale faces. Jack stands to join them – I pull his sleeve to stop him in his tracks.

'Jack, we have to get our story straight!'

He lurches back. 'Our story straight? There's no story, Fray. I told you. I didn't hurt anyone.' Jack rakes his fingers through matted hair. 'We just gotta tell the truth.' The crazy fool has no inkling of self-preservation. He's a boy again to me, staring down from the steepest jump at the skate park, fearless.

'The truth?' my voice shrills. I push him. He stumbles back; his heels dig craters in the sand. I pace towards him but he retreats with each step. 'What, that you wanted her gone, and now she is? Are you nuts? Can't you see how this'll look? You were the last one with her.' I poke his chest. 'You argued, came back white as a sheet, soaking wet and . . .' As if on cue, a dark trickle of blood meanders down his neck, pooling in a fold of skin. 'Jack, you're bleeding.' I can see white scratches on either side of the cut. Fingernail marks.

Jack's hand pats his neck, and hits thick wet blood. His face pales, as he seems to retrace the night's events in his mind. My guts clench. It has just sunk in for him, what this all could mean.

Fear threads the air between us.

I cross my arms. 'You know, no one knows all the facts except you and me.'

Panic rises in his face, boils over like an unwatched pot. He shakes his head and those slate-grey eyes bore into mine. 'What are you saying? I know what you're thinking and I won't let you lie for me. I did nothing wrong.' Jack chops the air with the heel of his hand but his steely words don't match his face, which is sinking like a sand-castle in the summer rain.

The ranger's car draws near; the guys wave him down. My heart races. I expect Jack to relapse into his ball of fear, but he is calm. Resigned.

'No lies. Tell them the truth, Frankie. I'll be fine.' His eyes are steadfast, determined. 'I didn't touch her. I feel shitty about what I did, but she knew it had to happen. She knew. It's no crime.'

I hear the roar of an engine over the pounding waves, and a white 4WD slows to a crawl then roars up the dune. My heart is heavy with some implied responsibility in all of this. Did he do this for me? We've skirted the idea for months but never spoken it in words. I suddenly have no time for Jack's problems. I can't think. There is no space in my head for him.

A balding man in cotton khakis leans out the window of a white ute. The four of us compete for air space, flooding the ranger with desperate rants, snippets of events of the night. The ranger holds up his palms as if under arrest. 'Whoa, whoa. Slow down, kids. I'm just on my way back from a call-out – I thought you just had a flat battery. Are you okay?' He gets out, wrenching his pants up by the belt. 'What's this about someone missing?'

Jack stands mute. I take the lead and say, 'It's Kate . . . Kate Shepherd. She's seventeen. She's been gone all night. She went for a walk, and we found this . . .' I gingerly pass him a crumpled pink t-shirt. 'It was up in the dune about half-an-hour's walk from camp.'

Nausea surges through me, fragments of the scene slideshow in my head – finding her shirt in the sand, a twisted rope in a frenzy of footprints. That shirt is the only trace left of her, the girl who never sat unnoticed. But she upped and vanished.

At first, the ranger doesn't share our concerns. He calms our thoughts, asks for Kate's details, assures us he'll go back to base and make some enquiries, check if the barge operator has seen her. He asks if any of us has a photo of Kate, a student ID from her purse perhaps.

Jack opens his wallet. 'It's about three months old . . .' His hand trembles as he passes a photo to the ranger.

I know the picture well. I remember every minute of the day it was taken. We were all in it. Me. Jack. Kate. His harem photo, he used to call it. It was taken in a two-buck photo-booth after seeing American Beauty. We were all making faces, poking our tongues out. Crazy happy. And now, three months later, a National Park ranger is using it to spark a missing-person's search.

He tells us to stay put. Keep calm. Try to sleep. The most likely scenario is she will turn up by morning.

I want to believe him. But seeing the yellow beams of light from his truck shrink small on the beach makes me feel as if all hope has left with him. He's taken the shirt. The photo. He has taken every last piece of her.

CHAPTER 3
House on wheels

Two muscle-clad lads, wearing support belts like suicide vests, lower the ramp of the removal truck. They busily unfasten the padded belts that are securing furniture like kids to a car seat. Jack and Gym-Barbie's post-war home had arrived on a crane in two halves, weeks earlier, and now sits like a stilted giant, shadowing my cottage. The two pieces are now patched up, the old and the new seamlessly intertwined to show a united front. I watched it take shape, still in disbelief that Jack is back. To look at it, no one would suspect that the house had been ripped apart and craftily mended to appear whole again. A lot like me, come to think of it. My own private wilderness in the burbs is gone.

Jack's ancient-looking orange Subaru follows the removal van. I plan to give them space but Bear has other ideas. He runs out to bark at the invasion of new sights and smells. I have to tie him up so he doesn't get squashed by the removalists and so I sneak out the back door, calling him.

'Bear, I've got a bone . . .'

Everyone but my dog turns to look at me. *Fantastic.*

'Morning, sorry about the dog,' I say to no one in particular.

Sara, wearing pink tights, a white Lycra shirt and matching runners, pauses from her unpacking. *Wait, is she wearing mascara? On moving day?* No wonder I'm still single. I have to lift my game. She raises her toned arm in friendly acknowledgement. I grab Bear by the scruff and pull him back to my side of the block. I throw him up the two back stairs, shut the door. He scratches and whimpers inside as Sara approaches.

'Hi, Frankie. We met a month or so back, at the auction,' Sara points out, as if it slipped my mind. It was Jack who has amnesia, not me. I'd seen her buzzing around a couple of times, and pretended I was out so she'd stay clear. Being buddies with Jack's wife is the last thing I need.

'So, here you are, house and all.' *Like a snail.* When she raises her eyebrows, I realise that didn't sound suitably enthusiastic. I'm hopeless at hiding emotions. One reason I suck at poker.

Sara surveys the finished product, commenting that the plans for the position of the house hadn't revealed how close we'd be in reality. She apologises for the noise, mess, disruption in general. I assure her it has been fine, yet the truth is, I'm totally over the tradies who had worked the house back to health. Loud crap singing at six am? Not my favourite. Especially after late shifts at work, when my head hums for a couple more hours – the patients' problems of the day pinging in my brain.

'So, Jack tells me you've met before,' Sara says, half her attention on directing the removalist. 'That he went to school with your *brother*, was it?'

So he *has* come clean, sort of. Not how I would have described our relationship, but true all the same. I'd known him since I was three (except for that thirteen-year gap).

'Well, and with me,' I clarify.

Her face turns, now ill at ease. I have her full attention.

'I see; well, Jack failed to mention that part.' Her nose is hooked high and I can see creases of foundation caked around her nostrils. Again, I'm pissed off. Surely I've earned a mention in the synopsis of Jack's life? What picture had he painted of us? Not an accurate one, it seems.

Jack appears from nowhere and my head is overwhelmed with thoughts of what to say, of how to be. I expected him this time, yet it still feels like the auction day freak-out all over again.

He makes polite greetings, reiterating Sara's regret over the tradies' presence in my world since the house arrived. When he pauses for breath, Sara seizes the moment. 'So you two went to school together, hey?'

'I told you that,' Jack says, eyes to the ground like he's counting ants.

'You said you thought her *brother* might have gone to your school,' Sara barks through her nose. Now I can't stop looking at her nostrils. They flare like a bull.

Jack shrugs, tight-lipped. It's as if I were a passing stranger he rubbed shoulders with once in the school hall. I glance at him for an explanation but his eyes slide sideways.

'Jack, were you gonna ask about – you know . . .?' Sara whispers, elbowing Jack in the side.

'Not now, Sare, we just got here.'

He rolls his eyes when he realises I've heard. 'It's nothing urgent,' he says to me, glaring at her. 'Sara just wanted to have a chat about the fence — perhaps we might look at increasing the height, get some 180s across here.' Jack gestures to the existing fence. 'This chain-wire doesn't provide much in the way of privacy.'

'This is true . . .' I say, but I wasn't sure a bigger fence would help, with their house towering over mine.

'It shouldn't cost much. Splitting it should only be, what, a grand?' Sara adds. Well, they have directness in common, these two. No beating round the bush. I like beating round the bush.

Jack looks at Sara with narrow eyes. 'I can put it up. We can pay for the palings, Sara. Fray has already forked out for her share of this one.'

Sara gives her headmistress sneer. 'I guess *Fray* can work that out with you then, can't she? Just like you said you'd deal with the mango tree issue . . .'

'Mango tree?' I interrupt.

'Oh, well, we weren't going to mention it,' she tucks blonde strands behind her ear, points her toe and folds her arms, 'but we did incur additional expenses with machinery hire, keeping that tree of yours alive.'

'Sorry?' I cross my arms. I have no idea what she's on about. 'Is there a problem with the mango tree?'

'No, no, it's all been taken care of,' Sara says. She stomps off to the truck without so much as a goodbye.

'Don't stress, it's all good.' Jack's eyes wander. He looks just like a kid again, and I know it's a lie. I shake my head.

He watches Sara glance at him over a brown box labelled 'kitchen'.

'Hon, can you grab that one?' she calls to him. 'We've only got a half-day hire.'

Jack steps backwards, to his side of the too-small fence, returning to her fold. Our eyes linger as he retreats, his lips buckle as he gives a quick hand gesture that barely passes as a wave, and he disappears behind the side of the removal truck.

I feel like a broken-heeled stiletto on a sticky dance floor. Abandoned. Misplaced. What else did I expect? Am I now just someone he used to know? Perhaps a bigger fence around their fortress isn't such a bad idea. A moat, even?

Six months. That's my sentence living next to Jack Shaw. I can't say it's kicking off well.

实

The next morning I wake to Bear starting his daily fierce guard against the early morning walkers and their canine companions. Someone rattles at my window. Who? Meg knows we don't walk Mondays. I try to drift back to oblivion. The tapping continues, but then it hits me like a migraine. Jackson Nate Shaw is now my neighbour and that removalist truck arriving yesterday was not a dream. I'd bet anything whoever is doing the tapping is him, and here's me: in an Elmo nightie short enough to cameo as a shirt. Not to mention that my hair usually looks like a cat is sitting on my head first thing.

'Balls to that,' I say to Bear, who barges his way out the pet door.

I'm right, of course. It's Jack.

'Hey,' he says as I poke my head out the gap in the door. His dark hair is more salt-and-pepper than my recollections of yesterday – in that cringe-worthy moment when he made me feel like a passing stranger in his life. Not the girl with whom he'd skipped naked through sprinklers and saved from kissing Ryan Murray. He squints and twists his lip. 'Can I come in?'

'Are you sure that's appropriate?' I survey the front yard to see if Gym-Barbie, Fence-Nazi, Tree-Killer is in earshot and I'm glad to find she's not. 'You know, given I am just some-guy-you-went-to-school-with's sister.' I will not get sucked into being his friend again. It's all too weird.

'Can I just come in . . . explain?' he asks again. Through the crack in the door I can see the boy he once was in those pleading eyes, big and round like a lost puppy. The look of him, *old*, still unnerves me. He has grown into his cheekbones, lost the gangliness of adolescence, and there's an earthy masculinity about him now. I grab my towelling dressing gown and pull it tighter across my chest. I'm in two minds about whether to let him in and it is too friggin' early to feel this rattled. I need to set *boundaries* here.

'I have donuts,' he says.

He knows my weak spot. Donuts convince me. I open the door.

Jack glances at my nightie, gives me the once-over. 'Elmo? *Seriously?*' he says, with raised eyebrows and a smirk.

I shut my gown on Elmo's grin. 'Treating me like some random? *Seriously?*' I retort.

'Hence the donuts. They haven't changed in all this time.' He takes a bite of one he pulls from a paper bag. 'Remember, we'd get them on the way to sport every Tuesday arvie?'

Now he decides to admit he knows a lot more about me than my gene pool and he still hasn't answered the question.

'If you think bringing me donuts means I forgive all, Jack –'

'I will tell Sara, Fray. I've felt like a real prick ever since – not telling her. It's just . . . I was too gutless to say anything at the start, and then you guys were talking and then it seemed too late to backtrack.' He holds the paper bag out to me. The sugar-and-cinnamon smell wafts out and my stomach growls. I haven't had breakfast. Who in their right mind has breakfast at this hour anyway?

I reach in. They're still warm inside the bag. 'I don't get it, Jack. What's the big deal about telling Sara you and I were . . . mates?' But I've hesitated just too long on that word and now there's a huge elephant on my porch.

Jack looks at me. 'She knows I know you from school. I just never told her about what happened with Kate, which means I never told her about you.'

I guess our stories are fairly intertwined. I think about the tumultuous ride he was stuck on back then. The community outrage. The suspicion. And I get it, but he's not getting off the hook that easily. 'It just puts me in a weird predicament,' I say, thinking aloud. 'It will get all blurry, the lines. How well I should know you. What can I say around her? You know I suck at lying.'

'But it's lying by omission. No actual falsehoods need to pass your lips. Way easier, all in all,' he says.

I take a bite of the donut as I think back to the last time we argued about lies. Thirteen years ago. And it was me doing the lying then. Look where that got me.

'Easier for you maybe.'

'Yes. Easier, for me. For you, I bring donuts.'

I take another bite. Somehow the sugar seems to calm my nerves. He must realise I'm not inviting him in, and sits down on the step. I notice my left leg has a hairy strip down one side that I missed in the shower, and I tug my robe over it.

'So what made you pick this place? You still got a thing for lost causes?' Jack asks, surveying my dilapidated front verandah. He gets up and sticks a finger in the rust hole in the roof, as if to make a point.

'You were the one who always brought home the stray dogs, as I recall, not me.'

'You saying my girlfriends were ugly?' he laughs. 'Crazy maybe, but none of 'em were dogs.' My breath catches. *Crazy.*

He realises what he has said and shakes his head, as if it'll erase the comment like an Etch A Sketch. 'Got your work cut out for you with this one,' he says as he picks a flake of paint off a greying weatherboard and kicks a rotten section with his shoe.

'Careful!' I yell, like he's smacked my child.

'Frankie, you gotta replace this whole side – it's stuffed.'

I roll my eyes. 'It's on the list.' The corrugated roof has rivers of red bleeding in ruts, and some of the window frames are covered with plastic. It isn't a short list, so that wall has to last a few months yet.

He relaxes beside me on the step once more. 'Look for long, before getting this one?'

I laugh. I remember the day I stumbled upon it. I'd run out of petrol and saw the 'For Sale' sign, crooked on a star picket. It was love at first sight. 'Nah. I went out for coffee, and came home with a contract of sale.'

'What, you just bought it on the spot?'

I shrug. 'Units weren't an option 'cause of the dog factor. The ceilings were high, the floorboards original and I liked the VJs, the quiet street. I looked online at the few others I could afford – there wasn't much in my budget – and decided the same day to make an offer.'

I fail to mention that it was just after ending things with Seamus. Just after the skank incident. That I was living out of my car. That my life had faded to grey and the idea of having something to do for all foreseeable Saturdays saved me. But I decide to bury that sorry-arsed tale, considering I'm supposed to be in *keep my distance* mode.

His eyebrows arch. 'Huh. I seem to recall you taking six months to decide on uni courses.'

'Yeah, and look how great that decision turned out. Anyway, enough about me.' I brush cinnamon off my fingers. 'So how the hell did you end up living next to me, Jack Shaw?' I can do direct too, under the right conditions.

He laughs. 'It's mad, ain't it? I mean, what are the chances? Landing back next to Lofty after all these years.'

Lofty. Now that takes me back. 'You stopped calling me Lofty when you shot up in grade eight.' He gives me a wry smile and I feel a somersault inside. We settle into an old, familiar dance. I feel my promise to keep my distance slip away as he unlocks memories I thought I'd cordoned off for good.

'I guess it's not crazy to return to where you grew up. Not too many vacant blocks around these old parts too, I suppose. Only a couple I know of, so not that weird,' I say.

There is a pause for thought. 'Nah. Still weird,' he admits, screwing up his nose.

'So, Jack, Sara knows nothing about why you left?' I ask delicately.

His face turns rigid, his eyes downcast as he shakes his head. It disturbs me that Sara is in the dark about all this, but I guess it's understandable. He moved away from Brisbane, so 'us', or more importantly, all the *periphery* that came with us, ceased to exist. Just as his parents had hoped.

'Tea?' I say. When words fail me, I offer hot beverages.

'Thanks, may never find mine at home. Wall-to-wall boxes.'

I retreat to the kitchen, hoping he'll stay outside but he follows me like a shadow. My beige bra is drying on the shower rail in full view, and I don't need the heat in my cheeks to know I'm red-faced.

'Won't your wife think it's strange, you being in here? She's already suss.'

'She's on her morning run. I've got about twenty minutes.'

'She's running?' I shake my head at him. 'While you eat trans-fats?'

He answers by taking another bite. 'And she's not my wife,' he mumbles through the stodge. His eating habits have not improved even though his body has.

Not his wife? Somehow I'm not surprised. No matter which way I look at it, I can't picture Jack married to Gym-Barbie. 'Oh. Sorry. I assumed.'

'Yeah, well. I bought her a rock about two years ago. After Oli was born. Thought – if she can manage to not shit-me-to-tears for an entire week, I'd propose,' Jack says, deep in thought.

I can't help but prompt: 'And . . .?'

He licks sugary heaven from his fingers. 'After a year, I pawned it, bought a new surfboard.' Our eyes meet, and I feel a surge of *deja vu* that rips through me. He still has a way about him. That way of looking at me that makes me feel like the centre of his world.

'So, how have you been, Fray?' he asks, taking me off guard. 'I mean, you seem good. Like you've got it sorted.'

I laugh inside my head. He hasn't seen the pile of clothes

beside my bed, or the floor of my car covered with Subway serviettes, crusts and dried-out jalapenos. Not to mention my half-hairy leg. Nothing about me is sorted.

How have I been? What – this year, this week?

'I'm okay, Jack,' I answer and I mean it. It was always my litmus test, growing up – if I said it to Jack, it must be true. 'I had a rough trot there a few months back, boy trouble, but that's all over now.' Seamus and I were done months ago, but now, after the last few stilted interactions, I'd say we were dusted.

Standing in my kitchen with Jack like this, I feel more exposed than I have in a long time. I always loved and hated that about him. His ability to draw me in, get the real dirt on a situation. I felt out on a limb with him at times, but I always went away with a clearer picture of how things really were. He was my truth serum. 'I started Law after school. It wasn't for me. More about money than truth. I wanted to help in practical terms, so got into social work.'

Jack gives me a sympathetic look. Again.

'I know, not very glamorous. Everyone had me pegged as the next High Court Judge, and I end up at the Queensland-friggin'-Health-Department. They can't run a payroll, let alone a healthcare system.'

He is thoughtful, quiet, staring through my milky-white louvres at his classic timber home behind mine. 'Actually, when you told me that was your thing now, I thought it was a good fit. Frankie, fixing the broken.'

'More like the druggos and binge-drinkers. It's demoralising.'

Jack raises an eyebrow at me. 'It's still strange. Francesca Hudson, all grown up. But in some ways you always were.'

I feel like I'm at a school reunion, my life being evaluated by the person whom I started becoming a person with. We've lapsed into that small talk again, and I relax in a way I've only ever been able to with him. There's so much about the last thirteen years I don't know. Has he missed me? Has he missed Kate? Has he made his peace with what happened on that beach when we were seventeen, desperately trying to be grown up in an adult world?

'Are *you* okay?' I ask.

'As okay as I get,' he says. Bear walks over to Jack, pokes his head in his crotch. Jack takes the hint and pats my dog. He grows quiet. 'I wrote you letters . . .' Jack says in a deep voice.

Letters? Never got any. I stop him short, shaking my head. 'You don't have to explain.' My hand touches his arm before I realise and then I instantly pull it away, tucking a hair behind my ear to camouflage the manoeuvre. 'I know it was hard. Especially for you.'

'I didn't know what you thought of me. What response I'd get,' he says, looking over at the wall, like he's thinking much more than he's saying. 'Then we moved so quick after . . .' He swallows hard.

I want to pinch myself. Am I dreaming? Am I really having this conversation? With Jack? In my Elmo nightie? At seven am? He's talking about stuff I've locked in my memory. In the *Before* files, never opened.

'I thought of you all the time, after. I kept thinking it would have been easier if you hadn't moved,' I admit to this man I don't know. Not any more.

'Same,' Jack says. 'I lost both of you. You and Kate.'

And suddenly I've got what I needed. It's as if his

acknowledgement of what we once had proves I'm not crazy. We've scurried around the edge of the issue but calm drifts through me and the silence is comfortable.

Outside, the world is waking behind my louvres. I see Meg in her dressing gown running after one of her kids in the back yard. Meg's dog barks at magpies caroling from the fence.

It dawns on me.

It is still us — the same Jack, the same me. Just in older shells. And in his case, fancier shorts. Jack fills me in on the years I missed. I find myself half-listening — too distracted by him just being Jack — in my kitchen, in my chaos, Bear's dog bowl at my feet — until he mentions Sara and my ears prick up. He met her three years ago when he was a head chef in Townsville. She was a waitress, studying marketing at the time. Jack's sinewy fingers stroke Bear's golden hair, rub around his ears the way he likes. Back and forth.

'Well, I'll work mostly nights once I get my head around the processes. I gave up the chef thing when Oli was born — crap hours when you have kids, plus my back was ratshit by then. So now I mostly do a management role, menu plans and stuff. Means I can get to pick up Oli when he starts Kindy, spend the afternoon with him before work.'

'Where *is* he?' I remember him from the auction, even though I'd been blind-sided by his dad.

'Oh, you'll *know* when he gets here, don't you worry,' Jack smiles. 'He's on his way back now so should be here this arv — we parked him up in Townsville with my olds, while we got sorted. Poor kid. I barely survived that family — I only want him subjected to it in small doses. You remember my parents?'

'Course.' I was like a boarder at their house until we hit puberty and Dad outlawed sleepovers at Jack's. I remember them fondly; Jack's petite, birdlike mother, his heavy-set dad who smelled like ear-wax and cigarettes. They were like back-up parents.

'Well, the grumbling between them has just festered a little more in their old age.'

I picture Jack's dad chain-smoking in that cracked vinyl recliner. I can hear his mum's monotonous nag echoing from the kitchen, I can smell the garlic she would be frying. But Jack has made his own family now. He has a son.

'Another little Jackson,' I say, shaking my head. 'Thought I'd never see the day.'

'He wasn't exactly in the master plan,' Jack says with a proud grin. 'I mean, we'd even broken up before we found out we were having him. But now I can't imagine life without the little tyke. I should see him more now, with the new job.' His voice changes when he speaks of him. 'You should have dinner at the restaurant one night, when I get on my feet. You and your friend from next door – Meg, was it?'

I realise how much I had yearned for this – the friendship we had lost. The friendship I had sacrificed so much for in order to keep, but lost anyway. Jack brings me back to reality with a thud as he shuffles his feet on my floorboards and says: 'Sara's probably gonna be here in a bit; I should head.'

I nod silently, and just like that the bubble of friendship he's inflated inside me bursts. Jack wanders to the front door, past my fibro walls bowed with water damage, past the casement windows that don't latch shut, still cradling his china cup. He stops, holding the doorframe with his free palm. 'It's good to see you, Lofty.'

I look at my feet, well aware that I've failed at my task to keep my distance. Failed dismally. 'Bring that kid around one day when he gets here. I'd like to meet him properly.'

'Not much chance of avoiding that.' He smiles at me, and I explore his face. The laugh lines are new, but the years have been kind to him. It's so unfair. He's improved while I've started sprouting greys.

In high school, Kate and I used to joke about how we'd grow old together with matching blue-rinse dos and a house full of cats, and I wonder what she'd look like now.

CHAPTER 4
The New Kid

Mitchelton State High, Brisbane
February 2000

'Class – this is Kate Shepherd. She has just transferred to our school from Singleton – I know you will make her feel welcome.'

Instead of the half-hearted claps that usually greet the latest army kid to arrive, there are heckles and wolf whistles from the lads.

I look up to see a girl with flawless skin and elf-like features that seem out-of-place here in this middle-class land of mediocre. Kate Shepherd has a fragility, a demure stance that makes you want to protect her. She curls a stray strand of golden hair from her green eyes, tucking it behind her ear. She sashays down the aisle, staring students on either side, and it is as if she is parting the sea. Mr Mason hushes the hecklers. I catch a fleck of fire in her eyes as she dips her head and gives a subtle smirk in the direction of the back-bench boys.

I want to solve the riddle of this new girl.

Even if fate had not placed an empty Bunsen burner next to mine, I have a sense we would have found each other anyway. It is like a light turns on inside me when she walks in. And for reasons I will never fully understand, she chooses to sit next to me, in all my mousey glory.

It is an unspoken kinship, at the start. But from that first day, Kate's presence sends tremors through my grade. I ignore the glares from Helena and Lanie at lunch that day, when I wag the student-council meeting to show the new kid around. Kate and I are sitting cross-legged in our burgundy-and-blue pinafores when Jack spots us. I'm shovelling ice from my popper in my mouth. He swaggers over, scratches the patchy stubble on his chin and scuffs his shoe on the bitumen. I'm surprised to see him – we usually only hang out after school since Jack started playing tackle with Matt and Dan and the other jocks at lunch.

'Hey,' Jack mumbles as he approaches us, sitting in the shade under C block.

'Hey,' I say. 'Too hot for footy today?'

When he doesn't respond, I look up. His head is directed at me, but his eyes are firmly focused on Kate.

'You were one of the back-bench boys,' Kate says to Jack, inspecting the ends of her ponytail.

He shoots her the two-dimpled smile. 'Yeah. I recommend sitting far away from the front desk – Mr Mason's meatball-breath can stun you for days.'

I start to worry when Kate laughs. He wasn't even funny.

'Shove over,' Jack says. He waves me up the bench like he is swatting a fly, even though there is plenty of room on the end next to me. He sits between us and suddenly, I am out of sight for both of them.

As Jack quizzes Kate on her life story, I rip my half-frozen juice open wider, flicking slushy ice on Jack's grey shorts.

'Jesus, Fray!' He steps back. 'Now it looks like I've pissed my pants.' He flicks the gravelly ice onto the cement.

'Sorry,' I murmur. At least I got their attention, and for a fleeting moment I see Kate's lips stretch into a sweet smile.

'You haven't got your stripes yet,' Jack says.

'Are you speaking metaphorically?' Kate asks.

Jack leans over and runs his finger over the cotton edge of her collar. 'Year twelves are supposed to have two burgundy stripes. It show's you're a senior.'

Kate raises her eyebrows and tugs on his tie. 'Thought that was what this was for.' A look shoots between them like lightning.

I swallow hard and look over at the buzzing insects circling the flower bed.

'Anyway, Frankie was just showing me around, so I'll see ya later . . . back-bench boy,' she says down her nose.

Kate loops the crook of her arm around mine, and leads me off with her head held high and I feel a buzz ripple through me.

At the final bell that day, she gently bumps her bag into mine. 'Come see my place?' she states more than asks in her aloof, yet endearing manner. Like a stray dog, I follow her home.

Her house is hidden down a steep cobbled drive, surrounded by a canopy of lush ferns and rocky crevices, the paint mouldy from never meeting the warmth of the sun.

Kate has her own key and lets us in. The galley kitchen, flanked by ceiling-to-floor windows, looks out to an atrium of rainforest, giving the home a crisp, mossy feel. I catch a glimpse of the lounge on the way through – double-brick veneer, brown leather couches, a wine-rack. There is a stack of vinyls, an art book on the mahogany side table, an ashtray on the mantel. So different to my light and airy home, with yellow kitchen cabinets, full of Women's Weekly cookbooks and Dad's stash of unread papers.

There is no mother waiting with a bun from the bakery. I have her to myself, first dibs, without the cool girls from school getting to know her first. I steal a glance at a silver-framed wedding photo – an older version of Kate, and a man with striking emerald eyes. Like the Mona Lisa, they follow me as I walk the length of the hall.

Kate dumps her knapsack carelessly, grabs some crackers, two drinks, and beckons me to her room. It is just as intriguing as her. The oriental lamp, draped with a scarf, and a print of Klimt's 'The Kiss'. Her audacious, eclectic style makes my pink wall-papered room seem embarrassingly childlike. I can't risk taking her there. Not yet. She flicks on an ancient record player and the sound of The Doors fills the silence in the room. Not the predictable Top 40 pop crap the rest of my group get obsessed with. She immediately leaps up, and stands on her unmade double bed, rips her school tie from her neck and throws it on a pile of lonely clothes. Kate dances like she is entranced by the sounds, engulfed by them, strumming her air guitar. It makes me uneasy – the candour of this girl I hardly know – yet I can't turn away. As she jumps around on her mattress, her long sheet of blonde hair becomes more dishevelled with each beat in a way that makes her look like she's auditioning for a sexy music video. She epitomises hot in a way I think I never would. At that moment, I don't just want to be like Kate. I want to be Kate.

As the music stops, so does she. Like the spell has been lifted, her breathlessness is the only evidence that her solo performance has even occurred. Was it for my benefit? Are these her usual antics to overcome the day's frustration? I can't say. I don't care, as long as I get to be part of it for another moment. She's just so other-worldly that going back to my boring life seems intolerable. It felt like a cool breeze of change blew in when she walked into that dusty lab, and I want to catch it before it blows away again.

Instead of a wardrobe, she has a clothes rack – with dresses of every colour, scarves and belts, matching bags. I notice her jacket strewn on a chair – and can't help but touch it, wanting to smell the leathery scent. She has a whole shelf of belts and hats. I have some similar stuff, but usually chicken out before actually leaving the house with them on. With each page I read into Kate Shepherd, the more I loathe my ordinary life. 'Do you wanna smoke some weed?' Kate says. This is the peer-pressure moment your parents warn you about when you are ten, right here.

'Oookay . . .' I say, surprising myself. She shimmies over to her drawers and rummages through to find a bag of dried green stuff. She expertly rolls a joint. She lights up, inhales, and passes it on. As I take a puff I try hard to give the impression this isn't my first. The resulting gut-wrenching cough soon gives me away, and to my relief she laughs, almost proud to take the role of expert hash-handler. We giggle on her bed, surrounded by twisted sheets and too many pillows for one person. Just then, a car door slams outside.

'Shit!' Kate whispers in an urgent tone. She turns the desk fan on full power, opens a window, in what seems like a well-rehearsed recovery act. 'It's Mum! She'll crack if she smells it!' She pulls me into the hall, swats the smoky air away and closes the door behind her. 'She thinks weed'll make me psycho.'

The elegant woman in the wedding photo walks through the kitchen door, groceries in hand. 'Well, hello, girls,' she says. She sounds as young as she looks. 'Who do we have here, Kate?'

'Mum, this is Francesca.' The lady extends her hand to mine, which I shake with a smile.

'Frankie,' I interject. I hate Francesca. It sounds like somebody's dead grandma.

'We met in frog study,' Kate says.

'Nice to meet you, Frankie – I'm Jess. Glad to see you are making friends so quickly, Katie. How was your first day?'

Kate fills her in on classes, the (apparently) hot PE teacher, the cool art room. We chat briefly about the reason for their move – her husband is a staff sergeant in the army. It is weird, the banter between them – more like a friendship than a mother–daughter thing. But cool. Like her mum knows every inch of her, even the bad bits. I envy this about their relationship. With my parents, I just project the image of myself that I know they want to see. I've become so good at it, in fact, I sometimes wonder who I'd be if I stopped.

Her mum leaves the room and Kate looks at me, as the laughter that has been caged up inside escapes us both. A close call.

Kate runs out the sliding doors leading to the back yard, and I follow her through to the shady cobbled courtyard. She leads me further, to an old rusty trampoline, perched next to the remains of a broken brick barbecue covered in leaves. She climbs up on the shaded tramp – explains how it was left by the previous owners. We lie with our backs airing on the circular mat, gazing up at the palm fronds that filter the sunlight from our eyes. Surrounded by trees, and obscured from the view of the house, it feels like we are floating in space on our own circular life raft. Like nothing can touch us.

Or maybe that's just the pot talking.

As we gaze up at the sky, Kate shares snippets of who she is with me, somehow more at ease now without the required intimacy of eye contact. And I latch on to every morsel with intrigue; how she is a transient, never living somewhere more than two years, how that is her normal. Her dad being away is her standard day. Her mum is her rock. I rack my brains for something intriguing about myself, something I can share, but come up with squat.

'So, Francesca – isn't that, like, an old-fashioned name?' Kate asks.

'You can't talk,' I say. 'It was my grandmother's . . . I guess I usually go with Frankie, or some people call me Fray.' Jack calls me Fray. Just Jack. I suddenly feel like I failed a test with the cool girl.

'So tell me about that jock at lunch? What's his name . . . Jack?'

My breathing stops when she mentions his name. It is like she has burst our bubble, injecting a slice of my straight-laced world into her perfect one.

'He wasn't too shabby. Are you, like, together?' Kate asks.

'Me and Jack?' I ask, the words catching like my throat's barbed with wire. I think back to the way she pulled his tie, how he gave her his two-dimpled smile. 'He's more like a brother – we kinda grew up together.' I turn to my front, start picking the leaves off a stray twig on the tramp. 'He asked me out once but I was too scared it'd wreck stuff. Besides it'd be too weird; I mean, I've known him so long. My mum babysat him when we were young, and we haven't been able to get rid of him since. He just keeps showing up.' I smile the words out.

'I wish I had that with someone. Someone to know my history. They always make sure that I don't.'

I wonder who they is. 'Yeah, also means there's always people lurking around, ready to throw stuff back in your face at the worst possible times too.'

I think of all the peed pants in Kindy, the bad hair, falling off my bike into a hedge of thorns – all these mortifications would cease to exist if the likes of Jack and my brother Ben were out of the picture. Erased.

Anonymity – it was like having a super-power. 'No brothers or sisters?' I ask.

She shakes her head. 'I don't think my parents could take another one of me. Anyway, Mum had trouble having babies. Dodgy plumbing.'

'She had you . . .'

Kate's lip twitches. She stands up on the trampoline and starts to jump with abandonment, almost sending me overboard. I step off and wander around the shaded garden, noticing the spread of ground cover in lieu of grass. Everything is different here. As if even grass is too pedestrian for the Shepherds. I notice a dilapidated fibro shed, and approach the small window to peek through, using my fingers to erase the dust from the pane of glass. Empty packing boxes obscure my view, but there is definitely some sort of vehicle in there – protected by blankets and tarps. At once, Kate is behind me, her panting hot in my ear.

'That's my Thunderbird – Dad likes restoring old cars. He reckons he'll have it ready for my eighteenth.' I think of my own father's offer to double my savings to buy a car when I get my learners. It will be a Magna, or a Ford Laser, or something equally void of personality. And canary yellow for safety, just to top it off.

'Wanna see it?' Kate asks.

She isn't the kind of girl to wait for answers, and opens the tilt-a-door. She kicks the boxes aside and removes the edge of a tarp to reveal the shiny panels of a convertible. It is retro, it is funky. It is so Kate.

'Dad had it imported – a hump of junk now but it will be fab one day. Cost heaps to have it moved up here. Told him he should just finish it so I could have driven it. Of course, he'd have to be home for that to happen.'

I hope I'll meet him one day. I wonder if I'll get to, or if she'll see through me before then. Something niggles at me. A fear I could be cast aside without warning.

The shadows grow long and the crickets start to chirp and I realise I never even called mum to say where I am. My brother Ben has just got his licence and wants any excuse to borrow Dad's car. I figure he can pick me up, and I call him for a lift.

We are listening to an old Smashing Pumpkins favourite on Kate's Discman when I smell rubber and hear brake-pads grinding in the cul-de-sac. My hoon brother has arrived.

The car door slams.

'Well, hello there . . .' he almost sings as he notices Kate leaning on the doorframe as I leave. I see he is still sporting patchy bum fluff that he likes to think passes as a goatie. 'And who might this be?' Ben asks, a swagger in his step as he approaches.

'Don't even think about it,' I whisper. She's mine.

实

The following weeks are different to any period in my life. We walk home via different streets, follow the creek bank home with our shoes off and feed the wild ducks, introduce each other to our favourite music, books, lip gloss. I am infatuated with all things Kate. We are inseparable. I keep up appearances with Helena and Lanie for a while. But Lanie gets cut when I change my spare to coincide with Kate's and I rarely see either of them now. I can't say I miss their clothes shopping and Destiny's Child obsessions. Kate helps me find the best stuff at op-shops now. She has a talent for it.

Kate's arrival doesn't go unnoticed by Jack either, so by default, I see a lot more of him in public. He swiftly dumps Charlotte, the glossy-haired sports captain, to free up his options, and starts joining Kate and me under C block at lunch. Before long, I am passing notes to Kate, as I had before with Charlotte and her predecessors, and my two best friends become the official It couple.

'You don't mind?' Kate asks one day. 'I know you said you don't like him like that but . . . I see you looking at him sometimes. I don't want you pissed at me.'

I shrug, unable to speak at first. 'As long as we can still hang out,' I clarify. So I guess I do give permission. I figure it won't last anyway.

I try to deny the dry mouth, the tight throat – seeing them all fingers and hands. I keep telling myself it is a good thing. That their union strengthens my position in the triangle. Most of the time our *friendship is equilateral, with the distance between the three of us fairly balanced. At times the properties changes, it is pushed out of shape, they fight or one of us gets lost in a fleeting friendship, but it is mostly Kate, Jack and me this final year.*

A perfect equilateral, until one side caves in.

I know from the start that Kate makes me want to live life instead of just use it up. What I don't know is that before the year is out, she will be gone from my life. And so will Jack.

If I could have known what was to come, would I have savoured every breath of her, or turned on my heels and run?

CHAPTER 5
Masterchef

I can't help but stare at Sara's skinny thighs as she stretches on my fence post after her run. I don't blame her for not looking happy about seeing her man on my front porch for no good reason.

'Can I borrow your iron?' Jack asks so loudly it makes me jump. 'I've got work later and can't find mine.'

I just stare at him. He winks on the side Sara can't see.

'Okay?' I say, and go back inside, to retrieve my iron and my cool. I roll the cord around it as I return to the front, and see Jack's not-quite-wife has joined him on my porch.

It really isn't fair. She shits me, this woman. She looks even better after exercise – glowing with vitality like an ad for Rexona. I'd only run if someone were chasing me with a gun, and even then I'd just look sunburnt and stink.

Then she meets my eyes and her face morphs into an insincere smile. 'Morning, Frankie,' she says.

'Okay, thanks,' Jack pipes in, reaching for the iron like an alcoholic for a beer. 'You're a life-saver.'

'Yeah. No worries.'

'So you've got the iron sorted, Jack. What about our other essentials?' she asks.

Sara shifts her weight. It makes my front step creak and I picture her pitching off and laugh on the inside.

'They're sorted too,' Jack says.

'I see, so because you have the music system connected, we are done?' Sara rolls her eyes.

'I did say the essentials,' Jack smirks.

'We still don't have the *gas* connected . . . Did you call them again? I am sooo sick of toasted sandwiches.'

'You haven't been able to cook up there yet?' I say. I store books in my oven though, so the kitchen wouldn't be high on my list of problems to solve either.

'It's fine. I can just bring leftovers home from the restaurant,' Jack says.

'Except you have the weekend off,' Sara points out.

A heavy silence descends on the three of us.

'You're welcome to use my oven,' I hear my treacherous lips utter. 'I mean – my kitchen is, well, ridiculous, but it does have gas . . . I think.' I have a vague memory of burning cupcakes once.

'See, Jack, I told you we should just *ask* her.'

'I would offer to cook for you too, but since you're a chef the thought scares me to death,' I say.

'Frankie, we can have a salad – it's no biggie. One more night won't kill us, Sares.' His brow ruts with tension.

'Jack, why don't you swing by the markets today, get some supplies to cook for all of us, then?' Sara suggests, eyes bright.

'I'll get some wine after work. Oliver gets in this afternoon, so you can meet him properly. It's a special occasion.'

She strikes me as an every-night wino kinda chick, special occasion be buggered.

My eyes meet Jack's. He looks like I feel — like a rabbit caught in a trap.

'Jack will see you around six?' Sara says, reversing off my porch and bouncing down the steps in a sickening display of energy.

'Why not?' I mutter half under my breath. I can think of a dozen reasons. A thousand, even.

'Don't be long, babe, Frankie needs to get dressed. Plus you have to get Oli's bed assembled.'

As she jets away I notice that her hair bounces, but her boobs don't.

Jack leans in to me. He smells of soap and donuts, and I feel my throat tighten.

'You don't need to do this, Fray.' He glances sideways at Sara, now rocketing down the easement, leaping up the steps to their house.

I hush him away. 'We're not kids any more, right? All in the past? I should be home from the hospital by five, pending any natural disasters.'

I could be in luck. Tsunamis were impossible in Brisbane, but you never know . . .

'Thanks for the iron,' he laughs, eyes crinkling at the corners.

'Yeah. Good cover, 007. Our secret's safe.'

He tips the iron at me with a grin and walks down the front steps, holding it up like a trophy. My iron has saved us. For now.

实

I survive my day at work on autopilot, my stomach in a knot. I cut and paste my way through reports to get home early. I only just finish fluffing around making my place look less like it's been burgled when I hear a knock. I haven't even changed. Jack is at the back door, eco-friendly bags in hand, sprouting green foliage.

'Am I too early?' he asks, tapping again on the door. The familiar tone of his voice makes me think of us in our teens. It was always distinctive, a decibel below other boys, even before it cracked.

'No, no. Come in,' I lie, shoving a Chokito wrapper in the couch cushions and patting at my crinkled work skirt. I am a sloth. Let's face it – I'll probably die living alone in my filth.

He looks scruffier. More tradie, less yuppie. For the first time since his reappearing act, his very presence doesn't shock me. I stand awkwardly in the kitchen like an extra on Jamie Oliver's cooking show as Jack unpacks ingredients onto the tiny excuse for bench space. 'Can I . . . help? I feel a bit rude. I could have attempted to cook . . .'

Jack shakes his head. 'As you were, Miss Hudson. I'll just do my thing, you just chill. Sara'll be over in a bit; the little man's in the bath. He's only been here three hours but my patience is already wearing thin. Figured the less time he's ransacking your place, the better. I'd remove all valuables if I were you.'

'What valuables?' I laugh. I relax a notch. Pieces of the person I knew have risen to the surface through the clothes and things that don't belong in the same sentence as Jack Shaw. Like *father*. Like chef. Like *property investor*. It is still unsettling – having him refer to things I have no knowledge of, when I had once known every layer of him. But I am hardly the same now either.

I screw the lid off the wine and pour two bucket-loads in oversized glasses.

'Is this okay? I know you foodies have rules about wine and certain food. My only rule is it has to be alcoholic.'

'It's fine, Fray.' He smiles, taking a sip. 'And what's with the "foodie" shit? You make me sound like one of those pompous old bow-tie-wearing freaks.'

I lean on the bench, my glass in hand. Jack expertly squashes garlic cloves, heats turmeric till fragrant and chops ginger into wedges. 'I'm guessing you don't have a mortar and pestle?' he asks.

'A what?'

Jack improvises, pounding coriander roots into the side of a soup bowl with a spoon. I watch his hands, familiar yet foreign; no longer nail-bitten or scribbled with pen the way I remember from school.

'So, Mr Chef Man, do you do that quick-chopping thing?' I ask.

His temples crinkle as he smiles and reluctantly performs for me, pulping the shallots to wheels of white in seconds.

'Pretty impressive, Jack Shaw,' I say, lightly poking his arm. 'Tamer of insects. Baker of mud pies. Donkey Kong King. And now, masterchef.' I could get used to this personal-cook caper.

'I'm a one-trick pony though. Although I do make a mean Moussaka.'

'You eat eggplant?' I refuse to believe it. 'You used to hide your carrots in your shoes.'

He shrugs. 'Still have to sometimes, when Sara cooks.'

The night stills as the shrill of the cicadas and shriek of the lorikeets ride the wind. The parrots squawk and scuffle over green mangos suspended high in my tree that shades my front windows.

'Are you gonna tell me about Sara's problem with my mango tree?'

Jack looks down his nose at me. 'Yeah, about that, and the fence thing. I know she can be *abrupt* – come across like a bit of a cow sometimes – but she doesn't mean anything by it. It took me a while to get used to that, but she's okay underneath. She's cool. She's a great mum. You'll like her, once you get past the bullshit she lays on sometimes with new people. And the tree thing – there's no problem, really. Not any more.'

'But there was?'

He huffs and rolls his eyes. 'Technically the base of the tree encroaches on the easement. Cost us a bit more as we had to get smaller trucks in for the site-prep stuff. She wanted to remove it, save a coupla grand, get me to get you to agree. I said no. That's it.'

My jaw drops. 'She wanted to cut down my hundred-year-old tree?'

'Well, not exactly, but it wouldn't have survived the haircut it would have needed to get the bigger truck down the side.'

I wonder who actually owns that tree. Isn't an easement just a right to access? Isn't it still my tree? Heat rages up to my cheeks. My volume switch is wrenched up. 'But the –'

'Fray?' He holds his finger gently to my lips. I freeze. 'I was never gonna let her cut down your tree, so can we drop it?' He removes his finger, and the taste of Thailand infiltrates my senses. I hear Sara approach with Oliver; her bangles chink as she walks to my back porch. I stand up straight, as if caught swapping notes on parade in school.

'Sara, hi, come on in.' Her musky perfume arrives in the room before she does.

'Hi, Frankie. Thanks for having us. Oh, sorry, you're still in your work uniform; are we too early?'

Uniform? Were my work clothes that void of style? Sara's outfit is an eclectic mix of accessories – a purple crocheted beanie kinks to one side, a funky scarf cascades down to her jeans and meets knee-high boots. Beads peek through a flowing blouse which is gathered by a plaited leather belt. She's sporting more accessories than I have hidden in my entire wardrobe. I needlessly adjust the waistband of my charcoal skirt (and mentally cringe as I notice an oil stain from the salad dressing at lunch).

'Love the beanie, Sara,' I offer in what we'd term *rapport building* at work. It *is* cute, softening her movie-star face perfectly. But in May? In Queensland?

Oliver appears from between her legs, every inch the catalogue tot, in that precious phase between baby and boy. He's a morph of his parents' features, with Sara's clear skin and Jack's dark hair and cheeky smile. As they circle each other in my kitchen I somehow feel like a guest in their world.

Sara's white teeth gleam as she passes me the bottle of wine. I scan the label and see it's French and unpronounceable. 'Thanks.' I put it beside my $12 bin special in the fridge. Next to the Miracle Whip.

'How's it going, babe?' Sara asks Jack, pecking him on the cheek as he stirs the curry paste. He adds the chicken and bamboo shoots to the wok. A chilli-red pucker mark now stains his cheek and he makes no attempt to wipe it clean. This irks me, and I want to lick my fingers and erase it like a mum outside a school-drop zone. But I don't.

The fragrant scent of coriander fills my teeny kitchen, triggering my hunger. The rice cooker pings.

Sara has brought an iPad for Oli, along with the alcohol for us. A survival kit. But after a brief exploration of my 'cubby house', as he calls it, Oli settles down with the Wiggles. Sara returns, making small talk while she supervises Jack, describing her day – *back to back consults, the arrogance of the doctors she had scheduled, how they palmed her off to their assistants.* I can almost feel the positivity in the room being vacuumed out as she speaks. My uni friend would have the technical term for her spirit, and describe her aura colour in detail. I just think she is as shallow as a contact lens.

'What is it again that you do at the hospital, Frankie?'

'I'm a social worker.'

'Oh, okay. Was that something you always wanted to do? I imagine it has its moments. I hate even being *in* hospitals and that's in a sales role.'

'Not really. I had this idea of being a hotshot lawyer when I was twelve. Watched too much *LA Law*.'

'And what, you didn't get the marks?' Sara says, swirling her wine, and every point she'd earned by making an effort so far tonight heads up the rusted old range-hood.

'I started it. Can't say it was what I expected – it can be so dry. Too many lawyers . . .' *And then I go and promise to marry one.* 'Anyway, one of the friends I met in justice studies was a rescue diver. I volunteered on a few of her call-outs with the SES on missing-person searches –'

Jack splutters his wine all over the bench-top, distracting me mid-sentence. He catches the drips with the back of his wrist as they dribble down his chin.

'You right, babe? That Chardy got bones in it or something?' Sara snort-laughs.

'Yeah,' he coughs, 'or *something*.'

What's his problem? I turn back to Sara. 'Anyway, that kind of sparked my interest in it, I guess, helping people through things.' *I just want to help people.* I must sound like a dick.

'So what do you actually *do*? Talk people off rooftops?' Sara asks. Another snort-laugh escapes and a loose strand of hair flicks under her nose. Oli comes in and she opens his muesli bar for him and he is on his way again.

'My job varies.' If I evade her line of questioning she might give up. Work encroaches on my headspace enough without infiltrating my social life as well and I sure as shit don't feel like discussing it with her. Not after that *didn't get the marks* crap.

'So, like, what did you do today?'

Man, she doesn't let up. I muster the strength I usually reserve for difficult patients.

'Today I had to work through some post-natal appraisals. Basically I have to assess if new mums are fit to be discharged with their babies. Often they're teen pregnancies.'

Jack coughs again near the stove.

'Sorry . . .' he adds, and returns to the wok.

What is with him? Am I such a disappointment? Is my career such a failure? I'm a team leader.

'Fit to be discharged? Like physically well enough? Wouldn't the doctors do that?' Sara says, flicking her fingernails on the wine glass.

'It's whether they're mentally competent. If they are likely to start using again, if they're on drugs, that sort of thing.'

'Wow, so they are on it when they're pregnant? Are their babies, like, deformed?'

'I've seen a couple of FAS cases –'

Jack looks up, confused, and I add: 'Foetal Alcohol Syndrome; underweight, premmie bubs. But, to be honest, it is surprising how much a foetus can take and still live to see the light of day. It's sad really – seeing these unwanted kids, probably accidents, going home to drug-affected single-parent homes, when I know so many loving couples on IVF, going crazy, wrecking relationships over infertility.'

'Just because someone has an accidental pregnancy doesn't mean she can't love a child,' Sara shoves in. I raise my eyebrows at the venom in her words.

'I wasn't suggest –'

'Dinner's ready, ladies, if you want to grab some bowls,' Jack interrupts. Sara and I shuffle awkwardly in the small space to gather plates, all pinned-in elbows and shifting feet.

We dine alfresco (due to my lack of dining room), with a fabulous view of their half-painted stilted giant shining down on my back porch. The Thai curry fragrance is delectable, but the heat of it burns my throat. I try my best to hide it, sculling water between each rice-packed morsel that I drain of all sauce.

'Too hot?' Jack says. 'Sorry, I should have asked if you like chilli. I can't get enough of it.'

'It's fine,' I lie, grabbing for water, my throat stripped of its lining.

'Have some bread, Fray,' Jack says, smiling as he passes me a roll. 'Water makes it worse.'

It registers that he called me *Fray*. Again. Sara stares at him, blank faced. He's got to stop doing that. I can't stand the stress. We're still recovering from the single-mums thing.

'I might check on that son of ours; Sharon said he hardly slept, so excited about seeing his new room,' she mutters, tiptoeing into the lounge. *You do that, hon, give me some air.*

'Have you *told* Sara how well we knew each other?' I whisper. He is so careless with his remarks I think surely he must have given her some sort of explanation.

He shakes his head at me. I had forgotten that *relaxed* is his default setting.

'Stop calling me Fray, then.'

'Okay . . . Francesca.' He smiles. For me, the limitations of our interactions are front of mind. The lines are fuzzy though – Sara doesn't know the half of it – but which parts of Jack and me are off limits?

Sara returns. 'Oli's asleep.'

The talk moves to renovations. She's interested in what I faced with my cottage (*start with the kitchen*, Jack pipes in), and she tells me what she and Jack plan to do in their place. It interests me, this focus on commercial aspects – using neutral colours for better resale. Stuff like that is always the furthest thing from my mind, but then I love my place. I'm not trying to do it up to make a buck. They leave me feeling inadequate in terms of my hardware knowledge.

'Maybe if you didn't buy the first house you saw, and a near-condemned one at that – I mean, you never really were good with tools,' Jack pipes in.

'Sorry?' Sara asks with an ice-queen stare.

'Oh, I was just telling Jack . . . earlier . . . that I didn't really look around much before I bought here. Nor have I done much renovating.'

Her lips tighten. 'It is unusual. A girl on her own taking on this sort of thing. But good on you though.'

I smile to stop my lips from sneering. Jack stands and starts clearing the dishes like he's at home. He always did when we were kids – he said it was the easiest way to win brownie points with mums.

'I've just done the wiring here,' I mention. 'Cost a packet, but the stuff in the roof was all spaghetti from 1940 – half chewed from rats. Nice to know it's safe now.'

I know my house is still cosmetically challenged. But I don't know why Sara has to sit so straight-faced, unamused by my rustic-cottage stories. I'm glad I haven't mentioned the mice behind the stove, or the natural air-conditioning (a hole near the pipe outlet in the toilet where the wind whistles through).

'That reminds me, Jack, I ordered those sockets. You know, the European stainless-steel ones?' She turns to me, her elegant hand grazing my wrist. 'I can order you some too, Fray, if you like – buy bulk. Cost a mint but look fantastic.'

I try not to reel from that fact that she's called me Fray. Only Jack calls me that. 'Think I'm good, but thanks.' My dad gave me a box that fell off a truck that he's had stored since he was a tradie twenty years ago. The switches have been gathering dust in his shed ever since, but they work just fine.

Jack's face hardens. 'I thought we agreed to get the normal ones. Save our dosh for the rewiring. Be cheaper in the long run.'

'It'll be someone else's problem by then,' Sara says with a chuckle, taking another swig of her French wine, emptying her glass and then pouring herself a top-up.

Jack can't seem to leave it alone. 'Buyers aren't stupid. It'll fetch more if it's rewired, Sare. People don't want to spend half a mil on a firetrap.'

'But it will *look* perfect. That's what'll sell it. Trust me. I'm *in sales*, babe!' Her Pandora bracelet sparkles along with her sales pitch.

Jack rolls his eyes. The playlist ends and another awkward silence descends. Jack fills it, not with speech, but with music. He walks to the stereo and in a moment has found another trace of the Jack I used to know. Powderfinger's 'These Days' blares from the speakers. It sends shivers up my spine. Does he mean it for me? Or did he simply want to hear it? The look he shoots me as he steps confidently towards us tells me it is by design. Without a word, without raising suspicion, he is acknowledging the good bits of our past. And the lads from Brissy were right – these days turned out absolutely nothing like I'd planned.

'Remember how long we had to line up to see these guys play?' Jack blurts, his eyes shooting over to me as he returns to the table. I raise my eyebrows.

'Huh? I don't even know who sings this. Too grungy for me. I need something I can dance to,' Sara pipes in from her seat, adjusting her blouse. She has no idea he's talking to me.

Jack flinches like he's been hit in the balls. My mind reaches back to the concert we attended at the Arena in high school. Back in the *Before* files. This plan of his – to downplay our connection – is fraught with danger, especially when the blood-alcohol level spikes.

Jack turns the conversation to safer ground and we chat about music we'd battled adolescence with. Our glory days, when everyone knew the steps to the Macarena, when we contemplated how civilisation was going to collapse from the Y2K bug, and there was only six degrees of separation between Kevin Bacon and anyone in Hollywood. Jack argues with Sara, asserting that our nineties grunge surpassed that of the *yooof* of today and their *doof doof* music.

We've all had enough wine for a school night, and the evening draws to a close. I thank Jack for the food, and joke that I hope taste buds can regrow after shock-chilli treatments. They make a polite exit – Oli swung over Sara's shoulder like a sack of flour – and the family stumble off home together. I wave as Sara opens the French doors and turns on the light.

I exhale. Thank fuck for that, I survived. Surely it will get easier from here on in. I sit on the narrow back step and finish my Pinot Noir in the night air. I like the refuge of the darkness – a moment alone. I don't have to pretend out here.

It smells like rain. There's humidity in the air, a sweetness that reminds me of Christmas-time mangos. I remember that I haven't called my mum in months.

A moment later, Jack is outside again. He hurdles the chain-wire fence back into my space. 'Left my phone. Sorry.' He gestures inside, and strides past my seat on the step. He returns with his phone, but then lingers like jasmine.

'Well, you're surviving the farce so far,' Jack says, a twinkle in his eye. 'It was always gonna be weird . . .'

'It's hardly been a week, Jack,' I qualify. 'Still, you're okay company I guess. Beats reality TV and Lean Cuisine.'

He hesitates. 'It's good to see you, Fray.'

A lump forms in my throat.

Then, as if taking pity on my lonely soul, he squashes in on the tiny step. His leg is hot against my thigh. My breath catches.

'She's still got a hold on you,' he says. 'The stories you told Sara – the SES volunteering, your job . . . She changed you.'

I frown. 'Who? Kate?'

'Who else? I mean, how did you get so lost, Frankie?' Jack slurs.

Am I lost? I was perfectly fine till he turned up with his instant house and his judgements.

'How did *we* get so lost?' He leans his side into me, like we used to do playing corners on the back of his dad's old XD Falcon. His shoulder presses on mine, his face inches away. 'I mean, I know I missed my window by, what, a decade or so. But why has it been so long?'

The thoughts that I had kept so neatly tucked in, race. Heat creeps up my neck, and it isn't from the chilli. *Do we need to go there, now?*

'You *know why*, Jack,' I say, trying to cut the thread before it unravels me. 'It was just too hard.' I was just too hurt.

He wraps his fingers round my wine glass, takes a sip. The intimacy of it shocks me. I feel the pressure of his cargo-covered thigh pushing on the thin cotton of my work skirt.

'Maybe it would've been easier if we'd made contact again . . . If we'd . . .' His eyes finish his words.

In my drunken haze, I think back to the turmoil. The lies. The scandalous gossip. The twisted nightmares. 'But we couldn't finish it, Jack. Not after what happened.'

'Why not, exactly?' he says, digging us deeper. His voice is harder now, cutting over the click of the cicadas, slicing over the distant hum of traffic on the main street. 'I mean, okay, straight away was too crazy, but after a *while* maybe?'

The wine he's downed is giving him the courage to mount this hurdle, but I can't. I wonder why Sara doesn't call for him. Surely she can see us perched on my step. Surely she must wonder what's so important he needs to sit with me after we've just spent all night in my kitchen?

When he looks at me, his eyes are unwavering, glossy with tears. 'I thought you might have thought . . .' Jack chokes on his words, his wine-fuelled courage fading. He rubs his forehead with one hand – the wine he's holding in the other almost spills and he looks at me with pleading eyes. 'I think of what you did for me. How hard that would have been for you – Miss Never-Told-A-Lie-In-Her-Life. But after, when you never made contact –'

'Neither did you,' I cut in, heat surging through me.

My words hit him like arrows and he throws his head back, eyes on the charcoal night sky, as if he's seeking answers in the stars. 'I wrote to you, Frankie. For months. But from what my mum kept saying to me, I figured you were like everyone else. That you blamed me.'

I stare into his eyes, my hand brushes his knee. I thought he knew me better than this. How could he think I'd believe he was capable of that? Except for Kate, he is the only person who really *got* me. Even still. There was another reason, and he knows it.

The security light illuminates yellowing tufts of grass and empty pot plants. Finally, Sara has had enough. She might as well have put out a flashing sign saying: *Jack! Get in here!* We are drowned in white, and a dose of reality. He gets up; a pained look clouds his features. His fingers brush mine as he hands back my glass and I wish I had words to ease his guilt.

'You seriously think that I could believe you hurt Kate?' My words spill into the night air. He turns his back on them and walks towards the light. I wonder if it's too late – if words are lost on him now. That his guilt has been carried too long, etched too deeply to be erased.

But he has it all wrong. The reason I couldn't be in his life, after everything, wasn't about Kate, or what they thought he did to her.

It was about what Jack did to me.

CHAPTER 6
Branded

Cooloola National Park, South East Queensland
3 pm, 18 November 2000

Once we have permission from our parents, getting here is easy. The car ferry pulls us across the Noosa River as we line behind a convoy of fishermen with tinnies trailing 4WDs. We are fringe dwellers coming here – anyone who's anyone is heading to Surfers for Schoolies. Our presence scatters the kangaroos, grazing in the bright green fields, as we hit the north shore and head towards Double Island Point. The road through the national park is lined with scruffy paperbarks, and ferns nestle in sandy wallum swamps.

Ben pulls over to the tyre-check lane, gauge in hand, to reduce the tyre pressure for the sand leg of our journey. We take the first cutting down to the beach. As the clumpy greenery parts way, we are hit by an assault on the senses. The humid heat is replaced by the fresh gust of sea air. I am blinded by the sudden expanse of white. At what point water becomes sky is uncertain. Then, I see it all. The unbridled beauty of it. The beach is a marbling of wet caramel patches and powdery soft whites, separated by shallow lagoons. The sand, like a flat bed of wet cement among patches of rippled shallows, is our highway.

Jack and Kate are belted in on one side of the troop carrier, Dan and Matt on the other. For once, sitting up front with Ben is my best bet. Kate is still cut at me three weeks after the formal for whatever she surmised, from whatever she thinks she saw. I have been too busy studying to bother fixing whatever broke between us. Maybe it is something else entirely. That I forgot to notice her new shoes. That she cut an inch from her hair – it could be anything, with her.

Ben stops the 4WD, roaring the truck behind a dune just between the last cutting and the headland. We all disembark. Our camp spot is dwarfed by a steep vegetated dune, dappled with blotches of red-coloured sands. The inaccessibility feels isolating but liberating all at once.

Ben unloads his swag and fishing-rod. 'I'm heading over the hill – take it easy, kiddos.' He stares at me and the bottle-o bag full of spirits. 'Don't get too blotto or Mum'll crack the shits with me, okay, Frankfurt?' My brother treks off with a wink, his swag and tackle box balancing him perfectly. He always is happiest alone, and knows all the good spots from camping with Dad.

The aqua terraces, laced with white peaks, thrash against the glazed black boulders nestled at the base of the headland. According to the park map, a steep trail leads north, past the rugged cliffs and lighthouse to the calm side. To the fish.

'Where's he going?' Kate asks – finally speaking to me. She is tying back the entry flap on the tent Jack has assembled for them. I am relegated to the smaller tent, while the boys plan on camping out in their swags near the fire.

'Fishing. Not exactly the chaperone Mum had in mind.'

She shrugs, and the cold war resumes once more.

We are finally here. We mark the moment by sitting on a dune, drinking Sub Zeros and Stollies. We talk crap, listen to Killing Heidi's 'Mascara' on the car stereo. We are on a mass high, our final exams finished.

Jack looks at me with a dare in his eyes. 'First to get wet . . .' he taunts as he sprints fully clothed to the water's edge, hurdling the set of scalloped white peaks. Kate's tawny skin is speckled with shade as she sits quietly, still in her uniform from her last exam. We had written final goodbye messages all over each other's cotton shirts in the school tradition. Yet the print smudges, the ink runs into the sea as she gallops into the waves, and the words are lost.

It is stir-crazy hot, my feet feel like charcoal bricks searing on a hotplate as I follow them into the surf. Once the other two boys catch up, the serious dunking and splashing take off, the laughter infectious. Jack swims up between Kate's legs – heaving her up onto his shoulders in the waves. Her smile is luminous, as her prince carries our drama queen high above us, her face glistening in the summer sun.

This is it – the start of our first independent adventure, the start of our real lives.

实

Later, the boys attempt to surf. Kate and I are alone, and I feel uneasy. She has to talk to me now. The sun slips behind the dune, and I relish the shade, the afternoon shore breeze. I pass her a vodka Stollie. She brushes it away.

'So Silverchair – the next Nirvana?' I throw into the breeze. Kate thinks their lead singer is a freak, and I know it will break her silence, but she doesn't fall for it. She stares out at the sea, trying to pick which black-blob is Jack.

'I reckon Daniel Johns is better looking than Bon Jovi . . .' I try again.

'Are you kidding?' she shrieks, scrunching her face up in disbelief. Bingo. 'I can't be friends with you any more if you think that . . .'

At least she considers us friends now, I surmise. The sand is grey with shade, like it has lost its life source without the sun. She sees me smile, realises I tricked her into talking, and her ice-queen face melts away. If only I had thought of this strategy before the excruciating two-hour drive up here. 'So, we're good?' I ask her. 'You're not mad?'

Kate folds her legs up to her chest, and looks out to sea.

'Cause I'm gonna need a wing man, at uni . . .' I say, and start dreaming about our new lives – take-away coffees, Friday arvie happy hours, new friends. No more tuckshop and school discos, and zitty boys.

'Yeah, if I get in. Probably end up working at Sportsgirl.'

She does have a point. Kate is hoping for a place in early-childhood teaching, but with her absenteeism and inability to focus, a place isn't exactly in the bag.

'You and Jack will probably hook up. Leave me alone. I know you, you have this *thing*.'

I panic. The guilt eats at me. I can't lie to her. 'I've known him like, forever, if that's what you mean.'

'It's more than that. He talks about you like you're all-knowing.'

'You think?' I screw up my nose.

'Like, he admires you. When I talk to him lately, it's like he's tuned out.'

I raise my eyebrows at her.

'You'll both go to uni, and I'll be in the dole queue with all the losers.'

I sit up straight. 'No you won't. Wasn't photography on your list too, at TAFE? You'll be great at that. You've got style and you can't learn that at uni.' I feel unease bubble in my chest.

'Huh, yeah, you'll be a criminal barrister, Jack will be a hotshot business exec, and I'll be doing Pixi Photos outside Kmart. Woo hoo.' She waves her hands in mock excitement.

'Beauty before brains, my fair friend,' I say to Kate, 'cause boys will always see better than they think.'

Kate looks thoughtful, perplexed. She peers up at the spiky Casuarina branches buzzing with insects. 'That's where you're wrong about us, Francesca Louise.' She glances at me with a rare moment of seriousness. 'Because you have both and don't even realise.'

Her words nest in my throat and make my cheeks hot. I link my arm under hers and rest my head on her shoulder. I relax. Things are back to normal. But for how long?

The boys are returning, boards under arm. I guess our chat is over.

Sand flicks in the air as Kate gets up, and she gives me a gritty kiss on the cheek. 'You'll be brilliant at whatever you do, Frankie. Don't forget that.'

Jack bypasses Kate making her way to their tent and walks over to me. I am hit with a spray of water as he flicks his fringe, shaking his head on the side to clear his ears. He sits beside me, filling the indent in the sand that she's left.

'I think you should go talk to Kate,' I say to Jack. 'She's in serious mode but at least she's talking to me now.'

'Yeah?' Jack replies, still puffing from his surf. 'Soon . . .'

We wave-watch. An endless army of waves. I am sapped by the intensity of my thoughts – swarming with Kate, with Jack, with me. I don't know how to be with him since how he was at the formal. The way he looked at me, all we didn't say. We just sit knees touching, but it feels so wrong.

'I got some clarity – in the water,' Jack says. I pray he isn't going to admit something I can't face. Something he can't give.

'What, that you can't surf for shit?'

'Yeah, that,' Jack scoffs. 'Plus, I don't think you should do Law.'

63

I'm somewhat relieved – this is a conversation I can handle. 'Why's that?' I ask, smoothing the sand patch next to me to keep my eyes away from his. His wet shoulder presses into mine, darkening the stretch cotton of my t-shirt. 'Are you going all Dad on me – that a girl doesn't need to waste time at uni, just to marry and have kids.'

'You think I'm that backward? My wife's gonna bring home the bacon,' he almost sings.

'And fry it in the pan. Not sure that's a good deal.'

He flicks diamonds of water off his gangly arms. 'You need to do something with people, Fray. Something that connects you, not technical crap. You're not anal enough for those finicky rules. I know you think it's about justice, helping people, but it's all bullshit in suits.'

'So what do you suggest, in all your wisdom, Master Yoda?' I close one eye, to try and focus on him in the glare.

He looks out to the heaving sea, as if the answer is written in the waves.

'You should teach, or lead people in some way at least.'

'Teach?' I baulk at his words. 'You think I can deal with teenage boys – putting dog shit in my drawer and stuff – every day? I'd probably strangle one of 'em. I have no patience for morons.'

'Whatever, Miss Hudson,' he says, giving me a two-fingered salute as he wanders off. 'Wise you are.' He picks up a long thin piece of driftwood, a makeshift walking stick, and hobbles off, like Yoda. Wise you are.

I smile for a second, and enjoy the warm feeling burning inside, the image of Jack and me at uni together, until it hits me again.

He's been branded by Kate already, and despite what he says, I am not convinced that will ever change.

实

'Who's coming to the lake?' Dan calls outside my tent later that day. 'My brother recons he caught a freshwater croc here.'

'Bullshit,' Matt heckles. 'We're not in Cairns, you dickhead. Might be a few Red Bellied Blacks but.'

'For real?' I hear Kate's voice chime in – he has touched a nerve with her: fiercely snake phobic.

'No more than here in the dunes, Katie Kate,' Dan mocks. 'Gonna have some snake action in your love cave later, huh? Find out if you're a howler or a screamer?'

'Shut up, Nympho,' Kate retaliates. We are outnumbered by blokes so have to keep the defence line strong.

'Your mum likes to howl – she tells me so every Friday night,' Jack pipes up in her defence.

We brave the bush track through the humidity and endless insults volleying back and forth. Kate plays the role of freaked-out city girl nicely, while I am appointed as the boring mediator.

At last we come to a clearing. I see cars with canoes strapped to racks like helmets, and a swampy mosquito-ridden puddle smaller than our school pool.

'I guess we are in a drought, guys.' Disappointment fills the air. The three boys trudge through the reeds, determined to cool off after the long walk. Kate follows quickly, after the comedians point out there are fewer snakes in the water.

The fellas splash and skylark, Jack and Kate frolic through the water entwined as one, and I try to look unaffected. Jack glances my way as Kate worms her slender limbs around him like a drowning child. A look of shame runs across his face.

I escape the world, and dive beneath the surface of the tepid water. I swim to a shady nook before sitting on the muddy edge. Kate finds me dreaming on the bank. I am cornered.

She starts her familiar monologue. The theme is always the same: Jack is distant, strange, avoiding making plans with her.

I notice the beard rash on her chin. Obviously he isn't that distant.

The boys get bored, and Kate complains about sunburn, so we walk back to our camp, sapped of all energy. The stop/start drinking of the afternoon has caught up with us and we find the campfire terminally ill with no one to tend it. A letter from the ranger is taped to our tent, warning us of fines for leaving a campfire unattended, and to store our food in dingo-proof containers.

Kate claims the tent and no one is game to question her ownership, while Matt and Dan top-to-tail it on the mattresses in the back of the truck – sleeping bags constructing a wall between them to fend off any comments about what team they bat for.

Which leaves me and Jack alone. I used to relax when it was just us, but since the formal – that tiny spark of hope that Jack feels the same way that I do – it just makes me nervous. My heart races.

I sneak a look his way, and find his eyes waiting for me.

'Can't do this any more, Fray,' Jack says as he gets up and gathers loose dry branches for the fire. 'I'll tell her tonight. It's doing my head in.'

My stomach somersaults. I feel equal parts excited and guilt ridden. After all the talks we've had, all the notes, is this actually going to happen? Is this the only way to be together – for her to be heartbroken?

'Maybe you should wait. Tell her when we're back home. She'll have her mum then if she doesn't cope.'

'She can talk to you – I can't keep pretending, lying like this. She knows anyway, I reckon – I've tried before. Chickened out. I just – I feel like a user. A liar.'

He drops the firewood, scans the camp for onlookers, then steps over to me, pulls me up from my chair and takes my hands in his.

He leans in so close I can feel his breath.

A wave of trepidation washes over me, and I step back.

His eyes dip low and he twists his mouth. He scratches his

head. 'Is it any better to just pretend I still love her? She'll get over it, Fray.'

I walk over to the campfire and pull up a chair. Jack joins me.

'But what if we don't? What if going out wrecks it?' I ask, throwing another branch on the fire. 'You might decide you don't like me after all and I'll end up with neither of you.'

He curls his finger through my belt loop. 'Fray, no one ever stacks up to you.'

I taste bitterness and wonder if it's the guilt seeping out my pores.

The fire blazes, the dry twigs crackle and spit, as we sit and ponder in silence. He passes me the Bundy Bottle. I swat it away. 'I think you need all the courage you can find.'

He takes another swig from the neck, the amber fluid draining from it.

I turn and make sure Kate is still over in the tent. 'I just feel like a horrible friend.' My shoulders slump, like my mood. 'She doesn't deserve this. I mean, she's always paranoid about feeling left out. Now she will be.'

'Fray, me and Kate are through, whether you're with me or not. Don't think this is your fault.'

The music slurs, slows and dwindles to silence. The car radio had been left on, the doors open all day. Just as the light fades on the beach, our car battery is flat. An argument ensues, with Dan appointing Jack and Kate to rustle up some other campers with jumper leads.

'I'll come with you.' I am not getting stuck with the guys' drinking-games for the next hour. The three of us head north, following tyre marks through the dunes, looking for signs of life along Teewah beach. On the way, we climb on the rusty remains of the old cargo ship. There is nothing for half an hour after that, until we stumble on a crusty old fisherman with a CB.

The man sits with his legs spread wide, on a burnt-out tree stump, rolling tobacco in a Tally-Ho. He has skin like leather and a long elf-like beard that has yellowed around his puckered lips.

'Youse kids in a bit of strife hey?' the man asks after Jack explains our predicament – that we have no other way home with our 4WD's battery flat. 'Shame you're not bogged. I've got a snatch-strap . . . but no jumpers.' He laughs and reveals grey crooked teeth. 'Usually youse kids are getting stuck on the rocks at high tide. You seen those photos at the pub – all them cars wrecked? Think they know it all.'

The fisherman licks the edge of his cigarette and gives Kate the once-over. 'Got a daughter 'bout your age. Course, not as bonny. Youse can call me Nick.'

Kate folds her arms.

'So can you help us call the ranger maybe?' Jack asks.

'How far south are youse camped?' The fisherman lights up his cigarette and walks to his ute full of crab pots and casting nets. He reaches under the sun visor, and takes down his CB radio.

'Just south of the wreck. We've got a Mal up on the dune as a marker.' The fisherman makes contact, relays the facts, and assures us the ranger will pay us a visit in the morning.

'Nick, was it? Thanks, mate.' Jack shakes his hand. He looks so grown up.

With our mission successful, we set off back to camp. Kate stops to collect shells, Jack powers ahead. I slow down to walk with Kate just as the sun slips behind the dune. Kate's eyes twinkle as she turns over a shell in her palm, inspecting its worthiness to join her collection.

'Do you have any fishing line?' Kate asks.

'Why? You don't strike me as the fish-murdering type.'

'I'm making you a necklace.'

And I'm stealing your boyfriend.

She flicks a matted hair from her cheek, dries a shell with her shirt.

'That fisherman would give you some. Seemed pretty besotted . . .'

'Very funny.' Her wide grin lights up her face. She has the grace of a movie star – I often feel like she is delivering me a line.

I take a breath of fresh sea air, and watch the gulls shadow the scattering of peach and orange hues of twilight. The rippled beach is littered with blue bottles clinging to drift lines laced with ocean foam.

'Did you know, down in Sydney, I was like, a total vegan for two years?' Kate says. 'Lived on potato salad and Mars Bars. I got so anaemic I had to get a blood transfusion.'

'You're full of crap. You wouldn't last a week without a cheeseburger. Besides, your nose always crinkles when you lie.'

She smiles. 'Okay, you got me.' She grabs a stick and carves out a heart shape with 'Frankie and Kate Forever' scrawled inside, and I'm overcome with guilt. I consider telling her Jack's plan to dump her. Maybe it will be easier if she gets in first? 'I've missed you,' Kate says, smiling sweetly. 'You never even asked me about what happened after the formal.'

'You weren't talking to me, remember?' I step closer to her. 'What was all that about anyway? You being cut at me. Because I danced with Jack?'

Her lips twist and she turns away. 'I had stuff to deal with, but it's all sorted now. It's all good.'

Typical Kate, never answering anything straight. 'Well, are you going to tell me?' I figure nothing happened at the formal or I would've heard about it by now – three weeks later.

Her eyes are wide. 'I've been desperate to tell you something!' She grabs my hands. 'I just was too shit-scared to . . . I mean, you're so responsible and I was so happy when I found out but I just couldn't live with you thinking I was some slutty trailer-trash.'

'Hey? Kate, what are you on about?'

'Pinkie swear you won't tell?'

I roll my eyes. 'How old are we?'

She stares me down and holds out her little finger.

'Okay!' I twist her pinkie around mine. 'I promise.'

She pockets her shells, and holds my hands once more. Her sand-speckled fingers are gritty and wet. She smells like frangipanis and sea salt.

'I'm going to be a mum!'

I choke on the breeze. It is like the air has been sucked from my lungs. 'Sorry?'

'I'm a week late, my boobs are sore, I have this funny metallic taste – isn't it fantastical?' Her eyes dance. I realise she'd been drinking Diet Coke earlier when we were drinking goon.

'You're pregnant?' I screech.

'Shhh,' she says, covering my mouth with her sandy hand. 'You promised not to tell.'

'Seriously?' I am nauseous just thinking about it. I try to remember to breathe.

'Would I kid about that? I peed on a stick. Twice. It's official. I so wanted your help but I was scared you'd freak on me.' She leans in and pushes my legs and we both collapse in a pile, Kate giggling with excitement. My palms break my fall. My thoughts race. My world collapses.

I can't hear my thoughts over the beat of my heart. Poor Jack. He's been played. She knew he was over it, and this would keep him close. Brand him for life.

There is no chance for us now. He will marry her. He will, the crazy good-hearted fool.

Maybe it serves him right. It takes two after all.

I push down a half-sob. 'And you're happy about this?' Like I need to ask. Her face is glowing like a commercial for some luminescent beauty product.

'Please be happy for me! I can't do this alone, Frankie. I know what you think of teen mums, but it doesn't have to always be such a bad thing. I can do this!'

'How did this even happen!'

She works a divot in the sand and settles in as if she's about to tell me a fabulous tale. 'It was formal night. After we dropped you home we went to Mount Coot tha. He had those little tea-light candles and petals and Peach Schnapps.' I feel my chest tighten. 'He parked near a picnic shelter and, well, we did it on a blanket under the stars.'

I feel as if there is a knife twisting in my ribs. So, what, about an hour after telling me I was the one.

'It was pretty quick but I can still feel him –'

As a self-preservation tactic, I feel a sudden compulsion to disprove what she is saying. 'Wait, he drove without a licence?' Jack couldn't even do hill starts last time I checked.

Kate's face turns to that of a petulant child. 'Fray, you are such a fun sponge. I've got my learners.'

Do two Ls make a P plate?

She rolls her eyes, but then her elated mood returns. She babbles on about his touch, his kiss, how she fell asleep in his arms. A lump forms in my throat. I feel like a beach ball that got snagged on a rock. I remember the bullshit Jack told me. How he always thought his first time would be with me. I feel stupid and suddenly want to go home, away from the lot of them. Her jubilant voice fades back in, still babbling. Grains of wet sand cling to her clear complexion like brown sugar. Her striking eyes glisten in the draining light. I am a fool for thinking he would rather be with me.

Her fingers wrap the shells safely in her pocket. She draws me near. 'Promise not to tell anyone? I want to see his face when I tell him.'

'How do you think he'll take it? I mean – most guys our age would –'

'I don't care. I've thought about this, and I'm doing it, with or without a boy. I know I can do this.'

I think of all the mornings Kate couldn't find her own shoes, how she thinks a Summer Roll counts as lunch, and wonder how true that is.

She looks up the beach to Jack who is now waiting on the dune for us to catch up. He is well out of range. He skols the last of the stubby he brought for the road, and gestures for us to hurry up. I shoot a dagger at him, but I feel I have a sheath-full left to hurl his way.

'Say you're happy for me.' Her eyes plead with me, batting away all thoughts of lecturing her on how crazy this is, how stupid, how moronic. 'Mum's just gonna die, so I need you, Aunty Frannie . . .'

'Who's gonna die?' I hear Jack's voice invade this nightmare in fragments. He walks towards us as we sit in the sand. I try to wipe the shock off my face, but I think it is etched there. 'What are you two doing? I wanna go back, my drink's empty.'

He falls in between us on the sand, puts his arms around us both. I fold my arms, and turn away. He turns and says, 'What crawled up your arse?'

I just glare at him. What I want to say is 'What the fuck, Jack? You shagged her? After what you said to me?' I feel the rage churn. Kate folds around Jack, wrapping her arms around his neck, kissing his lips. He falls onto the soft sand with her weight on top. I can't help but stare at them, trying not to imagine a tiny alien creature in her belly – cells dividing, multiplying.

I sit mute, shell shocked.

'I'm going back,' I say, my stomach in a knot. I feel like I need a hole to hide in, to cry all this out.

'On your own?' Jack says, coming up for air. 'It's getting dark. We should go together.'

Jack gets up, flicks the sand from his fingers. 'Where you going?' Kate asks Jack, and turns and winks at me. 'She'll be right. It's a full moon.' She traces the top of his boardies with her fingers. I want to puke.

'Whatever.' I can tell I'm not wanted. I had better get used to it. It sounds like they have a replacement for their third wheel all lined up, growing larger by the second.

As I wander off alone, my eyes flick to his.

'What's with you?' Jack asks.

'Nothing,' I blurt, but he hovers, unconvinced. 'Just go!'

He reluctantly trudges off.

'See ya, babe,' Kate whispers over her shoulder, turning with a smile. Her long arm twists around Jack's waist, sending a stab of anxiousness radiating through me. He can't dump her now.

He'll never be mine.

CHAPTER 7
Kids-R-Us

I can hear a distant clanging of pots. It is obscenely early. Who needs alarm clocks when your neighbours have kids? I make tea, and find my usual place in the sun. I hear a muffled male voice, presumably Jack's, followed by the shrieks of a child yelling like a limb is being amputated. I tilt the louvres to suss it out. Jack appears at the open French door, trying to catch his stomping son. He is in nothing but boxers, and I can see he is more triangular than lanky now.

'Oliver, you need to stay inside. It's too early for outside play,' Jack says in an angry whisper. Oli pelts him with pebbles that chime on the glass.

'Oliver – stop!'

'No!' the superhero-suited boy screams. Jack pulls him inside using an expert side-stroke manoeuvre. It doesn't seem that long ago that Jack had his own superhero shirt – covered in food stains – that he refused to take off. I smile.

I shower and dress, then realise I'm about an hour earlier than needed. I grab the paper to kill time when I see Meg watering her front garden. The weak winter sun is out, but it feels too cold to be awake. The birds chirp in the still morning air as I walk out to my front fence.

'Have some bad news, Megs . . .' I announce with a grim tone. 'Those plants are cactus.'

'Don't tease them, they can hear you,' she scolds. 'Look, there's a green leaf – green means photosynthesis.'

'Green means mould,' I mock. 'That plant is so old, it's decomposing.'

I am distracted by her youngest – well, out of the ones that actually *move* – running past with a bucket over his head, entirely covering his face. More disturbing is Meg's straight face and lack of corrective action. She's finally cracked and lost the will to keep them alive. I know she has three boys, and one of them is called Ken, but I refer to them as Small, Medium and Large in my head.

'Have you heard any more from them? The new neighbours? Other than the procession of tradesmen parking in your driveway.' The reference to *them* shits me, which shits me more.

'I try to avoid neighbours, as a rule. They make you do stuff like walk before the sun comes up, and ask you nosy questions. But yes, I lent them my oven. Sort of.'

'And you said you knew the guy since you were kids. Is that strange?'

'Kinda,' I admit. 'I grew up with him. Mum looked after him as a toddler when his mum went back to work. She was a nurse. We camped together as kids, that sort of stuff. But then . . .'

I feel the blood rush to my head. Do I *tell* her? About Kate, about everything. She *is* my bestie. I may need a vent hole for all this craziness. 'Then they moved away.'

Yes, I am a coward.

Meg is too distracted by her kids to notice the edge in my voice, the flush in my face. Her bionic ear — the one they must insert into mums' heads after childbirth — hears things I am oblivious to. It's the same story with the eyes in the back of her head. Accessories to motherhood. I wonder if I'll ever need either of those adaptations, and feel a hollowness. Perhaps I just need breakfast.

'So you don't know the skinny wench, then?' Meg asks, flicking the hose along the garden with her elegant wrist. She looks around to see who's in earshot. 'With the fakies?'

'Fake?' I ask, cocking my head to one side. I had dinner with her without noticing, and she figures this out from her deck? She is a doctor's wife, but seriously?

She gives me a knowing head bob.

'So the guy — Jack. Bit of a hottie. You don't like, *know him* know him, if you know what I mean?' Meg asks in G-rated code, her eyes narrowing like a hawk.

'Nope,' I say, tight-lipped. 'I can count them on one hand, and he is certainly not on the list.'

'Just one hand?' Meg comments, raising her eyebrows. 'Wow.'

'Four years with Knobhead kind of slowed me down.'

'What's a Knobhead?' I hear a knee-high voice squeak from behind the gaps in the battened-in laundry. *Whoops.*

Meg laughs. 'A type of vegetable,' she says back to the wall, and turns to me without missing a beat. 'Fair enough, kiddo. Philandering Pig.' She flicks her greying bob behind her ear.

'I saw him, the other day, in the city,' I recollect. It had been months since I had rid him from my world, moved here, moved on.

'Did you freak?' Meg asks, eyes wide. She really needs to get out more if my benign love life is entertaining to her.

'Hid behind a pole.' Hmm, I am noticing a pattern of behaviour here.

'Nice.'

'Real mature of me.' I thought I was over Seamus, but obviously not enough to actually speak to him in person. 'Then he caught me, said we should do coffee soon.'

'You owe him *nothing*, love,' Meg reassures me.

'I still have the ring,' I barely whisper to myself. She looks over to her brood. I was used to only ever getting half of Meg's attention.

'Sebastian!' she yells, in a voice so fierce it seems incredible that it came out of her petite body. 'Put! The shovel! Down!' She wags her finger menacingly. 'Don't make me come over there . . . Three . . . Two . . .' And then the fire mysteriously fades from her voice. 'Thank you.' Her eyes hide behind closed lids.

She takes a yoga breath and opens her eyes. I wonder if there's vodka in her Mount Franklin water bottle. I'd need it.

'Anyway, how are all the cherubs?' I dare to ask. I need to redirect the heat from me. She huffs like a dragon, as if she has been gagging for me to ask, and steals her chance to vent.

'I don't know, Frankie. They just make me feel like a horrible person. I used to be *nice*. Calm. Coordinated. Now I am just a fishwife, in a pair of unironed cargoes, living in a house of clutter and pee-ridden toilets.'

'Oh, come on – they are Lorna Jane *originals*, Meg, nothing to be ashamed of,' I say, grabbing her shoulders in a mock massage of support.

'People think because we don't leave 'em in the car at the casino with a litre of tang, then we're good parents. They were just so feral this weekend I really have to wonder what I'm doing wrong.'

'Nothing! They're . . . spirited – free-range kids, if you like. And you're on your own so much, with Mitch at work. Meg, if I'm ever half the mum you are, I'll be stoked.' She looks away from me, chews the inside of her cheek, and starts to sniff a little, signalling to me that we have reached our quota of sappiness for the day. The month, even.

Chipper Meg returns. She chats about her plans for the weekend. That was easy. I feel chuffed. She has picked me up after so many lonely Friday nights, and the shit days at work when I'd lost faith in humanity. I only have a few dozen to go to even the score.

As she drones on about family gatherings, I hear the chirp of a smoke alarm escape her window, lost in squeals of excitement. I see their heads bob, as the boys grab tea towels to act as fans to whoosh the smoke away. I am distracted from the chorus of mayhem when I spy a sleepy-eyed, bed-haired little boy wearing Shrek ears, straddling the front fence like a trusty steed.

'There you are, Mummy,' Medium yells, dismounting the fence. 'Daddy's making *powidge* but it looks like Clag. And he didn't do the smiley-face syrup, and he can't find my Thomas bowl, and . . . we need you upstairs, Mummy!' The smoke alarm is still singing. Meg cradles her son's protruding cheeks in her hands, brushes the curtain of fringe away from his rain-puddle eyes, and somehow fits that lump of a lad on her hip, where he melds in like a long-lost appendage. And he stays put, with just that one scrawny arm of hers loosely circling his waist, hanging like he was always meant to be there. Right there, on her side.

'Sanity time has come to an end. But don't think you're off the hook with this Jack person either. To be continued!' Meg's words fade away as she carries Medium upstairs.

I wave back, and walk to my porch.

As I retreat to my shack-built-for-one, I realise even *Jack* is a parent. All I have is a mortgage and a dog. I have a fleeting thought of Seamus, the life we planned. The life we would have had if I'd found it in me to forgive. Then I remember the fights, his unwavering view on *no kids*, and my heart turns to steel again.

And just to rub it in, there is Jack. With the kid. Standing on the easement. I can see him on a cooking show – *here's one I prepared earlier*. A bonus child, like a free set of steak knives. Can't they just stay *indoors*? He appears to be spotting his now-smiling son teetering like a drunk on a wobbly training-wheeled bike way too big for him. Oli's tongue pokes out in the corner pocket of his grin, as he concentrates on the task.

I would never have picked Jack as a helicopter dad. He was a latch-key kid, as I recall.

'Morning,' I call.

'It is indeed,' Jack says. 'Sorry if we woke you with . . . all the shenanigans. Oli's readjusting after a week with the olds.' Jack scratches his head, as Oli tracks up and down the drive more steadily now, through puddles of mud where the cracker dust thins. 'Oli! Come say hello to Frankie.' The boy loops and swings round towards us.

'Hello to *Fwankie*,' he says, coming to a stop near my feet. My heart melts. Maybe I have to settle for being an aunt. Although I doubt Ben will ever get his shit sorted either. Mum may have to rent grandkids.

'Hello, Oli,' I say, mustering my kid voice from mothballs in the attic of my head. 'You're pretty fast on those wheels of yours.' I crouch down to the chubby cheeks and oversized eyes.

'*My* bike.'

With that settled, he skids off, Jack tottering after. After a few laps, Jack lets Oli off his short leash, unrolls the newspaper and reads the headline. Oli skids back to him, through a sloshy puddle at the side of the drive. The paper shields Jack's shirt, but mud splatters his face like dots on a Dalmatian. He frowns as a thick drop hangs precariously from his ear. He scrapes it off with his index finger and, seeing me fail to contain my grin, flicks it my way.

'You remember that mud fight we had at biol camp, Fray?' He shoots me a smile and I stifle the laughter bubbling beneath the surface.

'How could I forget.'

Mud. Yet again, it gives me a sense of clarity.

Our class of fourteen were staying in cabins at Stradbroke for a week. I was one of only three girls. Kate was back at school – a drama queen more than a botanist, so it turned out. A deeper part of me was curious about how things would be with her overpowering presence snuffed out, when our galaxy of three had lost its sun.

It was on that camp that the dynamic between us changed. I remember thinking it felt like when we were kids, B.K. – Before Kate. I could barely remember a day without Jack in my shadow, or the sound of his tyres spinning behind mine. The thud of his schoolbag hitting the tiles outside our house after school, the plonk as he kicked his shoes off and came inside as if he lived there.

We had toured the shoreline in a group like crabs, inspecting the erosion, the muddy banks covered with mangroves – they looked more like spikey mutant Triffids to me. Our first exercise was to draw and label the elements of the life cycle of a mangrove. I took my clipboard and walked carefully to the stinky shore, the water lapping at my feet. I bent down to inspect one, poking at it with my pen.

'Fray, we're supposed to stay on the boardwalk, not go down there,' Jack said. 'You heard the man – take only photographs, leave only footprints.'

'They also asked us to sketch and label the parts of a mangrove.' I actually thought he was serious but the look he shot me highlighted my error.

Jack sat on the boardwalk and started to draw. 'Why lead guitarists need to know about this shit, who the hell knows.' You had to admire him for keeping the dream alive, despite him, well, sucking at music.

'So they can get a real job, so they can pay bills,' I piped in.

'Well I won't be dedicating my first album to you, Miss Kill Joy.'

I missed having him all to myself, the quiet ease when we were alone. I still felt the pang in my gut when I saw Kate and Jack making out, but it'd lost the edge it had that first day I caught them behind the janitor's shed. What annoyed me most was how they took me for a fool, like I didn't already know they were getting it on. Like I didn't read the notes

I was forced to deliver between them. But I could never work out who I was most jealous of. It was simpler when I saw them one-on-one. But that was rare.

After a few minutes, I finished my sketch, and tried to stand in the boggy mud.

'You done? The class has pissed off already,' Jack complained.

'Jack, I think I'm stuck.'

'What?'

'I'm stuck. It's like a sink hole. Can you help?'

My Dunlop Volleys were nowhere to be seen, nor were my calves.

'How? Shall I call Monkey to bring his trusty cloud?' He shook his head. 'Won't I just get stuck as well?'

He had a point, but I was starting to panic. 'Can you get a branch or something?'

He found a big stick that had broken off the canopy of trees on the shore, eased off his safe boardwalk, and extended his arm out to reach me with it.

Then I couldn't see my knees. I reached Jack's stick, and tried to pull myself free, but I just yanked the stick from his grasp.

'Here,' Jack said, exasperated, throwing his clipboard up onto the boardwalk. He stepped close to me and put out his hand.

My fingers found his, and pulled. I heard a slurp of suction, hoped I was free, but found I was sinking further. 'Jack!' I screamed, as the hem of my shorts descended into the brown lava that was eating me alive.

'Jesus!'

I hadn't heard Jack's serious tone since I had fallen head first into a thorny bush when I was five. This only made my breathing more rapid, my pulse race faster. I was in the shit. Just when I started to imagine what mud is like to breathe, he suddenly yanked my arm so hard, I felt like my shoulder was about to dislocate. He pulled me back, and we both landed hard on the rocky shore. The weight of me was on top of him, and we were caked with mud.

'Thanks?' I said to him, as I felt his heart race beneath mine. I gingerly tried to push myself up without breaking too many mangrove roots.

'Get up! I have an aerial root shoved up my arse!' Jack yelled, half amused, half concerned. We both managed to stand. Jack's entire back was caked in mud, as was the bottom half of my body. A flick of brown muck was splattered on his face.

'Fray?' Jack said, as we stood there, taking in our surroundings in disbelief. 'Where's your clipboard?' We both laughed, as we looked at the frenzy of bent and broken mangroves, and the brown pit of fury that must have eaten it.

I couldn't see where my legs stopped and my shoes started.

I looked up, and Jack was stepping over to me with a deathly serious expression.

Splat.

I kept my eyes on his face, too cowardly to assess the damage.

He had just planted a handful of stinky mud on my chest. The only territory clear of mud.

'You shit!' I said as I reached the mud and clawed a fistful to hurl at him. I had a big muddy handprint right across my chest. This meant war.

An avalanche of stinky wet was retaliated, spraying my face.

'Stop! It's in my eye!' I cried, in my weak-girl-under-attack voice.

He fell for it, ceased his fire, and grabbed a clean corner of his shirt, wiping my eye free of gunk.

I thanked him by planting a slosh of mud on his head, mashing it into his hair.

'Miss Hudson. Mr Shaw,' we heard Mr Mason bellow from the boardwalk, 'what on earth has gotten into you two?' Our class was assembled near us on the boardwalk. My two female classmates looked outraged. The boys were pissing their pants with laughter. We splodged our way over to them in fearful silence of what was to come.

'You two will be cleaning the toilet block when we get back,' Mr Mason added.

Jack grimaced at me, shaking his watch. 'You owe me a new Casio.' One dimple appeared on the side of his crooked smile. 'At least I got to grab your boobs,' Jack said with a wry smile.

'Jack Attack. Nice work, mate. Got her in the tits,' Matt called.

'Shut up, dickhead,' Jack said, returning to the fold. 'It's only Frankie.'

And with that he was gone.

CHAPTER 8
The Beach

Cooloola National Park, South East Queensland
8.20 pm, 18 November 2000

Jack and Kate still aren't back. To distract myself from what the heck's going on between my two best friends, I collect wood and throw another log on the dwindling fire. It seems like hours since they trekked off together. Matt and Dan have passed out half-cut in the back of the truck, and I'm thankful for the break from their skylarking.

I look out from the dune like a meerkat. I see a figure approach in the fading light and I know it's Jack by the way he drags his arms, like he still hasn't grown into those broad shoulders.

'What took you so long?' I ask as he scales the sandy rise to our scattering of Eskys, tents and tarps. Empty stubbies and chip packets litter the ground despite the fact that we only arrived today for our parent-free weekend.

His lip twitches and he walks straight past me.

'Where's Kate?' I cross my arms. The suspense rattles me. 'Did you do it?' I look to make sure the others are still comatose. 'Like we talked about.'

Our hatched plan.

'I said I would, didn't I?' His voice is grim.

Yeah, but he's tried before and failed. And then there's the other thing.

I notice his shirt is half satched, and water is dripping down his calves from the hem of his shorts. He sits in the sand and draws his knees up.

'Why are you so wet?'

He shrugs.

I thought he'd be relieved to have it over with. He was the one pushing to do it here when I wanted to wait till after. I sit close, fidget with a beer cooler and glance over. Jack's face is pale, his eyes red as if he's been crying.

I'm still reeling from what Kate told me before they left hours before, still piecing it together in disbelief. I'm not sure of anything any more, least of all Jack, but seeing him upset triggers a sliver of sympathy for his predicament.

I try to take the sting from my words. 'What did she say when you told her?'

He turns his head and wipes his face on his sleeve. 'That she was sorry . . . that she'd do better . . .' Shame bolts through me like an electric shock.

We sit in silence, a cloud of treachery hovering. I can't judge him. I'm as much to blame, an accessory to this cruel act of betrayal. I'm so caught up in self-pity I forget about what Kate said about Jack. I see-saw between wanting to dry his tears and kick him in the face.

'So, that's it? She didn't say anything else?' I'd imagined hours of wailing, screaming insults.

He shrugs. 'She carried on, started crying, you know, asking when I fell out of love, if there was something she did. That she could change . . .' A stifled sob escapes.

So she didn't tell him what she told me? That makes no sense. Had he spilled first, making her too heartbroken to go there? Surely he has a right to know. She told me not to tell. She'll be back in a bit and she'll kill me if I've blabbed, but it takes all my resolve to not scream at him for lying to me, for being so stupid.

'But you did actually break up? I mean, you didn't chicken out when she got upset or anything?'

'I thought that's what you wanted? So we could . . .' He lifts his hand to mine and I flinch. After what Kate said, I start to wonder if he dumped her just for that. To get with me guilt-free.

As I shrug away from him, I see him wince and my throat tightens. 'I'm worried. She should be back by now. Why did you let her walk off anyway, alone in the dark?'

'I didn't. I calmed her down, she seemed okay, so I went for a leak in the dunes and . . . she just ran off.'

'Which way? I mean, did you try to catch her?'

'I don't know. She just disappeared. I looked around then started to panic, but then it was so hot I thought she might have gone for a swim, clear her head.'

I consider him, with the knowledge of what Kate told me, and realise it could all be lies. Anything is possible now. Everything's in doubt. The one person I thought I knew to their bones turns out to be someone I don't know at all.

'I wouldn't have left her out there by choice.' He rests his hand on my shoulder.

'Don't touch me!' I'm surprised by the shrill in my voice.

His eyes narrow. 'What's with you? You've been in a shit since I found you two talking on the beach.'

I glare at him. 'I'm curious, Jack, about why you dumped her now. Is it 'cause you got what you wanted from her?'

His lip twists. 'What . . .' he shrugs, 'months of moodiness and grief?'

My heart pounds in my ears. 'This is all your fault.' I poke my finger into his sternum.

'That's not fair. I did this for you!'

Salty tears drip into my mouth. 'You're not who I thought you were, Jack.'

'Tell me, Frankie. What is it you think I've done that's so bad?'

When I say nothing he leans in and his eyes bore into mine. The vein in his temple throbs. 'You think this is my fault?' He gets up and waves his hands about. I follow his lead. His nostrils flare. 'That, what . . . that I did something to her? I didn't touch her!'

I stop pacing and cross my arms. The simmering boils over. 'Not today you didn't.'

He looks at me like I'm speaking Spanish. 'What are you talking about?' He's yelling now, his eyes livid.

'You know, Jack.'

That's all it takes. His anger stirs up every emotion in me. A fog washes over my vision and I have to step away from him, feet ploughing through the heavy sand. Here we are with no idea where Kate is, she might even be hurt, and all I can think of is that Jack lied to me.

Next thing I'm screaming like a banshee. 'Dammit, Jack. Don't play dumb with me. I know you did it!' I run up to him.

He just stands there, looking blank, and in a heartbeat I'm leaping at him. My hands make fists and I punch hard at his shoulders, but he barely flinches. He lets me hit my anger out and when I'm too tired to hit any more, he takes my forearms in his strong grip.

'Fray, you're not making sense. What do you think I've done?'

I stop the hysteria and take a long breath. 'At the formal you said . . .' I sniff. I'm petrified to admit it. 'I thought you liked me.'

He rolls his head in a circle. 'I do!'

My relief is short-lived. 'Then how could you do that?' I punch him again, but I'm just as angry at myself. My best friend is cold and alone somewhere, heartbroken, and here I am worrying about a stupid boy. About who likes who more.

'Do what!?'

'She's pregnant, Jack!'

Jack rocks back on his heels and his fingers grip harder, like clamps in the flesh of my arm.

'She's what? She said that?' he asks, his eyes blazing. 'When? Today, on the beach?'

I nod. 'I thought she might have told you before you had a chance to . . .'

His head lurches back. 'Why would she tell *me*?'

I glare at him. 'Cause you're her boyfriend. Duh.'

He rubs the nape of his neck. 'Yeah, well, last time I checked you gotta have sex to knock someone up, so . . .'

Here we go. 'Aren't you forgetting something? Formal night? On a blanket scattered with rose petals under the stars?'

'Petals?' His face screws up and I see a glint of white teeth in the black night. 'Seriously? Do I look like a guy who does that? It's all crap.'

Is he for real? He looks sincere, but so did Kate. Someone is playing me.

She had no reason to lie, but he does.

'You're telling me she actually said it was mine? Cause if she did, she's lost the plot, Fray.'

'Ahh! I can't even look at you.'

I turn and retreat into my head, trying to assimilate Jack's denial of all wrongdoing into my thoughts. Kate said it was Jack, didn't she? Or did I just assume?

Jack splits some wood and throws it on the dwindling campfire, our only light source. 'Yeah, well, when she gets back you can ask her yourself. I want to see her squirm.'

I try not to think of Kate and Jack making babies together, and retreat to my tent to let my head catch up to this farce.

实

As the night wears on, and Kate does not return, the ruminating thoughts won't ease. It's like there's worms in my blood. My legs are restless, the inactivity eating away at me. I find my watch and stare at the minutes as they're stolen away, each one heightening my fears. An hour or more passes with no sign of her. The guys stir from their drunken doze and I get up and rejoin camp so I can be the first to see her return. But I can't just do nothing.

'Kate's not back. She's on her own. It's been hours.'

'Huh?' Matt scratches his crotch and burps. 'She's prob'ly just cut at Shaw for being a prick. That's the usual story when she flips out.' He opens the top of the Esky, cracks a beer, returns the lid and sits on top.

My gut clenches. I hope that's all it is. *I shove my hands in my short pockets and approach Jack, who is moping on the dune. The moon shines on his profile as he stares out to sea in the darkness. His eyes don't stop scanning the waves. Ever since I revealed Kate's secret, his breath has been ragged, bumpy. Even as he sits mute, his body tells me everything I need to know. She's really missing. I try to repress my confusion, my anger, and concentrate on finding Kate.*

'Where could she go? I mean, the ferry's too far. It took half an hour at least for Ben to drive us up to the camping area. She could've hitched maybe, tried to get home . . . It's less than two hours once you cross the river.'

'High tide. No one's going anywhere,' Jack says.

I notice that the scattering of cars we dodged on the beach earlier is gone. 'Plus, the barge stops at midnight. No other way out unless she goes across the rocks at Rainbow.'

'That's good, right? She has to be here somewhere.' I try to think of all the possibilities. 'The lake?'

Jack shakes his head. 'Too dark. She hated walking there in daylight.'

I nod. She is the indoor type. 'Okay, so she'd stay on the beach.'

Jack looks thoughtful. 'She seemed obsessed with the wreck this arv – kept asking if anyone died, pretending she saw a ghost.'

'Maybe.' It fits with Kate's drama-queen nature. 'I guess it's shelter. A place to hide out. Make us pay. She's probably shitty as hell.' We exchange a look that acknowledges we're on the same page. It's worth a shot. A surge of adrenalin clears my mind and charges my limbs. I know what I have to do. I stride up the dune and stand in the centre of camp. Matt and Dan are half-tanked, pegging toilet paper bombs at the surfboard we'd dug in the dune as a camp totem pole, obviously terribly upset by it all.

'Fellas. Shut your gobs and get over here. Kate's missing. Jack and I are checking along the beach to the wreck to see if she's hiding there. You guys go south, search up in the dunes too.' My voice is surprisingly authoritative.

'What the?' Matt gripes.

'It's been ages! We have to do something! She might have hurt her ankle or something and need help. Come back in an hour, with or without her.'

He concedes, sets down his stubby and kick-starts Dan with a boot in his bum. Matt is the less idiotic of the *Dumb and Dumber* duo Jack insists on having around. They're both harmless, but hard work.

Jack and I pace off together, but I struggle to keep up. He is forever stopping, looking back, checking for me. I walk, run, stop, and walk again. I go as fast as my body lets me, sick with adrenalin, legs shaking. For an hour or more I scan the beach, calling, panicked, exhausted.

Finally I see the dark shadow of the shipwreck ahead. My brother Ben told me about the Cherry Venture years ago when he used to camp here with Dad, how it ran aground in a cyclone before we were born. It's a graffiti-ridden safety hazard now, with shards of rusty iron hull protruding from the sand. But it just might be the answer to our prayers – the place Kate has been hiding from us, her harbour.

I see Jack hoisting himself onto the top level of the wreck, calling out when he reaches the top. 'Kate!'

The wind kicks in, racing through the rusty hull. It blows strands of sticky hair across my face. With each corner I turn, with each corroded chamber I pass, I hope she will be huddled in a sandy alcove, her face wet with tears, her eyes full of anger – but safe. Yet the only movement on that wreck is the scuttle of sand crabs, and the panicked darting of Jack's feet as he searches every crevice; checks and rechecks every nook.

She's not here.

I fall in a heap and realise I feel exactly like the wreck. Run aground.

What now? Search the beach aimlessly? She has hours of lead on us. Unless she stopped and remained where she stopped, we will never catch her. Only a fraction of the wide open beach of hard sand remains. Any footprints from hours ago will have been erased by the incoming tide.

As my puffing abates, my eyes catch on something in the ocean. Hope and dread fill me all at once – is it her? Did she see us coming and run into the waves for cover?

A flash of bright. I wade out up to my knees in the rippling shallows. 'Kate!'

The moon flings shards of light on the object. It rises and falls.

I look closer in the darkness and my heart races. No. It's too stark – too pale to be her. Or is it just the illusion, the contrast of skin on a death-black sea? A huge swell lifts the shape and it hides once more. My voice shrills as I call her name, but it's hardly audible above the heaving waves. It's like I'm in a dream, screaming in deathly silence.

My foot hits something hard and smooth; I recoil in fear and look down at a flash of shiny white.

A plastic container bobs next to me, the label faded, like my hope.

I lift the bottle and hurl it against the rusty bow of the wreck. The sound echoes as it rebounds and is flung out to sea. I step over the waves back to shore. I stand in the incoming tide, rubbing my brow, water dripping down my legs. The moon slips behind a cloud, and I feel chilled to my core. Is this how Kate feels? Cold and alone?

The barricade of dunes is suddenly a haven for a stalking serial killer, the wind, a howling ghost chasing me. I hear noises, imagine stories around them. Masked men. Rabies-ridden dingoes.

'Jack? Are you there?' I fold my arms, but they're like icepacks against my wet shirt.

Jack appears from the wreck and the tension in me eases. He surveys my drenched clothes. My shirt drips, my shorts cling – I look like a runner-up in a wet t-shirt competition.

'You went in? Alone?'

'I thought I saw something.'

'You're satched.'

It's good that it wasn't her. It would have been a corpse. Not Kate.

'Stay on the beach, Fray,' he yells, 'or I'll be looking for both of you.' I see him eyeing off my see-through shirt. He puts his hand out to meet mine, pulls me up. His hand feels hot beneath my fingers, like a warm mug of cocoa on a squally afternoon, and the anger I was holding fades.

For a moment he looks at me, and I forget we're looking for Kate. For a moment, I'm glad it's just the two of us – like it used to be. And I feel hollow.

As if he can smell my shame, Jack's eyes dart away, and we stand, two figures on a wide open beach in the dead of night, with not a clue what to do next.

We've exhausted every possible hypothesis, played the blame game and come out none the wiser. All we can do is head back and hope to hell she is there to greet us. It's only a few hours back to Brisbane if she hitched and got to the barge before it closed for the night, so technically she could be home. As we walk, I hear the jagged edge in Jack's breath over the smooth pattern of the waves. I glance sideways and see the darkness in his eyes, etched with red.

'It's only been a few hours,' *I say, trying to find some hope to spread into my voice, wanting to soothe the hurt and fear I can see on his face.*

'Yeah, but this isn't like when we lost her at Westfield in City-Beach. We're in the middle of nowhere. And after what we did to her . . .'

'We?' *I yell.* 'You, more like it,' *I mumble.*

His eyes dip away and I try to scrape off the guilt he'd slung at me but it's stuck like gum. I scratch around for some optimism. 'I'm sure she'll wander back soon – shoes in hand, bitching about sand flies, telling us she fell asleep drunk in the dunes.'

Jack stops me in my tracks. 'What if she's gone, Fray? They're gonna think I did something to her! What if she's . . .?' *His eyes are wide and chilling.*

God, he is a rollercoaster – a zombie one minute, a raving loony the next.

I press my fingers to his lips. 'Don't even say it! She'll be back at camp,' *I decree. Even if I haven't convinced him, I've convinced myself.*

I can't even face the hypotheticals any more – they're becoming less ridiculous by the minute. I want to get back as quickly as I can so I can file this nightmare away under 'funny story'. The night at Schoolies when Kate pulled off the best Gotcha of all.

'She'll be at camp,' I chant like it's a mantra, as we march on. This will be a redundant conversation as soon as we get back. It's been over an hour since we left, plenty of chance for her to return. My calves ache from all the walking back and forth, but the pain distracts me from my thoughts, but then one dark fear trickles through.

I flick my arm out like a boom-gate and stop Jack in his tracks. 'What about that fisherman? Maybe he found her . . .'

'That old guy that helped with the battery?' His eyes are narrow.

'He looked dodgy. Think about it – he's the only other person we've seen all day. Maybe he's involved?'

'Yeah, right, Frankie, or perhaps aliens abducted her? Shall we call Mulder and Scully?'

I shove him. 'Shut up.'

His eyes are bloodshot, his hair full of sand and twigs, his stubbled chin crusted with salt. His face twists into a sob as he falls to his knees. I fall to mine, and cocoon his hands inside my own like we're in joint prayer. I brush his dripping hair from his eyes so I can see what they're telling me.

'You know I didn't hurt her, Fray. You know that, don't you?' His eyes plead even more than his words. I need all my strength to reassure him.

'I know that, Jack, I know that. She is fine. This will all be over soon.' Even on our knees I have to reach up now. I wasn't sure if the words were to appease him or myself. But I start to believe them. I hold him tight, feel the hard sobs heave against my chest as he cries in pain, sea water and tears dripping down his cheeks. A full moon peaks over his shoulder.

Then I see it. 'Look! The surfboard – it's just up the dune.' We'd rigged up a makeshift flag near our camp to act like a beacon to tell us when we were home. 'We're nearly there. The boys might have found her. I reckon she's just twisted her ankle – took her a while to get back, that's all.'

My assurance works, and he wipes his eyes, gets up from his knees. We turn up from the concrete-hard sand to the soft powder, and I breathe in, wide-eyed as I scamper up the scratchy coastal grass on the dune. She will be back. It will all be over.

I scan the camp.

Dan slumps by the fire, Matt stares blankly out to sea, both sucking on stubbies.

'She back?' I ask, as Jack races in and out of tents. No one answers. Jack returns and the look on his face tells me she's nowhere to be found. He sits on the dune, elbows resting on his knees. A calm replaces his hysteria. I think he stole it from me, as if it filtered through our hands before, via osmosis, and I'm left filled with his panic.

When I turn back towards the surfboard beacon, to the shards of broken friends that are now all that's left of our camp, I see Jack on the rise of the dune, hair blowing in the wind, his body a black streak against the stars.

'Found this up the dune.' Matt passes me a pale pink t-shirt, twisted and damp, smelling of Impulse.

I think back to when she walked off with Jack, a yellow bikini string tied at the nape of her neck, faded pink shirt, denim shorts. 'Show me exactly where you found this!' I'm unsure if this is a good sign, or a grave one.

All the way to the spot we alternate between trying to downplay the night's events, declaring she's just a drama queen, up to her attention-seeking pranks again, to panicking about what we are going to tell everyone if she doesn't turn up. Jack remains speechless, but his face says it all. We come to a freshwater creek that flows down to the ocean, and notice a frenzy of footprints in the sand – a blemish on the clean canvas since the tide started to drop.

'It was here.' Dan's voice is hollow. 'I remember the creek, how it forked left.' There is an eerie silence as we contemplate what the fuck we're dealing with. Four teenagers. Alone in the dark. Without a clue what to do next.

'Okay. We need to mark this somehow,' I say, 'in case they need evidence or something.'

'Evidence of what?' Jack asks, his voice stripped. 'What are you saying?'

'I just mean the police will want to know where she was last. They might want to get the choppers out or something.'

'The police? Just calm the fuck down, Frankie. Look, she's probably up in the dunes laughing at us now – or back at camp wondering where we all are,' Dan says.

'I hope you're right. But we have to look.' I think back to homicide shows. 'Okay, all walk out from this spot in a line for ten minutes. You know, like you see those SES guys do on TV when someone is missing. If you don't find anything, meet back here.'

So we do. Again. Part of me is desperate to find any trace of her, yet another fears what exactly I might find. At least if we haven't found her, she might be safe and warm somewhere – hooked up with a cute camper, hitched back with a night fisherman.

Jack and I stick together. We call till we are hoarse, search till we are wet with salt spray and tears, running on adrenalin alone – and find no trace.

I rack my brains for another option. 'We could head back to where we found her shirt. Maybe she did just go for a swim.'

Jack shakes his head. 'See that rip? The ocean's full of them. No one in their right mind would go in there.'

Yeah, but was Kate in her right mind?

Jack stares out to sea. His eyes fill with instant fear like he's spotted a tsunami approaching the shore. He stares north at the headland and rubs at his face, scratching at the salt that's caked to day-old whiskers. I don't think he even knows he's doing it. And then he springs into action.

'Jack?'

'I'm going to the point . . .' he shouts back over his shoulder, already streaming away.

The point? Heat fills my head. 'I told you, she's not going to go rock-climbing in the middle of the night, not when she's pregnant. Jack, you should've seen her. I've never seen her so happy!'

He takes three strides back and clenches my shoulders so hard I gasp.

'There is no baby, Fray! She's lying. Can't you see? You know how she gets. She's delusional!' He lets me go.

His words scare me. I know he wants me to see it his way, but I can't. It's true. I know it. I clutch Kate's crumpled t-shirt, draw it to my face, breathe her in. Kate was luminous when she confided in me; she had all these details. She wouldn't lie to me. Not about that.

But one of them is lying. Kate? Jack? My two most precious people in the world.

'Why the point? Jack?' My words dissolve in the night breeze because Jack has gone. He's running across the beach towards the huge rocky face of the headland like a man possessed.

This time, I don't follow.

CHAPTER 9
The Exorcism

It's just a drink, I tell the knot in my gut. Seamus may be out of my life, but there is no reason I can't be a mature adult and meet him socially. I'm in a crowded café – how bad can it be? Just a short catch-up to prove that I'm over him. That I no longer cringe at the memory of walking in on the man I loved in a twist of legs and sheets. I knew something was up for some time before – alerted by his jumpiness, the late-night texting, the midday showers. He never showered during the day, unless he'd just done *that*.

Enough. It'd been almost a year. I can do this. I said I would.

And now he's walking this way, so I've got no choice.

'Hey,' Seamus says in a soft, intimate voice, as he approaches my table. I forgot how striking he was – is, with the sexy two-day growth and European-cut slim-fit suits. How his sandy hair highlights the flecks of hazel in his eyes. Is this *nerves*, this heady, racy-heart feeling? Or have I just forgotten how I used to feel with him?

'Hey,' I say, still seated. As he leans in and brushes my cheek with his lips, I realise he still wears the same aftershave. The one I gave him last Christmas. What's he trying to say? Everything? Or nothing?

We make small talk as I nervously order a drink, my eyes fleeting, rarely meeting his. He is defence counsel for a fraud case – bound to be in court for months, he tells me.

'Guilty as sin,' he whispers behind his hand, 'but don't quote me.' He still gets off on the power of his position, so it seems.

'That never stopped you winning before,' I add, sipping my Coke Zero.

'I usually get what I want. Except with matters concerning you,' he says, stroking his finger down the side of mine as my hand rests on the table. I jerk it away instinctively, spilling my drink. I regret the scene it causes, the fumble for serviettes, the apologies. We're only five minutes into this thing and I have already sunk into the role of the muddled woman, and he the confident success.

He steers us expertly back on track, with just the right amount of intimacy to make me start to feel at ease, yet without crossing the line once more. Seamus sticks to work news, how busy he is, how lonely it can be in his new bachelor pad on the river. *Poor guy, barely surviving in the penthouse.*

'So the blonde you were wearing as a hat is no longer around?' I ask, but I honestly don't care. I just want to see his face, which is satisfyingly mortified with guilt and shame as my words land on him.

His eyes stay closed for what seems like forever. His jaw is tight, his frown heavy. I used to love that crinkle in his nose when he concentrated. Now it makes me wince at how naïve I had been, how lovesick. I'm embarrassed by how honest I used to be with him – how doting, eternally permissive of his needs. I was willing to give up everything for him at one point.

I take the black velvet box from my bag. The one he had offered on one knee a lifetime ago, on a deserted beach in Krabi.

'I think this belongs to you,' I say coldly.

My action seems to floor him. He leans back in his chair silently, stroking the soft velvet with his thumbs. I thought it would make him happy – probably worth a fortune. And it is not as if he thinks we are still engaged.

'You keep it. I bought it for you,' he says.

'It's no longer necessary.' The formality of my words seems to heighten the coldness in my statement.

'It symbolises a promise I made,' he says. *Here we go.* 'And would still meet . . .'

'Let's not go there. Take it. Pawn it. Give it to your next fling. I can't wear it, so . . .'

His bottom lip seems to tremble. Was this emotion from Mr Unflappable? One hint of reaction from him and the feelings I once had float to the surface; how sweet, how devoted he was, how brilliantly he performed in a courtroom, how his confidence made me feel safe. The time he surprised me with our 'substitute child' – Bear as a pup, complete with a blue bow on his collar.

He swallows hard. 'I know what I did and I'll never forgive myself. But you've got to admit your part in it. It was over well before that for you.'

I try to stay calm. 'What was my part, exactly? Wanting to have kids? Is that so selfish?'

'I was upfront about my feelings on having kids from the start. You never let on it was a deal breaker. You were never that sold on it until . . .'

My chest tightens. 'Seamus, can we just not do this? Please?'

He places his hand over mine. 'Frankie, I was thinking, what if . . .'

'What if *what*?'

'If I could be persuaded . . . to have one.'

Is he fucking *kidding*? All the raging arguments, the outings ruined by a cute toddler in a pram that he'd see me warm to. My outburst over spotting a stuffed bunny in Ikea – a stuffed bunny I knew I'd never have a use for if I stayed with him. He says this *now*? It's about a year and an affair too late, buddy.

I've given him the ring, I have to leave. I don't even want to entertain the idea of him in my world again. I've made an okay alternative life. It isn't hot sex, dinner parties with the law society and romantic retreats, but it is solid. It is mine.

'It's too late,' I mutter, my head in that familiar fog I'd fall in when having these discussions.

'Just like that,' he blurts, throwing his hands in the air and banging them down. 'I offer you the one thing you always wanted and it's still not enough?'

I don't have the emotional stamina for this line of questioning. I feel myself being sucked into his centrifuge.

'I gotta go.' I stand, grabbing my purse from under the table. 'Take care, Seamus. Don't work too hard,' I say to the wind.

I walk out to the quiet street, flanked by landscaped

gardens, feeling far less victorious than I had imagined when this scene had played out in my head. Finally closing the book on Seamus.

But I just feel cruel. How many nights had I hoped his views on kids would change, and I dismiss him without a second's pause? How long had I tried to convince myself I didn't really want kids? That they were just inconsiderate. And sticky. That I liked having a pelvic floor.

As the feeling worsens and hits my stomach like lead, I feel a tug on my arm, and look up to see his face once more. The face of the man who had nursed me through my knee surgery. Who had stayed in Brisbane, despite a job offer in Melbourne, because I didn't want to move. The person who'd fallen asleep on the stinky laundry floor next to Bear as a pup. The person who was once the best part of every day.

'Wait, please. I know we've done this to death. But not a day goes by that I don't regret what I did.' He delivers it like a line from Hollywood, so out of place in my world of sanding walls and mending the broken.

'You're the love of my life, Frankie.'

I melt. After everything, a part of me believes him, or wants to. We had so much good, until it ended with so much bad. I step across the footpath. I breathe in his familiar muskiness, brush my cheek close to his and kiss him long and hard. Is it to feel less mean? Out of curiosity? Or just to feel less lonely for a second – to bottle a piece of him, of what we once shared, to savour, back in my life void of romance? The passion still present shocks me, as I draw all of him in to me. His hands pull me closer, the kiss deeper. So familiar, yet so awakening at the same time.

I need to breathe. It takes all my willpower to push him away and escape the intoxication of him.

I have come so far, I can't go back.

实

I ring Meg that night from work. The one night I need distraction, it's eerily quiet. 'Be strong, Frankie,' Meg says down the phone. 'He stomped on your heart, hon. It sounds like you were a mess for a long time. Can you live through another dose of that?' I cradle the handpiece between my jaw and shoulder, feeling my resolve strengthen with each word.

'No. But he's changed his mind on the kid thing. Maybe he's matured?' It still twists in my guts, the image of him in our bed with that woman, but what if the arguments over wanting a baby led him there? Am I dismissing the love of my life, my last chance to have a baby, without even considering it? I'm not getting any younger.

Now she is brainwashing me. 'Once a cheater, always a cheater,' Meg bellows down the handset, as I sit in my cupboard of an office at the hospital. All right for her, three boys in tow. I feel like that postcard of the career woman slapping her face in shock as she checks her smartphone – *Oh my! I forgot to have a baby!*

I still blame that god-damned Ikea bunny.

She has started on all the clichés and one-liners now. Those I can supply for myself, so I politely hang up and head for home, feeling lower than before.

It's after ten at night, and I arrive at my crippled cottage to see Seamus leaning against my front door, Bear curled asleep next to him. My stinky dog must be twice the size since the last time they've seen each other, but he doesn't seem to have forgotten his (human) father. They look adorable.

'Shouldn't have kissed me, Esky,' Seamus says, throwing his hands in the air. 'This is your doing.' I slide down the door next to him. I used to hate him calling me Esky (it started as Cheska, then Eska, then Esky) but now the familiarity of it makes me feel like he is where I need to be. He kisses me gently, and I let him smooth away the misery. His hands slide down my side, his fingers claw at my chest, as his pace speeds up. Is there any real harm in letting him in?

'I stink like dog. Can we go in?' he asks.

He grabs my arse with both hands as I unlock the door. I start to panic about what underwear I put on earlier. We stumble together into my room like drunks. He takes off his shirt, unbuttons mine. I've always loved his brazenness, his confidence; it made me feel wanted. I realise I physically need this – need to feel sensual, alive. So what if it is impulsive, crazy?

Misguided, stupid – completely insane.

'I couldn't get this out of my head, since today,' he whispers.

I stop. His forehead rests on mine. '*This*, or me?' I ask. What arrogance he radiates, thinking he can just come round and I will pick him up like the daily news. Has Meg not taught me anything, these past few months – building up my self-worth one measly shred at a time?

Of course she has.

I pull away, suddenly repulsed by him. By what giving this to him says about me. I know where this is heading, and it isn't where I first thought.

I say as much to him, which doesn't seem to penetrate through the hot haze he has fallen under. The same one I have just fled. 'I can't do this.'

He takes a step back, puts his hands on his hips. 'It doesn't have to mean anything – you don't have to commit to . . .'

'Get out,' I scowl, pointing to the door.

He puts on his shirt. I cover mine over me, and head to the door to make sure he gets there.

'Can't we just talk, as friends? Hang out?' he asks, as he stands at my door. 'I miss you.'

'I've got enough friends, Seamus. What I lack is a man I can trust. One that wants kids, not one that'll *tolerate* them.'

As I watch him squirm, a trail of headlights flashes across his face. The crunch of cracker dust. Jack's Subaru is home, and parks in the easement. It stops short of his usual spot.

I see Jack glance over at Seamus as we stand awkwardly at my door. He then looks back at me with a furrowed brow. He hesitates, looks uncomfortable and gives Seamus a proper once-over.

Seamus looks back at him with equal distrust, yet neither man utters a word.

'Who's that? Is he the reason you're making me leave?' Seamus asks me.

'He lives out the back,' I say, frustrated that I am explaining myself to this man.

I breathe in, as Jack meanders over to us. 'Hi, guys – sorry to interrupt. Just wondering if that's your car, mate. Kinda blocking my gate.'

'It's okay, Seamus was just leaving,' I pipe in, arms crossed.

Seamus finally concedes defeat and wanders off down my

porch. He scowls, shaking the wobbly banister as he leaves. 'Nice house . . .'

I burn with an overwhelming desire to defend my life, but rise above it.

Seamus's Mercedes is in the driveway tandem to the old car Jack was trying to garage. 'If you move that shit-box, I'll get out of your way,' Seamus sneers. 'See ya, Esky.'

This time, the name just reminds me of why I hated being called Esky. They're cold, and empty. I am neither.

'Easy on, mate,' Jack says, getting back in his Subie to move it out of the drive. With the coast clear, Seamus skids off and is gone. Jack hops out, unlatches his gate, the car still running.

'You okay?' Jack mouths over the engine noise. He looks all grown up in his work clothes – his black and whites.

I nod unconvincingly. I just want to withdraw, run inside and mope, but that seems rude now he is involved, so I go in, nestle into the couch and leave the door open. I hear the engine stop, Jack's keys rattling, and see his double-dimpled smile at my door. I apologise for my uninvited guest's attitude, which Jack shrugs off. He holds up a container of food.

'Did you get a chance to eat at work?' he asks, putting the food in my microwave.

'Don't you own a microwave?' I ask. 'Is it illegal for ex-chefs to own such a layman's device?'

'We have one, but Sares gets the shits when I use it late – wakes her up. It's just risotto. Plenty if you're hungry.' Obviously he has pilfered it from the restaurant.

It smells better than anything that comes from my kitchen when I cook.

As he tries to find two bowls, Jack comments again on the ridiculousness of my kitchen – a small rectangle with a series of old cupboards and boxes of plates, all in a line. When I found holes chewed in the backboards of the pantry, I started putting my plates in sealed boxes. It's a work in progress, but I rarely cook more than toast or soup, so I can live with it till my overtime cheque comes through.

Jack brings out two bowls and sporks and finds me on the couch, still disconcerted by the Seamus thing. I am tired, teary, but I guess I can try to forget that and distract myself with food. I have spent enough nights tormenting myself over that man.

We eat in silence, Jack slipping Bear the bacon from his serve. My throat relaxes, and I find I can eat.

'So did you wanna tell me why you have stooped so low as to be dating a Merc driver?' Jack asks casually.

I well up, try to respond, but no words come out, just squeaks and snorts.

'Hey, hey,' Jack whispers, taking my bowl and placing it safely on the coffee table. 'I didn't mean to . . . you don't have to tell me.' He rubs my shoulders as I start to bawl.

'Merc drivers aren't that bad,' he jokes, which sends me half laughing between my sobs.

I start to explain he is my ex, that he'd resurfaced again, promising change, but that his sincerity is dubious at best. I dab my eyes dry with my work shirt, which I realise is still half unbuttoned. 'Thanks for telling me,' I yell at him, fumbling to do up my top two buttons, crossing my arms over myself.

'I thought it'd just embarrass you. I don't tell people when their fly's down either, although toilet paper stuck on shoes I usually point out. That's just wrong.'

I have composed myself enough to eat. I feel a sense of calm – like the tears had washed the confusion from my mind, leaving a tidemark of positivity.

'Have you ever been ambiguous about an ex?' I ask Jack, who is licking his bowl clean like a dog. His manners have not improved with his cooking skills, I see.

'I was a bit with Sara after we broke up, but having a kid kind of kicked that back into the *on* mode,' he says, putting his finished bowl down. 'The others, I was pretty sure were no-goes when they ended. Not to say that I wouldn't have had another chop at the hot ones if they'd asked.'

'My point.'

Jack's lip twists. 'He looked all right, besides being a prick. Maybe you should have,' Jack says. 'Any real harm in one last shag?'

I elbow him. 'Did you just call another guy *all right*?'

'Why not? I can appreciate another guy is attractive without wanting to bone him. Other than the car, he had style. Nice threads.'

'I notice you're a bit of a yuppie now.'

'Coming from someone who associates with Mercedes drivers . . .'

'Jack. My entire outfit came from Target, including the shoes. I am not exactly a fashion connoisseur. But look at you, Mr Labels. Mr Jag Hat.'

'You taking the piss out of my hat? I love that hat,' Jack says, clearly mystified.

'I just didn't think you'd turn into one of the trendies you used to mock. Last time I saw you, you were sporting elastic-waisted ruggers, a Hypercolour t-shirt and those high boot runners from Kmart with the fluoro-green ankles.'

'You can talk, Miss half a can of hairspray in your fringe on a daily basis. We were late for roster half the time – you brushing it out, having to get it just right.'

I cringe at the thought that half the time it was to impress him. 'So how else have I changed?' I ask.

'That's just it. You haven't. Still the goody-goody you always were. Still single. Still clueless about cars and sport.' He gets up, grabs the dishes from the table. 'And, evidently, about men.'

I hear a bang from the kitchen as he sinks the dishes before returning. 'Speaking of which, I better see if there is any action waiting for yours truly at home.'

I screw up my nose and scowl at the thought. 'I thought you said she's always asleep when you get home?'

'She doesn't have to be *awake*,' he retorts as he disappears down the back steps.

The steps again. What is it about them that makes me remember?

'Jack? Do you ever wonder how it changed us? All the Kate stuff?' I throw out into the night air as I lean on the door.

He looks into the dark sky clouding over above us. 'Every day,' he says, his lips turning to a half smile. 'Shit, we even had a shot at being normal . . .'

CHAPTER 10
The Arena

Fortitude Valley Mall, September 2000

I regret wearing heels as I walk the cobbled mall in the cool night air, past the overflowing bins, the buskers, the cheery Hare Krishnas with their orange skirts and chiming bells. Kate and Jack crowd onto the escalator, limbs wrapped around limbs, and I feel a pang of loneliness as I take a step all to myself.

A short stroll later we arrive at the venue. Ben and his mates are lined up already, and we push in next to them, despite the grumbling musos who've been waiting before us.

With no windows, The Arena is cave-like; a cathedral of noise, floodlights and smoke, with a terraced level full of drinkers. A constant hum of voices back-drops the obscenely loud bellow of the beat.

'This place smells like feet,' I yell, but my words are eaten up by the hum. I scan the crowd. Ben, Kate and Jack are lost in the sea of arms as we enter. I try to appear unfazed. I catch a glimpse of Jack and

Kate, busy groping each other in the mosh pit, an ocean of gyrating bodies separating us.

I grasp at any sense of purpose for company, and decide on alcohol consumption.

The bartender shakes his head, and yells something I can't hear, pointing to my wrist. Then I hear a voice from behind. 'No armband, no alcohol.' I turn. The stranger smiles at me. He is much older, with short spiky platinum blond hair, and muscle bound. The way his eyes undress me makes my throat tight. He orders my drink and passes it to me when it arrives. I fumble in my jeans pocket for change, but he waves me away. 'Don't tell,' he says, his finger to his lips.

I smile, and skol half the glass.

'I watched you come in before. Your mates desert you?'

'Seems that way,' I say. 'My brother's too cool to hang round his sister for long and the other two, well, they're in their own universe.'

He takes my hand, and leads me to a retro-looking lounge in the Chill Out room. I thought I would relish the relative quiet, but I start to panic at having to make conversation.

'I'm Jasper,' he says, beaming a Hollywood smile.

'Frankie,' I say to my feet.

'And the tall guy with the floppy hair – is he stupid, or blind?' he asks. I give him a quizzical look. 'For not picking you.'

My eyes roll and drift to the floor. I feel out of my depth with this man, who bears no resemblance to my native species – the lanky limbed, pimply faced adolescent male.

'Hey, isn't that your friend?' he asks, giving a head bob in the direction of the band.

I focus past the crowd and see Kate climbing up on stage. I wait for security to haul her arse down, but to my surprise, the support act's lead holds out a hand, and helps her up with a smile. She joins him at the microphone for the next song. I smile and wave in disbelief, but she is oblivious and my enthusiasm for her fame wanes.

'She's trouble, that one,' he says, wagging his finger at her dancing, the crowd cheering on.

'Kate?' I say. 'She hasn't got a bad bone in her body.'

'I don't mean like that.' He sips his rum and coke. 'I mean, she's gorgeous. Just looks like the type that would cut your dick off if you got on her wrong side.'

I'm insulted on her behalf, but he's probably fairly perceptive. Kate's passion, unchecked, could be dangerous.

'But, like I said, he must be mad anyway, to walk past you.'

I lower my eyes, embarrassed. I can't stand flattery from strangers.

'Another?' he asks.

'Oh, I don't actually drink much, so . . .'

'That's okay,' he says. 'I do – I'll teach you.'

He returns a few minutes later with two more drinks, and I finish mine surprisingly easily for a binge-drink virgin.

'If you are trying to get me drunk, it's working,' I say, a little too loudly.

Bernard Fanning has taken to the stage, and the crowd erupts. The familiar riff in 'These Days' makes me feel at ease.

'Do you dance, Jasper?' I ask.

'Nuh uh.'

'C'mon!' I pull his arm.

Who is this person I've become? The vodka must be kicking in. I take another swig, and pull him up. The mosh pit near the stage is an army of elbows, of grasping hands, of strangers sloshing drinks. I'm poked and dripped on. And it smells like nowhere else – a salty mix of stale beer and sweat.

'Dance with me?' I say. I cringe, when I remember the same line from Dirty Dancing. I should know; Kate made me watch it a thousand times on DVD. I know it verbatim. We push through the crowd. The squishy floor is stiff with decades of spilt drinks. I look up to see a ceiling misted with cigarette smoke. A speckling of lights glitter in the dark mob – which I realise are lighters when one nearly singes my hair.

'Hoot, hoot,' the chorus of ragers chant, egging on the music. My heart races like the day I was dared to jump from the high dive at the swimming carnival.

It's okay. I can do this.

I wrap my arms around his neck, as we feel the music together. Maybe I shouldn't have picked a slow dance. He kisses me gently. I taste old tobacco and bittersweet rum. I feel his hot tongue near my ear. I turn and spot Jack and Kate towards the front – a glimmer of comfort in an ocean of uncertainty. Kate sees me with my new friend, gives me an air-punch and mouths 'go girl'. Jack spins her around. Now he can see all of me, all of my friend. He catches my eye, and his face hardens. He shoots me a steely glare with a rutted brow. As his stare stays with me through flashes of light in the darkness, I see a sliver of rage in his eyes. What is his problem? Hasn't he been mauling Kate all night?

I turn my attention back to my new friend.

Was it Jasper or Jacob?

Suddenly the man's tongue is in my mouth, thrashing away. All I feel is frisking by strange hands, all I taste is ash and alcohol. I feel his teeth tease at my lip, his body pushing hard against mine. I'm in way over my head. The confidence I found at the bottom of my glass suddenly wears thin. Thankfully, the violent pashing stops, but then he twists me round, grabs my waist from behind, grinding himself into me. His hands wrench round my chest, as he claws at me. It feels more like a body search than affection.

'Wanna get a cab?' he asks me.

To go where? This is more than I can take, and we're still in public. But what can I do? I look up at him, but no words come out. He takes silence as a yes, and grabs my hand, leads me through the crowd.

This is not happening. This is not what I want.

'I better just tell my friends,' I say, pushing his hands off me as we approach the exit sign. *I need an exit – from him.*

'They'll work it out,' he says, grabbing my wrists. I back away, but he walks forward into me, forcing my back onto the rough brick wall at full steam.

'No!'

He's got me cornered. His strong hands fumble with the button on my jeans, his fingers search down. I try to release my wrist but he overpowers me. I look around, desperate for something to take away this fear. Now all I feel is despair. Blood rushes to my head.

I hear the crowd roar, smell a gust of pot, see a flash of light – and Jack! Through the smoky kaleidoscope.

'Fray?'

Thank God.

'Get the fuck away from her!' he screams as he rips the groping giant's shoulder off me. *This is my chance.* My wrists still pinned, I find my knee, and I kick it high into the guy's nuts. He releases me; his hands cover his groin as he riles in pain, crouching on the floor in agony.

Jack grabs me, shepherding me away.

'You can have the bitch – cock tease,' the man scowls.

Jack guides me over to an old cloak room, his arm protecting me.

My eyes well with tears. My hands shake. 'It's okay now,' Jack whispers. He sits down on the floor, as I remain cradled in his arms, his Band-Aid voice purring in my ear. I hide into him like a child. The sobs pour out, wetting his shirt. He holds my cheek in his hand, nudging my chin up so our eyes meet. 'It's all over,' he whispers gently.

I notice for the first time that his eyes are grey, not blue, and I have to stop myself from kissing him.

'Where's Kate?' I slur. 'Can you find her?' I ask, looking around in circles. 'I need to go home.' I want this night to end.

'I'm not leaving you alone again,' he says. 'She'll find us.'

'He just wouldn't stop. I thought I could handle myself but he was so strong.' My lip trembles. We sit in silence as we wait for Kate to turn up. He rubs my shoulder, I lean into him with the other. 'You know what this reminds me of?' he says. 'The bumper sticker Ben stuck on his truck, the one your mother made him take off – Neigh Means Neigh.' He laughs, and I feel my lips curl into a smile.

My brother always was a sicko.

I just sit in my safe haven, surrounded by lockers blocking out the nasty world, with Jack calmly stroking my hair.

I'm brought back to reality when I hear my brother's voice through the beat as he intrudes into our quiet corner.

I blush with shame at my disappointment when Kate's face appears from the crowd, triggering the release from the safety of Jack's arms. She's found my brother. She's found us.

'There you are!' Kate yells. 'You're missing Bernie!'

Ben shakes his head at me sitting on the floor. 'If you're drunk, Frankfurt, Mum'll ground me.'

I guess we can go home now. Yet moments before, it felt like I already was.

'You're not going home already?' Kate blurts to me in frustration as Jack leads me to the door.

'That guy freaked me out. It's nearly midnight; I just want to go. Ben, can you stay with her?'

I take his grunt as a yes. Kate looks at me in disbelief.

'Fine, just go!' She folds her arms.

Jack and I meander through the markets and cobbled street, and

I start to relax. Jack tries to cheer me up by trying on knitted beanies from one of the stalls, pays a balloon artist to shape me an animal that vaguely resembles a pig, and orders me an Italian hot chocolate at a café just as it is closing. As we approach the train station, we decide to split a large fries to soak up the alcohol. Jack seems deep in thought. Is he lost without Kate?

'My dad always told me the hot ones were trouble,' Jack says, dipping a chip in tomato sauce as we dodge the crowds in the night air.

'Are we talking girls or chips here?' I ask.

'See, it's never easy like this with Kate,' he says with a laugh in his breath. 'Everything is so . . . difficult. Never just "being", like with you.'

'Well, she likes her drama. Likes to feel grown up.'

'She can be pretty immature for someone wanting to feel grown up.'

'Jack, if you want low maintenance, you shouldn't have picked someone like Kate.'

The fights, the making up, it's been like this all term – me being the mediator between my two best friends. They were the It couple most of the year, but lately things have started to change. Their bubble is about to burst, and I don't want to be around when it does. I feel a little responsible for his predicament. It was me who brought them together. She was my friend, he was always around – things just happened. A flutter of guilt buzzes in my stomach with all this talk of her. This wasn't me, bagging my best friend to her boyfriend. I don't do bitchy well. 'She can also be pretty amazing.' I laugh, thinking of all the crazy stunts she's pulled. 'Remember when she spoke in nothing but song lyrics for, like, a whole day?'

'Yeah. That was cool.'

'And how she snuck us all into City Rowers fire escape, and we got drunk on $2 Vodkas. What was that crappy Destiny's Child song she danced on the table to?'

'"Say My Name".' A half smile slides across his lips. 'She's pretty amazing in other ways too,' Jack says, raising his eyebrows, poking my ribs.

'Gross,' I say, making gagging gestures. 'Like I don't hear enough of that crap from Kate.'

'Well, can you blame the poor girl?' Jack asks, gesturing to his physique like a game-show hostess with a grand prize.

'Each to their own.'

'She's got some heavy shit going on at home though – her dad grills her about everything, by the sounds. Me, especially. Like he thinks she's still eight.'

'You can understand him trying to protect her from the likes of you.'

'At least her mum is nice,' he says.

'Yeah.'

'I mean, they reckon you should pick a chick with a hot mum, as, like, that's what you'll wake up next to forever, you know?'

A twang of annoyance hits me. The thought of Jack and Kate together forever is nauseating. I picture them – matching greying temples, talking about being high-school sweethearts. I'm not sure where I fit in this picture. Stashed in their granny flat with a freezer of frozen meals and a Crossword Digest? I walk off, leaving Jack stepping along the landscaped-garden edge, like a balance beam.

'Hey, wait up, Lofty!' he calls, grabbing me gently around the shoulders when he catches up. My moodiness has set in now, and started to unpack. 'What's up with you?' he asks.

'Nothing,' I scowl.

We walk into the Brunswick Street train station. My heart sinks when I see the next train isn't for twenty-eight minutes and wish I had the finance for a cab. I hear a ruckus echoing from the end of the platform, some guy screaming.

I hear a laugh like a hyena. Like Kate.

Jack and I rush down to the commotion. It is *Kate – on the track*. My heart stops.

Ben is on the platform, arms out, trying to coax her back. Pleading with her, his voice bumpy like when he was in trouble as a kid.

She is oblivious – heel-to-toeing along the metal track like an acrobat on a tightrope, her elbows up near her ears. I see a bottle of something sloshing in one hand. She takes a sip with each step, the shine of it dribbles down her chin. She's singing like a drunken sailor to no one in particular.

Crazy drunk.

Her words are erratic, her eyes dart from one thing to the next.

'Get her off the track!' I shout at Ben. Now I'm hysterical too.

'What the fuck do you think I've been trying to do for the past ten minutes?' Ben snarls.

My throat tightens. 'She's been down there that long? Why didn't you get some help?' I scream, my fingers raking through my hair.

'Because I'd have to leave her, that's why, Einstein! I got her off once, she just went back!'

I scan the scene, racking my brain for ideas.

There is a light in the distance. A train.

I can hardly hear with the beating of my heart thudding loudly in my ears.

In an instant, Jack is down on the tracks. He grabs her, pulls her to the platform, where Ben guides an uncooperative Kate to safety.

Jack pushes himself up onto the platform and scoops Kate in his arms like she is his bride and the station platform, her threshold.

I breathe heavily, my wobbly legs collapsing under me. She is safe.

The train stops, and leaves, without a soul getting on or off. Jack hides her as far away from the tracks as he can. 'I am not letting you go,' I overhear him say to her in that voice I thought he saved for me, for when I skinned my knee or lost a swimming race. But it's wasted on her. She is elsewhere.

Her angry words show she realises whatever stunt she'd planned is foiled. She starts swinging in vain; her arms are pinned. She tries kicking. Jack gets clocked in the head by her foot. He grimaces, but stays calm, his grip on her unwavering.

Ben starts at her, hurling abuse, fear, relief.

Do I go for help? But that means adults.

We decide to wait it out, see how Jack manages. I try to calm her. I think back to mothers in the grocery shop, using distraction for their toddlers. That is what she reminds me of – a terrible-two having a tantrum, only she's seventeen.

I try to ignore her aggression, and start babbling on about the Formal. Describing the antique lace dress she'd adored for months, what shoes we should look for. I sit next to them, Jack and Kate as one, and me, staking out the corner of the platform. I'm surprised not to find a security guard arrive.

Jack holds her in his lap; his arms, stronger than they look, circling her, make her seem small. He's her life raft. The deep muscle pressure, the weight of him, seems to calm her. She stops, the kicking wanes. The erratic chatter, the quick lyrics, all stop, like the pink Energizer bunny – and her batteries just run out.

Ben checks Jack is okay with her, and decides to get the next train.

'Maybe a train is not the best way home,' Ben adds.

Jack subtly sends him the bird. Kate seems to sink into Jack, like he's a protective cocoon. I know she'll be safe with him. Seeing the suddenly happy couple, wrapped together in their own bubble, I decide to join Ben and go home.

Jack Shaw – the Kate Whisperer.

'Are all the hot ones psycho?' Ben asks on the way home.

I raise my eyebrows at his rhetorical question. I think of my boring brown features – my level headedness. Maybe he is right.

'What was it they said about Marilyn Monroe – if you can't handle her at her worst, you don't deserve her at her best?' I say.

I'm sure mental illness isn't predisposed to the beautiful. I've seen plenty of crusty old men chasing their tails in the streets. But there's nothing wrong with Kate. Her moodiness is just one element in the chemical equation that results in her being the vivacious and unpredictable Kate.

And like any relationship, you take the bad with the good.

CHAPTER 11
Boundary Lines

It has been three months since Jack, Sara and Oli infiltrated my predictable life at 83A Lovedale Road. And slowly, my world is becoming less about working late with nothing to pull me home. Most of the awkwardness surrounding Jack's return has been washed clean, as we develop unconscious filters of mutually acceptable topics when Sara or Oli are home. Yet often, when I have a night shift or day off and Oli is at Kindy, I might hear Jack banging around in his shed, and find a reason to be out back too.

The tin shed, perched on the property line between our blocks, has been the first thing to fall into the communal property list. The boundaries are fuzzy around the washing line too, after I brought in some towels for Jack before an afternoon storm. And Oliver has determined that the strip of weedy grass between where my pergola ends and his fence begins is decidedly *his*. The old cast-iron bath at the side fence, once a thriving vegie garden I soon forgot about, is now a cooking pot – a home to the many concoctions a little boy can invent with sand, stones and sticks as key ingredients. Already a mini-masterchef.

The property lines, originally pegged out with stakes, are becoming elastic. It started slowly, with a knock on the door to borrow a wrench, turning into an open invitation to borrow whatever you need. Hardware is our common ground, our safe zone.

This morning is no different. It is the third day in a row of sanding and painting. I feel like my tongue is thick with paint, it is all I can smell and taste. I am sore in places I don't know the name for – even my thumbs seem to ache from constant flicks of the brush, up and back. Before long, Jack pops his head over the fence, mug in hand.

'Going to Bunnings in a bit – need anything?'

'Nah, thanks.'

'Sure? That paintbrush's seen better days.'

'It's all right. I buy cheap crap – that way when I'm too lazy to wash it properly I feel less guilty about my negligence. I've got a ten-pack of two-dollar brushes in the shed.'

He shakes his head at me. 'You need a good one – horse bristle – makes the finish better.'

'Why so fussy? You think the dudes that buy your place will notice the difference?'

'You're the expert, Frankie . . .' he trails off.

'Actually, I need masking tape, please.'

'You know a careful painter doesn't need masking tape,' he says. I just glare at him. 'Okay – the cheap stuff, I assume?'

'Thanks. Oh, and some rollers?' I add, thinking I left the other one in the sun last time and unsurprisingly it fossilised.

'Rollers? What kind?'

'You're the expert.'

'Nah, don't like that sort of pressure.' He looks down at my paint stash, which is empty. 'You're done here. Just come with me.'

'Come with you?' I am only used to him in context, in my easement. The shed. Maybe my porch. 'I'm covered in paint,' I say, gesturing to my shitty clothes, my blue-speckled Nikes.

'Then you'll fit right in.'

'Won't it look a bit suss?' I say, seeking out witnesses, lowering my voice for Oli's sake. 'I mean, Sara thinks you barely know me . . . still.' I give him the evil eye.

'Frankie. It's the hardware shop, not a motel. Don't be so uptight,' Jack replies. 'Plus, she's at the gym — which is code for gym, coffee, shopping, see you this arv half-tanked. I'll just get Oli dressed, come over in a sec.'

My protests fall on deaf ears, and five minutes later I am wandering sheepishly up the stairs into Jack's house. The change since the last time I snuck in here is inspiring. The crisp white gives the traditional home a modern feel, yet it is in keeping with the original character — the VJs and ornate cornices retained. The floors are gloss, the scuffs of a thousand journeys sanded away. And their furniture finishes the room perfectly — streamlined and elegant. She has style, I have to give her that.

But what strikes me is the enormous family portrait, a professional black-and-white photograph covering most of the main entry wall. Life-sized versions of Jack, Sara and Oli, smiling, crisp and neat in their all-whites and jeans.

They look like a life-insurance ad.

I have to step back to fit all of it in view. I cross my arms and start to feel strangely unwelcome. 'Wow. It's –'

'Ostentatious? Precocious? Grandiose?' Jack comments like a talking thesaurus. 'Big.' He wrestles his son's squirming leg into his overalls.

'Sara likes to maintain a particular image,' Jack says, almost hanging Oli by his legs to get the final boot on. The tininess of his shoe gets to me. It's just so miniature. 'She'd be aghast that I even let you in here – with dishes in the sink, cereal crumbs on the floor.'

It surprises me, his candidness. We're not strangers, yet these unbecoming anecdotes about Sara are unnerving. I look around and see a pristine room – cushions intentionally aligned, bench-top free of clutter. 'How did you, sloth boy, end up with a neat freak?' I ask. It barely looks like a child has even sat on the couch, let alone lived here. No crayon scribbles, no toys.

'Oh, she's just as messy as me, don't you worry. Shit all over her side of the room. Bathroom looks like a ransacked make-up department. She just likes to keep this bit like a museum.'

I wonder about people like that, projecting this image of living a life of perfection, when often it is a house of cards that a puff of wind could unravel.

Oli is finally wearing two matching shoes. Jack gives me the tour of the living area, and I can't help but try to work out what exactly they can see of my place from theirs. Thankfully the pitch of my back roof monopolises most of their view. Naked bolts from the shower to the bedroom? Check.

Jack grabs his keys, and a moment later I am in his passenger seat on the way to the hardware store. Jack speaks freely about his family. How his brother Charlie is working in London as a freelance journalist. I picture him hiding with the paparazzi, hoping to catch a glimpse of Kate and William in a compromising position. I fill him in on my brother Ben – loveless and penniless in T-bar, as he calls Toowoomba. The short trip is turning into a bit of a timeline of our recent lives. I feel like a sponge, soaking in all the Shaw family details that I had wondered about. Oli is unusually quiet in the back – the Wiggles are singing 'Vegetable Soup' and he is totally absorbed. Pure genius.

'You too will be subjected to torture via your ear canals when you have kids.'

'What makes you think I'll have kids?' I shoot back. Why do people think the reason you're childless is public information?

Jack jerks his head back and puckers his lips. He shoots me a sideways glance as we stop at a red light. 'Sorry. Just assumed that was on the cards for you. You did have their names all picked out. Rachel and Ross ring a bell,' he laughs, as he parks the car. My hope that all knowledge of my *Friends* obsession from the nineties is dead and buried is lost. 'No one ever liked Ross, you know. He was lame-arsed.'

'You mock, but I seem to recall you pretending to pash Jennifer Aniston on my *Friends* poster, so fair's fair.'

'Daddy? What's "pash"?' Oli asks as the engine stops, and I rethink my earlier assessment that the Wiggles had forged a cone of silence in the back seat.

'A type of fruit,' I serve back to him.

Jack unfastens Oli's car seat and walks his son through the parking lot. As we enter the giant hardware superstore, the temperature rises ten degrees – it's like a sauna, and smells like enamel. Jack grabs a few items he needs, while Oli asks me the names of gadgets cluttering the aisle. I surreptitiously substitute the word 'tool' for the unknown ones as we walk through the crowded store. Jack dawdles in the brush section, reading labels, comparing brands, then moves on to the paint-tinting queue. I realise now why he wanted company – another person to supervise his active son.

Jack approaches us with paint in hand. He ruffles Oli's hair. 'Well, I hope they're right when they say it's darker on the wall – or Daddy'll be on the couch tonight, Ol.'

I feel lately I know more about Jack's bedroom than I need to.

As we walk to the checkouts, Oli holds his puffy hand out to mine. His fingers are so tiny, so trusting. My heart warms. Jack takes the other, and we swing him gently between us. His giggle is infectious.

A staff member approaches Oli, gives him a tickle under the chin. 'Enjoying your morning out with Mummy and Daddy?' the old codger asks, crouching down to Oli. The little boy hides in Jack's pants leg. Jack and I smile weakly and move to the exit.

'Don't know why you thought this was gonna be weird,' Jack remarks with a wink.

I turn my face so he can't see the flush on my cheeks.

In a look, I remember the reason I lied for him.

CHAPTER 12
Crazy as a Coconut

Cooloola National Park, South East Queensland
2 am, 19 November 2000

As the hours mount, I watch the fire, sitting and waiting for Jack to come back from the point. To come back with her. The other boys are off somewhere looking for Kate, leaving me alone with my wandering thoughts.

I retrace the night in my head. Kate telling me about what happened at the formal with Jack, the ranger, Jack's face when he heard the news of Kate's pregnancy, his race to the point. His fear was real. Why the point? Had she said something about it earlier? Something niggles. She's a drama queen. This might all be a script, a story she has created for us to play out, with the final scene set high on a windy peak. I shudder.

I do occasionally have my doubts about my choice of best friend. I think back to a sleepover when she'd first moved here.

We were up late doing Cosmo *quizzes. Kate put her bed socks on her hands, imitating our least favourite teachers' voices perfectly, as* she acted out R-rated scenes with her sock-puppet doubles. Her long tanned legs thrashed around as she jumped on my bed, laughing at the spectacle she had created. She finally crouched down, grew small.

'If we like, died, do you think any of them would come to our funeral?' Kate asked. I told her, half delirious, that they'd all be dead by the time we carked it, and to shut up. If that weird statement didn't already have my attention, she then went on about how she caught my brother perving on her once from the pool area, how she yanked her shirt up so he could have a proper view. Before I could question her further, she'd run out to the kitchen for a drink.

After what seemed ages, I'd gone after her, slid my door open, tiptoed out in the dead of night. I could hear her talking to someone. I thought, who would still be prowling this late? Ben with the munchies, maybe? I braced the wall and listened. I could see half of her. Kate's arms were crossed, which had the desired effect of pushing her boobs up and half out of her thin, cotton nightie. Her head was flung back as she laughed, then she did that dumb thing where she sucks the chain on her neck. Poor Ben, being led on again, I thought. I heard her muffled voice. 'So, you must do weights and stuff?'

A male replied, an embarrassed laugh. 'I'm a landscaper.'

It was my dad.

I had just about choked at the sight. Kate had her hand on my father's arm, squeezing his bicep. 'What are you doing?' I'd asked, freaked. Dad ordered us to bed in a strange, high-pitched voice, and we never spoke of it again.

Then there were other things she did that felt strange at the time. The night she freaked out at Jack over missing their three-month anniversary. The night she danced on a tabletop like a stripper at a nightclub. Okay, she was unpredictable, but that was part of her charm. Was this just another prank?

实

I leave my dark thoughts in the tent and pace the dune. Finally, I see movement and light ahead in the darkness. A shape on the beach. A torchlight, erratic, swinging from someone. My heart flutters, but I can tell it's too tall, too bulky to be her. And there is only one shadow. Is he carrying her?

It's Jack. Without her. My stomach sinks. That was my last hope. That he'd find her, crying at the point, waiting stubbornly for him to find her, say he's sorry. Take her back.

'She here?' he pants. I realise we just drowned each other's hope.

I shake my head. 'Nothing? No sign of her at the point?' I sob, unable to keep the panic from my voice.

Jack sits on the dune, puffing madly, staring blankly out into the darkness.

I touch his shoulder. He shrugs my hand away.

'I think you should prepare for . . .' His eye twitches, a tear is suspended on his lash. 'She's gone, Fray.'

'It just means she's not at the point.' The panic that I'd parked, that I'd retired and let sit idle while he was gone, now takes centre stage.

'Or the coloured sands, or the wreck, or anywhere in between.' His voice is void of all expression, sucked dry of hope.

'She's got to be somewhere. We just haven't found her. I mean, even if she was . . . gone, there'd be a . . . body. Why did you think she'd be at the point anyway?'

Jack's eyes fall, and he sniffs, can't say the words.

He grows quiet again.

'There's stuff you don't know, Frankie. She was sick.'

'Sick? She was pregnant – it's not a disease.'

He rolls his eyes. 'You still believe that?'

'She wouldn't lie to me. She told me details.'

'So? She was full of shit half the time! She'd make up these elaborate stories. Like, once she told me her mum was gonna die – had

ovarian cancer. I asked Jess about it, and she laughed and said, "She's still telling that one, is she?" Then she told me she was adopted but they never told her. I mean – hello, her mum could be her sister they're so alike.'

'So, it doesn't mean she's suicidal! Isn't that what you're trying to say, Jack? Spit it out! I can take it!'

His lip quivers. 'When I'd ask why she wasn't at school sometimes, she'd say she doesn't sleep for days, then her mum lets her catch up.' He pauses, his eyes trace the shifting clouds in the night sky, hazing over the moon like mist. 'She says some mad shit.'

He used to tell me she said weird stuff, sometimes when it was just Jack and me walking home, but I figured it was the same 'poor ugly me' crap she pulled, so we all had to say how pretty she was.

'She talks about feeling different. Like we should take the Thunderbird and run away together. Sometimes her moods will shift, and she'll like, start wailing shit.'

Seeing his face, all worked up, I think – is this the same boy who Nikko-penned a moustache on my lip when I fell asleep watching Melrose Place? He is serious.

I remember that week she was away from school. It was months ago though. She'd been pissed at the world the week before, hardly speaking to either of us. Jack made me come with him to check on her, said he was concerned, that we should talk to her mum in case she didn't know she was wagging. We'd rocked up to Kate's place, her mum had opened the door and said she was asleep, citing 'lady problems', which made Jack blush and run. Kate was at school the following day, as if nothing had happened. She was chirpy, even – and had braided me a purple friendship bracelet, cut out pictures of some formal dresses she thought I'd like from a mag. Sometimes, it was like remorse. The calm after the storm. Jack said he'd never tried to speak to her mum about his concerns since.

He never spoke to me about it again, not in words. But they lurked in our peripheral vision, waiting to pounce.

Is that what really happened tonight? Did whatever darkness that was lurking, finally pounce?

CHAPTER 13
Outed

Madness. It's a Friday afternoon. Most singles are at the pub, ordering their third drink by now. I, however, am covered in paint-dust. In a harebrained moment, I decided hand-sanding my weatherboards to preserve their unique curved shape is the way to spend my weekend off.

Jack has a beer in hand, setting up a car track down the stairs with his son. I can't help watching them – the picture-perfect family: him – tall dark and handsome; her – fashionable and blonde. Sara is relaxing with a mag, a bottle of wine on the table as she watches her boys from their porch. After initially declining their pity offers to come over, I finally succumb and join Sara for a quick drink.

I rarely see her, which suits me well. She's always at work, or out, or recovering from being out. She has made no attempt to hide her distrust of our set-up. I probably come across as skittish to her, always on edge about what I can and can't say, given she doesn't know Jack and I grew up together. I am kind of over it.

Sara pops inside, presumably to retrieve a glass for me, but I know she won't leave me with her man for long. I seize the opportunity to join the boys in the yard – it still makes me nervous to be around her alone. It takes all my mental energy to self-edit my words – delete all references that may result in slipping out something I shouldn't know – that I am flat out keeping up a meaningful conversation.

Jack fills me in on his new menu at Duck Duck Pig, something about trying to achieve so many hats at the restaurant – how Brisbane is great for fresh produce but how the prawning restrictions are doubling the crustacean prices, wrecking his cost base.

Oli gets over the car racing, and sits contentedly filling a bucket with sand, then tipping it out, the same motion, over and over. Jack watches Oliver, then looks at me, cocking one eyebrow like he used to do to teachers who were rattling on with rubbish during class. It always made me laugh.

Jack's dad's seventieth is coming up, he explains. The family are flying up to Townsville next month – he wonders if I could drive them to the airport if I am not at work? I am happy to earn a credit. One day I might have a life and he could drive me to it.

Sara joins us around the sandpit, has a whinge about having to go back home for the party – how Jack never gets weekends off for her family, but managed to swindle it for his. Jack's eyes glaze over.

I skol the last of my wine, seeing their bickering as a cue to *exit stage left*, when I hear my front gate squeak.

The footsteps in the cracker-dust driveway grow closer.

'Frankfurt – you out back?'

It is my brother's familiar but unexpected voice. How very like him. Turning up unannounced (and usually hungry, with dirty washing).

His unshaven face appears around the side. His eyes grow wide as he takes in all of the instantly appearing house. Then suddenly his eyes fixate on Jack and widen further.

Fuck. I haven't seen Ben in months. I haven't told him about Jack turning up again.

'Well, if it isn't Jack-fucking-Shaw!' Ben says, a swagger in his voice, and a palm raised out to shake.

I jump up, spilling the dregs of my wine, eager to divert Ben back to my place before he does any more damage.

But it's too late.

'Ben?' Jack says, with equal parts surprise and dread in his voice.

'What are you doing here?' I ask my brother. My heart races.

'I could say the same about your friend here, sis. Thought you were in Townsville, mate.' My brother seems taken aback, shocked almost. He swallows hard.

'Moved back, start of the year. This is my partner, Sara. That's our son, Oli.'

'Right, shit, hey,' Ben says, scratching his head. 'Big family man now, huh? So, you visiting Frank?' he asks, dropping his knapsack on my outdoor table and walking over to us. Is it my job to do damage control?

'Ben, Jack and Sara bought out back. They live here.'

Ben looks at me like I have lost my mind. 'What the *fuck*...?'

Time seems to stop.

I can see Sara's reluctance to speak – as if she wants to see how this line of questioning plays out. Trying to stop the damage would be like attempting to control an avalanche. I don't even try.

'Well, ain't that cosy,' Ben says sarcastically. 'Of all the people . . .'

'So you're Frankie's brother, the one Jack said he knew from high school?' Sara asks.

'Technically I was the year ahead of them at school.'

I mentally cringe.

'The year ahead of them?' Sara asks. She turns to Jack. 'You were in the same *grade* as her?' She stares blankly, as if all her cognitive resources are being utilised to figure out what is going on. 'I figured she was much older than you, which explained how you barely knew her.'

Much older? *Cow.*

Jack looks like a deer in the headlights – mesmerised by the steely glare of her eyes.

Ben just seems muddled. 'These two?' he says to Sara. 'Nah, they were tight *as*, ever since they could walk. Mum used to babysit Jack when he was a rug rat.'

Sara shuts her eyes and puffs out one cheek. She looks like a bullfrog.

'So, let me get this straight,' Sara says to Ben, arms crossed. 'Frankie – your sister – and Jack Shaw – standing here – were *tight*?' Sara turns and shoots a glare at Jack, who seems remarkably calm given his world is collapsing. Or perhaps it is relief, as if the decision of how and when to fess up to his little lie-by-omission has been taken from him, left to chance, and finally over with.

'He's right,' Jack admits, with a vacant stare. He looks over to Oli, still happily filling his buckets in the sandpit. I wish the little guy would cover me with sand so I can sink down into a mine-cave out of reach.

'Jack?' Sara says, turning to her partner, 'am I missing something here? Why wouldn't you have . . .?' Then she turns to me, as if seeing me for the first time. She starts waving her finger, pointing. 'The photos – I remember now. He has an old photo of a brunette girl, with a nineties fringe – of you!' Sara closes her eyes, her hand to her mouth, as if she could hold in the emotion with her fingers. 'Is she some sort of old flame? You didn't want me to know we were living next to your ex-girlfriend, so you lied?'

Jack stands mute, forcing me to go in to bat.

'It was nothing like that. We grew up together, but we were never *together*,' I explain. That much is technically true.

'So, why the secrecy, Jack? Why all the lies? If this was all so innocent, why cover it up?' The hurt in her voice niggles at the guilt inside me. I feel the acid in my stomach rise in my throat. I am part of this charade, an unwilling participant, but involved all the same.

Ben just looks in awe, scratching his head, trying to piece together what he's walked in on – what he unwittingly caused. He saunters over to me with a scowl. 'You mean to tell me this chick didn't know you knew each other?' Ben tries to whisper, but his anger spills over.

Now I'm mute.

'That's fucked, man. Good luck with that,' he says, grabbing his bag and storming through my back door.

I stand in their yard, desperate to flee, to let Jack face the interrogation alone, in private. Yet I somehow feel like I have to be dismissed. That I'm an accessory.

'I am sorry, Sara, if we misled you. Jack was uncomfortable with . . .' I start to say, but can't find the words. They are Jack's words to say.

'Things were fucked up, complicated, the last time we all saw each other,' he finally utters. 'I just didn't want to bring up all that with you right at that moment. I didn't plan it; it just got harder the longer it went on.'

Sara throws her hands in the air, grunting with exasperation as she storms inside.

Jack leans on the old saw horse, arms crossed, eyes to the ground, deflated like a beach ball.

'My mess,' he says, walking past to go inside and face the inevitable.

I feel my throat tighten. I retreat home to Ben, to face my own music. Ben is usually quick to step up to his high horse when it comes to matters of his 'perfect' sister showing questionable morality.

I am relieved to hear the shower run. I have a few minutes' grace. I never had to ask him twice to make himself at home.

Disastrous. It's like we just acted the script from a bad sitcom. Yet part of me is relieved – no more pretending. And part of me warms, knowing he kept a photo of me all this time.

实

I tend to be a tad reluctant to take in my older brother when he is in Brisvegas for something. It usually starts well, for the first few days. Then things go downhill. And smell. He did take me in after Seamus, for those weeks between lives, so I could hardly say no.

'So, things have heated up a bit here, by the looks,' Ben says, appearing in my faded pink bathrobe. A waft of steam is in his wake, his wet hair dripping. He smells like my deodorant. 'The most exciting thing in your newsflash usually relates to trialling a new treatment for canine hot-spots,' he teases, in his documentary voice.

'Like your life is so dynamic,' I rebut.

'No, I think you have the monopoly on that one today.'

He starts searching my fridge for sustenance, scratching his balls through my gown and I make a mental note to wash it the moment he goes home.

'So tell me how Jack Shaw goes from a safe distance away in Townsville, to living within spitting distance,' Ben hits me with, as I walk into the lounge.

'Thirteen years have passed, Ben. He wasn't a convict from Colonial London. People move back.'

'Yeah, but what are the chances they move into your street, let alone your fucking yard?'

'Slim, but evidently possible.'

'Slim is very generous. Right up there with "*Magic* fucking *Happens*".' My brother, the anti-hippie.

'Are you suggesting this was orchestrated somehow? Because that would make you certifiable.'

And I thought Jack would be the one on the heat tonight, although from the bellowing coming from their house, he isn't missing it. My stomach churns.

'I am just saying it's hard to believe it happened by chance,' Ben pipes in.

'Well, it did.'

'Out of all the vacant blocks in the land, they chose yours.'

'It's not unusual for people to return to their roots. And vacant blocks around here, in an old area, are rare.'

Ben looks blank. 'You don't think Jack could have done a title search, found where you live?'

'Why would he do that?' I say, slamming the back door, hoping it will hide our petty argument from the neighbours. If we could hear them, perhaps it worked both ways.

'Because you're *you*, Frank. And he's Jack, and that is just what you guys do.'

I shake my head at him. What is he on about?

I shut the windows. 'Ben, if he wanted to see me, suddenly, after thirteen years, he could have called, visited. He didn't need to buy that land.'

That shuts him up. He suddenly calms, starts to scratch his head, as if unsure of his logic.

'It's still fucking weird, Frankie.'

'Don't you think I know that? Don't you think my heart skipped a beat when he turned up at my door?'

'Okay. So why the secret squirrel crap? Why not tell his missus?'

'He never told her about what happened before.'

Ben looks at me, stunned. 'It was in the papers, Frankie.'

'Half a lifetime ago.'

'And besides, he could have acknowledged knowing you, without bringing all the shit up.'

'Who knows?' I shrug. 'It might be a slippery slope to all things Kate.'

I see Ben's face drop when I mention her name.

I lean on the kitchen bench, feeling sick with guilt. Why had I gone along with this stupid lie? I didn't feel at all sympathetic towards Jack now. He had it coming. I can't say I had warmed to Gym-Barbie but she deserved some respect. I was part of the charade despite Jack being the creator. I was never entirely sure why he didn't just come clean – it seemed like a storm in a teacup, heavier now than it should have been. I had imagined that Kate's story, and all of us, would have been broached at some point in their relationship, if they had any sort of real intimacy.

As Ben and I hear the raw emotion escaping from out the back, I realise there was no such thing as privacy at 83 Lovedale Road since they hacked it in two. I am torn between the grown-up thing to do – turn on the TV and let them bicker – and my desperate curiosity to hear how he scrambles his way out of it.

I always thought you acted strange around her. Are you sleeping with her? I hear Sara bellow. *Just answer me, Jack!*

My heart sinks as I hear the hurt in her voice. It was all so unnecessary – avoidable.

'Had it coming,' Ben says, taking his pilfered supplies from my pantry to the couch for immediate consumption. An open box of rice crackers falls to the floor, and he expertly hooks it with his toe on the way through.

'None of our business, Ben.'

'My arse. You were in on this too. Don't play the innocent card. And how long have you been playing this strangers thing?'

'You were the one to let the cat out of the bag.'

'You didn't tell me shit! Couldn't you have texted me – *BTW Jack Shaw moved in next door*? And why would I have assumed his wife didn't know anything about you two?'

'She's not his wife.'

'Same shit. May as well be.'

The ear-splitting emotional shrieks from Sara, rebutted by Jack's short, sharp, emotionally void responses, are still audible through the closed windows. Next I hear him get going, the temper flares, and his deeper voice retaliates.

'Do you think he will have to spill about Kate now?' I ask. He is being tortured by a pro, by the sounds of it.

'Brave man if he does,' Ben says, raising his eyebrows.

'I just thought it might explain why the big silence. Stop her thinking it was something to do with me.'

'We'll you're kinda part of it.'

I glare at him. He shows me his palms like he's under arrest. 'Whatever,' he says, dismissing me with a flick and finishing off his makeshift dinner. We start to relax when the verbal gunfire from out back infiltrates the room through the closed windows. The shrill of Sara's voice makes us both stop and brace ourselves.

So the cops think you killed her? Who are you, Jack?

My heartbeat races.

'Well, that answers that one. It's all coming out now,' Ben offers, to lighten the mood. We both move into the lounge to avoid the firestorm.

Ben starts chewing on a toothpick, an old annoying habit he has never grown out of. His ability to find straws, toothpicks, bits of plastic to chew on in any setting is remarkable. Ben is nothing if not resourceful. I don't even own toothpicks.

'So, besides there being a friggin' monstrosity of a house in your back yard – and the kid we grew up with living in it – what else has been happening?' Ben asks with a laugh.

'That about sums it up,' I concede, staring blankly at the TV screen. The cyclic hum of the argument next door drones on.

We chat comfortably over a flagon of red.

By about the third drink, it comes to light that Ben's been dumped. The latest flame in his bachelor life has been smothered, no doubt by his lack of career aspirations and pot-addiction. Yet no good would come of me highlighting this possibility. The lease of their flat is in her name, of course, so he sits, broken-hearted, homeless, and *here*. A gentle suggestion that perhaps our parents would like a 'visit' from him is met with quick dismissal. Mum and Dad still hover in our lives and live locally, but somehow seem distant. Things have never quite been the same since I left school. Since our disagreement.

Ben has always been a tortured soul. His music, his movies – always eccentric, intelligent and dark. It gave him an air of mystery, but an overarching sense of being high maintenance. I love my brother, admire his passion for life, yet he can only be taken in small doses.

'Just don't get it. Wouldn't all that shit have come up? It must have packed a punch,' Ben says. 'Doesn't say much for their relationship.'

'I can't say I tell people about it. Only Seamus.'

Ben turns quiet. He pales. And I know how it feels to have the locked box of **all things Kate** wrenched open unexpectedly, so give him some space to play catch-up. He had been around her enough in high school for it to have left a mark. I had wondered how much of the months of boozing when I left school was related, or something that was on his roadmap regardless. He had attended uni less and less the following year, until finally pulling the pin. It didn't slow him though, with contract IT work keeping him in supply of beer and burgers, and suitable non-fussy ladies.

But I dare say concern for Ben was overshadowed by our parents' constant worry over me during that dark patch of our family history.

'I am surprised you went along with it – lying to Sara. You are always on your high horse about honesty, especially since Seamus trampled you.' He is right. I wonder how Sara will act around me now, how much of the dishonesty she will attribute to me. I have never willingly deceived someone for so long.

'I'm not proud of it,' I tell Ben, sipping my wine. 'I guess I felt the pull of loyalty to Jack, to protect his need to keep all that under wraps.'

'Not the first time you've covered for him,' Ben says. A shiver trails up my spine. Does he know more than I think about that harrowing night?

'Remember when Mrs Marsh's car got scratched with his handlebars?'

Phew. No. 'Whatever,' I exhale. 'Besides, I wasn't in the firing line from the media like he was. I can understand him wanting to live a life without that clouding him.' Yet it surprises me that he hadn't even broached it with the woman he lives with.

Ben talks about apologising to Jack for the consequences of him arriving unannounced, but I want to stay right out of that minefield.

I bite my nails. 'What did you mean before, when you said something about "because it's me and Jack" like we were a single entity or something?'

Ben, still slumped in the couch like a wilting palm, seems deep in thought. He skols another glass like water. 'Just how you two were always . . . connected,' Ben slurs.

'Well, I was kind of *unconnected* there for a decade or so.'

'I mean, you always gravitated to each other. On the same page with stuff.'

'Like what?' I knew we *got* each other; I didn't know others knew.

'The duet you did at our street's New Year's Karaoke party.'

'We were eight, Ben.'

'People had you geared up for an arranged marriage after that.'

I shake my head.

'Or with games – we'd play Pictionary, and you would draw one stick figure, and he would guess it.'

'He was probably cheating.'

'My thought at first, but I realised it was just like that between you. Like with charades – you would think it and he would say it. I could never compete. I was always the third wheel.'

'Funny, that's how I always felt when he was with Kate. Like the extra person.'

Ben grows quiet. 'See, I reckon Kate felt it was always her.'

Our isosceles triangle, forever being wacked out of shape.

'How would you know that? They were always all over each other,' I say, swirling the dregs in my cup.

'Why was that, you think?' Ben says, then burps. Loudly.

'Because she was hot and Jack was a teenage boy?'

'Because that was the one thing she could do with him that you couldn't. It was the only trick she had.' He takes another slug of wine.

'Since when are you Mr Psychoanalytic?'

'Since I have clocked up a few failed relationships.'

Since he had the truth serum in him.

'You seem to have taken a lot of interest in Kate. Then, I always did think you had a thing for her.' I sneak a glance over my glass to see his reaction. His expression changes, his lips tighten.

'Let's just say I am not new to the torture of unrequited love.'

I clean up his packets, his crumbs, and throw his washing in my machine before it stinks out my house. I start to feel like Mum. Ben's slave.

'So, what's he like now? Jack, I mean,' Ben yells down to the laundry, getting up. 'Mr Family Man?' I return upstairs and slump on the couch.

'I take it you don't intend to stick around to find out, come by for dinner or something?'

'I am not sure that is an option after our reunion.'

'Fair enough. Well, I guess he's not going anywhere in a hurry.' It suddenly occurs to me that Sara may have a 'For Sale' sign out the front before I know it.

'So? What's he like? And what is it with Jack and the hot ones?' Ben asks again.

Is Sara hot? Fit, sure, but *hot*? Apparently so.

I frown. 'You mean, does Jack still rate girls' "hooters" when they walk past, and burp the *M.A.S.H.* theme?'

'I am sure he still does both of those things, just not in mixed company.'

'He's much the same. Still a smartarse, still fairly relaxed. Blokey with his tools. It is weird, though, seeing him as a doting dad. Makes me think we are supposed to be grown up now.'

'You're not exactly a senior citizen. Although you do act like one, but that's nothing new.' He smirks. 'It's the kid. They age you. Wear you down. Chicks I date with kids seem far more clapped-out than those without.'

So I should look on the bright side of childlessness thus far – at least I can date men like Ben without feeling *clapped-out*. Joy. Then I think of Jack again, how he is with Oli. There is nothing like it. Being a parent. It makes you extraordinary – to someone at least. I realise I am smiling to myself, picturing the time Jack did his Elmo impression for Oliver one afternoon, keeping us all in stitches.

'Jack's turned into a bit of a foodie though. He's a restaurant manager, trained as a chef. Get this – he has a pepper grinder with a light on it. And actually cares what wine he drinks with what.'

'After playing Goon-Of-Fortune on our washing line when he was fifteen – who would have *thunk* it?' jokes Ben. I have to smile at the image of Jack tying a wine bladder to our backyard clothesline with my mum's dressing gown cord. We would spin it, and whoever was standing under the spout when it stopped had to skol. A giggle escapes.

'Look at you, Frankfurt, talking about that nincompoop. That is the happiest I've seen you since Shithead cheated on you.' Ben shoves me along the couch. 'Don't try to deny it.'

I choose to ignore his comment outwardly, but secretly what he says irks me.

Deja vu creeps up my spine. I recognise this feeling. I have had it before. But after what happened last time I tried to act on it, I can't go there again.

实

Things are eerily quiet at 83 Lovedale Road after the storm that unsettled us all.

Ben is gone the next afternoon when I return from work – as unannounced as his arrival – and Jack is conspicuously absent for the days that follow. I overhear the odd scuffle between Sara and Jack – usually in the morning, as he works most nights – but if we cross paths, even at a distance, Sara's eyes skip mine. Jack has not been careless enough to place himself near me, by design I am sure. I am yet to hear his signature knock on the door. No requests to lend tools, share a bottle of red, ask me to watch Oli while he has a shower for work, or provide some wrongly delivered mail. Whether this stems from annoyance towards me for not protecting his story, or from some order from Sara to stay clear, I'm not sure.

My predictable life – life before Jack was back – returns. Work. Eat. Sleep.

What did I do before this soap opera landed on my doorstep?

And now it's a standard Friday night. I pop in to Meg's for a drink after work. I'm always shocked at the mess when I turn up unannounced at her place. Not a skerrick of bench space can be seen, with piles of papers and half-built Lego cars cluttering the tables. Uneaten crusts and apple cores are stacked between plates next to little plastic cups upturned in milk ponds. A ball of black wool has been strung between every chair, pole and table leg throughout the room – appearing like an oversized spider's web. And I am about to get caught.

As I duck and weave the string, Meg appears from the cacophony of sounds emanating from the kitchen, toddler on hip (I think it's Small, but it is hard to tell when they're not all together and I'm not sure where Medium and Large are).

'Sorry, kids have run riot.' She has her usual frazzled but welcoming face, and the same yoghurt-stained skirt I saw her in yesterday. Without a word she dumps the kid on the couch, grabs a Sav Blanc from the fridge in one hand, hooks two glasses in the other and nods her head in the direction of her deck. 'Quick, let's hide. *Peppa Pig* is on but we don't have long.'

Stepping over the intricate web, I follow her out back.

'So, what was with all that scuffle the other night? Dish it up, girl!' Meg asks me as we sip our wine.

Knowing Jack is out, and out of earshot, I fill her in.

'But how could he not have told her anything? Is he a closed book?' I realise Meg is a hopeless gossip.

'I guess he moved away, no one knew about it, he just compartmentalised it all. I mean, it was just one chapter in his life, I suppose.' I am somehow defensive of him, knowing how difficult it was back then.

'A pretty tumultuous one, though, by the looks. Sorry, I Googled it after what you said the other night,' Meg admits, and I mentally cringe. She caught me in a weak moment over a wine last week and I spilled about Kate. About Jack. She did warn me she would get to the bottom of my history with Jack. But I have second thoughts about telling her, now it appears she's *researching* us.

'You Googled *what*, exactly?'

'Frankie, if it happened, it is on the net. Don't tell me you haven't sniffed around a bit.'

'Not really. It was a long time ago. And I was pretty happy with it staying that way until Jack did his reappearing act. I mean, I didn't even tell you about it till you got me drunk and did that stare thing – it's like a truth serum, you know,

I've seen you do it with the kids – so, yeah, I get his reluctance to tell people.'

'People, yeah, but his *partner*? I mean, he has seen this woman in labour. Surely they have at one point been stripped-down-bare with each other to a level that he could tell her? If only to avoid her finding it out on Google. Or from your dickhead brother.'

'That was my fault. Ben was ambushed. I am sure Jack has his reasons for wanting to keep it out of the present.'

'Makes me think there was more to you and him than you let on.'

'It wasn't like that. He was in love with my best friend, for one.'

Meg's neck tilts in a pity nod as she gives my knee a squeeze under the table.

The kids' show ends and noise erupts from the lounge. Boys appear from every corner, all demanding something in whiney voices. Meg rolls her eyes. Knowing I'll only get a fraction of her attention now, I decide to retreat home.

'I'd give Jack a wide berth if I were you, hon.' She hugs me and it feels slightly indulgent to go home to an empty house where I can do as I please, after all that mayhem. Then I see Jack's Subaru fly into his drive. Our drive.

He gets out, flinging his car keys round his finger like a baton; he pauses when he sees me hop the fence out of sheer laziness. I cringe as I realise my three-quarter pants are stuck on the chain-wire fence.

I have never looked less graceful.

Instead of offering to help, I hear him laugh.

'Were you waiting in the bushes for me to come home?'

he teases. 'Well, it's nothing worse than me buying your house, just to stalk you,' he says with a smile.

Shit, he did hear us – or at least Ben's foghorn the other night. 'You heard that?' I ask, appalled and embarrassed. 'Ben does have some issues with paranoia. I put it down to his history of drug use.'

I struggle with prying the wire free. Jack stands by, motionless.

'What happened to chivalry?' I call to him.

'Feminism, I think,' he replies, walking over to the fence.

By now I have successfully unhooked my hem, thankfully with no embarrassing rips. He walks me to my door.

'So how deep are you in it, at home?' I ask.

'Up the creek,' he says. 'I have actually been grounded, and banned from speaking to you. Bit like a restraining order, really.'

'Since we are having an affair and all,' I tease, revealing what I overheard.

'Well, at least that would make buying this friggin' swamp land worthwhile,' Jack says. 'Your brother always felt the need to paint the worst picture of me to you.'

'Protective,' I say, walking over to my front steps.

I stand on my porch, Bear at my side. The security light welcomes me home, shining on me as I hold my shoes in one hand, the railing in the other. 'I am sorry he got you up the creek though.'

'Had it coming, almost a relief,' Jack says. 'Felt like a prick every day, lying to her. Used to make me feel sick.'

Oh, I know that feeling. 'I guess. Still, I'm sure all this was not what you had in mind when you moved down here . . . everything coming back.'

'It hasn't been all bad,' he says, his eyes softening as he smiles. His eyes hold mine and keep me there. My insides warm, and I picture Kate – her turquoise eyes glaring at us through branches in the moonlight.

In that moment, it is ever so clear to me. The need to keep the boundaries firm.

'I better go in,' I say, dipping my eyes.

He bids me adieu with his two-finger salute and disappears round the side, to his family.

Where he belongs, I tell myself.

CHAPTER 14
Lies. All of It.

Cooloola National Park, South East Queensland
4.30 am, 19 November 2000

After another hour of hearing Jack's stories on how crazy he thinks Kate is, and me questioning him on why he would dump her on a deserted beach if he thought she was so crazy, I decide to hide from it all and try to rest in my tent. It's nearly dawn, and I am struggling to keep my eyes from closing. I turn and toss, despite being physically and mentally spent, thinking – hoping – every noise is Kate returning. My puffy sleeping bag sticks to my legs like cling-wrap, a lather of sweat trickling down my neck.

I must have dozed, because I wake with a start and a pounding pain behind my eyes. For an instant I forget Kate is missing. I hear birds. I see light. It's daybreak. My ears detect someone rummaging through boxes. An anonymous foot trips on a tent peg, my canvas chamber wobbles, someone swears.

Male. Not Kate.

I poke my head out, squint in the blazing sun cresting over the horizon, shimmering on the aqua terraces. It all looks so innocent in the light of day. Like nothing sinister could hatch in this setting. It is the picture of postcards.

As I stretch I am hit by a wave of nausea. I find a water bottle and a chair, and slump into it like an old woman. The tide is out. The beach will become a highway again soon, convoys of Patrols, Hiluxes, Landcruisers, all flicking their indicators to warn which side they will approach oncoming cars. The barge will start ferrying campers across the Noosa River. Will Kate be on one?

I see Jack stir in his makeshift swag – a surfboard cover stuffed with towels. I hope he stays there. I don't know how to be with him now, and I'm talked out. The events of yesterday have crystallised in my mind overnight in the silence of my tent, but how I feel for him is shaky at best. My gut tells me he speaks the truth – that he didn't sleep with Kate – but my brain is wary. What if he's telling stories, covering his own mistakes? Trying to keep me on-side?

I hear the roar of the ranger's ute growing closer, mounting the dune. My throat tightens with the thought of what he might have found, what news he holds for us. I try to make out if he has a passenger.

The ranger has returned with his partner, but his face, his tone has changed. There is a frenzy of activity, not all of which I seem to comprehend. The ranger, Bob, dispatches a search team that scours the coastline. He explains how timing in these matters is paramount.

'Look, I don't want you to get your hopes up, it may be nothing, but the ferry operator did report that a young blonde girl and a middle-aged man crossed the river at first light this morning, so we're investigating that lead.'

My heart fills with hope.

'But you had the photo, right?' Jack asks, arms rigid on his hips. 'Did they say it was Kate?'

'They couldn't be sure. They remained in the vehicle, so it's hard to say.'

'What kind of car?'

The ranger pats Jack on the shoulder. 'It's being investigated.' His tone is smug. 'There's another lot of school-leavers down in the camping area, so it may have been one of that crew – you know you lot are out of bounds up here. We're doing everything possible. You don't need to worry.'

Jack shrugs his hand off and exhales loudly. 'I don't need to worry? Are you hearing us? She's been gone all night!' He looks like a thug at a pub, ready to start swinging.

I shoot Jack a glare and he pulls his head in. I see him readying to fire again, and grab his arm, pull him away. Ranger Bob wanders back to his truck.

'Don't piss him off, Jack,' I whisper through gritted teeth.

He shrugs me off too and sulks under a tree. I'm still angry at Jack, but I can't watch him orchestrate his own arrest.

I sit on a chair and hug my knees, watching the action unfold. I welcome the direction, the newfound hope, but it is as if we kids had been rehearsing a bad play, and the grown-ups have arrived to pick us up, take over the plot. But the play carries on without us.

As more and more adults infiltrate our world, our camp, we all retreat into being children – longing to be protected. Grateful someone else is making the decisions, asking the questions. All our brashness of yesterday afternoon, our independence, seems a distant memory. My gut is a twisted mess, like I've swallowed barbed wire.

Our world is shattering.

As the sun beats down, the sand heats up beneath our feet. We potter around camp distracted, unfocused, worried sick. We all retreat into ourselves. All the blame, the theories, have been voiced already. Now all we can do is wait. And hope.

A marked police 4WD skids up to our camp – now their headquarters, by the looks of it. The two cops stand in a semi-circle, arms crossed, heads bobbing as the ranger fills them in.

On what? The nothingness? The absence of news?

A red-faced policeman in a navy Akubra calls us over to his makeshift station – two camp chairs and an Esky under a tree. The officer, with more hair on his face than his head, gets a sense of who's who in our pack, before picking us off one by one. Jack is called over first. He asks the rest of us to clear off out of earshot. Jack gives me a determined look as he paces away, with a half-hearted thumbs up.

Yeah, Jack, everything is just peachy.

A second officer, a woman with cherry-red locks in a tight bun, calls me to another 'interview room' under a blue tattered tarp. I peer over my shoulder at Jack as I follow her into a sheltered pocket. Jack's arms are folded tight, his heels forming arches in the sand as the officer starts the interrogation. I stumble, off balance, before finding the cop waiting for me in the shade.

My throat tightens as I perch on the canvas sling chair, unable to relax enough to sink into its folds. I fiddle with the empty drink holder on the arm rest. The red-head reveals a recording device, and presses the small grey button. An amber light appears, along with a sickening feeling in my gut. She takes my details in that soft tone teachers use when they're trying to make friends. I relay the easy parts – how long I'd known Kate (can it really only be a year?), how she was dating Jack, how the fisherman helped us call the ranger about the flat battery.

'What time was it then? The last time you saw Kate?' she asks when her hand, scrawling quickly in her little blue book, catches up with my words.

'Um, not sure. It was getting dark, so I'm guessing six something?'

'The ranger was called at six forty-five so it must have been after that.'

So I'm already fucking this up. Why ask me if you already know?
'Really? Oh okay. Well, it was after that . . . say seven.'

'Do you think you could identify where this fisherman was? How far along the beach?'

'I guess. He had a white beard that was all brownish. Do you think he's involved?'

'We're just gathering information at this early stage, Francesca.' She wipes sweat off her brow. 'So you, Jack and Kate were walking back after the fisherman called the ranger. You stayed together the whole time?'

'Kinda. Jack walked ahead for a while. We were dawdling, collecting shells.' *Kate told me she was growing a belly full of arms and legs.* 'About halfway back they decided they wanted to be alone, so I walked back.'

'Was there a particular reason for that? Wouldn't it have been safer for you to walk back together – you said it was getting dark by then . . . seven pm?'

I couldn't bear being with them another second, I was so pissed at what Kate told me. He'd played me.

'I think they were planning on, you know, getting with each other. So I kinda wanted to leave them alone.'

Red-head's pen pauses, her eyes seem to pierce mine. Did she have a lie detector installed in her pupils?

'So, between calling the ranger, and Jack and Kate walking off together, how would you describe her demeanour?'

'She was fine. Like, happy. She was making a shell necklace for me. She was excited about the end of school.' *About being a mother.*

'She didn't share any concerns with you? About her school results? Her future, nothing like that?' *No, she wasn't at all concerned that she was up the duff at seventeen.*

161

'Well, she did earlier that day. She joked she might miss out on uni. But I wouldn't say it concerned her. She isn't really the studying type.'

There it is again, the lie detector in her eyes, staring me down. Niggling at my conscience.

'So, nothing else? She didn't mention any problems she was having with her boyfriend? At home? Nothing like that?' An image of Jack in handcuffs, the headline 'Boyfriend kills pregnant teen!' race through my muddled brain. Jack's unwavering eyes. His thumbs up. I don't need anybody lying for me.

'Nope,' I tell the ground, as I pick at the seam on the chair, unravelling as quickly as the lies from my lips. Yes.

'And Jack? How would you describe his mood when they left together?'

Shit-scared. Fed up with her.

'He was pretty relaxed. Fairly normal.' Readying himself to dump his girlfriend for me. He'd already tried, twice, and chickened out.

'Nothing unusual?' red-head prods.

'Nuh,' I say to my feet. I won't let her eyes see mine.

She stops writing, sits back in her chair, twirls the pen in her hand.

'You're sure?' Her tone is unconvinced. 'Because the ranger said that when he arrived you said,' she flicks back some pages, 'there was an argument, and then she ran off.'

Shit. My eyes slide sideways to the trees. 'Yep. Jack said they argued. I am not sure about what.'

'How much had Jack had to drink?'

'Maybe three beers?' I won't mention the rum.

'How long was it, till Jack returned alone?'

'I'm not sure. A while. Maybe twenty minutes?' Or an hour or so.

'And the other boys. They remained at the camp the whole time you were gone?'

'Yep. Far as I know.' Exploding farts. Drinking under-aged. Wanking into socks.

'And when Jack returned, how would you describe his mood?'

Oh God. I can't avoid her eyes again – she'll know I'm full of shit.

I look straight at her. 'He was a little shaken up. Worried about where she went. Said they argued. That he went for a pee in the dunes. When he came back she was gone. She must have run off.'

She taps her pen on her clipboard.

'Quite quick, is she, Kate? Bit of an athlete? Jack looks fairly light on his feet.'

We dawdled during cross-country a few months back, and tied for last place.

'She's a good rower. She swims in squad.' I look at the glassy waves, tranquil in the light of day, and wonder what they know.

'Have you been with Jack ever since he returned?'

'Yes.' Except for those hours when he charged off to the point like an unstoppable train.

'Did Jack elaborate on the reason she went off? Say what they argued about?'

'No.' Yes. He broke her heart. She said she'd do better.

'You are her best friend. And from what I hear, you know Jack pretty well too. You grew up together, right? Tell me what you think they might have disagreed about.'

My knee jitters, along with my nerve. I peek over the dune to see if they still have Jack. I picture his arms wrenched back in handcuffs, his head being pushed down into a police car. I know he didn't hurt her, but red-head won't think that. That's not how it will seem. To these people.

A rush of blood fills my head. I panic in silence.

She stares at me blankly. 'I'll give you some possibilities. Were they sexually active?'

Bingo! Give the girl a medal. Kate says yes, Jack says no. So that equals an average response of who-the-fuck-knows?

So I tell her what I am sure of, and look her straight down the line.

'I don't know. They made out a lot. They were thinking about it. But I'll tell you what I am certain of. I know Jack would never hurt anyone.'

She considers me with a crooked smile. 'Who's saying he did?' she asks, kinking her head to one side. 'So what do you think did happen to Kate?'

'I don't know!' I yell. 'Maybe she hooked up with those other schoolies the fisherman said he saw? Or hurt her leg trying to walk back? I don't know.' I rake my fingers through my hair, feel the knotted mass of salt-stiffened strands. 'I just want you to find her so everything can be sorted out!'

A quizzical look finds its way onto the red-head's pale complexion. 'Everything? Is it Kate you are most worried about, Francesca?'

'Of course. She was my best friend.'

She nods. I realise I am using past tense. I turn again to see if Jack is done yet, or still trapped.

'Because it seems you're more worried about Jack.'

Her eyes lower. Her pen clicks closed. Her finger stops the tape, and my nerves uncoil.

'That's it. For now.'

CHAPTER 15
Duck Duck Pig

The cold war lasts a few more weeks at 83B Lovedale Road, before Jack devises a plan to see me without detection from his wards-person. He scrawls *Duck Duck Pig. 7.30* on my right hand, reminding me not to be late – apparently people wait for months for a table at his restaurant. It is like we are back in school – biro marks all over our forearms. After sneering at my pitiful excuse for a wardrobe, I settle on black pants, a grey knit and boots. I don't leave home in winter without boots. I glance down at my outfit, the absence of anything resembling colour of any shade, and wonder if Ben was right – maybe I do dress like a communist.

I hear Mitch's car pull up next door – Meg's ticket out of her home-cave. In a nanosecond, she is at my door, beaming like an overexcited labrador, waving a bottle of wine around like a game-show host. Come to think of it, she is dressed like one too. Heels were never my thing.

I tower over most women in ballet flats, but they make her petite frame even more elegant. 'Time for a roadie?' she asks.

'Bring it on. Oh, only problem is, I have a camping toilet for a dunny, so you may want to ease off a bit on the liquid intake.'

She cocks one eyebrow. 'I hope that is temporary?'

'Plumber comes Monday.'

'Just checking. I never know with you. Given you live with a kitchen that is, well, about on par with the standard Mitch fashions for us when we're camping.' The quality of facilities has obviously dropped below Meg's fairly low standards, and we decide to head off.

We arrive at Jack's work. I am immediately taken aback by the character of the place. Usually these formal venues are wide open, brightly lit, sparsely furnished seas of crisp white and chrome, devoid of personality. But Duck Duck Pig is like an explosion of eclectic charm, huddled in a dark cave. The mismatched wooden furniture is rustic and funky. Corner booths for larger groups are adorned with candles and oversized cushions, hidden from the crowds by Indian-inspired fabric curtains. Antique bird cages are chained to the roof, a retro phone booth houses the ATM, and an old rusty bicycle is perched on one of the rafters. The galley kitchen is sunk into the floor in the centre of the restaurant, with a huge wooden wine rack barricading it from view. It feels a little like we are guests in a funky Spanish friend's home, who's part hippie, part modern-style guru. It is bold, it is madness, but it works.

A charming, elegant woman seats Meg and me at an intimate table near a window. Or, more accurately, a porthole.

'Mr Shaw has requested this table for you,' she informs us.

Mr Shaw. She sounds like she's referring to Jack's dad. Then I remember we are grown-ups now.

It's cosy. Through our porthole to the outside world, we can see the glimmering river meandering along the edge of the botanic gardens. But my eyes are continually drawn back to the trinkets, the hidden embellishments and ornaments adding to the ambience that had engulfed me when I entered.

As we sit, I can see Meg's jaw drop – she is as impressed as I am. It's so unexpected. Standard brick pillars adorn the external façade – you would never imagine a stylish world of intrigue is contained within its walls. It's like we entered a scene from *Harry Potter.*

'I heard one of the mothers at school say this place was cool, but this is divine.' Meg is a star-struck teenager.

When we settle in to our new universe, we catch up – Meg describing her trouble finding a family holiday that wouldn't just be *same shit, different place,* and I vent my usual work crap – procedures, shift changes, the norm.

The food and wine seem to arrive by magic. I start to wonder if this is standard, yet the waitress informs us that Mr Shaw has selected a menu for his 'VIPs'.

I have no idea what I am eating – other than being Spanish-style tapas – but it's like nothing I've ever tried. How had I not known such flavour combinations existed?

Meg is rattling on about the P&C when I see him. Her rant, along with the oriental chimes of the music, fade away. His back is to us, but I'd recognise the nape of that neck anywhere. Jack heads up from the kitchen, a clipboard under arm. He is dressed in the black tailored pants and crisp white shirt I have often seen him race out to the car in as I get home. But now that I see him in context, he seems different.

The staff are his disciples, shadowing him as he snakes from the front desk, to the back office, to the kitchen. Asking his permission, asking for advice, who can tell? But he has a way about him, here in his little world. He beams with the effortless confidence I remember him exuding as a teen – stopping to chat to a chef, giving a waitress a wink as she passes. Jack Shaw – all dressed up; the clipboard, the pen tucked behind his ear, they give him an air of authority that makes me proud of him. He may not have become a rock star, but he has become something that makes him light up inside. That he is good at, and respected for. He's become a rock star after all.

I see him wander past the bar to the mezzanine level. With all tables full, a line has formed outside, complete with little crowd-control ropes and a sturdy bouncer. I watch. The beautiful hostess smiles at him, touches her throat, throws back her hair flirtatiously. She nods at Jack, and points over to our table. He touches her arm and turns to us.

He's coming over. I quickly tune back in to Meg's voice, still rattling on about the benefits of independent public schools. I uncross my legs, and unwittingly bump the tiny table. My red wine spills down my front.

Scarlet. All over me.

'Oh, Frankie, you are worse than the kids.' Meg grabs napkins to mop up my mess.

Jack arrives, just as Meg is leaning over the table, stroking my chest with a napkin. He's grinning at me, his eyes alive with amusement.

'Hi, Jack!' Meg says, and starts to gush about the amazing

food, the ambience, all of it. I just sit, awkwardly, trying to soak up the wine, dabbing at the stain. This is why I wear grey. I am constantly spilling stuff.

'Hi,' I sheepishly interject when Meg comes up for air.

He assesses the spilt wine. 'I ordered it for you to drink, Fray, not wear.'

I roll my eyes and pray my cheeks are not the colour of the wine I am trying to expunge.

'Well, what do you think?' he asks. 'I hope you like the food. I didn't want to come across like the big hero ordering for you, it's just that we use these artsy terms that don't sound anything like what you're getting, and I didn't want you to get stuck with the spicy stuff.'

'No, it's all good,' I say. 'The décor is unbelievable.'

'Well, I can't take credit for that.' He scans the place. 'Concept was designed before I got involved. But it works, huh?'

'It's great,' I reply, still trying to pull out the serviette I wedged between my bra and my shirt.

Jack shakes his head at me, takes my hand and pulls me up.

'Meg, you'll be right with your wine there for a bit?' he says over his shoulder as he leads me away. 'I will bring this one back in a sec.'

With my hand in his, he guides me through the labyrinth of tables and antique artefacts decorating the corridors. I feel like a bargain hunter, weaving through a crowded bazaar in an exotic land, and suddenly wish I was, with him. As we arrive at an office door, Jack extends his keys from his belt and unlocks.

'Are you making me do dishes for spilling wine on the linen?'

He smiles, and I unravel a notch. 'Just getting you cleaned up,' he says, turning on the light. 'Welcome to my lair.'

'Don't worry about me; you're too busy to –'

'Will only take a sec. Otherwise you'll fuss all night.'

I follow him through, our pinkies linked, my heart in my throat.

The office is small and dusty. The desk is cluttered with in-trays, documents and spilt staples.

'Your office. It's so *dull* for a place this mystical,' I say as Jack opens a cupboard door. 'You should have a little cave or a tent or something.'

A half-dozen plain white men's shirts, all still wrapped in boxes and cellophane, fall to the floor. He rips one open.

'Get your gear off,' he orders me, shaking out the shirt. 'I won't look.'

'Is this your way of avoiding ironing? Get a new shirt every night?'

'Don't mock. I've tried that,' he says, sitting on his desk, twirling round so his back is to me. Once I am sure his eyes are away, I quickly strip off my wine-soaked knitwear and pull my arms through the crisp new shirt.

I roll up the sleeves, trying to look less ridiculous in a size 43 standard sleeve, the front still agape.

Jack turns around, glances at me half dressed, and quickly looks away laughing. 'You look like you've been stabbed.'

My eyes dip to see my pale blue bra speckled with rich red blotches. I fumble with the buttons, trying to end this humiliation, and realise I have misaligned them.

'Hurry up, girl,' he says, walking over to me. 'Meg will think I've kidnapped you. Here,' he whispers, 'line up the bottom first.' His voice is thick in my ear. His sinewy fingers fasten the first button. 'Even Oli knows how to do that and he's two.'

As he works his way up, knuckles pressing on my stomach, I feel a warm shudder through my spine. 'I can do it!' I nudge him away. 'Do I look ridiculous?' I ask as I adjust the collar, and try to tuck the tails into my pants so I look less like a duck.

'Only a bit,' he smiles, turning the light off as we exit his lair.

When we return, Meg has finished the bottle and is singing to herself.

'Thanks,' I offer.

'No wucking furries,' he smiles. We used to get grounded for saying that as kids, then tried to argue our way out of it due to the technicality that no swear words passed our lips. 'I have some other fires to put out. You ladies enjoy. I'll see you before you go,' Jack adds, giving me a wink as he rushes off. I exhale, uncoil like a spring.

'How friggin' embarrassing.' I roll my eyes as I take my seat once more.

'You look hot, hon. Don't stress.' Meg pats my hand like a child then glares at me over the top of her glass suspiciously as she sips.

She gives me a knowing smile. 'So how well did you say you knew Jack? Before?'

For a moment, I just sit and think about it.

I look my friend straight in the eye, and say all matter-of-fact: 'I was in love with him. In fact, I think I still am.'

实

I could pinpoint when it started. Year twelve. The formal. I remember every detail of it. It's etched in, along with the guilt. As I retell it to Meg, I feel like I am seventeen again.

It was warm that night. I'd escaped the music and emotion of the dance floor, and gone outside for some solitude. I needed to breathe. I'd stumbled up a dimly lit path. It led to a hexagonal pergola, bathed in fairy lights. I'd taken off my stupid heels and wandered to it. The beat of the music inside faded to a woolly hum. I leaned on the rail, inhaling the solitude, when I heard his deep voice. 'You having a joint or something?'

'Yeah, right,' I replied. 'Have you *met* me?' I felt a hand brush my back, feather lightly down my arm to my fingertips. My toes curled. Jack took my hand, and led me to the centre of the pergola. He slipped the strap of my shoes from my fingers to his to free my hands. 'I haven't had that dance yet, Lofty.'

He'd abandoned the guff, and was donning just the bare-suit-basics. His hair had lost the greasy product he'd gooped in.

'When did you get so tall?' I asked him, as he spun me under his arm.

'Maybe you're just shrinking,' Jack said. 'Old age . . .'

The distant beat inside, slowed. He pulled me close, which I liked and hated all at once. I thought back to what I saw earlier in Kate's bag – the condoms.

'Kate tells me you guys . . . that tonight's the night.'

He was silent for a second, pulled me back to see my face. 'Is that right? I dunno about that.'

'I had wondered if you two had – you know – already.' I felt heat rise in my throat. I didn't want to picture it. I looked at my bare feet, my fire-engine red toenails, painted under duress.

'What?' Jack asked, lifting my chin. 'The night to cash in the V card? Sink the pink?'

'Okay, you can stop now.'

'Nah, just everything but . . .' He laughed. 'I've become pretty good at imagining it, though. Since I was about twelve. I imagined it all the time, alone in the shower.' Jack could only tolerate eight seconds of serious at a time. 'Under the sheets,' he said, spinning me faster. He twirled me around confidently in the night air, as we circled groups of imaginary classmates. I felt like Cinderella. Every time I lifted my gaze, I saw his eyes waiting for mine to return.

'Seriously though . . .' His hands were sweaty in mine. He still had my shoes hanging from his fingers. I diverted my eyes, unable to face him. I placed my chin on his shoulder as we swayed back and forth in a token attempt to look like we were dancing, to justify the physical contact.

'Serious? When are you serious?' I said, daring to lift my head and glance at him.

But his face was. His confidence, his commanding lead on our makeshift dance floor had gone. 'I know how it's probably looked this year, me going out with Charlotte, with Kate, but even when I'm with them, I still thought, I mean, I imagined,' Jack started, all reluctant, 'the first time . . . it'd be with you.'

At the time, his words had bounced around in my mind, flooding it with a new perception of us, rewriting all the cloudy moments I'd tried to interpret between us that final term. So, I wasn't going crazy. I panicked, and employed an avoidance strategy from the master himself – mocking.

'You've probably pictured *losing it* with half the Spice Girls too, so I'm not sure that says a lot.'

He dropped my hands. 'Always with the fucking jokes.'

As I closed my eyes, the hum of the party inside returned to my ears. He did warn me he was serious. 'Jack . . .' I caught his arm.

'What, Frankie? What are we doing?' His palms were to the heavens in question. The warmth in his eyes was replaced with hurt, frustration.

'What are *we* doing? You're the one going out with someone else. Did you think I'd just hang around, wait for you to have your fun? Did you even notice when I didn't speak to you for a month when you starting pashing Charlotte after school? And now Kate –' My heart thumped in my chest. 'My best friend . . .' I managed to utter, my throat tense and dry, '. . . is your girlfriend.'

'Yeah. I picked up on that.' He started to pace, leaned on the rail, his knuckles tense. 'What if she wasn't?' he asked, turning, moving to me. He dropped my shoes, took my hands in one swift movement.

'But she is,' I said, his face close, his hands warm. I knew I should pull his hands off mine, but I didn't. 'And even if she wasn't, it would still feel . . . wrong.'

He inspected the mesh of our entwined fingers woven tightly. 'Yeah, I know.' He pulled me into a waltz, my head resting on his shoulder once more. 'Do you wonder, if she hadn't moved here? If there was never any Kate?'

I had. In glimpses of jealous rage, seeing them pashing every chance they got, I had wondered if Jack and I would have turned down a different path if she had never moved here, if she had not side-tracked us with her overwhelming presence in our lives.

But I would never have wanted that, not even for him. I raised my head, our cheeks pressed so close I felt his poor excuse for stubble on my skin. The song playing inside faded to silence; our friends cheered, turning our attention to the path, to the entrance. To the figure standing in the doorway.

To Kate's piercing eyes staring us down.

Perhaps it wasn't the beach at all. Perhaps it was that moment that started it all.

What we led her to do.

CHAPTER 16
Losing the Plot

Double Island Point Lighthouse,
8 am, 19 November 2000

The hours march on. Fifteen SES volunteers arrive and scour the area for the remainder of the morning. They work tirelessly, as we wait at the ranger's shed nestled in the trees on the point a few kilometres north from camp, rehydrating and fearing the worst. The guys' rum-induced courage has worn off, and they suffer through a hangover they'll never forget. We all head up to the lighthouse and rest in the shade among the wildflowers, when a cop approaches with a clipboard and a frown.

The policeman asks me to escort them to identify where we saw the fisherman we spoke to last night.

I ride silently in the ute, feeling small, thinking that people who know what they're doing can't find her any better than we could, so it seems. Positivity is fading fast.

We pass the Cherry Venture, and I realise we've overshot. It all seems different in daylight, from a truck. I ask him to turn around, but then everything clenches when I see our camp marker up ahead. The very sight of it – viewed from a search vehicle – makes my head spin.

'Should we just go in and check she isn't back?' I blurt out. 'She might have found her way in the light.' I feel an overwhelming sense of urgency to open the door and run to the camp – a vision she'll be waiting for me on the dune. This will all turn out to be a storm in a teacup. I start to panic, grab the door handle.

'Take it easy, love, we have a team at the camp. It's okay. If she comes back you can be sure it will be all over the radio. We have procedures for this,' the ranger says. The red-head cop in the back seat gives my shoulder a reassuring pat. I recoil – *her touch reeks of patronising pity.* The poor girl, without the sense to realise her friend is lost for good. *I can see it written in their expressions. What good will this team be for finding Kate if they have already given up?*

As the ute slows as we approach the little freshwater creek just past our camp, I yank the door handle. The door lurches open and the vehicle comes to a sudden stop as I run.

I fly. Fly towards the picture I see of Kate on the dune, smiling at me.

I splash through the shallow trickle, scale the dunes, past the surfboard – like if I run fast enough, I won't miss seeing her smiling, waiting for me, twisting her hair the way she does when she's bored. She'll just be sitting there, wondering why I got out of a cop car. If only I run fast enough to catch her.

As I make it through the gap in the dunes, panting for breath, I see the team of investigators methodically measuring things, dusting the door handle of the troop carrier.

Like a crime scene.

'What are you doing?' I scream at them, hysterical now. 'Why aren't you out there, looking for her? Instead of wasting your time here?'

I am physically stopped by the ranger and the red-head cop

grabbing one arm each. They firmly, but gently, sit me down on the dune, and I collapse in the ranger's arms, sobbing like a baby. I cry unashamedly. Nothing matters if she's gone.

The wretched fog in my head lifts, and I become aware of the police glancing over at me, the mental case, as they root through our stuff with their gloved hands. My pride resurrects and drives me to composure. I wipe the sandy tears from my cheeks. I am suddenly conscious of the stiffness of my shirt – now starched with dried seawater, the white tidal marks of salty residue staining the blue.

One, or twenty minutes could have gone by; I wasn't sure and didn't care. But I shake off the pitying gestures of the officials, dust the sand off my shorts, and walk back to the truck without a word. I feel like a drunken girl at the races, gathering her self-respect after falling on a broken heel.

The officials join me in the vehicle and we drive silently till I point to a clearing in the dune between the wreck and the point. 'It was behind here. I remember, because it was just past the day camp area.' We disembark, the cop making notes of something, and walk into the shaded grove. 'I remember – his truck was here, and this was his camp. I remember the rope tied to that tree. He must have left.'

The two of them scan the area.

'Do you think he could be a suspect?' I ask, as we trudge back to the truck.

'We don't even have a crime yet, but it's best to cover all bases with this stuff while we can. Cast a broad net, so to speak,' says the female cop again.

We drive back to the headquarters at the point in silence. I realise I have stopped scanning the dunes, endlessly searching as I had on the southerly journey.

I think about what Kate's like – an indoor girl, hates the wind blowing her hair, the sand in her shoes. And she's easily bored. She wouldn't stick around somewhere she'd lost interest in, not by choice. That is when I know she is no longer at the beach. She is elsewhere. With other schoolies? In Noosa, sipping a hot chocolate in a café? I just don't know where.

The walls of the information centre (now Find Kate headquarters) are adorned with eco-friendly messages and pictures of native animal habitats. Jack has pulled two lines of plastic chairs together, a makeshift bed, but he wrestles with more than the discomfort of the sleeping arrangements. I sit on the end of his row and look at him, still with slumber. He seems younger. His sleeping face reminds me of the time Ben taped Jack snoring, after Jack fell asleep watching Home Alone. It seems like a lifetime ago.

Jack's jet-black hair is stiff from salt-spray, his cheeks wind-burnt, his lips chafed. By late afternoon, the cops direct us to leave. We protest at first, but physical exhaustion seems to motivate our decision to comply. Being here only highlights our uselessness. It is clear that we're actually in the way, using resources to manage us, feed us.

Leaving those barren dunes without her feels like another act of betrayal.

The troop carrier that had delivered us here in such high spirits is detained – the police want it to remain at camp until 'Kate returns' as they delicately put it. All we can do now is wait. Matt and Dan, the only others in our group besides my brother, are long gone. They seemed distraught too, but desperate for an opportunity to retreat from the intensity of it all. To vanish into anonymity. The ranger called all our parents, and advised they would meet us at the barge. It is time to go.

Ben turned up at camp at dawn apparently, wondering what all the fuss was about, and had been informed Kate was missing. He had wandered round in a dream since. Like someone forgot to invite him to the party of the year. Left him out again.

But this ain't no party I want to be at.

The police salvage our belongings – those not required at the scene. They take Kate's bag, keep some clothes for the sniffer dogs, promising to return them. They apparently found her denim shorts up in the dunes, not far from where Jack said they 'talked'. It makes no sense. Nothing does. The image of where the boys said her twisted t-shirt was found, strewn on the sand in a frenzy of footprints, flashes in my mind. It tells a much more sinister message now, twenty-four hours later. My heart sinks.

We have all our belongings, except for one irreplaceable person.

Jack and I sit and wait in the shade near the cable ferry loading zone. Ben is still withdrawn like a druggy waiting for his next fix. He sits on his own in a smoky daze, rolling endless durries. We're told our parents are on their way and will be here to take us home. Back to civilisation.

As I wait, surrounded by the crisp dewy canopy of green, I continue to invent many plausible, however unlikely, explanations for why Kate isn't here with us. I feel a surge of energy charge through me. We just need signs – media coverage, all of that. There is still hope! I run, determined, into a circle of cops, chatting to the barge owners. I begin blurting out my strategy – that we aren't searching for a body, that she is probably at Noosa by now, in a bar. Or nursing a hangover.

My speech is manic – I can't get the words out fast enough, the plans I have for them. If only I can make them listen to me. I know I am just a kid, but I will make them listen, goddamn it! Make them see that we need people searching the local clubs, asking for sightings of her the night before. That I have pictures at home I could give them to put on TV. Proper ones – not that distorted one from the booth. That people will not have forgotten if they had seen her – collided with that face, those eyes. That she is unforgettable.

Unforgettable.

I am shouting now. I am in a daze, screaming my thoughts aloud, full of adrenalin, feeling a surge of limitless energy to devote to this cause. Like it's impossible to not find her with this epicentre of rage and determination at my beck and call. That this is all that matters. To find her.

Ranger Bob presses his clipboard against his overalls, crinkles his brow and speaks firmly. 'Frankie, Frankie, calm down – we're doing everything we can.' As he placates me I tune out. He's not listening!

A flash of blonde catches my eye from over his shoulder. A blonde girl is leaning against a pole on the toilet block, less than twenty metres from us. She's facing the river, but tugs her ear the way Kate does when she's tired. The shirt is new but . . .

I tell my legs to leap but I'm running in slow motion.

'Kate! Kate, it's me!'

It's her! As I race over I think how it makes sense that she came to town – we searched the beach but all this time she was hiding in plain sight!

I'm just metres from her now. 'Kate!'

Why isn't she turning? My voice must be so hoarse she can't recognise me. I reach her, yank hard on her shoulder but she pulls away.

I yank on her sleeve. 'It's Kate! I found her!' I announce with a flood of relief. I put my arms around to hug her but I realise my hands are being held back.

Am I being arrested? Is that where my hands are? Do they think this was just a prank we planned, a waste of taxpayers' money? It's all a blur. Like when the movie is stuck in slow motion and the contrast is all wrong. But I can still yell, I can still kick!

Let go! But no, it is only Jack. He has my arms, pulling me back away from Kate. Trying to rein me in.

But like the scratched DVD getting unstuck, the picture suddenly becomes clear. The image steadies. No one is talking now. Just staring.

'Mum!' the girl cries as the toilet door opens, and a woman scoops her away like I'm a crazy person.

'It's not her, Frankie. It's not Kate,' I hear a voice say.

I blink and see that the girl is about twelve, with freckles and a strawberry birthmark. As her mum guides her away, she peeks over her shoulder and stares right through me.

Not again, I think. I'm not losing it again, surely? Not after the blubbering on the dune. At least I should aim to melt down with the same cops. They already think I am insane. But we're in public now. These are new faces of sympathy – different expressions of pity.

The high-pitched ringing in my ears had stolen my orientation, but now normal sounds start to sneak back. I can hear people trying to calm me. And Jack. He is holding me. When I protest, admit that, all right, it wasn't Kate, but she's out there! That we still have to tell the TV people!

Ranger Bob reassures me they have.

She is breaking news. The fact that Kate is missing is everywhere. Not at first, he explains to me; drowning was assumed, yet when nobody washed up in the areas expected, the search widened. Not only in terms of ground to cover, but possibilities to explore. They are now investigating other hypotheses.

The ranger leaves us and Jack holds me till the sobbing abates. I have no choice but to steal any breath of air I can gasp, to help save myself from this strangling fear, this dread of what the future may hold. My face is burrowed into him like a baby being rocked to sleep, as he silences my hysteria.

'I thought it was her,' I mumble into him.

'I know, Fray.' He stares at the ferry, the pulleys jerking it further away from us, the girl and her mother no doubt in one of the vehicles. 'But it wasn't.'

His self-assurance irks me. What knowledge makes Jack so composed? Ben, I get. He's using his usual coping mechanism – nicotine and withdrawal to the point of being catatonic – to stay sane. Me, the odd public meltdown. What is Jack doing? He's an extrovert, always solving his problems aloud – to anyone with ears. Yet he is eerily still, silent. Like he's been given a gag order.

Or already knows the answer.

I realise that the others have now left. I break free from his support. I turn his face to see it freely, my eyes asking his what they know, what they saw, what happened at the beach. What was the truth about Kate's kid? I feel complete assurance to my core that Jack did not, could not harm anyone. He is the same boy who saved moths that were drawn to our camp lantern – he thought their translucent wings were beautiful. Yet he knows something, and that something isn't being said by his mouth, so I look to his eyes. Yet just as quickly, he turns his head. I see nothing but sadness as he pulls away.

And not a hint of hope.

CHAPTER 17
Aftermath

Noosa North Shore,
6 pm, 19 November 2000

Crunching gravel against rubber draws close.

'That was fast. Didn't the ranger only just call the parents?' Jack asks.

'What?' To my surprise, my parents' car pulls off the asphalt onto grit. 'Mum?'

My mother's lily-white arm rests on the window of our 4WD, as she peers down her nose at Jack and me, our knees touching. She steps down out of the passenger seat. Her face seems aged, as if she's been as tormented as we are. Dad, steadfast by her side, looks grim.

I run over and hug her, feeling the tears well, the relief swell from my throat. 'Did you just get here?' I ask in a husky voice.

'The ranger called us. Are you okay? I was so worried!' She turns to my brother. 'And you. You were supposed to be supervising the girls! Why didn't you call us? We could have helped!'

I shake my head. 'No mobile access, and anyway you were hours away; not much you could've done back home.'

Ben moves faster than I've seen him move in days and escapes to the back seat.

'Well, we were . . . nearby actually,' Mum mumbles, rubbing my back. 'Your father decided we should make the most of the child-free weekend – it was a last-minute thing.'

I step away from her. 'And you decided to stay here? Where I was going? Are you serious? It was humiliating enough having Ben come with us!'

Ben huffs from the car.

Mum reaches out to me. 'Honey, it wasn't like that. Just come on, let's get you home.'

I stomp over to the back seat of our car, and pull Ben's earphones off. 'How long did you know, Ben? That they were going to be here, spying on us?'

Ben grimaces, and I flick the earphone back with a whack. I walk back to the roadside where my mother stands. 'Have I ever given you a reason not to trust me?'

Concern wafts across Mum's face. Dad raises his eyebrows in response. It is a dance they often step together – when I was caught with biscuit crumbs on my lips as a girl, or talking to older boys at the blue-light disco. But this time they are the ones caught out.

'Love, it's not *you* we don't trust. You hear all kinds of things about these Schoolies things. And besides, it was with good reason – look what happened! It was a ridiculous idea, coming up here.'

I return to the shade where Jack remains, looking sheepish. I thread my arm around his, lean my head on his shoulder.

Mum stands tight-lipped. 'Honey, c'mon, we're getting the next barge.'

I just sit.

'Goodbye, Jack, your parents are on their way,' she says through gritted teeth. Her eyes fixate on my arm, loosely linked in Jack's under the shade. So that's what's got her in a flap.

He unhooks his arm. 'Better go, Fray.' His mouth is crooked. 'See you back home.'

Dad takes my bag and puts it in the boot. Mum grabs my hand, leads me to the open car door. As my fingertips are dragged free from Jack's, I feel a sudden lurching inside, an urge to refuse to go. To stay with him. The only person who knows what's going on inside my head, who can understand that it's been de-fragged, the colour and light sucked away, the hope drained from every cell. All that remains to leave this place is a wax museum statue of my former self, an impostor who looks and smells like me, but is nothing like the person who arrived.

I've got to just keep breathing in and out. Until Kate is found. Until Kate can tell us all what really happened on that foam-swept beach, under the orange sky.

'Stay away!' Mum waves her finger at him. Jack stands and retreats in shock, like she's switched on an opposing current to repel him away.

'What's your problem?' I yell.

'Get in the car,' she orders, shoving me in like a drunk in a paddy wagon.

I want to defend him, shout his innocence from the rooftop, but I find I have nothing left. My sweaty fingers fan wide against the window as we pull away, leaving him. I stare at the long straight path that leads to the beach cutting, as we backtrack along the road on which we had arrived, jubilant. It seems like a lifetime ago.

Six foot three of smelly sibling is sprawled out on the seat, his hairy legs and sandy feet extending across the centre console. His headphones chirp next to me. The same beat over and over. My parents' anxious monologue bellows from the front. The same words, over and over. Kate is right, my brother is just a Teenage Dirtbag. I do the 'L' sign on my forehead and Ben responds with the bird.

We wait as the vehicular ferry waves us on board.

'So do they have any leads, the police?' Dad asks from the front. 'Was there something about a fisherman?'

I grunt but Dad doesn't get the hint. He keeps asking questions, what I said to police, if they've let on what they really think happened.

We're across the bank in less time than it takes Dad to say, 'Jack Shaw has a lot of explaining to do.'

'What do you care anyway, you never liked Kate!' I cry from the back seat. 'I guess you got what you wanted – the bad influence out of your daughter's life. Congratulations.'

实

I wake surrounded by the familiarity of my own bed after a sleep that seemed like death. For an instant, I forget my incredible reality – a stolen moment of normality before the fact that Kate is missing hits me like a train. A surge of nausea jerks through me. I run to the toilet, dry-retch bile in the bowl. I have another instant where I am distracted to ignorance of it all, but then the truth pounds me again like a series of waves.

Waves.

Flashes of super-coloured light flick past my eyes as I lie on the cold tiled floor. The smell of Toilet Duck hits me. This is hell. This is like the morning after the night I sunk a bottle of vodka in Kate's garage, yet without the vodka. As the nausea abates, my vision clears. I see her reaching for me, a tiny flash of silver blonde in a sea of darkness. Another wretched need to purge hits me.

Keep them coming, I whisper to no one. No physical pain will match the misery in my mind, my bottomless pit of wretchedness, loneliness, helplessness, guilt. All rolled up in a ball of fury that seems to be eating me from inside out.

When I decide it is safe to move, I shower for what seems like hours – surprisingly, Dad doesn't bang on the floorboards to get me out. I guess I'm being given a wide berth, particularly after their little stunt, spying on me.

I meet the sympathetic faces in the kitchen – offers of help. I ask if there is any news, and Mum shakes her head.

'Can I get you anything, love?' she asks through her pity face.

Yeah, I need my friend. I need my life back.

Ben is conspicuous by his absence.

I look over to Dad's coffee table. Something catches my eye. The paper. Kate and Jack – their formal photo, the headline 'Missing'. Dad slaps the pages shut when I peer over his shoulder; the smell of fresh ink fills my senses. 'Nothing newsworthy in there,' Mum calls, placing a plate of scrambled eggs in front of me.

'Nothing true anyway,' Dad mumbles. 'Makes you wonder how much of what they print is ever true.'

'Dad. I'm not a school kid any more.' I need to know what the world knows, what I'm up against. He shoots Mum a glare, and passes it to me.

The story fills a page, yet is padded with rumours, hearsay, fabrication – hinging only on the most basic of facts. The world, it seems, is obsessed. The journo paints a picture of Kate being from a mysterious new family, part of a love triangle that somehow went wrong. Even Jack's family church (which was described more like a cult) is deemed worthy of a mention. Thankfully there is no picture of me. Jack, though, is centre stage. They don't go as far as to say he's a suspect, but every chance to tarnish his reputation is exploited.

I try to call him, but it rings out each time. Perhaps they are screening calls. I see footage of his house on the news – his father taking rubbish to the wheelie bin, oblivious to being filmed. There are hourly updates on the nothingness. The same absence of anything new, over and over. A flash of Mr and Mrs Shepherd, sunken-eyed and weepy, flicks on the news on every channel, with the Crimestoppers number scrolling below.

I'm a prisoner in my own home for the days that follow. My parents are the guards – advising me it's best to give Jack some space, have some time away from the group to clear my head. Our quiet neighbourhood is suddenly scrutinised, swarming with people like a movie set.

A trip to the bakery for chocolate milk opens my eyes to the spread of the disease sweeping through my suburb, plaguing people with symptoms of delusional thought. The local IGA seems to be a production company for lies and intrigue about what really happened. The insincere sympathy nods, the whispers, *there she is* – *the friend or some sort of love triangle.* The bold, intent gazes from the school mums burn into my back, but just as quickly flick away when confronted.

'Take a picture, it lasts longer,' I let fly as they tut-tut and stare. As I line behind a group of old ladies, everyone has a story. Even the ones that mistrusted Kate and her left-of-the-middle demeanour, her short skirt rolled up at the waist. *She went rowing with my daughter, I hear one say, she had the face of an angel, she was destined for greatness.*

I pay the pimply cashier without a word and back down the alley to the loading dock. I slide down the besser brick wall, lean against it, the smell of rubbish less offensive than the comments I hide from. It's like they enjoy thinking of our sleepy suburb as something sinister. I wait for what seems like long enough before scurrying home, my eyes scanning the fading light in the street from under my hoodie, like a vandal on the run.

I get home, I smell something cooking. I yell out that I'm not hungry, that I'm going to bed early, but I can't settle.

I open my bedroom window wide, and slide down the weatherboards, jumping the final few feet. I walk the few blocks to Jack's house, the fresh night air cool on my face. I figure I've got half an hour before Mum figures out I'm gone and freaks.

I meander through the overgrown stepping stones down the side of his boxy sixties home, and see light escape the window of Jack's room. His lanky limbs are strewn on the bed. I hear Led Zeppelin blaring. My shadow breaks the warm light cast from his lamp, and he removes the dowel from the window frame. He opens it wide, and I slide in.

His room always resembled a yard sale. Dumbbells, surfboards, guitars, even mag wheels for the car he didn't own yet.

'Hey,' he grunts. I'm shocked by his appearance, how battered he looks – the stark contrast of his red eyes and pale face. 'You heard anything?' he asks.

I shake my head, fiddle with the hem of my cut-off jeans. 'Nothing true anyway.'

'Oh,' he nods, flopping back on his dishevelled bed. 'So you heard the one about us being a threesome, in a cult.'

I roll my eyes. 'Yeah. If only we were that interesting . . .'

He half-smiles. 'The threesome I could be persuaded about, but the cult? Not so much.'

'Gross,' I snarl, flicking through his CDs as 'Stairway to Heaven' ends and silence threads the air.

Heaven. I shake the thought. 'You got any idea what that song's about?'

He shrugs. 'I don't think anyone does.'

We argue about what to play next, and settle on Nirvana's Never Mind – the last album we heard with Kate.

We don't say her name. We don't talk about her. We have enough of that in our minds without having it in the air too. For a brief moment, lazing on pillows on his floor, I almost forget she is missing, until reality jerks me back.

'Tried to shoot some hoops at the courts – friggin' vultures, trying to get me to spill some dirt,' Jack says. I cringe. Poor Jack. I want to comfort him, but I need to get us back to feeling normal first.

'I guess that's what happens when you're famous.'

His smile falls. He bites his lip, gets up, stretches, then flops on his side on the doona, the navy-and-white cotton checks skewing out of alignment. 'Weird though,' he says. 'They're bringing all this bullshit up – they searched Kate's house, you know, looking for clues. They have her diary, letters from me and stuff. It was all over the news, but nothing about her being pregnant.'

The word stabs at me like a knife.

His eyes dig into mine. 'You didn't tell them, did you? Is that cause you realised it's bullshit?' he glares.

'I still believe her, Jack.'

'Meaning you think I'm lying.' He shakes his head and puffs out a breath. 'So, why didn't you tell the cops? I mean, they hammered me about every friggin' detail.'

'Why would I? You want that all over the news? You'd look like a murderer and she'd look like a skank.' I cross my arms.

He springs off the bed and paces the room, fingers raking his fringe, before he stops to glare at me again. 'Fray, I told you I didn't need you to lie for me!'

'I was trying to protect you!'

'Protect me from what? I did nothing wrong!'

'I know that. But how would it have looked? Me saying hey, that guy over there, the boyfriend? Yeah, well, he dumped the girl five minutes before she went missing, came back white as a sheet, soaking wet, bleeding from the neck. And, by the way, the last thing Kate said to me was she was preggers with his kid. Doesn't sound a tad suss, Jack? Doesn't scream motive to you?'

'I told you to tell the truth, that I didn't need your help, that I could take it. I've got nothing to hide.'

'Yeah, that's great, Mr Noble, but kinda stupid. Grown-ups won't see it like that. They'll see a guy with his future ahead of him, and a pregnant girlfriend in his way.'

'Well, she either cheated on me or lied to you. Take your pick. Either way she's no friggin' angel. You've always had her pegged wrong, as this perfect being. She sucked you in.' He stops, a sullen frown reaches across his face. 'She had me too for a while.'

His words feel like treason. Is it true? Did she have me fooled? Or did he?

The music fills the space between us.

'You've got this complex,' he grunts, joining me perched on the bed, 'like you're never as good as her. But you are. You're so much more.' His thigh presses on mine. He leans over and tucks a strand of hair behind my ear.

I spring up away from him. 'Are you making a move? Now? Seriously?'

'No,' he grunts. His arm tucks back next to his side. 'But us fighting won't bring her back. It won't change what happened.'

'Do you think I would ever have let you dump her if I knew this would happen?'

'What, and you think I would? No fucking way! Don't get me wrong. I wanted to be free of her, Fray, I did. But not like this. Not ever.' The depth to his voice returns, as he points in the air. 'I would have friggin' married her if it meant saving her.'

He would have, the crazy fool. I examine his face, as familiar to me as my own. I notice the patterns on his eyebrows, the extra-long lashes, the grey of his eyes, chipped with the warmth of steel-blue flecks.

'They're not going to find her, Fray. Not alive. She's gone. The way she was before she took off – she wasn't right in the head.' His tone has softened to a whisper now. He is a rollercoaster, pivoting between fasts and slows. 'That's why I ran to the point. I was scared that she . . .'

'Don't say it!' I'm sobbing, overwhelmed that he could think that. He can't leave me alone in hope.

'I've racked my brains for days. I'm paranoid. Man, I was even pinning it on your old man at one point cause I was that desperate for an answer. I was sure I saw a white Patrol on the beach early the next morning.'

I laugh. 'Yeah, good one. There's only about a zillion of them around.'

He grabs at his hair, pulling it in clumps, and folds his knees up under him. 'Well, what the fuck else could have happened out there? The tide was in. We were the only ones around.'

'Ben was telling Dad something about that fisherman we saw. They've got that artist's impression of him on TV, apparently, from the description we gave. He's well known up there, they call him Old Nick – some local guy who's been fishing on the point forever. Got a caravan hidden up in the dunes where he keeps rabbits in cages.'

He stares at me like I'm stupid. 'Rabbits? It sounds like crap.'

'Dad said he used to see him getting aggro at people for stealing his crab pots years ago, when he used to fish up there.'

'You think he kidnapped Kate?' Jack scoffs and shakes his head. 'He was harmless. You saw him. Why would he call the ranger to our camp if he was gonna murder someone? Suicide's far more common than murder.'

Are they my only two choices?

He's given up. Anger curls in my chest. 'You think I'm stupid, don't you? For still hoping.' I feel a shudder in my throat and try to push it down. I sit on the edge of the bed, and he joins me.

His arm curls over my shoulder, like it has a thousand times in my lifetime, but now it's different. I sweep the wetness from my cheeks, my nose, as Jack brushes hair from my eyes. His fingers fold over mine. I've watched those small pale fingers change into the strong dark hands of a man. Since that night at the club, I've wondered how his touch would feel. His hand, resting innocently on my knee, feels electric. I close my eyes, shut out the shameful feeling of wanting him. It's not real, I tell myself, this feeling; it's just the release of all the charged emotions, the pain. And as much as I know my actions will cut like a knife, I push him away.

'We . . . can't,' I cry. My splintered words are threaded with stolen breaths. I'm confronted with snippets of Kate everywhere. A scrunchy, stringy with hair on the bedside table, a bear she'd given him for their half-year anniversary, her handwriting on a post-it.

She is gone, but the room is full of her.

His eyes smoulder, glazed with tears. From hurt? Regret? For once I can't read his face.

'We did this! Can't you see, Jack? If she is gone, if you think she did something to herself, it's cause of this! You and me!' I pace the floor. 'Her worst fear was being left out. Remember that time after Seaworld – she was cut at you for days just for riding in the dodgem car with me instead of her. And when we made leader body and she didn't she went home early.' Suddenly it's so obvious. 'Imagine what dumping her would have done?'

'She didn't know you were the reason.'

So I was the reason. I did this.

It was the best and worst thing he could have said.

I jump out the window in one great leap, my head heavy, my body brooding.

'Fray, wait!' he protests, bracing the window with his arm span.

'You needn't have bothered, Jack. Whatever we thought we had, we broke,' I cry out in one sorrowful breath.

Without turning back, I race into the street before Jack can stop me, and escape in the night air. Did I really believe we broke us? Or did I just hope this warm feeling for Jack would push down and get lost, so the guilt would escape too. I sprint, wanting to feel the hurt seep through my muscles, wanting the physical pain to drive out the emotional agony.

I see my front yard up ahead. I know he's not following now. I've lost him.

I've lost him too.

My front steps are bathed in light, my mother's profile shadowing the rail. I figure she's caught me sneaking out, guessed where I went and cracked. But as I draw close, I see her hand veils her mouth, and sense doom.

'No! No!' I call, scanning the footpath for other options – anywhere to go but to her news. Was Jack right? She comes out to meet me, leads me to the stairs, gently sits me down. My hands are shaking. My head knows what she has to say. Part of me wants to spare her the deed, but I suddenly need to hear it.

'Honey?' Her tone is soft, like when she told us our dog died. 'The police called. She's gone, love. They found her.'

'They found Kate?' I feel a spike of hope run through me.

'Her b-body.' Her hand reaches up, her fingers abate the tremble on her lips. 'She washed up several kilometres north of the point. She drowned.'

I hear the vibrations of her words, loud and quiet all at once. The balance in my ears shifts. I lose all equilibrium as if I'm ascending in a plane.

Mum explains that Kate's parents have been informed, and identified the body.

It is Kate.

And so our lives are free to fall in around us like a house of cards.

When I start to comprehend what I'm hearing, I imagine I'll just sink into a deeper pocket of whatever has already engulfed me. Yet despite it being the worst outcome, I actually feel relief. All the 'what ifs' fly away from my mind. I am freed from all the misguided conjecture, the speculation intruding on our lives. And so is Jack.

The shock I am expecting doesn't arrive.

I think the knowledge that she is gone was already there. It had loitered for a while as we searched, darted in and out of the doors in my mind as we waited, but then stubbornly planted itself in my stream of consciousness for good. It had been sitting there since my return to camp.

As I sit on the step, my mother by my side, the puzzle pieces all fall into place, flashing before my eyes. There was no hitchhike to Tewantin. There was no suspect fisherman. No axe murderer waiting in the dunes. The ranger had warned me as much – explained that accidental drowning was the most likely explanation with the absence of any evidence to the contrary. I just didn't want to believe it. I felt disloyal for even thinking it. Then, or now.

And to think she was a champion rower, an avid swimmer.

Drowned.

A burst of uncontrollable laughter surges through me, exploding. I alternate between sobs and laughter like a crazy person. The irony.

My mother looks at me in wonder.

'Francesca?' Mum says. 'Frankie?' she repeats, almost slapping my cheeks so I will come to. 'Are you okay?'

Her words fade in my head, as I keep on laughing. Loud, raucous laughter – the uncontrollable snort-laugh kind. Like my brain's trying to regain some equilibrium. And the only way back is via hilarity.

At some stage my mother shoves me inside, fearing the neighbours will add my little outburst to their collection of stories to tell at the checkout line. I catch a glimpse of Dad, bleary-eyed, beer in hand, as I escape to my room.

And on my bed I stay. In my room I hide, until they make me pretend to be alive again.

实

Kate's funeral.

It is just too bizarre to even put those words together. We were meant to grow old and grumpy together, plait each other's long grey ponytails while we rocked in our patio chairs, surrounded by dogs. So much unsaid, undone.

I'm here in this dusty church, staring at a shiny coffin. Kate would hate all this solemn stuffiness. I can't say the service so far – painful pictures of beautiful Kate, kind words from all and sundry – achieved anything but deeper sorrow for me. It brought further clarity to the loss that's being felt by all who knew her.

I am eternally distracted, looking for Jack. Where is he?

There is a gut-wrenching parade of speakers, poems and songs, all preaching the same message – our shining light had blown out way too soon. No shit.

My best friend is dead.

The service finally ends, and no Jack appears.

'Just as well,' Mum mentions. 'It would be inappropriate, given the circumstances.'

'She drowned. Can you get it through your head, Ma? Please?' My voice echoes through the church.

'Keep your voice down, young lady! Show some respect!'

'How about you show some respect for the truth?' I whisper back. 'What, you think he held her under till her lungs filled with water?'

She sits white-knuckled, tight-lipped, with Dad steadfast by her side, until the music starts and I can breathe again.

The wake is held at Kate's home. Their funky lounge is filled mostly with old people I don't know sitting in a circle of chairs, smelling like moth balls. They don't fit here.

I give up on looking out for Jack, and sneak away from the masses through to Kate's room; it's surreally quiet. It smells of Impulse. Memories lean on me. Her laugh brushes against my hot cheeks. I feel dizzy, and put my hands out to break my fall onto her bed.

I knew the first time I came here that her presence in my life would be short-lived. I predicted a falling out, a move away perhaps? Not this. Never this way.

I compose myself and return to the group.

I have only just entered the room of mourners when Mum gives me the nod that we're leaving. 'It's a place for family,' Mum whispers through gritted teeth as we politely make our excuses. Yet Kate is my family. She knew my deepest secrets, my wildest dreams, my most embarrassing moments. Why am I relegated to a mere school friend, when she was my person? My reason to go to school, the best part of every day. Kate was my wild card. She could upturn any typical Tuesday into a day I'd never forget. She could put a smile on my face with a look.

I think of one night we'd bought slurpees at the 7-Eleven and were walking home together in the hot breeze. I was dawdling. Kate slowed. When I caught up she hooked my arm in hers. 'C'mon, deary,' Kate mocked, in her wrinkly pensioner voice, 'I need to do my purple rinse tonight before bowls club tomorrow.' Kate's mood sweetened. She said how we'd grow old together, once we'd earned our millions and worn all our husbands out. 'I'll braid your hair as we read Jane Austen on the porch in our rocking chairs,' she painted with words, 'with all our cats.'

'Screw the cats. I hate cats,' I said as we walked arm in arm up the street. 'Make them dogs. And besides, you'll be married to Jack Shaw, surrounded by grandchildren – while I knit in your granny flat alone, talking to myself.'

About halfway home, we passed our school. It looked latched up and lonely in the moonlight. The only sign of life was a stray piece of litter skirting the path in the hot night breeze. I had this epiphany – a flash of the future – the legacy I would leave at this place. The teacher's pet – the debate champ.

'C'mon, my legs are tired!' Kate called, as I lagged behind again.

I ignored her. Was that how I want to be perceived by my peers, even now? The straight-A girl who helped Kate pass her assignments?

I observed the lit signboard, high above my head, the plastic Perspex letters in random colours spelling out:

'TUCKSHOP ASSISTANT: LONG-TERM VACANCY APPLY WITHIN'

I wondered who got up there? The janitor before school? My eyes scanned, and stalled on a tall step ladder, leaning on the shed behind the pool filter.

I carried the ladder to the sign, double checked the legs were stable, and scaled it.

If I stopped to think, I would never start again.

'What the hell are you doing?' Kate whisper-yelled from the front school gate. It was as if the place were heavily land-mined – her reluctance to penetrate the perimeter. 'They have security dogs now – after that school was lit on fire.'

I hushed her like a fly and stepped up. My footings were holding, so I scaled the ladder to the top of the sign. I could reach the letters; I started my handiwork. I felt like a giant, peering down at Kate, as she ran the length of the fence, back and forth, like a rat in a cage. Was she securing the perimeter for me? I could see her panic from there.

'You know, it was all bullshit, that crap I said about me shop lifting.

I have never stolen anything in my life.' Kate spoke as if I didn't know she was a story maker. Half of her intrigue was in deciphering her words, wondering which parts were true.

From my castle I arranged and rearranged – throwing down the letters superfluous to my needs.

Done. I paused for breath, my heart beating fast. I glanced up and admired my handiwork.

'ASS LICKRS ANONYMOUS: APPLY WITHIN.'

Two days later, my sign was still intact, as the students paraded through the gates before first bell. Clumps of kids pointed and cracked up, and I felt proud, until the principal wanted answers, and called a special parade. My conscience was eating away at me, taking over every thought. My fingerprints were on the letters, so strong circumstantial evidence did link me to it, if they chose to go there. I felt acid burn my throat, my stomach a pit of fire. So much for changing my reputation – I couldn't even own up to what I did. But I had to or they'd call the cops.

The principal's door was ajar, and I heard his nasal voice bellow through it. My thoughts slowed enough for me to make out the principal's words. 'Since you've come forward with this information I'll stick by my word and I will not involve the police.'

'Thank you, sir,' a girl's voice said.

It was unmistakably Kate.

My head spun. Had I misjudged her? Was she a rat?

'But consider this a formal reprimand. Mr Mason will expect you in detention for the remainder of the week, while the staff discuss any further action on the matter.' His voice was firm but fair. 'If that is clear, Miss Shepherd, you may go.' I looked up to see the back of her walk briskly to the exit, her head down, without a word. I just stood outside his room like my legs were cased in concrete.

'Everything okay here, Francesca?' the principal asked. 'If you are here to shed light on your more flamboyant friend, you needn't bother – she has come clean and turned herself in.'

'But –' I only had a matter of seconds to make it right, but he was gone.

When I asked Kate why she took the rap for me, she consistently denied it. But I waited every day, on a rock outside detention, to wander home with my beautiful friend.

I only knew her a year but I was more to her than these people sipping tea in her parent's house. I was by her side every day since she moved here. I'd walk her to the office when she needed a Panadol for cramps. I'd take her homework when she had the flu. I knew she had one dimple, her favourite colour was lilac, her biggest love – Johnny Depp; her greatest fear – being left out. Her favourite food was pancakes with bacon, but only when smothered in maple syrup. She had to have the full bandwidth of flavour experience, she'd say – sweet and savoury, all at once.

She lived life the same way.

CHAPTER 18
Baggage

Rain speckles my sunglasses like chips on a windscreen as I walk home from my afternoon shift at the hospital, brain-dead and famished. As I drag my heels on the footpath, my last patient plays on my mind. A runaway teen, a heartsick mum reunited finally after a week of wondering. It was a rare happily-ever-after ending, but wrenched open the *Before* box in my head, as missing-person cases often did.

But this time I let the lid stay open.

As I dawdle home the brief shower eases, and I think of Kate. I think of her mother's pain at her only child's funeral, the image as raw as if it were yesterday instead of half a lifetime ago.

I had seen Kate's mum only once since the funeral, about two years ago. She had been shopping, cradling her basket in the checkout line. It was weighed down by a carton of skim milk, oats, a single pear. I wonder if she lived alone now. Kate's parents' marriage may have been another casualty.

Her face had aged in the years that had passed, appearing more drawn, pale, framed by her pewter bob. As I'd watched her in awe, obscured from her view by a flower display, she appeared like any other well kept, attractive fifty-something woman as she smiled politely at the cashier, making small pleasantries. Yet to me, it was like she'd been whitewashed – all lightness and colour leached away. I wanted to approach her, but it was fear over what she thought of me that fixed my feet to the floor safely out of view.

As I arrive home, the rain scurries away like the skinks on my front cobbled path. The sun is low in the sky, the dogs bark at the wind. I gingerly open the back door, hoping to catch that window of time when Jack will be in the yard, and Sara will still be at work. I sigh in relief as I see him planting seedlings in a raised garden bed, Oli a foot behind pulling them out as quickly as they are planted. I am spent, but my need to talk overpowers my tiredness, and I wander out to say hi.

'Sara still out drug dealing?' I say, as I bite down on a yawn. Did I say that out loud? My filter process is on the blink.

'You don't like her much, do you?' Jack laughs, his dimple making an appearance.

'That's not true,' I fluster, pulling a plastic chair from the faded outdoor table and taking a seat. 'I just don't know her well.'

'She's never got on with other chicks,' he says, smearing potting mix on his cheek as his gloved hand wipes his face.

'Well, I can see how she would get on with men . . .'

Jack raises his eyebrows. 'She's okay once you get past the fake stuff. We're not all as self-assured as you.'

I settle, feel guilty.

'So, did you save some people from themselves today, Fray?' Jack teases. 'Leave the world a better place?'

I reposition my chair to cut the glare from my eyes and it scrapes on the pavers. I wipe the rain speckles off the seat with my palm. His tone pisses me off. 'What, and your job changes the world? How does hospitality impact people's lives?' The words are harsh on my lips.

'Impacts on their wallets,' Jack shoots back, but seems unperturbed. He is hard to rattle. It had irked me before, and still did. 'Money makes the world go round, business keeps people employed, income tax funds our valued public servants . . .'

My ankle tapping on the spare chair next to me speeds up with my stress level. 'Is it that you think my job is *easy*, Jack? Or *pointless*?'

He huffs and pauses from his planting. Finally he reacts. 'You are a real barrel of laughs this arv,' he says, throwing an empty seedling tray in the pile. They scatter. 'I'm just taking the piss.'

I huff to myself as I shift my gaze over to Oli and Bear. I know I am shitty. Why has today unleashed all these memories of Kate's mum? I have dealt with dozens of missing teens, grieving mothers – stories closer to hers – without this cloud following me home. I blame Jack, and his selfish reappearing trick. Ben, for outing it all with Sara the other night. As I've become older I've learned to acknowledge my moods, yet I still haven't mastered the art of changing them. I figure I'll use him as my sounding board.

'I saw a teenage girl today. A returned runaway. Off the rails a tad, in her final year at school. Made me think of the old crowd. Did you keep in contact with anyone after you moved?'

'Nah. Part of Mum's ploy. Divide and conquer,' Jack says. 'You? I mean, you must see some of 'em, still living in the same place?'

'Not really. I mean, Helena and Lanie, but not anyone that was there.'

I see their happy family posts on Facebook, but I'd run the other way if I saw most of them in real life. But Dan, Matt – they vanished after Schoolies. I rarely saw anyone from back then. They can't have all moved elsewhere. It's strange; it's like we are ants, going about our work in the same nest, anonymously. 'I kept in contact with a few of the girls in early uni days – I think they were addicted to the drama of it all. Just staying in touch to extend their dalliance with the dead girl's best friend.'

'So you haven't even seen the guys around? I assumed they were still in Brisbane.'

A montage of images – the guys skylarking at the beach, flashlights searching in the dunes – slideshow in my head.

'I thought I saw Dan at a pub once, a bald version, but he looked straight through me.' I leave my chair and sit on the shady lawn, playing with the grass next to Jack. 'I saw Kate's mum at the shops once – a couple of years back now.' As I say the words I'm surprised they don't sound like there's holes in them, like my voice box feels.

Jack looks up at me, as if trying to extrapolate more information from my expression. 'I dodged her, of course. I couldn't face her. She looked so frail.'

Jack, squatting in the dirt, pauses from his planting.

'I followed her for a bit . . . out to the car . . .'

'Yeah?' Jack says, standing to a stretch. His t-shirt rides up. I drop my eyes away, but that just seems to draw attention to the fact that I'm trying not to look. He smiles wryly. 'So you didn't talk to her, you just stalked her, in the bushes?'

'Kinda.' I shrug. Have I brought this up too soon? Been caught in a false sense of intimacy with this boy I knew once?

Jack abandons his yard work and looks over to Oli, who is now happily lining up cars along the pathway.

'She's still got a hold of you, hasn't she?' Jack says. He pauses and scans my face for a reaction, but continues despite my appalled look.

Not this again.

'I mean, I admit, seeing you again has brought a lot of it back,' he says, 'but it's like you never left, like you're stuck.'

'Stuck?' I manage to utter. 'What makes you think that?'

His lips thin. He sizes me up. 'Your safe single life, your Wonder Woman job . . .'

I raise my eyebrows. 'Thanks for your advice, Dr Freud, but I didn't ask for it.'

I get up, wipe the grass off my hands. Suddenly I feel lost. I start to stomp away, but the anger surges in my throat. I begin to form words in my head, but suddenly they are coming out of my mouth in fits and starts. 'You think because I'm not some property-mogul restaurateur with a picture-fucking-perfect family, I must be a stifled lonely sack of shit who, what, never got over her best friend dying?'

'Picture-perfect?' he laughs. 'Can I remind you that I'm sleeping on the couch after your brother's little stunt?'

'Not half of what you deserve.'

Jack raises his eyebrows, but ignores me. He gazes up at the trees, the flock of birds sweeping the darkening sky.

'I just think you'd be in a different place if Kate hadn't died,' he says. 'You had the makings of . . . something big.'

'And what, I threw it all away to work in an underpaid healthcare job?'

He looks over to me, then away, as if he's thinking long and hard about his next words.

He turns back, his eyes soft and warm. 'It's too late to help her, Fray.'

I shake my head. 'And you base all this analysis on what? A few months of sharing a driveway? You don't know shit.'

'I know the only time you get mean is when you know you're losing an argument. I know how your nose scrunches when you're drunk. I know how fiercely loyal you are and that you'd see living your life fully as betraying her.'

'And what? You're so sorted, so at ease with what happened to Kate, that you couldn't even tell your de facto any of it? Real *together*, Jack.' Just as I exhale, ready to hurl another mine, I hear the gate. I see Oli turn.

To his mother.

'Hon?' Jack calls to Sara as she approaches him. 'I thought I was gonna pick you up from the station?'

'Decided to walk.' Sara ruffles Oli's hair as she starts to usher her son inside. I may as well have been a fence post.

'Sorry to interrupt,' she says with no inflection, her face void of all feeling. But her eyes stare me down. 'I promised Oli McDonald's, so I'll take him now.'

'I was gonna make pizza,' Jack says to Sara. 'I've started the base already.'

'I might go in,' I whisper, turning to leave.

'Don't bother,' she shoots to me, crouching down to Oli and whispering their plans in his ear. The smile splits his face as Sara gathers him in the car, and backs out without so much as a wave to Jack. He seems relieved she is gone, but then kicks the empty punnet cases flying over the patchy lawn. The car drives away.

He turns his attention back to me. 'Fray?' He stops me. 'Life's short. I think you should look her up. Go see Kate's mum.' He takes off his gloves and leans on the metal handle of the shovel. I see his biceps flex. 'No more hiding behind poles. It's fucked up.'

The suggestion surprises, and frightens, me. 'To what end? It's cruel to bring that all back for her.'

For me . . .

'She might fill some gaps for you. You headspace-dwelling-freaks call it closure.' Jack gathers up his garden tools and empty plastic punnets. 'I mean, they protected us from a lot of it. We were kids. Even before we left, my dad stopped the papers, as if we couldn't handle the gory details.'

'Like we couldn't imagine worse.'

Oh, how I had. In the days before they found her, in the nights after, in my dreams, in my waking moments, in my worst nightmares. 'Do you ever wonder if we could have changed it?' I ask.

'Every fucking moment for a while.'

I lean against the wall. I need its strength to prop me up. Then I slide, kneeling on the wooden porch like a kid. The niggling feeling of sorrow starts — first at the back of my throat, and then it seeps lower into my chest, to the depths of my stomach. I hadn't felt it this strong for years. And yet, in an *instant* it feels so familiar, so well-trodden. I can feel the tears well. I do the usual tricks, looking to the sky so they pool and don't shed, as if I can hold it in if I just think about something else. He walks over, drops to my side, his shoulder against mine. I want him to make any sort of noise, to conceal my sniffing, sobbing self. Yet he is silent, as if by allowing me all the airtime I need, I will find my way out of it sooner.

There is always a sense of shame when I feel things this hard, after so long. Like a more well-balanced person would have dealt with losing a friend far better than I have. She wasn't my daughter, after all, or my sister. She wasn't even a *lifelong* friend. I had known her less than a year – a tumultuous year, but just a breath in a lifetime.

But Jack is right. Leaving her behind that night left a blemish on my perspective on life, a wound that will always leave a scar. Just at an age when I should have been embracing life, I was learning to bear it. Living the worst of it. Is it the proximity to the event, the tragic nature of how she was taken, or my guilt, that keeps me riding with this dark passenger after all this time? Or is it simply the uncertainty of what actually happened? Did she plan it? Was she hoping to end it all, when she stripped almost bare, and wandered in, surrounding herself in water, surrounding herself in nothingness?

'Do you still think she did it?' I ask him. I realise I have thought of this often, but never articulated it to another person before. And here I am, on my back porch, with the last man to see her alive. 'I mean – on purpose?' My mouth is dry. 'I have always hoped not. At least an accident wasn't our fault. But if she had planned it, *meant* it, we could have stopped it – tried to help. Like if we'd told her mum some of the things she said . . .' I think of the suicide risk assessments I have completed on patients. Did she really behave that way?

I recall a lecturer telling me suicide risks, or those that present as risks are often indifferent about when they die. They can present as being so apathetic about life they don't even care when it ends, that suicide hovers like a cloud they can use when it gets too much.

Kate was nothing like that. She was effervescent. Engaged with life.

'Fray, she had problems. More than I realised at the time. More than I admitted to you, to myself. I was just too young and stupid to see the signs were real. If only I had.'

'If *we* had.' I lift my arm to cap his shoulder with my hand.

He shrugs. 'Don't give me the *not your fault* shrink crap. I *know*. Shit happens.'

I always liked the accidental-death angle myself. 'You really think that she wanted *out* that bad?' I hate the thought. 'I mean, suicide? It's just so selfish. A permanent solution to a temporary problem.'

'Easy for you to say,' Jack murmurs.

'Meaning what?' I glare at him. 'I don't know the extremes people can face? I see it every day, Jack. I just like to think there is always an out.'

Jack's eyes linger on mine, and I see a glimpse of the scar that Kate left him with. Her residual effect. It hits me that he knew. He knew that night how bad she was. He just wanted to protect me from the harsh reality.

'She was like fireworks, Fray. She was never made to last.'

CHAPTER 19
For Rent

Mitchelton, Brisbane
28 December 2000

Now my best friend's gone, she's all I can see. My room is a shrine to all things Kate. The flat indents in my carpet from the legs of my chair – she would rock back and forth when I was trying to study. The Friends poster she gave me for my birthday. Her spare bikini – I don't have the courage to return it now. What's the point? I suddenly rush over to her jacket, grab it with both hands, and bury my face in its folds. I think of how she lent it to me walking home from the train, even though she was cold too. I breathe her in, the scent of apple shampoo. A gust of her engulfs me and I drown in her.

'Why does it always have to be about you?' I yell to the walls, hurling her jacket as far as I can. 'Teenage Dirtbag' is still playing in Ben's room, over and over. I stomp down the back stairs to his man-cave, barge into his room, which I never did without knocking once I realised what he did alone in his room. I press the eject button on his stereo and pull out the Wheatus album that had haunted me for days. My brother is such a loser. I stomp on the case with all my weight, cracked plastic splintering beneath my shoes. I expect a torrent of rage from him. Yet he stares blankly at me, without a word. It hasn't even hit the sides.

'What's wrong with you?' I yell. 'She was my friend!'

My prodding words still fail to penetrate the inner world of my brooding brother. I collapse on the edge of his bed, staring outside at the weeds that poke through exposed aggregate coping. The pool is a watery pit of leaves. I suddenly need to reconcile all the snippets in my head, the stories she told that were now put into question.

'Is it true, that you perved on her getting dressed from the pool?'

'What?' Ben says, arcing up. 'I wish . . .'

He curls back into himself after a momentary lapse of interaction.

I storm back to my room. Even poking the hibernating bear has not provoked a reaction. He is a vacuum of feeling. Part of me envies him.

I grab my swim bag, and hope that following the black line to the T one hundred times will take my mind elsewhere.

'Where are you going, honey?' my mum calls from the kitchen, fingers from one hand stuffed inside a dead chicken's cavity.

'Just to the pool,' I utter. I have learned to say what she wants to hear, but in as few words as possible. I have just about reached the steps when she approaches, hands drying in a tea towel.

'Hon, if you are looking for him, he won't be there.'

'I know, Mum.' The twisted rope of my swim bag cuts into my shoulder. 'The Shaws aren't back yet. Not till Saturday.'

'That's just it, love,' Mum says, stopping in her tracks. 'I'm not sure they're coming back.' She folds her big white arms, the way she does.

I turn to her, as we stand at the top of the stairwell.

'Sharon and Richard came back alone, to clean up the place

to rent. Charlie's started a job, so he and Jack stayed in Townsville with his —'

'Rent?' The words feel like a sword being thrust in my throat. 'They're gone for good? You're lying! You just don't want me to see him!'

My bag, and my life, drop to the floor.

Her eyes avert from mine. 'Honey, I know it's hard,' she says as she folds the tea towel in her hands.

'Hard?' I yell. 'My life is falling to pieces around me, and you're all crazy if you think moving him away will fix this.'

'My darling, you are about to start a whole new life at uni. You may have drifted apart anyway, now you've left school. You will find nice friends you have more in common with.'

'More in common than a lifetime?' I ask. 'Didn't you meet Jack's mum – your best friend – at Brownies when you were, like, seven?'

'Well, yes, but —'

'But what?' I say. I realise my mother seems fine about this change, losing her friend as well as mine. What's with that?

'I am not sure we're on speaking terms now.' Her words are threaded with pain. I look over to her, as she stands there stoic. She places the towel on the handrail, stops and takes my hands in hers. 'Jack's still being investigated.'

'What? But she drowned.'

'It's not that simple. There are still tests being done, honey. It's not something I need you to be involved in.'

I pull away. He isn't. He was cleared.

'After knowing him since he was in nappies you still think that he killed her? Strangled her, dumped her body in the ocean? Is that what you think?'

Her eyes close tightly as she turns away. I'm ashamed of her. 'Some role model you are! You don't even have the guts to admit it! What did you always teach me about loyalty? Friendship? Trusting your instincts?'

Her face sinks like a beach ball snagged on a rock. I see a tremor in her chin.

'What makes you think I didn't help him then, huh? Get rid of the hot blonde – so I can have the guy all to myself?'

'Don't be ridiculous!'

'No more ridiculous than what you think!'

My mind races. I have to speak to him. He will think I believe all this.

'You don't know anything about what happened, not for sure! He wouldn't do that!' I cry.

Mum looks pale, her eyes glassy. Her hands tremble as she edges them to her lips. 'Frankie, I know you had feelings for Jackson that you thought were real.'

Had. Past tense. I hate this patronising tone. Like I'm some kid with a crush, blinded from reason. 'Oh, come on, Mum, it's not about that and you know it! Can you honestly tell me your gut instinct when you heard she was missing was that Jack did it? He's not even the father!'

Shit.

I suck my breath back, hoping the words will be erased with the air.

'Excuse me?' The whip in her voice returns.

I feel the colour rise in my cheeks.

Her eyes are dark and wide. 'Kate was pregnant?' Her knees buckle. She grabs the rail to take her weight. 'Why wasn't that mentioned? It wasn't in the papers. The police know this?'

I turn away, stroke the banister. I feel my stomach coil like a snake.

'Tell me you didn't keep it from them . . . something like this . . .'

She yanks my face close to hers.

'Francesca, what have you done?' Her spindly fingers cup my shoulders, her nails indenting in my back as she stares me down. 'You lied to the police? Oh, Frankie! Have I taught you nothing? You stupid girl!' The tendons in her neck strain like a weightlifter. Her words fade. I feel only the vibrations. Saliva sprays on my cheek when she emphasises a word. Stupid. Why. Honesty. Station. Statement. It's all a blur.

'He's behind this! He left his pregnant girlfriend on a deserted beach. What else are you covering up for him?' She shakes me now.

My height towers over her, yet I feel like a robot, genetically programmed to obey her. Her nails dig in hard now as she holds my shoulders firm.

She releases me like a wrestler at the final siren, and sits wide-eyed on the wooden stool near the phone, her hands cupped neatly on her apron as she scrunches the fabric in her fists.

So, I've said it. It's not just my secret now. Now that the initial shock is gone, it feels like a wet towel on sunburn – a relief to let the weight of it go and float away.

Her eyelids lower in slow motion. She exhales like a bull. 'I never thought of you as naïve, Frankie.'

I swallow the venom creeping up my throat.

Silence stretches out before us, like an eye in a cyclone, and I panic about the other side.

'You will tell the police,' she states all matter-of-fact. 'I will take you first thing. The police, her parents, they deserve to know.'

'No.' No more. 'You can't make me. I'll deny it.'

She stands up, her fingers tracing her brow as she paces the hall. 'You will go to jail as an accessory; you have to retract your statement! Have some sense, dear!' She says it with such distaste that my skin crawls. She touches my shoulder, but every cell in my body wants to recoil from her.

'I have the constable's number.' She wipes her brow, exhales with relief as if all is good again in the world. 'I'll take you there tomorrow to make this right.'

'You don't control me any more! I am not you, Mum! This is my life! I'm not a re-do for you – a chance for you to do all the stuff you wished you did. It's mine,' I ramble. It is a conglomeration of all the thoughts from all the fights through my teens that I never had the guts to say out loud.

'If you don't, I will,' she says blank-faced as if I had said nothing at all.

I panic. What if she does tell them? What if they reopen the investigation?

'You're bluffing!' I yell.

'What were you thinking? Putting this irresponsible boy before your future?'

'He is my friend, I can't do that to him! Even if it was his kid, he didn't hurt Kate.'

'Francesca Hudson,' my mother's steely voice commands, 'if you don't do as I ask and do the right thing, you can find somewhere else to live!'

'Crap threat, Mum. Moving out suits me just fine.'

I race down the steps, the shudder in her voice in my shadow.

I grab Ben's speed bike from the entry before she can stop me, and race the two blocks to Jack's house.

It looks the same. No 'For Rent' sign – it must be a mistake. She is lying about all of it. He's just escaping the circus, having Christmas with his gran. It's not forever. He has uni applications to come back for. His band . . .

He has me.

I dump the bike on his front path, more at ease.

That's when I see it.

Their garage door. Vandalised.

MURDERER!

It is painted in red; the letters drip like a bleeding wound.

The M, faded, scrubbed, scarred from an earlier attempt at erasure. But the word is etched in my mind.

I feel my breath become jagged, and hope he hasn't seen the stupid cruel stunt.

I take a breath and knock. I hear muffled noises of crockery being stacked behind the wall – these cavity brick walls that were rich with secrets and lies, that had heard our stories for the past decade or so. Could they really leave their home, over this?

'Aunty Sharon?' I call, tapping harder, with a sense of urgency now. 'Jack?'

I raise my fist to bang again, yet the door falls away, and his mum's weary face fills the doorframe.

'Dear, it's just me, I'm afraid,' she says, looking small and birdlike, her apron dusty on her waist. Her eyes slide sideways, eyeing off the hurtful scrawl on her home, but neither of us mentions it.

'Is it true?' I plead with her. 'He's staying up there for good? Without even saying goodbye?'

Her silence, her blank face, void of hope, is all the answer I need.

I feel the tears glaze my eyes and spill over. There is no more room for them inside, no headspace for this. I am already full. I am going to start losing pieces of me to fit this in too.

'Frankie, dear, he would have loved to have said goodbye, truly. He is heartsick. But you know it's for the best – a fresh start for him. All of this,' she gestures to the vandalism, 'it isn't healthy for any of us.'

'Is that what Jack wants? Have you even asked him? What about uni?' An idea hits me. 'Maybe he can live with us if you have to move?'

She shepherds me inside, and I see the house is stripped bare of any trace of them. The cupboards are clean and empty; the doors spread open to air. My eyes are drawn to a bright patch on the wallpaper, like a fossil of where a family portrait previously hung.

Without invitation, I wander up the hall. I remember how we used to count the steps to the kitchen so we could sneak out during sleepovers to steal supplies. How the floorboard near the linen press would always creak. I show myself down the stairs to his room but there's not a trace of the yard-sale scrum it always was. The Doors poster is gone, another dark patch surrounded by faded wall. It used to be strategically placed to cover the hole – the one Ben punched out, that we used to stash things in. A pile of boxes are stacked on the corner, his guitar case among them.

If his guitar is leaving, this must be real.

I hear footsteps and she enters.

'I don't get it. You'd take him away from his friends? You'd move away from your home just cause of the gossip? Some graffiti?' My stomach is tight with anger.

Her stormy eyes spear through me. 'Charlie has work up there, Mum's health is fading, and besides, I would do anything for my son. For him to escape this thing,' she tells me, revealing an inner strength her outer skin fails to disclose. 'I understand you two have always been close, but you're both good kids, you'll find other friends.'

I see red. I hate how grown-ups belittle our lives. Miniaturise them. Like our problems, our relationships, stand short next to theirs.

'It may not be forever, Frankie. Just till the dust settles on all this.'

'You think it's that simple? All the hurt will just go away if you do?'

Her eyes have lost their warmth, replaced by steely determination. 'I won't let this . . . girl . . . define his life,' she says through gritted teeth.

I think of my safe life before Kate – predictably benign in every way. Even before she blighted my life by leaving me, she had altered its course just by being my friend.

'You're too late,' I tell her, as I turn to walk away. 'She already has.'

CHAPTER 20
Three Seconds

It's the kid-free, nearly-wife-free bachelor weekend Jack has been looking forward to. It started with a boys' night, by the laughter springing from the cab in the driveway late last night, and continued with a surf this morning. Jack has only just returned home after heading off early with his board, wetsuit and shoeless, with a van full of sun-kissed surfer buddies.

Sara is away with Oliver, at a friend's for a couple of days apparently, so I am also feeling a newfound freedom, with a chance to loiter in my yard without any friendly gunfire. I take the opportunity to immerse myself in paint. No death stares, no neighbourly screaming matches, just paint.

Well, paint and Jack. It's like he can smell the acrylic from his kitchen bench. I have only tapped the edge of the can when he comes running like a dog to a rattling packet.

'Don't you have a golf course you can divot, or something to fix?' I ask, as he strips off his shirt and grabs the spare brush. 'Where'd your mates go?'

'Had my dose of them. Need to recover. Besides, most of my real mates are all back home, and work mates . . . well, they're at work. So you're it. Mate.'

The sun highlights a tan line at the small of his back. His abs ripple as he stands, and I wonder how he got them. He's more likely to be seen with a donut than a dumbbell.

'You call that prepped?' he asks, screwing up his nose at my sanding job.

'Fair go. I did it by hand.'

'It's not like you had more than three square metres to do, since you live in a cubby house.'

He starts on the side wall, feathering light expert strokes back and forth with his wrists.

'Strong hands. That from all that stirring?' I ask, my tongue firmly in my cheek.

He ignores me. 'So, Fray, why is it I don't see any blokes sneaking out this back door of a morning?'

I laugh. I guess I did lower the tone first. 'The only blokes to see the inside of these walls lately have been Ben, my plumber, and you.'

'Waste,' Jack teases. 'Although you're probably seeing as much action as me at the moment.'

'Just hold it,' I grimace, stopping my paintbrush for a second. 'I've heard enough of your bedroom . . . stuff. We don't do girl-talk.'

'So, you're not going to tell me about your tickle fights, and slumber parties with your friends with bi-tendencies?'

'If I had any, the answer would be *no*.'

We both resume our painting.

'You have never really been an open book with this stuff. Very private. I remember you going out with that guy you met at that disco – what was his name?'

'Dillon,' I remind him, with a cringe.

'Dillon! Now he was a smooth operator. Older guy, at uni or something. So I am guessing there was some sort of action?' Jack says.

'Do you mind? I am trying to paint!' I cough. 'Anyway, there was no actual action.'

'Okay. Well, I'm assuming there has been since. Merc guy perhaps?' Jack asks.

'I'm nearly thirty. Ya think?'

'Well, you were always a bit . . . prudish,' Jack says.

'Prudish?' I scream, flicking the end of my paintbrush at him. 'Just because I wasn't the town *bike*?'

'I'm just saying you never flashed too much boob action or pashed guys behind the incinerator. I can't imagine you actually *flirting*.'

'I'm not a nun. I flirt . . . when required.'

His ears prick up, and his brush slows. 'Okay, give me your best line.'

I glare. 'I don't have lines. I have looks.'

'Looks?'

'You know, like the three-second stare.'

'The come-hither eyes?'

'Not even that. I reckon I can suss someone out, see if there is a connection, in three seconds. You forget, I work people out for a job.'

'It's that simple, huh?' Jack says. 'No need to live together, just a quick stare will tell all?'

'You mock, but I swear it works.'

He pauses and then looks at me with determination in his eyes. 'Try me.'

My throat tightens. Maybe he's right. I can't even handle talking about it.

'Doesn't work that way. Can't muster the mojo to do it right when there's no genuine interest in the merchandise,' I say. I won't mention it's the only trick I have. I'm a terrible flirt. Always have been. Too much pride and not enough courage.

'Gee, thanks,' he says, slapping a big pile of paint on my wall, feathering it out. 'How often do you put it to use, this three-second stare? Perhaps you need the practice.'

'Never you mind.' Which is code for hardly ever. He looks at me and a smile splits his face, makes me blush.

'So, I am guessing you are not the random sexing, one-nighter typa gal.'

'Which makes me what, Jack? Ethical?'

'I was going to go with *frustrated* but stick with your word if you like.' He smiles.

I grimace. 'I think now would be a great time to reinvoke the no-girl-talk clause.'

Jack rolls his eyes. I feel like a bore. A frigid one, apparently.

'Well, we have two walls to go, so what can I talk to you about then?' he asks.

I pause to think. 'Paint?'

'Wow. Can we watch it dry together too?'

I see now that the off-spray from my earlier brush flick has speckled his face with a blue rash.

'Come here a sec,' I say, grabbing a rag to wipe off the paint on his temples before it dries. I erase the colour from his skin, turn the cloth over, and rub his ear free of paint. I walk back and continue doing the lower section. Jack bends over to the paint tin to replenish his brush, but a flick of blue splashes across me, speckling my arm.

'Sorry,' he says. The smile on his lips tells me otherwise. 'You sure you don't wanna show me your stare thing?'

I roll my eyes. If I don't, I'll look like a complete lame-arse. He will pester me as long as he lives in my yard like a stone in my shoe. 'Fine!' I huff.

Even as I get up, I can't believe I'm doing this.

He stops, pretends to look like serious business is about to be discussed. 'I'm listening.' He puts the paintbrush down, as if he needs all hands on deck for this.

'First, you ensure physical proximity . . .'

He stands blank-faced, hands on hips. I shimmy over to him nervously until our noses are almost touching. I can see the lines on his lips, I'm so close. 'Direct, unwavering eye contact – no blinking,' I explain, but he is bashful, his eyes linger too low to meet mine. I notice how long his eyelashes are, wasted on a man.

To finish off my demonstration, I prop his chin up with my fingers, turn his face to meet mine, a breath away. I look right through him; my eyes are fixed, absorbed in the flecks of blue blending with shades of grey. I realise I've stopped breathing.

What am I doing?

I feel my face flush, and pray it isn't obvious, but I can't back out now.

And I hold his gaze for one, two, three terrifying seconds.

Jack's the first to look away, stepping back suddenly, tripping on a roller tray with his boots. I use the distraction to breathe out, compose my nerves.

'So you believe me now, about the three seconds?' I ask, my voice full of holes, handing back his paintbrush.

'Nah,' he says, screwing up his nose. 'Needs some work.'

After a telling silence, he hands the paintbrush back again. I suddenly feel cruel.

'Think you should finish up,' he says, wiping his hands on a rag. He throws it down like a yo-yo and retreats to his side of the world. 'Got some shit to finish while Oli's away,' he says to the ground. I stare at him as he walks away.

He's taken his bat and ball, and called stumps.

When we were ten, I remember us learning to pash with our hands between our mouths so never our lips should meet. Or sometimes, we'd pretend to be doctors and nurses, checking our heartbeats, our pulse – it was a little wicked, but mostly a laugh.

It didn't feel like that any more.

This is why I never flirt.

CHAPTER 21
Drunken Shenanigans

Meg — every inch of her geared to taking in strays — has invited Jack and me over for dinner. Sara is visiting her aunt with Oli apparently, so I don't need to fear her inclusion. She seems to be away more than she's home, and I wonder if that's by design.

Chargrilled something wafts through the windows from the Weber on her back deck. Marinated capsicum and chilli perhaps? It smells tantalising. That woman never stops amazing me — I'm surprised she has time to brush her teeth, let alone cook for lonely neighbours.

I stare at the slim pickings on offer in my wardrobe and wish I spent more time shopping than painting. Work threads, the odd chiffon bridesmaid's dress, and a few pairs of jeans that all seem like different versions of the same. Joy.

Jack's boots clod up my back steps. I grab the closest shirt in reach that doesn't require ironing and throw my arms in, just as his head pops around the door.

'Jack!' I say, turning away as I fasten buttons – fast.

'Sorry,' he says, yet continues to stand there.

'Are you right?' I ask.

'The main bits are covered. Besides, it's nothing I haven't seen before,' he adds, heading off to my kitchen.

'What, when we were eight? I don't think that counts,' I call out, flicking my door closed with my foot.

'More like sixteen,' he mumbles on the other side of it. 'Biol camp, remember? White t-shirts kind of show it all when wet.'

I squeeze into jeans and walk out to him. 'We were never speaking of that, remember?' I remind him, finding my boots.

'Total recall. Sorry.' He smiles, and starts pouring the wine I assume he intended to take to Meg's. 'Don't you love screw tops?'

'Can't you wait? That's rude, opening the bottle before.'

'I took some cleanskins over the other day for having Oli sometimes, so I'm in credit.'

I suddenly remember my upgraded fuse box – the electrician had finished it off that afternoon. 'Check it out!' I ask Jack, presenting my kitchen appliances. 'I can turn the toaster and kettle on at the same time without blowing a fuse.' Jack's eyes narrow and I feel a flush of embarrassment at my excitement. 'Not that much of a biggie, I guess.'

He lifts my chin, as if to reassure me. 'It's good, Fray. I get it.'

I avoid his eyes, and step away.

'Upgrading ours is still on the To-Do list, thanks to Sara. Everything looks pretty though, got our priorities straight.' Jack sips his glass. There it is again, the lingering look. He's been different ever since that stupid stunt with the stare thing. Or maybe it's just some flirtatious mood he gets in when Sara's away? Which seems to be every weekend lately.

'Come on, piss-wreck, before you get tanked,' I say once my boots are sorted, shepherding him outside.

We arrive at Meg's late, and Jack's hand lightly grazes my arse as he ushers me up the steps. 'What's with the hand?' I ask. 'We are not on a date, Jack,' I whisper, as I hear footsteps approach the door.

'Don't flatter yourself – you had masking tape on your arse.' He holds up a small wad of used tape for me to inspect, then chucks it over his shoulder.

'Oh.' I pull my head in. Perhaps I am imagining all of this. A reluctant twinge spirals in my stomach.

'Guys! Hello! Hit bad traffic, did we?' Meg jokes, gesturing to the time.

'Sorry we're late,' I say.

'Fray couldn't find anything to wear,' Jack adds, rolling his eyes.

'Just listen to you – you're sounding like an old married couple.' Meg laughs. I sneer at my friend for the image she has inserted in my head.

Meg parades us through her home and out to the expansive back deck. The kids are conspicuously absent – already settled watching *The Clone Wars*, she explains.

As we walk through, I admire the metal fretwork, the restored VJs and picture rail, and feel overwhelmed, but inspired by what I still hope to achieve at my place (on a much smaller scale).

I head to the kitchen to help prepare, a large glass of wine in hand. I need to catch up to Jack's early start. As I toss a salad, I peek through the servery to the deck. Meg and Jack are engaged in foodie conversation – comparing marinade recipes, what works best with different cuts. Jack's almost finished his bottle.

'Hey, save me some of that!' I call. 'I don't want to have to carry you home.'

I hear Meg's kids (Small, Medium and Large), bicker in the rumpus room over who ate all the salt-and-vinegar chips.

As I rescue the bread from the oven, the chill of the night air blows through the bi-fold doors. Jack stands to fire up the gas heater Meg stores in the corner of the deck. I place the bread on a serving platter. I take it outside, and notice Jack reaching up to start the pilot light, his right bicep filling his sleeve as he flexes to push the start. His shirt slinks up his chest, baring a mere few inches of rippled abs, a trail of hair from his navel to his fly.

I miss the door track, and the plate crashes to the floor.

Their heads turn. Jack steps over to help as I apologise to Meg for the mess.

As Jack and I both squat to pick up the pieces, he says with narrow eyes, 'What was that about *me* having had enough wine?'

He takes the broken pieces to the bin, while Meg gives me a sideways glance and says down her nose, 'Be careful there, hon.'

The weight in her voice tells me she isn't referring to watching my feet.

Meg carves the rosemary-scented lamb in thick chunks, and serves it beside chargrilled corn and garlic herb potatoes. I admire Meg, competently filling the role of both husband and wife as she hosts this simple but elegant dinner. Mitch is always working.

But her comment to *be careful* irritates me. Does she really think so little of me that, even if I do have feelings for him, I'd go after someone spoken for? Break up a family?

I expect the drinking to wane as the food settles, yet Jack is steadily climbing his stairway to drunk.

It doesn't take long before the conversation hones in on Sara not knowing our past until recently. Meg comments on her own experience, having returned from a dinner party years ago, only to be told by her husband that he had once dated the host back in university.

'I could understand her feeling hurt, feeling stupid – being left out of the picture,' Meg says, empathising with Sara's mistrust of Jack since Ben's visit. 'Lots of hard yards to make up, I'd be guessing, hey, Jack?'

'You could say that. I'm still in the doghouse. At least I get to sleep in my own bed when she's not home.'

'Not good, Jacko,' Meg says, pouring another drink and slapping him on the shoulder. 'But when there's kids you have to try to live out the dry spells. Talk to Mitch. It won't fall off.'

In an attempt to avoid further details about Jack's – or Meg's – sex life, I clear some dishes, rinse them off. The wine is making me heady and I decide my token effort to clean up will suffice and walk back out.

There is silence when I return. I'm concerned. It's like I left a toddler out of sight for too long.

'You didn't mention you were engaged,' Jack says to me with squinty eyes.

I glance at Meg but she ducks for cover. 'Oh good, it's not just me she's cagey about with that one,' Meg says. They smile at each other, yet Jack grows quiet. I leave the conversation for two minutes, and come back on the outer. Jack, the rock from my childhood, and Meg, my new bestie, have joined forces against me.

'I was. Past tense.'

Meg and Jack pick at me for sordid details, which I deflect poorly. I am suddenly offended by this line of questioning. Even half drunk, I feel bullied. I know they mean no harm, but it is time for me to call it a wrap. Jack reluctantly leaves too, thanking Meg for her hospitality, and I promise to have her and Mitch over soon (for take-out). I trudge up to my front door, and find my key as Jack babbles something behind me.

'Go home, Jack,' I order, as he settles on my front step like a stray cat.

'It's weird, thinking of you with some guy I don't know,' Jack says. 'I mean, I knew everyone you ever met, your whole life. Now I find out you were *engaged*? Were you, like, living with this guy?' he slurs.

'Pretty much,' I admit, turning the key, hoping to make a quick entry. Meg's warning echoes in my head.

Jack has different ideas and remains sitting on my front porch. 'What was he like?'

'He was beautiful. Charming. Successful. And wrong for me.' I realise it is the best summation of his character yet. As usual, Jack makes me see things clearly. He is still my litmus test for the truth. 'You met him actually. He swore at you for asking him to move his stupid car.'

He frowns and then it hits him. 'The Merc guy?' Jack almost yells – he loses all sense of volume when he drinks. His jaw drops as I join him on the step.

Jack leans his head on the banister, his eyes gazing up at the stars as he sits on the bottom step.

'Don't get mad,' he almost laughs. 'But I used to think you and Kate, that you were, you know . . .'

'Me and Kate *what*?' I ask, flabbergasted.

'Well, you were always so *close*. With all your sleep-overs and shit, lying around in the same bed, doing each other's hair.'

'You *wish*, more like it,' I say, kicking him off my step with my boot.

'That would have been something,' he laughs, as he stumbles home half-tanked.

'Goodnight, Jack.'

I undress, forgo my final pee, with full knowledge that I'll regret it in the early hours when I have to get up to go, put on the last clean nightie in the drawer and crash on my unmade bed. My head is spinning from the wine, the night. Did I really drop a plate of bread, I think, as I fall asleep.

实

It's pitch black when I hear a disturbance. At first I reassure myself that it's possums in my roof, or bats bickering over green mangos, until I hear the distinctive tinkering sound of rocks being thrown at my kitchen louvres.

'Fraaaayyy?' I hear Jack call. 'You shit me, you know,' he calls, slurring his words on my back porch. 'That stunt you pulled. That "look" thing. Are you that cruel, Francesca?'

Here we go. Lonely Jack. Still drinking. Alone. And why is he calling me Francesca?

I can only ignore it so long.

'Jack, it's three am. What's wrong?' I ask weary-eyed from my back door. 'Are you locked out again, cause I gave you the key you stashed here last time you were locked out.'

I open the door a few inches, which sees his size 11 foot being wedged in the gap, levering it open. He is standing in my kitchen, a half-empty bottle of Bourbon in his hand. I smell gusts of it when he talks. He fumbles for the light switch.

In the sudden brightness, I realise I'd put on my lace-edged black nightgown – the good one, the one no one ever sees. He double-takes, glaring at my more-than-usual northern exposure.

'You're *mean* to me. So *mean*!' he slurs, swatting imaginary flies as he babbles on. 'Why are you torturing me – wearing *that*?'

I make an attempt to cover up, make sure nothing serious has escaped.

'It's three am! I wasn't expecting visitors. I was asleep,' I say, crossing my arms. I'm in that annoying twilight between pissed and hung over.

'That cruel stunt the other day – you are doing my head in, Fray!'

I know what he means. The three-second stare. So now he is admitting it got to him too.

'You made me! After you called me a nun, I had no choice – I was just mucking around. I didn't expect –'

'It to fucking *work*? Well it did, Frankie. It woke me up. You have my attention.'

'Well, you shit me off, Jack – that afternoon – saying that crap about me, like I was this, this non-sexual being. It bothered me.'

'But that's how I have to see you. I am stuck with this chick who can't stand me. And yet I see you every day. I watch you bend over to hang your clothes, I watch you drink your tea through the louvres, I imagine what you look like behind that friggin' frosted-glass bathroom window. I want you, every day. And I've learned to tolerate it. Accept it. Knowing you've never wanted me like that. Remembering that night in my room.'

'Jack!' God, here we go. It's all coming out now. I shake my head awake. 'I couldn't, *then* –'

'Don't remind me. I know, I know what you said. I can still see your face saying it.'

I cringe, realising what I'd put him through back then. But just as quickly I remember, he went out with my best friend instead of me. 'I couldn't think of anything but Kate that night.' Back then, everything was irrelevant but my reeling sadness. Jack included.

Jack slides down the wall of my kitchen, flops on the floor. I join him, feeling sober at the thought of her.

'I know. But I needed you. I needed to have a second of good, in all the misery. I needed to know we were okay. That you didn't think . . .'

'What? That you'd hurt her?' I shake my head at him, at his sad, sorry drunken self. 'I never thought that for a second, Jack. Not then, not now. No one does.'

'*She* does.'

'Who?' A cold shudder passes through me. *Kate?*

'Sara. After she found out I lied about us knowing each other, she was convinced I was screwing you. I had to tell her the whole story – get her to trust me again.'

This isn't news to me. I heard it all in stereo through the windows after Ben's introduction.

'Okay, that's good, right? It's all out of the closet now.' Should have been all along.

'She thinks I *killed* her. I know she does. She just reeks of accusation. This is why I never told her.'

I shut my eyes to it all.

'I know that must hurt, but you have to understand it from her side – you kept her in the dark so long, she didn't know who to trust. Figured you were hiding something big.'

'But to think I *killed* someone? That's fucked, Fray.'

'You don't know she thinks that. She just doesn't know what to think.'

'She *told* me. She keeps asking me details, over and over. I can see the doubt in her eyes. She's wary of me. Asks me if I raped her first, got scared. How can I live with someone who can think I was capable of that? The worst fucking thing imaginable.'

I close my eyes, cringing for him with every breath, every word he speaks.

He rests his head on my shoulder. I thought I'd heard a lot of their fights, her threats to leave him if he talks to me again. But all this, I had never imagined. How could you have ever seen the light in his soul and thought it possible?

His head, hot with emotion, has now made its way to my neck, my chest. A drunk, desperate, broken man. His hand spreads across my waist, and I shudder at where this is leading.

He curls his finger under my shoestring strap, lets it fall, as he caresses my shoulders with his hand. His fervent eyes meet mine for a second, fall away as he kisses a trail down my neck, to my chest, cupping his fingers around me. I feel the roughness of his hair tickle against my chest as he buries himself in me. His lips skirt along my breast bone.

I shamefully feel myself react. Despite our drunken state and knowing his heart of hearts doesn't want this, his touch tempts me. My mind races. My Jack, my security blanket, touching me. Wanting him to touch me more.

But when I open my eyes, the haze I am under dissipates.

The new version of Jack is a father. A good one. And he wants his son more than this. He wants to mend things, not break them beyond repair.

I close my eyes, and wish the pleasure rising in me away. I think of Seamus. His affair. I've been on the other side of this.

Jack isn't mine to have. He never was.

I guide his fingers down away from my chest, holding them safely in one hand as I lift his chin to look into his eyes.

'We can make her see, Jack.'

'It's no use, she doesn't love me!' he pleads.

I wonder where all this has been hiding – he was fine at Meg's. But he found this sorrow at the bottom of the bottle. 'Maybe not, Jack, not right at this moment. But Oli does.'

With the mention of Oliver, he suddenly recoils like a switch has been pulled. As if saying his name has orientated him.

He leans back against the wall and a frown settles on his face. Here we are, two grown adults, sitting on the floor like toddlers on a play date.

He gets up and walks out without a word, leaving his half bottle of Bourbon overturned on my kitchen floor, messing with my head.

Perhaps I'm going to need that bottle.

实

The next morning, brave with the knowledge Sara should still be away, I order Jack and I two flat whites from the local, and plan to pay him a visit – my justification being to get things out in the open and brushed away before she returns. To put things right.

He's left the door wide open, his keys in the lock. I find Jack slumped face down on his front-room couch, with Bear sprawled next to him. Traitor. So I'm the only one who slept alone last night.

I decide I should let Jack sleep it off and tiptoe out, when he stirs. The smell of coffee must have roused him.

'Hey, stranger,' he says to me in a husky voice, rubbing his eyes.

'Hey.' I am suddenly nervous.

I make small talk, trying to ascertain what, if anything, he recalls from our earlier kitchen-floor antics.

'You're sussing out what I remember, aren't you?' he groans. 'Well, I remember it all. Every last piece of you . . . it.'

I'm not embarrassed. I want him to know every piece of me. I realise I always have. There is just always something in the friggin' way. Dead girlfriend. A few thousand kilometres. A ready-made family.

'I'm sorry, Fray-Fray.' A loose arm flings out from where he lies.

The way he says it reminds me of how he started calling me *Fray*, when we were four and he couldn't get his mouth around the 'K'.

I gaze at him – his eyes are bloodshot, his usual Hollywood hair is flattened on one side, and a trail of salted saliva has crusted on his dry lips. And yet he is the most adorable thing I have laid eyes on. My past and my present, rolled up in a ball of man.

'*Downuus*,' he murmurs, in the haze of half sleep.

I frown. 'You wake me up at three am and now you are demanding I get you *donuts*?'

'I *bought* donuts,' he slurs. 'Last night. I went for a walk,' he says, lying down again, then suddenly sits up as if he remembers something critically important. 'Did you know that the 7-Eleven is actually open all night?'

I nod.

'So why isn't it called the 24/7?'

He's still drunk, I think to myself.

I see there is a huge bag of donuts on the bench, two of which are squashed and half devoured.

'Here. Take some. I got lots.'

He has bought me donuts. Had he walked all the way to Everton Park for these half plastered? He then adds, 'They're Oli's favourite,' and falls back asleep. He's out cold.

Oli.

It hits me with a jolt, as I realise what I've done.

He is all I want, and I have sent him home, to her.

CHAPTER 22
Options

I am scraping flaky paint from windowsills later that morning, when I hear it. The front gate unlatches. The hairs on my neck rise.

Sara is back. *Jaws* theme music tones in my head.

I sneak along the side wall like a burglar to avoid her path. I hit my shin on the tap and stifle a scream. Bear comes and sniffs me and I whoosh him away.

As the car drives down the easement into her garage, a dishevelled Jack greets her at the door. I can see the sleep lines from here. She grabs Oli from his car seat and approaches Jack. He leans in for a kiss but Sara shows her palm to him. Jack's eyes flinch, the hurt closing across his face. Oli reaches to Jack, arms open as he calls 'Daddy!' and Jack's face lights up.

I stand under the eaves, considering if sufficient time has passed for me to escape inside. A muffled argument overflows from Jack's walls, then almost immediately Jack and Oli fly out of the house. I lurch my head back against the wall out of sight. They head off down the road, one silver Razor scooter collapsed under Jack's arm. Obviously his hangover is easier to bear than his partner.

I retreat inside, and the tension in my neck uncoils. I scan my near-empty fridge. I am glad for the boys. They escaped.

Then I hear footsteps, rapid ones, growing louder down the side.

It seems I have not been so lucky. A knock. Sara has come for me. Has he told her about his late-night visit? Jack was always crap at keeping things he'd done buried. When we were kids he'd say he had to have his outsides matching the inside. They had to align, or he didn't know how to be. I bet he told her. He's learned his lesson.

I try not to wince as I turn the door knob. Her black roots are gone, her talon nails back to their fire-engine red. Her arms are crossed.

Sara's expression primes me. I am in the shit. Up the creek. Stuffed.

I'd hoped she'd return from her girls' weekend rested, resolved to work things out calmly with Jack. Yet it seems to have only bolstered her confidence.

'I heard about your *dinner* together last night. Just tell me, did you sleep with him?'

I am thankful I can handle *that* one. 'What? No.' I feel a grenade of guilt foraging into my throat. She's fishing. He hasn't told. 'We went to Meg's for dinner. Jack got pretty drunk, ranted some stuff, went home to sleep it off.'

It is mostly true.

'Tell me the truth for once. I need to know!' Sara pleads

with me, a hand to her temples in sheer desperation. I can see the veins throb.

'We haven't slept together.'

I feel empathy for her in her desperate search for the truth. It's the logical first step in self-preservation for the suspicious woman – finding facts, so you can apply feelings to them, and not waste emotion on conjecture or fear.

'So, what, never?' she asks, looking straight at me, tapping her foot.

I shake my head. 'Not before, not now.'

I see the relief ripple through her. She believes me. Is this out of love for him? Or competitive pride? In any case she collapses in a mountain of emotion on my front lawn.

Now that she has calmed, her eyes glaze with tears. The ice queen is melting.

'I was hoping it would be our new start, you know?' She places her hand on her forehead, her face softens and she looks fragile and human for a moment. 'I hate Oli hearing all this fighting, seeing me crying all the time. Jack's been lying to me ever since we moved to this fucking place. About knowing you, about this Kate person.' Her calmness evaporates again with the sound of Kate's name, and she points her red talon at me. The usual Sara returns. 'Something just doesn't add up and I am going to find out what it is.'

She backs away, retreating to her house of cards.

I close the door on it all.

实

My hair drips a wet patch down my robe as I waft the cloud of steam from the mirror. Mental note: get bathroom exhaust fan installed. I've been too busy being a harlot home-wrecker, apparently, to keep up my home improvements. It's late, and I hope the heat from the bath, still warm in my muscles, will help me sleep.

I hear a knock at the back door and my stomach vaults. Surely it's not Sara again? I'm still recovering. A pasta, a movie and a bath later, and I still can't get her out of my head. I feel sorry for her.

Another, almost hesitant, knock.

Unless Bear has grown opposing digits, I'm guessing it's Jack. I suddenly dread and hope, all at once, that he is here for the same reason he came last night.

'Can I come in?' His voice is thick.

I fasten my robe, take a breath and open the door.

His eyes are direct, and make me unsteady. Not again.

'Sara's asleep,' he says, stealing a backward glance.

Her name stabs at me.

He double-takes. 'You look younger with your hair wet.'

I blush and fold my robe tight.

He notices and scratches his head. 'I just wanted to come over to –'

'Jack –' I show my palms like an arrestee.

'Just,' he grabs both my hands, cradles them together in his, 'hear me out.'

His mouth starts moving but I can't hear what he's saying. His hands are warm. Thick. Rough. I can't think. I feel heat rush to my face, and pull my hands away. I slide down into the chair at the breakfast bar and sit on my fingers. He slips into the stool beside me. At least now there is airspace between us.

We stare across the table like a Mexican stand-off, less than a metre between us.

'I'm sorry,' he says, his face twitching. 'For last night. For what I did. Said.' He swallows, his Adam's apple bobs. 'It was . . . inappropriate. I was drunk. I wasn't thinking. It was a mistake.'

My lungs fill in my chest. I know all that. I don't need to hear it. Why can't we just be juvenile and, after a few awkward silences, forget it? We both know it can never be.

Fuck, last time we tried someone didn't come home.

He looks studious. 'I need to try and work things out with her. Like you said. For Oli.'

I nod silently. I don't want to speak. It will come out in squeaks.

He squints, as if the light is glaring, instead of the truth.

'I'll try to stay out of your hair. Only a few months left, couple of last jobs and the place'll be ready to flog.' He stares at the floor. 'I could even take time off work, get it done sooner. Be out of your way.'

He is leaving. Again. I'll be free to return to my pedestrian life. This is good, right? Simple?

It is so quiet I can hear the night air whisper past my ear from the open door.

He peers outside nervously, and his eyes don't return to mine. I used to think I am the most authentic version of myself around him. That there is no self-editing required. But we're in definite bullshit territory now. Bullshitting each other. 'Anyway, I just wanted to check that we're okay. Apologise. It won't happen again.' His voice has a formal tone and I hate it.

My mind races for the appropriate response. I don't do that with him. I just talk.

'I know, Jack. We can never be. I get it. If it makes you feel better to say that, then okay, say it.' My words have a whip in them that I hadn't planned on. He taps his thumb incessantly on the table, and I wrap my arms around myself.

'Meaning what?' He squints, the thumb-tapping stops.

'Jack, it's fine. I'll stay out of your way. Just go home.'

He chews his lip. 'What, so now you're mad?' he huffs. 'You're not making this easy for me. I'm trying to put this right! You played the moral high ground last night, made me think of Oli. Now I'm trying to fix this, and you, what, get *offended*?'

'I'm not,' I grunt like an eight-year-old. I don't know what I am, but it's not good. My throat swells.

'This is my lot, Fray.' He slaps his hand on his thigh. 'Sares. Oli. It's far from good but it's the hand I got. Plus she . . . she wouldn't cope if I . . .'

I see what this is now.

What is it with him and crazy hot chicks? There is always one standing in my way, and I always let them.

'You're acting like you think I expect something more from you,' I say. 'You're doing just what I expect. Being loyal. Doing the right thing – that's what you do.'

He looks at me with narrow eyes.

'You think I do the right thing? What, like leave a supposedly pregnant chick on a beach to go kill herself? Drink my life into a shit pile for a year or so, knock up someone I never loved. Yeah, right. Jack Shaw: citizen of the fucking year.'

I feel a twist inside, thinking of him struggling alone after Kate died. Is he never going to escape all that? 'You told me you thought Kate still had a hold on me. Ran my life. What about you, Jack? Sticking with someone wrong for you for too long, out of obligation, fear of how they'll cope – sound familiar?'

'What the . . .' His voice rises, then he checks himself and lowers it. 'Last night you're telling me to go home where I belong, now I'm a sucker to stay. Which is it? Pick a fucking side, Frankie.'

'There's no side cause there's no other option.'

He looks like his chest has taken a bullet, and emotion rises in my throat. His eye starts twitching again. He rubs it away.

'Isn't that what you came to tell me, Jack? Well, I get it.'

I walk to the door and hold it open for him. My heart races.

'Well, glad it's all so crystal clear to you,' he says, jumping from the chair.

As he steps closer, a shiver runs the length of me as my mind reaches back to last night. We stood in this very spot. In the dark, in a drunken tussle, and I want to be back there. For once in my life, to do what I want, not what I should.

He lingers, looking out into the darkness, both of us fuming. I want the world to shrink away, to grab him, pull him close, wrap my mouth around his.

To scream *pick me.*

I'm your other option!

He stops at the top step, closes his eyes as he exhales.

I can't breathe. He turns, strokes my face, the tip of his finger grazing my cheekbone, my chin.

My hand covers his palm, pressing on my face. He strokes it with his thumb. I want to push his hand lower, down my chest, waist, to ease the burning in my thighs.

But I don't.

I breathe him in, savour him, and watch as he drops his hand and walks away.

All the while knowing this is as close as I am ever going to get.

实

I dodge him all week. I wait till his car leaves before venturing to get the mail. I avoid the common ground, the shed. I keep Bear inside, out of everyone's way, so we have no need to meet. I return to my predictable pre *Jack-Shaw-returns* life.

And I feel lonelier than I have in a long time.

When I open my eyes the following Saturday morning, I realise Jack and his lot are in Townsville. Some family thing. I'm relieved to have some space to breathe, swear, slam. That fluster of emotion from my off-his-face neighbour, and his piss-poor attempt to apologise, has redefined the boundaries of our relationship. Or highlighted the need for them. But since they're away now I can finally get that washing done without seeing him. Or her.

I tiptoe out to get the paper, dressing gown and all. Bear gets there first, decides it's a game, and I chase him round the mango tree dodging low-hanging fruit like grenades.

'Long time no see . . .'

Fan-fucking-tastic. 'Jack,' I cringe. He hasn't left yet. Superb.

'Frankie,' he says, with his eyebrows raised.

We both look at each other uncomfortably. What now? Are we allowed to even talk?

'You know,' Jack says, breaking the silence, 'the old codger across the road waits for these sort of front-yard peep-shows,' he says, gesturing to our neighbour, who seems to be dawdling behind a rosebush.

'Good luck to him,' I say. 'Morning, Mr Wilson!' I call across the road, retying my dressing gown. Why am I never in actual clothes? I'm going to sleep in them from now on.

The old man scurries away like a rat. Jack hovers, out of place, like he doesn't know where to look. 'You could have just stolen mine like you usually do,' Jack says, picking up his paper, 'instead of chasing the mutt around.'

'I know what's mine.'

And I wasn't talking about the paper.

He looks up from the lawn, over to me. 'Yeah, I got that.'

We stand awkwardly, just days after his promise to stay out of my hair.

'Anyway, Sara is driving me and Ol to the airport, so we don't need a lift. But thanks anyway.'

Shit! I forgot I'd even offered. I'd rather poke sticks in my eyes. I breathe a sigh of relief. 'Sure. Just re-mortgage your house and pay to park at the airport for the weekend.'

'No need,' he says, tapping the rolled paper on his palm. 'She's not coming,' he adds. 'Work shit.' But his eyes say something else. He breaks eye contact when he lies. I figured that out when he got caught with a sling shot in grade six and denied all knowledge.

'Okay. Well, say happy birthday to Mr Shaw for me.'

'Will do,' he says, stepping away. 'Fray?' He stops in his tracks. 'Can you look out for Sares?' He stares up at the trees, deep in thought. 'This weekend, can you maybe check on her, or something?'

I am taken aback. Is he fucking kidding? Approach the *ice queen*? On *purpose*? 'Jack, I am not sure that's –'

'I was gonna pull the plug – stay with her – but I can't do that to the old man.'

'Surely I am the last person she –'

'Please? She's fragile.'

I am dumbfounded. Fragile like a tank.

'She thinks I'm sleeping with you!'

'Yeah, I gathered that.' He squints at the sun filtering through the tree.

'Why would she want me near her?'

He just looks at me, tilts his head like a puppy. 'Can you *try*?'

I look at him in disbelief, shaking my head. 'Okay, Jack,' I promise.

But the very idea of it makes acid bathe my tonsils.

'Thanks,' he says, walking home. 'Owe you one . . .'

实

I feel the weight of Jack's words on my back. I can't actively knock on her door – the very *thought* if it makes me shudder. The way she's avoided me, accused me, the last thing I feel is neighbourly. The days where we brought in each other's towels before a storm are well and truly over. I have spent all day avoiding being home – groceries, coffee with work friends, shopping for Ben's birthday (a month early, just to be out of the house). Now I'm stuck at home alone, with my task infiltrating my headspace. What did he mean, 'fragile'? I'm sure all the Kate crap, all the stuff about me rocked her boat. But that was weeks ago. Surely I'm the catalyst for her fury now, so why exacerbate the situation? Yet something niggles. The last time a girlfriend of Jack's needed help I was too cowardly to act.

I start chores, feeling sorry for myself for equating Saturday mornings with Toilet Duck and washing. I'd rather be ripping away at some old tiles than doing this mundane repetitive cleaning. As I wipe the benches, my mind digresses to last week. To the night Jack knocked on my door – what he told me about Sara doubting him. Am I arrogant to assume I know him better than she does? What did she say about something not *adding up*?

But it's not possible.

I throw the whole bag of doubt to the back corner of my mind. I dump the cleaning products and go outside to sand something. The doors, anything.

I go to the shed – no sander. I'd sanded the weatherboards manually to preserve their curve, and my hands are still sore from it. I can't face the doors without the electric sander. It must be at Jack's.

Forget it. I can try to use paint remover to get in the crevices of the casement window frames, but with rain predicted I'm not keen on pulling the windows off this weekend.

The neon sign flickers. I guess this is the ticket to 'check' on Sara – ask for my sander without appearing too obvious. Get the monkey off my back.

Okay. Do it now. Before the nerves cripple me.

I march right up and knock on her door. I hear a bang, footsteps. She appears at the door, a glass of wine in one hand, a durry in the other. My mind wanders – Gym-Barbie doesn't come with a *durry* accessory, surely?

Sara appears smaller without Jack's bulk by her side. Her face is softer without the usual thick foundation clogging her skin. She seems fine – yet it is almost as if I caught her being herself.

'Well, if it isn't my favourite fucking neighbour,' she slurs.

'Sorry to disturb – just realised Jack must have borrowed my sander. Wondered if I could get it perhaps?'

She just stares at me like I'm speaking Spanish.

'Do you mind?' I ask.

'Sure, help yourself. You do to most things around here.'

This is ugly. She could at least *pretend*.

A puff of smoke trails from her lips.

'That's okay. I can get it later, at a better time,' I say, hoping to escape this nightmare.

'Actually, I'm better than I've been in weeks.'

'I can see that,' I say, as she stumbles inside. I hesitate, then follow her. An empty wine bottle lies lonely on the couch. 'Might want to slow it down a little, or tomorrow might be a little ugly.'

She scowls unattractively. I want to sink into the floor.

'The do-gooder, always trying to *do good*. Think you can *fix* everything.'

'Actually, I think he needed it for the bathroom. It's probably in there if you don't mind checking for me.'

'Why don't you?' she says, waving me in. 'I'm sure you know the way.'

She never misses a hit. I cross my arms and stop in the hall, unwilling to follow her to their bedroom. She enters the bathroom. I see their bed, her nightgown over a chair, portraits of Oli as a baby. I feel claustrophobic.

'This what you're looking for?' Sara asks. The very movement of holding the sander up near her head totally unbalances her and she lands in the wing chair near their bed. She giggles like a twelve-year-old, her feet kicking in the air.

'Thanks,' I say, grabbing the sander. 'I'll let you get back to your Saturday.'

I have checked on her. She's alive and kicking. I am off the hook.

I hightail it out of there, through the door and onto their front entry.

'You could probably help me actually. Figure it out.'

My eyes slam shut. I am so close. 'What's that?' I ask, turning back.

She stands, leaning on the doorframe with one hand, tapping the ash from her fag with the other. 'Which is it? The big secret. Is it you are both lying about being fuck buddies, or did he do something to that girl?' She pauses, grabs her wine in tandem with her cigarette. Multi-tasking. 'He never much went for giraffe features in a girl. But he never much went for hurting chicks either. So which one is it?'

She puffs a cancer cloud at me that I dodge like a left hook.

'You don't mind if I smoke?' Sara asks, leaning on the wall for stability. 'My house, after all.'

Honey, I don't mind if you burn.

Her cheeks hollow as she sucks down hard on her cigarette. She looks like a stick insect. 'Or did you do it together? Did she trip and hit her head or something? You panicked, dumped her body . . .' Her eyes are void of warmth as the words spill from her mouth. 'How romantic – your little secret, all this time. Covering for each other.'

A lump wedges in my neck. 'Jack has never hurt anyone.'

'Ah, well, you see, that's not true. You don't know everything about your precious Jack. He got done for assault once, you know.'

My heart surges, my balance shifts. Assault?

'Hit some bitch, few years back. Maybe it wasn't the first time, huh?'

I shake my head. 'I don't believe you. There must be more to it.'

A wry smile skirts across her plump lips. 'You've got it bad, don't ya? Think he walks on water.' She flicks the ash from her durry on the pavers. The pavers Jack took such care to cut to precision. She grinds it in. I feel a snarl curl in my nose. 'I see the way he looks at you,' she says, exhaling smoke like a chimney, 'like the way he used to look at me.'

Now the lump in my throat is getting an acid wash. 'Well, I don't know about that. I just know there's nothing physical between us, never has been.'

Except for that nearly-snog the other night.

She looks deep in thought. 'Maybe that's the whole point.' She wags her birdlike finger at me. 'He just wants what he could never have. Perhaps he should just screw you and get it out of his system, so we can get on with our lives.'

'I'm not listening to this,' I mumble to the vulgar cow, striding out of her yard. Thanks, Jack, for five minutes I'll never forget. *Fragile* my arse. I feel like I've just poked a grizzly, but in this case I'm running for my life.

'I can't even trust him now.' She half-sobs in fits and starts at my retreating back. 'Could hardly visit his friggin' family – them thinking I trapped their precious son, getting knocked up. And Jack barely looks at me now. He hasn't touched me in months.'

I stop in my tracks. I fill with shame – in all this grief I feel a surge of relief. They are worse off than I thought.

'He is hiding something. I know it. And if it's not shagging you, then what the fuck is it?'

Blood rushes to my head. I try to slow my breaths, employ the strategies I use at work to hold it in, but the blood pulses louder.

'Do you know him at all?' I look at this cold-hearted, durry-smoking, foul-mouthed creature before me like an insect. But I still can't walk away. Maybe she's right – I am just a do-gooder, trying to save the world one person at a time. 'He has lived his adult life with the guilt of her – feeling responsible. You may not trust him now but I have no reason to lie to you. I was there. I believe him without question. Always have. Just like I know he now desperately wants to stand by his family.'

'For Oli! That's all he fucking cares about!'

I can't lie to her. Their problems are plain to see. I shrug. I am done.

'Go on, you bitch!' she yells. 'Go play house in your shitty shack, you thieving whore! It was probably you who drove that girl mental! Sounds like you're not above stealing people's boyfriends.' She hesitates, her mouth opens, 'when he comes back, he's all fucking yours!'

She throws her glass across the lawn, straw-coloured liquid splashing in the air, as she watches me in my walk of shame, retreating to the safety of my half-painted walls. I shut the door behind me, sander in hand, and sob tears of guilt, salty on my face.

实

I go to bed that night stroppy as hell. How can I live next to that woman now? Jack said it would still be months before they sell up. How can I stay? The inside of my place is liveable now, except for the kitchen. And the bathroom. But someone would rent this place, surely? And I could get on with my life without all this. Rent a townhouse with a yard. Even moving in with my parents seems more peaceful than living in their shadow. I can't even bear to see him with her.

I lie there, eyes livid, contemplating where my life's at, when I hear a car engine stop on the roadside. No headlights. They are trying to keep it low key. Boots on cracker dust. Someone is outside my window in the easement. Bear is inside, twitching in canine dreamland. *Useless watchdog.* I peel the blind back. A tall figure. Sara coming to kill me? Jack home early? I get up and navigate the dark hall to the louvres. Sara's security light floods her door with glare. My eyes flick to the navy-blue badge on a pale cotton sleeve – a cop. Was she robbed after I left? Is she turning Jack in, reporting a suspected crime from thirteen years earlier? Where is the cop's patrol car? His partner? I squint to see. Sara opens the door in a half-open robe, and proceeds to wrap her lips, her arms, her legs around the cop. My jaw drops. Straddled by her, the visitor stumbles inside, closing the door behind him.

Not on duty then, I'm guessing.

Somehow this makes everything clear.

I should be sad for Jack. A good friend would be.

But I am more than a good friend to him. Aren't I?

I think back to what Sara let slip earlier. That word *assault*. How he wasn't the man I think he is. Is she right? The Jack I know, the Jack I grew up knowing, wouldn't hit a girl. Not for no good reason. Not pissed. Not stoned. Never.

Okay, the chick is living with him. They've been together for years.

But I know him better.

I lie awake and remember the exact moment when I knew he was different from other boys. The exact moment when things between Jack and I stopped being simple.

CHAPTER 23
Some things change, some stay the same.

**Fletcher's Cattle Station,
December 1994**

We are eleven and we are camping. But the event starts out like it always does. Our bottle-green wagon is so loaded with tents and tarps I fear the rust-speckled floor will give way, and I'll end up walking the car to the camp like the Flintstones. Yet our convoy of cars arrives intact at Dad's mate's cattle station. We clear the three gridded gates before the alpha males disembark and analytically ponder the pros and cons of each camp spot (and settle on the same as last time, the shade near the creek). As I peek over the half rolled-down-window, I know what the day will bring: licking popsicles in the speckled shade, climbing trees and skinned knees. Slumping with sun-kissed shoulders on the foldout picnic table that collapses if you move. At dusk Jack and I will argue over property deals in Monopoly while the grown-ups drink till they laugh like hyenas. We'll laze on lilos on the lake, battle Donkey Kong in the hammock. I will beat Jack at Canasta, he will be the king of thumb wrestles.

But first, there is always the race. The weekend always starts with a race – it is a tradition. A battle to see who'll get wet first. Once our tents are up (Jack shares with my brother Ben), we can hit the creek and lose the sweat.

'Beat ya, Fray!' Jack brags, walking his shorts to his ankles as he runs to the creek. 'What ya waiting for?' he heckles from mid-stream, naked but for Y fronts. He is all shoulder blade and elbows. We were exactly the same height on our first day of Kindergarten. But I have shot up, and he is still scrawny. His dark hair looks like shiny wet bitumen, like a Lego man's, slicked to the side. I didn't think Jack was capable of looking dorky. 'C'mon, Lofty!'

'My shirt,' I say. 'It's white. It'll get all yuck.' My tank top is still crisp and fluoro-white like hospital sheets.

'Just take it off then.'

I stand on the bank. Through the murky tea-tree-stained water, my ankles brown, a crisp line marks where they meet pale shins.

'You worried I'll see your double-barrelled sling shot?' Jack teases.

'Shut up, Spackhead!' I rake my fingers through the water, flicking it high like scattered diamonds.

It was no secret. I'd been fitted for a bra the week before. A Double A, tawny beige, a bow in the centre. The whole class knows. Jack had felt it when we were wrestling, so now there is no hiding the fact, and it is too hot for wearing jumpers to hide the strap.

I shimmy my shorts off and jump in, undies, shirt and all. So what if my shirt gets stained? It is my own fault for wearing it. First rule of camping: never wear white.

The fresh water cools my skin, leaches the heat from me as I slowly sink deeper. Setting up at midday was nuts. Second rule of camping: never set up in the heat of the day.

We float. The tea trees shade us from the blistering sun that glimmers in patches on the water's face.

'Isn't that thing, like, annoying?' Jack asks, his eyes dipping low. I glance at my chest. My plan to wear my t-shirt to maintain some level of dignity has been foiled, the outline of my bra (and what is under it) plain to see. It is nearly as mortifying as the day I realised my togs were transparent when wet.

'You big perve,' I say, my arms springing to my chest. 'Just cause you still act like you're five doesn't mean I am.' I splash him again, which starts a war that I am destined to lose.

'Do you even need it? What does it do?' Jack asks. 'I mean, does it stop your boobs getting all long and droopy like those African jungle chicks?' He is such a git lately.

'Think I'll get out.'

'Whatever.' Jack shrugs. 'Smell ya later.'

I keep my arms crossed as I slosh back to camp, my clothes slicked on like Gladwrap. I am glad Jack's older brother Charlie stayed home. He'd have a joke about my wet clothes for sure.

实

I keep to myself the rest of the day, retreating to my tent after snags-in-blankets for tea.

Summer camping days always feel stretched. The sun's shift starts before five, and extends through till the twilight chatter is replaced with country quiet, nothing but the buzz of insects circling cow dung, and bats bickering. The amber glow of the mild morning sun streams through the thin veil of my two-man. I can smell the woody smoke of the fire – hear it crackle in the still. Someone is up and organised. Dad has yet to untie the canoe from our roof-rack, and I can make out its distorted shadow on the wall of my tent.

I hear a yawn, and it isn't mine. I remember now. Jack and his sleeping bag had wound up with me somehow last night, and now it is rustling next to me like cellophane. I had overheard Dad telling Mum he thought Jack and me still sharing was a bit off, when Ben's the off one. Jack was a refugee, he claimed, retreating from the toxic fumes being emitted from my brother's bum the night before. The Gas Tank had created a gas chamber.

But I didn't care. Jack and I had thumb wrestled in the dark, and made shadows on the roof with his Dr Who torch. We drank Mellow Yellow from the bottle. He taught me how to burp the alphabet.

'Fantale?' Jack's mouth asks, before his brain is even awake. 'Only half melted.'

He pulls a stash from his windcheater pocket.

'Before breakfast?'

He rolls his eyes.

'Okay,' I reply with a smile. I sit up and pull the blanket up to reach him.

I look down, and see it.

Blood on the sheets.

My heart is in my throat.

I quickly pull the covers back, yank them up to my chest as if I am trapping the horror like an insect caught in a web.

'What's wrong?' Jack asks, staring at me.

'Nothing,' I say, a quiver in my voice. 'Can you go? I just wanna get dressed.'

'What are you hiding?' he asks, with a smile. 'Did you steal my Donkey Kong? You do need the practice, but –' He yanks the blanket down.

He sees the stain before I can hide it and looks as mortified as I feel – a hybrid, half shocked, half curious.

I want the earth to swallow me whole. 'Just go!' I shriek, before the look on Jack's face makes me cry. That's the last thing I need.

He gives me an affronted look as he trails out like a dog kicked out for farting.

With him gone, I look again. I feel the thick wetness between my legs. I sense a dragging pull inside. My clothes are still in the car. How am I going to fix this?

A voice startles me. 'Are you okay?' he asks from outside the tent.

Why is he still here? 'I just need you to go!' I plead, my arms springing the sheets back.

I hear him scurry away like a possum. I find some tissues in my day pack. I pull up the sheets, but my efforts to erase the stain only smudge it. I turn the mattress over. Of all the times I'd worried when this would happen, it has to happen here, with him. My head pounds, so I lie back, take it all in. It has finally happened.

I hear a thump outside the tent.

A delivery.

I poke my neck out like a bashful turtle. A pair of shorts. A shirt. And a pad. 'Mum?' I call. But no one is there. I stretch my arm out of the tent and grab it all. My eye catches something on the grass – and I notice Jack's half-empty pack of Fantales tucked in with my supplies. It is excruciating, not only having him know, but needing his help. I sort myself out and leave the tent.

I approach the circle of ownerless camp chairs with dread. I keep adjusting things, the surfboard, all foreign and fat between my thighs. What has he said? Where did he get the thingy from?

Who knows?

I fear facing a scrum of sniggering boys, pointing fingers at the girl on her rags. But nothing is amiss. I find a chair. Mum is nowhere to be seen, nor is Jennifer, my aloof older cousin – either of whom

I could have used right about now. The girls have gone up to the main house for ice, someone informs me. Jack walks over, and I cringe at the thought he will say something. Without a word, he places a hot milo in my hand, in my favourite chipped Alf mug.

'Thanks,' I squeak.

I need a distraction – to make breakfast. When it comes to toast, Jack always picks Penis Butter, I have Vaginamite. Three pieces each, cooked slow and with care on the mesh toasting rack over the coals. It is our turn for the dishes on the Shaw–Hudson families' roster. Jack rattles the billy. It echoes with emptiness. He fills it and sets it to boil for the wash-up.

Everything is long-winded when you are camping, except Jack.

'We're taking the canoe down the lake, if you wanna come?' Jack asks, shattering the awkwardness.

'Nah,' I say. 'Think I might just listen to my Walkman. Taped the Top 40 before we left.' Jack nods as he wipes the dishes dry.

'Why not, you big nerd?' Ben pipes up from the foreground, appearing out of nowhere.

'She doesn't have to if she doesn't want,' Jack growls, which sends my brother packing. You wouldn't guess Ben is nearly two years older than us, hovering like a bad smell, desperate to be included.

We wash up in silence. No towel flicking, no Chinese burns.

It feels strangely adult.

'So, who'd ya tell?' I ask when I can't stand it any more.

He looks disgusted with me. 'No one.'

'But you got . . . where'd you get the . . .?'

'Stole it. Mum always has 'em in the band-aid box. Always freaks me out. Ever since I figured out what they're for.'

'How'd you find out? The talk last term?'

'Nah, Mum. When I was little. Caught me using them as knee patches when I fell off my bike. I even used one to patch my tyre once, when I ran out of puncture squares. But Mum said they were not for boys.'

I could see Jack standing tall next to his BMX, sanitary pads stuck on his grazed knees, on his bike tyre. 'Did it work? Stop the leak?'

'Nah,' Jack says with a smile. 'They sucked.'

I spend the day enveloped in a dusty hammock, re-reading the same words of my book, while Mum has the Women's Weekly cryptic crossword open, and pesters herself with the solution to eight across – five letters, starting with 'm', final stage of metamorphosis prior to mating.

'Morph?' I suggest to Mum.

'Nah, doesn't fit.'

I peel spuds, strip carrots as I listen to the ladies reminisce about glory days. Last trip I was scaling trees, grazing knees, bruising shins like the rest. What was next – crochet? It is like someone has stolen my life.

I miss Jack. I wait for the boys to return from the lake. When I finally stop waiting, they all appear in a row – like pall-bearers, except with a canoe on their naked shoulders, all elbows, drips and grins.

That night, Jack sleeps in Ben's tent. I wait for him to visit, escape the gas chamber, but he never arrives. As I invent mythical creatures out of shadows on my canvas ceiling, eight across finally hits me: Moult.

It is as if I am looking at a spot-the-difference. The game with two sides, where everything seems the same at first, but when you squint, nothing really is. That night, I realise things with Jack and I will never be the same on either side again.

CHAPTER 24
House of Cards

I feel restless for hours, wondering what Sara's cop-booty-call next door means for me. For Jack. For Oli. I finally doze off in the dead of night, when I hear the distinct pipping of my smoke alarm. Have I left the dryer going without the window open again? I stagger bleary-eyed to the sleepout/laundry/study, then realise it's coming from outside. Meg is known to burn bacon early, but it's the dead of night. Nuts, even for her.

I hear Bear yapping. Barking at Jack's house.

Sara.

The cop. I check the street. His car has gone. Their shag-fest must have ended.

I race to the back.

A cloud of smoke engulfs the fence. As it clears, I look in horror at Jack's house on fire. The windows fill with the flickering flames. I fling open the back door and race through the grey cloud, my arms flapping. A small stream of smoke billows from the cracks in the casement windows. I think through the layout – the bedrooms – the main, ensuite, and study on the right. Had she left a candle burning?

The cigarettes.

I try all the doors – locked. Windows – locked. I need a weapon. My eyes stall on the sander lying idle on my back table. I use it to smash Jack's new French doors. The fire erupts, accelerated by the rush of air filling the room. I grab a shirt from the line and twist it around my hand, forcing it through the shards of splintered glass. I fumble to turn the key, release the door. I'm through.

As I enter the room, thick with smoke, I feel the heat brush the back of my legs. I hear a whooshing sound. Wood splinters and the air pressure changes. A roar of heat erupts, feeding off the oxygen from the open door. A curl of smoke dances away from me. In its wake, I see a lump. Sara is right there, lying on the couch. She's motionless – unconscious? The curtains above the couch are ablaze – the roof, I can't see for the smoke.

I drag her by the arms to the yard, place her under the light. I try for a pulse, but my hand is trembling. Nothing. I can't focus to keep my hands still. I put my mouth on hers, breathe, pump her breastbone. I pull her head to my ear, but all I can hear is the howl of the fire. I shut my eyes, trying to feel it. It's there, the faint rush of air. Thank God! Thank God!

I breathe for myself and the trembling abates.

I run inside, snatch the phone, calling 000 – fire. I give the address, tell them 'the back one' and leave the operator hanging. No time! I grab my own extinguisher from under the sink.

I skim the cautions on the label – fat fire only – fucking what? What does that matter? Fragments of fire training at work merge in my scattered head.

The hose. I grab it and race back in; the amber trim licks the exposed rafters. It seems to have tripled in seconds. I start douching the flames in water. It sizzles. I'm like a sprinkler, flicking it anywhere I see orange licks of light. This cheap kinked hose won't cut it. *Stop buying cheap shit!* I hear Jack say in my head. I need a bucket. I can't stop the coughing now. My eyes burn. I squat low to try to find air. I try to stay orientated in the smoke – I don't want to lose track of where I am in relation to the door, my only exit.

My foot kicks something hard – a hollow chink. A bottle. A Polar Bear on the label, on the familiar orange background.

I see a ribbon of light race across the floor towards me – a river of rum darting in the darkness.

I need to get out. The cop isn't here. Everyone is out.

I race to the door with my eyes closed to stop the burn, coughing all the way. I hear a crack behind me, feel something hit my shoulder, and I am reminded of those adventure scenes where the hero jumps on the train to escape danger without a second to spare.

Except the only music in my adventure is the crackle of wood, and the hero is just me.

I return to Sara, just as a roar comes from inside and a wall of invisible heat hits us, ten metres out. I drag her further away, over to Meg's fence.

'Meg!' I scream, my voice stripped. But I know she mustn't be home, couldn't be sleeping through all this. I wonder if they've stayed over at her sister's as they sometimes do.

I hear the sirens.

Bear is lying next to Sara now, licking her ears. *Surely his halitosis will wake the dead.* But she is still unconscious. I make sure she's on her side.

The ambulance. A medic examines her. She is placed on the stretcher, and slides inside the ambulance.

'Where are you taking her?' I ask.

'Hop in,' they say. 'We need to check you too.'

Me?

'The fire?' I ask the fireman. My house! It's too close. I can't leave it.

'Isolated to one room, under control, ma'am,' he tells me in a deep voice, directing me to the ambulance. 'You go.'

I feel like I am abandoning a child as I step into the ambulance. I realise how much that stupid dump means to me. It's all I've got.

'Are you sure? Can't fires jump roads? I haven't cleared the gutters, there's flammable stuff, paint in the shed, and my dog –'

'Like I said, all under control, ma'am.' He tips his yellow hat.

From the ambulance door, I notice a large branch of my mango tree has been ripped off. Long yellow leaves litter the easement, broken and trampled from when the fire engine had squeezed down the drive. *Sara always did want that tree gone.*

The stench of vomit fills the small back cabin. Chunks of it cling to Sara's honey-blonde hair, her face pale and drawn.

'We induced her,' the paramedic says. 'Got rid of some of it out of her system.'

How did this happen? I'm in an ambulance. With the woman who abhors me.

'We need to know what she took – if gastro-irrigation is needed.'

'I wasn't with her,' I explain. 'Just heard the alarm. She'd had wine before. There was a Bundy bottle on the ground . . .'

I can smell the alcohol, even over the stench of bile. But she is moving. Alive. Okay.

There's no siren. I'm guessing that's a good sign. No panic.

We arrive at emergency. The brightness of neon signs stabs at my eyes, gritty and irritated. A gust of wind feels like knives stabbing my eyeballs.

They whisk her away. A kind man ushers me in, sits me down. He speaks to another, who carefully holds up my hand. Dried blood. Black soot.

Pain in my shoulder.

I am wearing my Elmo nightie. Again. The one that could cameo as a shirt. I stretch it over my knees, and Elmo's grin sags. They give me a blanket for the shock, but I really wish I'd committed to my idea of wearing real clothes to bed. I notice the sleeve is ripped. Scalded. They take me through to a different room, smelling of clean.

They run tests to ensure I have not injured my lungs, breathing in the heat.

My eyes are irrigated with saline.

'Ouch!' I yell, as they carefully try to remove my nightie without taking off more skin.

'How did I get that?' I ask.

'One of the beams came down,' they said. 'Must have hit you.'

'Beams?'

I don't remember that.

They care for me selflessly, but it feels like a blur. A procession of health professionals. A series of needles – antibiotics? A lot of careful cleaning of my shoulder, my hand.

Glass, in my hand.

The sander! I remember now. Can smoke cause amnesia?

I have a dressing on my hand. A patch on my shoulder. Stitches. I remember the sting of local anaesthetic as the needle pierced my hand.

I am a little proud; I've never had stitches. 'How many?' I ask.

'Well, we just do one big continuous stitch now,' they say. It disappoints me. That won't sound good in my story. I need a number.

'You were lucky. No damage in your fingers,' the nurse says. 'We get that a lot. Often it's toddlers – tendons in their fingers being sliced off from soft-drink cans.'

I am asked to tell the police what went down, I am not sure why. I relay how I heard the alarm, smashed a window, got her out, tried the hose, felt the bottle then got out. That's the gist of it. They tell me I can go, that they can show me to my friend.

'She's not my friend,' I clarify.

'You're her friend for life now.'

Super.

The nurse takes me over to a ward. It smells like work; ammonia and sorrow.

'Here is Ms Mcleod's room,' they say to me, directing me to her. 'She's asleep – probably best. She'll be fine to go in the morning. No major burns, thanks to you. We have given her a banana bag – an IV, some liquid charcoal to soak up the rest. Get a few of these types.'

Dread fills my stomach as I think about having to tell Jack of the night's events. I hope someone has already informed him. It hits me that I should have known things were out of hand with her. I had been so stunned by her insults it never crossed my mind to call him, let him know she was livid, drinking heavily. What if my efforts to 'check on her', as he termed it, actually fuelled this? Boiled her blood. Or maybe the cop brought more than his libido with him tonight. A little stash of something he picked up from a raid? Who knows?

I close my eyes, and find myself nodding off. I'm exhausted. I want to shower the soot from my skin, slip back into bed and pretend all this never happened.

I think of Jack. Do I tell him what I saw before the fire? Sara's bit-on-the-side? What if he does go home – finds the damage, us all missing? He'll think the worst.

I call Meg. She is panic-stricken because I wasn't answering my phone but I explain I'm fine. They just returned from her sister's. My house, my dog, are fine, she tells me. She's on her way.

She arrives in a frazzled state, and I realise her usual frazzled state is nothing on this. I feel her chest heave, choked up, as she hugs me, then passes me some jeans and a t-shirt.

As she takes me home, I call Jack. I figure his dad's party will be over so I won't be ruining anything.

'What's up? You okay? Is it Sara?'

My body seems to unravel, hearing his voice, in realisation of everything. I suck it up and try to sound normal.

'We're fine, Jack.'

'Shit. Had me worried, ringing this early. Thought she'd got at you with an axe. Boiled your bunny,' he jokes, oblivious. He starts rattling off details of his dad's party, says it all went well, except for the egg salad (that made some great-aunt puke). No one called him. Great.

'Jack, I have to tell you something that's happened.'

'What?' he asks. 'She *did* boil your bunny?' I am almost reluctant to spoil his mood. I hear Oli's high-pitched laugh in the background.

'Just a sec, Ol, no more space rides. I have to talk to Aunty Frankie.'

I summarise everything, leaving out the late-night booty call.

His silence tells me he's in shock. 'But you're both fine?' he keeps asking over and over in a frayed voice.

'Drugs?' His whisper-soft voice is muffled in the earpiece.

'Not sure, Jack.'

'I thought she was over that shit. I told her, once Oli was in the picture I won't have that near –'

It is as if I can hear Jack's blood boil, all the way from Townsville. He seems to distance himself, his tone formalises. He sticks to the facts – he will try to catch an earlier flight. He doesn't care about the house, he's just glad we both got out, grateful Oli went with him, and hangs up.

His voice is suddenly gone. I stare at my phone. I feel hollow as the screen fades to grey.

When Meg and I arrive home, I realise my stomach muscles are tightly clenched. I don't want to see their house – all Jack's hard work – gutted and black. I am relieved to see my cottage untouched, as Meg assured me it was.

I brush off Meg's offer to sit with me. I just want a second to catch up, and wave her off.

I soon find that trying to dress with a taped-up shoulder

is tricky. One hand in a plastic bag makes turning taps interesting too. The bruising seems to be getting blacker, sorer. But I have privacy to get my head straight.

I dare not look out the back. It smells like a campfire after you've thrown the dirty dishwater over it. Sloshy and sad.

Despite the early hour of the day, I have to sleep. I sink into my flannelette PJs and slip into bed. Bear has balled himself up next to my bed on the worn patch on the rug, still clingy after the strange smoky loudness of the night just gone. I know how he feels.

实

I wake to find I have lost a day. I'm surprised to hear the cicadas hum and the birds bicker in the palm tree outside my window. It is dusk again. I don't remember falling asleep, yet I am woken by a commotion outside. Oli's distant voice, sweet and familiar in my eardrums, tells me Jack is back.

I am alert with need. I want to know how he is, how the house fared. She'd be discharged by now, surely? And I can't intrude if she's there. I know my place, and it is here. The thought of facing Sara again makes me sick. Is she even home yet? I can't see signs of her. Will she ever be again?

My skin is healing – the stitches pull as I start the kettle. My mouth feels like an ashtray, my eyes extra-sensitive to light and breeze. Clanking echoes from Jack's garage. Oli has found his sandpit and starts to create a concoction of sand and grass in his bucket, but I see it is covered with soot.

In the twilight I notice the lower level of Jack's house has been taped off. The front ground level looks like a greyscale print – void of all colour and life, laced with dark etchings of black and grey.

Jack comes out of his garage – the only room not taped off. He has a tent bag, an Esky and a folding chair in the shape of a frog. I watch him anxiously as I think of the male visitor I witnessed the night before. I had almost forgotten, with the fire upstaging the cheating-with-the-cop drama.

Jack threads sectioned poles through blue canvas, pushes silver pegs into the clay soil with bare feet. I watch his biceps flex as he rolls out the tent, and feel my face flush. Oli throws his twiggy arms in the air with excitement when the tent's finally erect. He rustles inside with his pillow underarm.

I eat my toast, sip my tea in a twilight breakfast for one, listening to Jack sing 'Twinkle Twinkle Little Star' completely out of tune. I feel my lips turn up at the thought of him lying under canvas, metres from me.

Sara is conspicuously absent.

A while later I hear the gate, and Jack is on my back porch. Up close he looks as if he's aged five years – unshaven, puffy-eyed, a startled expression. His shirt is actually inside out, and he has his painting shorts on, the old elastic peeping through the waistband. I can see 'Ecru' splashed on the rim.

'Hey. You okay?' he asks, his eyes livid. He sees my bandage, takes my hand, strokes my fingers with his thumb. I feel a shiver. I want to crawl into his arms and never leave. 'Is this all?'

'Yep,' I lie. 'How are *you*? Better than you look, I hope?'

He just nods, his eyes lower. He bites down on a yawn. It has been a big day for all of us. I see a glimpse of the blackened shell that was once the base of his house.

'So where's my biggest fan? She's been discharged, I assume?'

He swallows hard, and his cheeks seem to quiver. 'She was gone when I got there.' He bites the curve of his lip. 'Some guy . . .'

He can't finish the words. His eyes are vacant and dark. He knows, without me telling him what I saw.

'She's left me,' he mutters.

My heart melts. I assumed I would feel elated if this day came. The liberation of the man I wanted all for myself, but his gutted face rips me up.

'I thought we could get through this, give Oli a shot. But it's fucked. It's over. She's done.'

I raise my good arm around him and he seems to collapse into me. I feel his short sharp breaths rise in his chest. I well up. I know this is about him, but I struggle to keep strong. I feel like a kid who's had a bad day but managed to keep it together till Mum arrives.

His nose nuzzles into my damp hair as he hugs me. I am at once distracted from the pain. It's replaced with a smoky haze of warmth, the smell of him invading my head as his rough cheek scrapes my face. His coarse fingers find mine. He brings my hand up to his face and I cup his cheek in my palm.

Just as I start to sink into this, Jack's hands move over to my shoulder, and meet bandage tape. I wince, and he pulls away.

'What the?' he whispers, gently brushing my shirt off my shoulder to reveal the bandage, the bruised edges. 'You're hurt? You said it was just your hand!'

'It's fine. They said the beam must have fallen –'

'A *beam*?' His voice is threaded with anger.

'I don't remember everything . . .'

'Is it burnt too? Did they check you for smoke inhalation, all that?' The dressing has soaked through in dappled red. 'You need to change that. I can help.'

'It's fine,' I say. Plus, it hurts too much to have his clumsy big man-hands all over it.

'Big fucking hero saves dying woman in fire, but can't bear thought of bandage removal?'

He takes me inside under duress, and places me on the side of the bath. He gets the lamp, plugs it in as if he's about to commence surgery. I turn away, remove my shirt with a wince, feeling his eyes burn holes in my back as I place a towel over my bare chest.

'Ouch!' He starts to rip the plaster. 'Why must they tape stuff down on sore stuff?'

'Shut it.'

Carefully, he peels the dressing back and replaces the pad with a fresh one from the stash the short smiley nurse gave me on the way out. His fingers gently smooth over the sticky edges on my shoulder.

'Thank you, Dr Shaw.'

I expect him to get up, to leave so I can dress, but he doesn't. I wait. His fingers roll down my backbone like a painter at work and I forget everything. I suddenly wish he would throw me against the wall, shoulder and all.

We're at a crossroad. Thirteen years after we got to it the first time.

He leans in and kisses me on the cheek. He starts to linger, his nose tracing my ear, smelling my hair.

'You better check on Oli,' I breathe, hoping he'll say Oli's fine.

Instead he steps back and says, 'Thank you.' He swallows

hard as he looks over his tent in my yard. 'For Sara.' The canvas walls start to wobble, and I hear a high-pitched cry. 'For Oli's mum.'

I breathe out, clumsily feed my arm into my shirt, take his hand and lead him to the back steps. Somehow I can't look at him, with the mention of her name.

'Daddy!' Oli calls in a sleepy growl.

Jack stands a breath away from me, so close I can feel the heat of his skin radiate. His fingers fall away as he takes a step back to safety, and slowly makes his way through the gate. To his man-cave.

He calls to his son, 'I'm here, mate, I'm right here.'

And I'm over here, alone.

CHAPTER 25
Kitchens R Us

Sleep does not come easy. As exhausted as my body feels, my state of mind stops me from deep slumber. This only irks me more, grinds at me, breeding the anxiousness that prevents me drifting into sleep. I relive the sensation of Jack's touch. His hands feathering my back. The unspoken words in the look that passed between us.

When I wake, my shoulder is less painful; the black bruises have started to turn a mottled yellow and purple around the edge. I shower and eat, and feel almost normal again. I notice the calendar behind the toilet door, and realise I've got a conference in Melbourne the next day for work. It will focus on the rehabilitation of young sexual offenders – an element of my job that makes my skin crawl, but mandatory in my role at the hospital. If I don't go, next year's budget will be redistributed. Physically I'm fine. I just feel mentally stripped. The thought of airports and hotels fills me with dread.

So does leaving him, the way things are.

Jack's mug appears around the front door. His four-hourly checks have started today (making sure I didn't suddenly cough up a lung).

'Marco?' he calls, like we're eight in his pool.

'Polo,' I stammer. 'Yes, I am still breathing.'

'Good. Can I stuff some beers in your fridge?' Jack says, walking through with a carton. It's like what nearly happened last night never happened, which is both bad and good.

'Still no word on the power?' I ask.

'Nuh,' he calls from my kitchen. 'And the ice in our Esky looks like warm piss, but with floaty bits.'

'Doesn't insurance cover emergency accommodation?' It seems unfair, him living like this.

'All in her name,' he says, joining me in the lounge. 'And I am not asking her for squat.' My stomach lurches at the thought of her. I know that ambiguous stage of a relationship can last for months. Years even, when there's kids involved.

'Have you heard from . . . her?' Surely she would miss Oli by now.

'She's staying with him. Some cop who booked her for speeding or some shit. Been going on for months, apparently. Probably move in. That's what she does. Won't move on till she has the next shag in the bag.' He sounds detached but I hear the dark and twisted edge in his voice.

'Seriously?' I ask. Although I was an eyewitness to the makings of it.

'Well, the last thing she screamed at me on the phone was *he tastes like you, only sweeter.*' He seems composed, yet sends the empty beer carton skidding across the wooden floor with one swift kick.

'It might just be the hurt talking,' I say. 'Trying to hurt you back, for . . . what she thinks you have going with me.'

'And what is that exactly?' he says so matter-of-fact.

My jaw drops. All I can do is stare, wait for the words to come out. He looks over at me, this side, then that. 'Still nothing?' he asks. 'Don't you, like, talk for a living? Deal with people's emotions all the time?'

'That's easy,' I mumble. 'It's not about me.' I lean on the bench behind me.

'Tell me I'm wrong.' His eyes look directly at me. 'The way I feel with you, can you tell me I'm wrong?' His words are laced with anger. At me? At her?

He opens my fridge and cracks a beer. He skols half of it in one quick movement. He takes the rest out back, pulls up a chair.

I walk out, throw him a key. He looks at me with one brow cocked.

'You want me to move *in*?' he asks, holding up the key.

'I've got a work thing in Melbourne tomorrow. For three days. You and Oliver may as well sleep here instead of in that alfresco oven you call a tent.'

He looks at me, grateful but somehow unsatisfied. 'So you're asking me to sleep in your bed, but you won't be in it?' *What's he saying here?*

I suppress the smile that sits just below the surface.

'Oh, and don't forget to feed the Bear,' I say, kissing him on the hair as I walk back inside to pack.

实

Three days later, the taxi pulls up outside my shabby shack. I have butterflies. I had received a text from Jack earlier, asking me what time I'd be home. Now, as I roll my suitcase across the bumpy pavers, a waft of something delicious pours over me. For the first time, I feel like someone is welcoming me home. Independence is nice, but this is addictive.

As I approach the porch, Oliver's little feet stomp along the floorboards to the front door. It seems a bit late for a two-year-old. Before the trip, Jack seemed to have abandoned all traces of rules since Sara left. Oli's bath was optional, or a spray under the hose. Food was out of a can or a Happy Meal box. And the kid had never been happier.

'Fwankie!' Oli shouts at me, his eyes lighting up. My heart melts.

I hardly recognise my house, speckled with toys. There's a tent assembled indoors, with some sort of flying fox strung along it. It's a mess, but it paints my little cottage as a picture of happiness, rich with life.

I leave my case in the lounge, and walk the short hall to the kitchen.

The back door is open, and I see straight through to Jack's ute. The tray is full of crap, old cupboards and broken doors. He must have been busy demolishing already.

Then I recognise it. That crap pile used to be my kitchen.

I am in disbelief. What is going on?

I turn.

Jack is stirring something, wearing my apron over his cargoes and bare chest.

Yet that is not what startles me.

My kitchen is transformed. A shiny, stainless steel Smeg oven has been expertly countersunk in a new crisp white laminate cabinet. A Caesar-stone bench-top has been cut to size, moulding round a new double sink, with a flick-mix tap like the brochure I had cut out and stuck on my wish list. The boxes I was using to store my food have been replaced by a corner pantry. I am not only amazed that he has created my dream kitchen, but he did it in three days – with a two-year-old in tow.

I am overwhelmed. I can feel my toes curl with warmth.

'You *like*?' Jack says, a smile beaming from ear to ear. 'I still have to get the splashback glass fitted. Got it custom.'

'Jack! I can't believe it!' My hands cover my cheeks in shock. 'How did you do . . .? Where did you get all this?'

'It was all on order for my downstairs kitchenette. It turned up the day you left. Figured the insurance should rebuild my joint for free, so I didn't need it,' he says, like it was an extra bag of oranges that he thought I could use. 'I did have to get the corner unit changed around, but that was okay. Most of it worked like a charm. Even the plumbing was pretty much where I wanted it.'

I am flabbergasted at his generosity, his skill. He is beaming, so proud, so happy to have helped. 'Plus, I needed a distraction,' he says. I notice bags under his eyes, and my heart sinks.

I am astounded, yet part of me is annoyed. What if I wanted something different? This is my thing. Project Independence. I'm not sure I want a guy taking over.

'What is it?' he says. I realise I am yet to thank him, or say anything in response to his monster gesture. 'You don't like Caesar stone? I would have picked you as a hardwood person, fitting with the house, but I had this ordered, so . . .'

Oli is standing next to him, bouncing up and down like a jumping jack. 'We bashded it, bang, bang!' Oli says. I ruffle his hair in thanks.

'It's not that, Jack. It's . . . perfect. I love it. I can't believe you did this for me. And in a few days, it's amazing.'

He walks over to me and puts his arms around my waist. I tense up. Oli joins in, grabbing Jack's legs like a tree trunk. Jack touches my chin with his fingers, lifting my gaze to his. 'But . . . what?'

I consider my words, but then they just start gushing out. 'It's just too much. Too soon. This house. It was *my* thing. My distraction, after –'

'Too much? Too soon?' he says, dropping his hands away, his eyes turning dark. 'I have known you my whole life, Fray! I spent twenty-hour days busting a gut for you this week – to surprise you. And you wish, what, I let you prove you could do it yourself?' He sits Oli outside with a piece of garlic bread to entertain him, but comes straight back. 'You were living in a shithole! The rats had eaten through the wall, Fray!' he yells. 'Weren't you getting quotes for people to fit it, anyway?' he says, glaring at me. 'What's the difference?'

'I don't know. They would be working for me. Doing it my way,' I say, but I am not sure that is what I mean.

'Is it the bench-tops you don't want to be stuck with, or is it me?'

I feel my chin quiver. 'Jack –'

He chucks a ladle in the sink and water splashes. 'Tell you what, I'll send you a bill if it'll make you feel better. Man, I can't win with you chicks, I tell ya.' He walks over to the new stovetop, stirs something vigorously. It smells divine. I take a look around at all his work, the soft-close drawers, the modern fixtures. It is truly beautiful.

He keeps his back to me as he checks pots, stirs a sauce.

His shoulders seem even broader, with nothing but my apron over his neck. It has been years since I've seen all of him up close. The small of his back, the bulk of his biceps, his shoulder blade flexing as he stirs. That neck. Why am I such a cow? This is a good thing! Over-analysing what I should feel, how things should be. Why don't I just do what I feel for once? Just *be*?

Who am I kidding? I have a dozen reasons not to. I am tired. His availability is questionable. Oli is just outside. And I can't get his dead ex-girlfriend out of my head, not to mention the survived-by-the-skin-of-her-teeth current girlfriend. He is still standing at the stove, oblivious to my thoughts.

Jack turns to face me, his eyes zealous. All I can hear is my pulse. Before I left, hadn't he asked for honesty? Why can't I tell him I want him? What's stopping me?

I can barely breathe. I trace my finger along his arm, up to his shoulder. I find the guts to look to his eyes, and find his waiting. I can't speak, but somehow it doesn't matter. He threads his fingers through mine, pulls my hips onto his.

I hear a sound but ignore it. I've thought of nothing else for days but this. Starting this. 'Daddy! More bread, Daddy!' a little voice demands.

Oli is at our feet. He has one hand yanking on Jack's cargo pants, the other holds his empty bowl. His big brown eyes are oblivious to what he has interrupted – that look between us, that line we crossed.

The trance is lifted and Jack springs into action. 'Buddy, you scared me!' he says. 'More garlic bread?' he asks his son. 'With magic sprinkles?'

He taps Parmesan cheese on top.

Although my body wishes the kid would get lost, my nerve has dried and shrivelled up. I can't do this. He has a kid with her – who is five feet away. She left like five minutes ago and could be back in a week. Am I crazy?

'Can I come sit with you, Oli?' I ask, taking him by the hand. 'Tell me how you and Daddy made the kitchen so nice!' I walk us both safely away from the heat of the stove.

Oliver tells me how he used the big hammer to bash the yucky kitchen up, and how they found Mickey Mouse living in the corner, and how he had eaten a hole in the wall, and . . .

Jack arrives with two plates. He hands me one, with a lingering look.

I say thank you, trying to minimise eye contact.

The ravioli looks simplistic but is divine – silky smooth, with a rich tomato ragu that tastes like Italy.

And as I eat, all I can think is Sara is a fool.

Has she really abandoned this cabinet-making, gourmet-cooking Super-Dad?

Or do I just want to believe that she has?

We eat, watch ABC Kids, do dishes with the tension of what we started, lurking. Oli drifts off on the couch, Jack transfers him to the tent erected in my lounge. I feel alive. I feel wanted. I feel like I'm being exactly myself, yet with someone else along for the journey. Is this actually going to happen?

When my eyes return to his, he confidently stares me down. 'I want to kiss you,' he mouths, almost inaudibly, with a pained expression on his face.

I lift my chin and kiss his forehead sweetly. Jack lingers,

and looks at me as if to say *is that it*, and goes to lie with Oli who seems to have stirred since being moved to bed.

'That's not what I had in mind,' Jack whispers, ducking into the tent.

I hear a little chirp – *Goodnight moon. Goodnight stars.*

When he returns I realise this father thing is an aphrodisiac, and I melt again.

'Sure you're off duty now, Mr Dad?'

'You never are, once you're a parent. I'm surprised anyone has siblings, but I hope he does. Well, half-siblings, I guess. One day.'

He scans my face for a response, and I sit blankly.

'You didn't sound so sold on the kid idea, that day in the car.'

I remember. I had jumped down his throat – the images of Seamus, his stoic view on kids wrecking relationships, sapping all personal freedom, had sprung to mind. I had snapped.

'Sore point,' I mutter. He raises his eyebrows and bites his lip.

'Yeah, well, if they have to be called Rachel or Ross, I might have to rethink,' Jack teases, and a smile escapes my lips.

'Ha ha,' I say. His face flattens, as he bites his lip again.

Have I offended him? Is he seriously talking about *us* having kids? He hasn't even kissed me. Or am I imagining all of this? We are talking in riddles.

'So. What's the deal here, Fray?'

I tense again. My mouth freezes. He sits on the office chair next to my desk and wheels it where I sit awkwardly on the edge of the bed.

He takes my hands. His are warm, and I can't think straight.

'Your gut didn't ping when I turned up in your yard, out of nowhere? I knew it the second I saw you again. I had no idea you would be there, but somehow it all made sense when you were. The move back. I thought it was a last-ditch effort to get a fresh start with Sara. Bring Oli up in my old stomping ground. But it was the step back I needed. It was you. Seeing you.'

He touches my cheek with the back of his fingers. The light roughness prickles my skin. I take his hand, and notice it is scarred with white lines. The hands of a chef.

'You were always beautiful, but it was as if,' he strokes my hand, 'you'd grown into yourself, your face.' He traces the lines of my cheekbones. 'Like I'd missed a whole chunk of your life and wanted to get it back. I knew I missed my best friend, all that time, but didn't realise how much.'

I am taken aback – his thoughts on us, even then. I was just freaked.

'I take it, it wasn't like that for you?' he asks, doubt in his eyes.

'I liked seeing you, but it made me think of . . . the beach.'

He turns his body away, scratches his head.

'You see me and you think of Kate? After all this time?'

He stands, his hands bracing his neck from behind. He paces to the window, does a u-turn and faces me again. 'You still have doubts?' he asks. The hurt in his eyes fills me with fear. Have I wrecked this? Again?

'Not about you. I know you, Jack.'

He grabs my hand and stares at me like a hypnotist, psyching his patient into submission, gleaning the truth. He *seems* satisfied with what he sees.

'What would you say to someone like you? Say, one of your patients at the hospital. Someone whose life was set up so well. So planned out to be a hotshot lawyer, marry some successful guy, pop out a coupla cute kids. She's smart, but she can't get over her best friend's death. Her plans change. Her relationships fail. She finds a job that can never really end, fixing a procession of lost causes. She is stuck trying to save someone that was never gonna last.'

I pull my hand from his. 'Yeah, we've done the one about me being a real fuck-up.'

He grabs my wrists. His eyes click with mine. There is no escaping him, his face invading my space. I inhale, confronted by his confidence. 'It's not that at all. Your life is fine. But this responsibility you feel, your loyalty, it's still fucking with you, Fray. Do you not believe me when I say I'm yours?' he pleads to me. He seems choked up and angry all at once. 'I've always been yours.' His fingers grow flaccid on my wrists. His charcoal eyes are looking deep into me. We have circled it for years, and here we are.

'I'm not just after a quick shag here. I'm talking about our lives, Fray. I will pack up her shit. I will write it across the sky if it'd help.' He holds my hand in his. 'I know it's weird, after all these years, but it also seems like it was inevitable. You want it guilt-free. I get it. You're still hung up on the Kate shit. I get it. But you have to get over all that.'

I feel him slipping from me, and want to grab at the thread, but fear it's too fragile, that it could break between my fingers. I try to find the words. 'I do want this, Jack, it's just – it's complicated.'

He looks into me. 'All that really matters is if you love me. The rest is just bullshit detail.'

My lungs freeze. *I want you, I love you. Please stay.*

But my lips stay tightly pressed.

When he gets no response from my cowardly self, he stands, the chair rolling out from under him as he stomps out of my room. I hear him unzip his sleeping bag, throw the cushions off the couch, punch a pillow, and leave me alone, with my regrets, with my dirty thoughts.

CHAPTER 26
Foundations

The sun rakes through my kitchen window the next morning, as Jack cuts Oli's toast into star shapes. Shards of light dance on the bench-top. I feel like I opened a box of cereal and wound up with an instant family. I'm deep in thought as I glance at their stilted giant towering over my humble cottage. I think of their renovations – full of beautiful finishes, shiny appliances, stainless-steel light switches. All the trimmings, but none of the basics. The cracks were plain to see, and already it had started to collapse. Was the fire related to the wiring Sara mentioned she skimped on? I recall the premium fixtures she was going to order, in lieu of making the wiring safe. Maybe I wasn't so crazy – reworking mine from the ground up, prioritising the essentials. Still, it was beautiful while it lasted. The matt-finished VJs, the hardwood floors. Mine still looks like an abandoned storage shack with an out-of-place kitchen.

The sound of urgent thumping over the kettle singing brings me back to the here and now.

'I know you're in there with her, Jack.'

Fuck. She's back. I stand at attention. My stomach churns. I suddenly don't regret where we left things last night. But the guilt still resonates. The intention was loud and clear, despite being physically distant.

Jack and I look at each other, and then at Oli. We know what she has come for.

Jack takes a breath and turns the doorknob. Sara charges in, Louis Vuitton bag in hand. She looks fully recovered. Groomed. Immaculate.

She checks the tent. 'Where is he?' she says erratically.

It's a small house. It won't take her long to find the train set in the sleepout.

'Sara, slow down. We need to talk about all this – the fire. What happens now.'

'No. I need to go. I need Oli!' She shakes her head, her chunky necklace jingling. 'I can't be here with you . . . two.' Clearly she isn't my friend for life, despite the doctor's predictions. I shrink into the corner, but I fear I am not invisible as I hope.

A sliver of sympathy starts, until I remember the cop that night. I have no tolerance for hypocrites.

'Well, leave Oli – until we can discuss all this. He's happy here with me.'

'He's my son, Jack! He's not yours to have!'

'You think you can play the mum card and trump me? What if he'd been home! He's just as much mine as yours, and you need to sort yourself out before I can let you be alone with him.' He walks over to Sara and gently puts a hand on each of her shoulders, trying to reach her. She looks up at him, and for a moment is deathly silent. Has he got to her?

'If only that were true, Jack. If only I knew for sure,' she says in a bleak tone.

His hands drop from her shoulders. 'What the fuck does that mean?' He spits the words at her, his eyes wide with fear.

I go to the sleepout, scoop Oli up and take him outside. This is getting nasty.

'There was someone else, after you left me. I was never completely sure . . .'

My God, is all I can think, as I guide Oli onto my back steps, asking him to come feed Bear with me, but he hears her voice. 'Mummy!'

Parts of me feel a surge of relief. Of hope. This breaks all ties, all obligations to her. No more hesitations about hooking up with a guy on the brink of a complex custody battle. Yet I pull it down, like a sheet on the line, and a pit of guilt starts in my gut for my fleeting pleasure. I hear them hurl abuse at each other. I have never heard Jack so angry. I try to distract Oli from the heated words his parents are using as weapons of torture. I put the headphones from the iPad on his little ears.

'You bitch!' I hear Jack shriek at her. 'You lying fucking *scrag*!'

He is out of control.

'You told me he was mine! I asked you straight – you told me there was no one else!'

I have never heard him so irate. He is like a patient we called security on. Livid.

Poor Jack. My heart aches for him, hearing the rawness in his voice, so distorted with pain it's hardly his any more.

'He probably is! The other guy was just a few times. Besides, you saw me throwing up at work before I was even sure I'd keep it. I wanted it to be yours! I wanted you. You were my way back. And when you took us on, started planning with us, I couldn't take that away from my baby, or from you. I didn't want to find out.'

'He's nearly three! You have made me live a lie!'

They are both shedding exasperated tears now. Sara is hysterically crying – is it the relief? The sorrow? I never knew the ice queen had this depth of feeling.

'You don't know that. I knew you'd save us, Jack. Look after us. And then he looks so much like you, I didn't think it could be Romeo's.'

Jack runs out the back door, shaking his head. Sara follows. Jack swears a few times as he circles the yard like a bull in a fighting ring.

'Romeo? What sort of fucked-up name is that?' He scans around him for little ears. He starts to orient himself back to reality, rolls his fingers over his two-day growth.

Sara just looks at him, shaking her head. Her face is wet with tears and has sunk with shame.

'So that's the name of the prick I've ruined my life for, raising his kid?'

Her face is sullen and forlorn. She has become a hollow sack, blank and pale.

I pity her, the lengths she has gone to, the lies she has told to do what she thought would help her baby.

But hadn't I lied for love once? On a beach, to a cop, about a boy? Or so I thought.

'Get out of my fucking sight!' he yells at her.

Sara runs towards Oli, her hand to her mouth, the tears rolling down her face.

'Oli, we're going on a plane to see Granny!' she says, clearing the panda eyes from her lower lids.

'Plane!' Oli says, taking her hand.

Her eyes evade mine as she guides her son out to her waiting cab. Oli's stumpy sausage fingers squash into a wave as his rain-puddle eyes gaze back at Jack. 'Daddy come?' I hear Oli ask as she pulls him away. Daddy. The only one he knows.

I scan what damage she's done to the one sole survivor of the bomb she detonated.

Jack is leaning on the fence, his eyes turned away from the sight of Oli leaving. I am sure the post is the only thing keeping him from falling to a heap of clothes and bones.

He kicks empty buckets and boxes flying, then calmly walks to his open garage, feels along the rafters. He enters his garage and comes out a minute later with a cigarette in his hand, trying to light it with a butane kitchen torch – like the ones the cooking shows use to demonstrate how to make crème brûlée.

'She can fucking set my house on fire without trying, and I can't manage to light a fag.'

I hold the torch for him, as he positions the cigarette in his mouth and inhales.

I think he deserves one.

'I can't believe it, Jack,' I say. 'I'm so sorry. Is it possible? I mean, you don't think it's just to hurt you? To keep you away?'

'I don't know,' he half-sobs, then regains control. 'Aches like a kick in the guts though,' he says, a full sob escaping.

I fold my arms around him, but he is rigid beneath me, tight with anger. 'Can't they test for that shit?' His voice is raised again. He is a rollercoaster, alternating between anger and despair.

'We will find out, Jack. You need to know for sure. So does Oli.'

'I don't know how she could look at me every day, with Oli, knowing it was based on a lie!' He looks at me, eyes searching mine, like I have all the answers.

'It may not be. She did it to keep you, Jack. I mean, it's unforgivable, but she wanted you for Oli. She knew he would be the better for it. She wanted to have the perfect family with you.'

'Far from perfect.'

'But the love Oli has for you is real. No less real now whatever the truth is.'

He huffs, surveys the yard. 'Except I'll have no legal rights to see him if he isn't mine,' he says. 'I'll be nothing to him. She will shack up with this new prick, and he will replace me – I mean, he's a fucking *baby*!' Any control he had harnessed escapes him once more. 'What would I be to him? The guy he can't remember changing his nappies? Buying his car seat?'

'Teaching him to ride a bike? To pitch a tent? Make damper?' I add. And that is just what I have witnessed in a few months. 'Jack, I am sure you have rights to see him. Despite what she's done, Sara loves him. You told me yourself that she was a good mum. She wouldn't want him to suffer, to miss you, surely?' I shake my head. 'Besides, we don't even know if she's just making it up to keep him. To hurt you. I mean, Sara's not my most favourite person but I find it hard to believe she could be that deceitful, and she'd do anything for that kid.'

He sniffs, shakes his head as if it will rejig his mind. 'So what now? Tests probably take ages.' His thick lips turn down at the sides, his chin crinkles. 'The thought of not seeing the little guy for weeks – it kills me! I didn't even know how much I wanted kids, until him.'

We sit on the edge of the cement in silence, letting it all sink in. My gut is heavy like lead, so I can only imagine how his feels. I am reminded of Seamus, and the exact opposite reaction he had to our nearly baby.

'I know what you mean. I wasn't sure I wanted kids either for a while. So much pressure to bring them up right. And the world being so – well, fucked. But when I thought I was once . . . it changed. The concept is overwhelming, but the thought of your own little person? This little tiny person you made with someone you love? It's intoxicating. The way nature hopes, I guess.'

Jack's eyes soften, like the steam has evaporated. 'With the Merc guy?'

I nod.

'You *lost* one?'

'No, I never had it. It was just a scare. Well, for him it was *quite* a scare. For me, more of an awakening. A sign that we weren't meant to be. That I needed someone who wanted the same things.'

I swallow hard. It seems so simple in hindsight.

'I thought you caught him cheating?'

'Yeah, there was *that*. Another sign. A big blinking neon one.'

He smiles at me, and wipes a tear from the corner of his eye.

He eyes the froggy chair under the tree, the sippy cup strewn on the grass. The remains of the campfire he had made for Oli. 'I can't even imagine being here without him.' He stands and takes my hand as I get up. He raises it to his cheek and kisses my palm, nuzzles his head into the crook of my neck.

I will miss the little guy waking me with his noise each morning. But I hope Jack can do that instead. If only I had the guts to say the words out loud.

实

That night, my heart skips a beat when I hear Jack's car pull up. The headlights arc over my bedroom wall as I lie, half reading, half waiting for him to return from the restaurant. I open the door to his unshaven face. Jack in his black and whites, his eyes swollen with tears, no doubt shed once he hit the privacy of his car on the journey home.

My arms envelop him. 'The tent. It smells of him. Plus, I can't face that fucking air mattress another fucking night.'

'Do you want to crash on the couch?' I say with a smile. I can't use the Oli excuse tonight.

'I wasn't thinking of the couch,' he smirks. 'I was thinking of sleeping with you. Or *not* sleeping with you.'

He casually walks in, de-shoes, checks the back door, fills Bear's water dish. Like he lives here. I suddenly feel protected. Like my father checking the back steps for spiders when I was eight. There's a man in my house, taking care of things. It feels good.

'What's up?' he says, catching me in thought as he enters the lounge.

'You locked up for me.'

'Did *you* want to?'

'I have locked up that door every night for the past year or more.'

'So that's a *no*?' Jack asks. 'What is it with chicks?' he murmurs.

He takes a shower, and we crawl into my sheets. He lies down beside me like a spoon in a drawer, his arm over mine, and grabs my hand. A cloud of warmth engulfs me as he pulls me close. He traces the scar from the glass the night of the fire, now healed into a white line. He brings it to his mouth, kisses it gently. Yet somehow the eagerness of last night has festered – baked in my over-thinking brain overnight. Oli. Sara. Kate.

'It's been a long fucking day,' Jack says. His eyes are bloodshot, bags burden his eyelids.

I wonder about parenting – if the day your kid is born is the best, is the day you lose them the worst?

'I'm not sure I have anything left,' he says. 'I want this to be right, not remember it being today. On the day I found out –'

'No. I know. We've waited this long . . .'

Stalling is good.

I can work through the fact that when I look at his face, I see Kate's.

实

I have been half awake, off and on, for hours. I watch the clock by my bed. I keep it company as it reaches its journey to six. I am too shy to turn to face this man who lies sleeping in my bed, in the harsh reality of the morning light. I relive every moment, the ache returning as if he is touching me still. I savour the memory of my hands, reaching under his shirt, following the ridges and grooves of his abs. How I found the rise of his chest, and travelled along the hardness of his collarbone with my fingertips. I wanted nothing more than to rip his shirt off, feel his skin against mine. Surrender, share this want with him.

Yet I only allowed myself to kiss his neck, his lips, his stubbled chin. I moved to his ear, my tongue teetering on the rim, my teeth gently grating his lobe. The five senses, all in overload, but never out of first gear. But that is where we left it.

I kiss him on the forehead, so tentatively I merely disturb the fine hairs on his soft skin, afraid to wake him.

I need to piece it all together in my head, breathe my own air. Recover.

And so I rouse myself from my surreal memories of the hours before, and dress for the brave new world that waits for me outside my bedroom door. As I get up, and leave our pocket of warmth, I'm weak in the knees. I tiptoe to the bathroom, splash water on my face. I cup fresh water in my hands, and skol it down till my mouth loses that parched feeling. My eyes feel dusty with tiredness.

Would it have been like this if we had been together all those years ago? Or did it take half a lifetime to mature? Is Sara right – the tension is all we were feeling here? Years of pent-up curiosity? Either way, I feel like an addict – as if, after last night, I will yearn for a daily dose of Jackson Nate Shaw.

I grab my shoes for my walk with Meg. It is the last thing I want to do, but if I don't go out, she will come in, bang on my door like an over-zealous personal trainer. She will see him.

I peek out the blind. She is already out front as per our usual schedule, so any thoughts of pulling out are lost. It's cold but I welcome the chill on my skin after a sleepless night.

Meg taps her watch. I am late.

We pound the footpath, as Meg vents her domestic woes. I try to listen to my friend, happy to be doing something normal, but my mind is still in bed with Jack.

I thought the decision had been made about what was not happening in that bed last night. After the day he'd had, the tears shed from the crushing news about Oli, there was nothing left. Yet each time I drifted off, despite feeling the wetness on his cheeks, it would just take a slight change in the position of his arm, holding me, to bring me back to a sudden state of aching, warm arousal. His breath on my neck as I lay in his arms, his fingertips tracing the bow line of my stomach from behind, edging close to the rim of my underwear, feeling the rough lace trim.

I am lost in it, lost in the memory of Jack.

I must have missed a key point, as Meg suddenly stops pacing and stares at me. 'You look different, flushed. You feeling okay?'

I want to blurt out my happiness all at once, but it seems so private, what went down in my bed. Or what didn't, more to the point.

She pushes me further for answers and stumbles on Jack. My attempts to divert her to other matters only drive her conviction that she's on-the-money with her first instinct – something has happened between her two closest neighbours. She teases out from me that Sara is gone for good, that their relationship was built on a lie, that Oli's paternity is in question.

'No way. She made him think he was the father for two years? No. Oh, she's a piece of work, that one. Cruel.' Meg composes herself after hearing the *Days of Our Lives* plot playing out among her neighbours, then stops in her tracks. Her eyes dance, like she is reorganising her thoughts. 'So, he's suddenly single?'

I raise my eyebrows at her, give a little shrug.

'And?' she blurts, her hand on my arm, bracing herself.

'He . . . stayed over.'

'Aaaaah!' she squeals, jumping on the spot like a child on Christmas morning.

'Nothing happened, really.' I didn't mention that I am exhausted from him, infatuated, excited, fearful – all of it. That even now, her even speaking his name, sends a shiver within me, like my heart will break if he doesn't feel the same.

'So what's the problem?' she asks. 'The wench is gone, the father thing might not even be an issue.' My friend is happy for me. So why can't I be happy for myself?

That, perhaps, the last hurdle I have to cross is in my sight.

It hits me – the last thing stopping me.

'I keep thinking of Kate.'

'Oh, no. No. No, you gotta get over that thing. This is your shot. I need some good news stories.'

'I know. Don't worry, I have a plan.'

CHAPTER 27
Closure?

My plan hatched the very same day. I had rung her from an echo-filled corridor at the hospital. The familiar voice on the phone had agreed to meet me after work.

After all these years of wondering what became of her, I found her in the phone book. She had moved from the designer home I had known, but still lived just a few suburbs away.

As I pull up at her house, I see it is a modest little cladded home, with neat old-people plants, and well-tended garden beds. I called her Jess – she never liked the formality of Mrs Shepherd. I fondle the jacket bent over my arm as I knock on her door. She opens almost immediately – the woman I hid from in the store, with the pretty face spoiled by sadness.

Her teeth have lost their Hollywood white, but her smile is still bright and welcoming. I wonder what Kate would look like now, if she would have been more beautiful than her mum. Nerves gather in my throat. She offers tea, her eyes continually flicking back to my face. I haven't frozen in time like her daughter.

'Do I look *that* different? I need to start with those anti-wrinkle creams,' I say, trying to keep it light. I think back to those months before, seeing Jack for the first time on my porch. She must feel the same with me. It unlocks corridors you thought you'd never walk again.

'Oh, no, you're just as lovely, with your long limbs and all that chestnut hair. You don't know how much I have thought of you – what life you made for yourself. You were always such a good friend to Kate.'

I choke back a surge of guilt rising from my chest. I wonder if she knew we were both in love with Jack back then. That it was the catalyst for everything.

We sit in the sunroom, a small dated space with woodgrain-panelled fibro, and framed yellowing pictures of flowers and landscapes. It is pleasant, but void of any personality. There are no photos in sight. No reminders. As an icebreaker I fill her in on my life, which doesn't take long. I don't mention Jack just yet. I sense she is like a little bird – too much movement all at once and she will flee.

She speaks articulately about her grief. 'It's funny, there's no word for losing your child, like there is for losing a spouse,' Jess says, stroking her neck, 'when for many, it is so much worse. It's as if our culture is accepting of the loss of a husband, but not a child.' She is momentarily distracted by a bird's wings fluttering past the window. 'It's just not the natural order of things.' As I see her composure wane as she digs deep into her memories, I feel selfish for bringing it back.

'"Why couldn't it be me?" I would think,' Jess says, as she

describes the journey she had struggled through after Kate was found. 'The grief, it doesn't dwindle off like people say. It just gets diluted – gets mixed in with good memories. I can smile at a sweet memory of her now, but can be cut to the bone with the realisation that it'd be her birthday soon. It's the permanency that bites. People say it gets better, but the facts don't change. She was my world, and she is gone forever. That will never change.'

I feel like I have to evict her words, not let them dwell in my mind, or I will lose it. I have no right to trump her grief. If there's a kind of hierarchy in the 'who's who' of loss, I am far from top dog, and I feel I have to swallow my sorrow in her presence.

We finish our tea, yet the spread of pastries are left, untouched on the delicate rose-embossed plate. 'More tea?' she asks. I nod politely. Jess seems pleased by my acceptance, a request she can easily oblige. After a quick sip of her own, she continues.

'The community support was immense at the start – almost overwhelming. I still have the letters, the condolence cards. They remind me of how people can be so kind. In some ways it was easier that first year. You were expected to fall apart. It can feel even lonelier when the burning pain is still there years on. You imagine people questioning why you were still "not getting on with things", when I *was*. It was just that the new "things" were in a place that would never have her in it again. And I hid from that newness for years – holding on to the past, as at least she was with me then. But, after I stopped work, and my friends were around less and less, I realised that by trying to keep a thread of her with me, I was letting everything else slip away.'

Jess spoke of how she had separated from Mr Shepherd not long after it all. They were initially a comfort to each other, yet as time passed, the pressure of it, the blame game as she called it, was too much. 'It was like looking in a mirror, seeing his sorrow, the sadness grow on his face. The vacant stares – I couldn't bear it.' Jess places her teacup down with an unsteady hand. We sit in silence for a moment, as Jess seems deep in thought. I sense she wants me to stay. That it would be inappropriate to have released this pressure valve, only to escape the outpouring. I feel it is helpful for her to tell her story. As if speaking the words is reorganising all the stray emotions or thoughts from recent years.

I was wrong to think I would disturb this woman's day-to-day life coming here – as I'm sure not a day goes by when this saga isn't far from her mind and heart. It makes me wish, for her sake, that she had been blessed with other children – something to distract her, enrich her life, make it less about loss. Less about losing Kate.

I wasn't sure what I expected, meeting Kate's mum again – how I thought it would help. Did I imagine she would provide some closure? Some information I had not gleaned from the media? Forgiveness?

All I am hearing is that the ocean stole more than one life that night.

Jess leaves the room, and returns with something in her hands. She is seated once more, and places a small hessian pouch in my palm. I pull open the drawstring. My breath catches. Inside is a necklace of shells, Kate's collection, knotted tight on fishing line. The necklace she said she was making me the day she drowned.

'They found it in the pocket of her denim shorts on the

beach. It was so dear to me, the last thing she touched. I couldn't part with it before now, but seeing you today . . . she was forever making you friendship bracelets. I think you should have it,' Jess says.

A lump forms in my throat as my fingers caress the smoothness of each shell. I picture her collecting them, all those years before. I smell sea salt, frangipanis – Kate. 'It's my last memory of her, collecting these.'

I cross my legs under the table, and Kate's jacket falls to the ground. Jess's eyes click to it.

'Is that hers? I noticed it when you walked in.'

'Yes. I brought it for you. If you would like it . . . Kate gave it to me at the end of term, before school ended. I couldn't throw it away in all this time.' Jess touches the coat gently, stroking it, smelling it. I feel guilty having kept it from her. 'I'm not sure why she gave it to me, she loved it . . .'

'I think we both know why, dear.' Her eyes give me a knowing glance. 'She often did it, gave away her prized possessions to those closest to her, just before an attempt.'

'An attempt?' I ask. My thoughts race, my fingers sweat.

'Yes, dear. That was one of the reasons we moved here. A fresh start. In Sydney, we knew we were in trouble when her favourite shoes would disappear.'

I can't believe what I am hearing. Part of me is shocked, yet another is simply angry that this knowledge was out in the world, all the time I was wondering. I explain how I had no idea. That I knew she could be moody, have dark thoughts, but it always seemed like part of her drama-loving nature.

'Yes, well, her meds did curb a lot of it.'

'Meds?' I ask. I had never seen her take a thing – in all those sleepovers, weekends away . . .

'You were kids; we didn't think it was appropriate to inform you of her bipolar history. She was monitored, we had good doctors. The school knew. But we thought it was important for Kate to feel as normal as possible, without a stigma. I mean, we thought we were over the worst. She went through a rebellion where she would refuse her meds after we told her she was adopted.'

'Adopted?' I try to cover the awe in my voice. 'She never told me.'

Her eyes dip, her weak smile falls. A shudder trembles through the folds of her loose skin. 'Well, she didn't know herself until she was thirteen. Took it pretty badly, understandably.' She holds her hand out and rests it on my forearm. 'Before you judge, it was . . . complicated.'

'It's not that. I just . . . I had no idea – you look so alike. You could be sisters.'

'Well, she was *family*. She was Carmen's – my sister's child. She was only nineteen, single, unstable – they diagnosed schizophrenia, among other things – and well, she just couldn't cope. Carmen took her own life when Kate was still a baby, so we adopted Kate.' Jess rubs her finger along the side of the table, deep in thought. 'I loved her like my own though, and we looked so alike so it was easy to pretend. But as Kate got older, her likeness to her real mother worried me. It took its toll on us, and her friendships. Anyway, we all know how that story ended. My worst fear . . .' She stifles a sob. 'The media was actually pretty understanding, preventing it coming out. I think they have some code about suicide – not reporting it.'

I am slowly putting the jigsaw together, after finding the missing corner-piece years after starting the puzzle. Poor Kate, living with all those complexities. 'They did insinuate she was taking drugs at one point, I think.'

'All prescription. Nothing interesting there,' Jess says. 'Except for the pot, of course.' She looks down at her hands, straightening her sleeve. 'I gave up trying to curb that – it only added to my concern, particularly when the doctors told us marijuana can trigger schizoid personality traits for those predisposed to it. It's like she smoked it just to prove me wrong, that she wouldn't take the path her mother did.' Jess's eyes turn glassy as she stares past me. 'Her neck was broken from the jump.'

My eyes slam closed. The point. Jack was right.

'The headlines – they made it sound like she drowned.'

'Well, she may have. She landed in the sea.' A tremor wrinkles across her lips. She presses her mouth to quash it. 'A drowning was far more palatable for their readers, I think. Christmas time 'n' all . . . and they couldn't *not* report her death, after all that build-up. I was always mindful of what message to send to other girls like Kate. I didn't want it glorified. Being under-age, the specifics were left to us to reveal.'

'So all the conjecture about Jack . . .'

She rolls her eyes. 'Oh yes, that was unfair, horrid really. I always knew he was a good kid – not capable of murder. Once I revealed Kate's family history, the police were agreeable to wind things up, so to speak.'

The issue of the pregnancy burns in my throat. I have to get all this out.

'You didn't blame him?'

'For her death? Oh, I blamed everything and everyone for a while. But no, her demons were her own.'

'You didn't think the pregnancy tipped her over?' I blurt.

Jess chokes on her tea. 'Sorry?' Her voice is stripped.

Oh God, what have I done? I always assumed Mum told Jess and the cops like she threatened. It was the reason I moved out when uni started. The reason I had to work two jobs through uni to pay my rent. I still resented her lack of support of me when I needed her.

'I assumed when they found her, the tests would have shown she was . . . you would have known.'

Was Jack right? She made it up?

Her eyes soften and are glazed with tears. 'She told you?' Jess flattens the tablecloth with her slender fingers. 'She knew?' Her hand covers her mouth. 'It was so early, I wasn't sure she . . .'

So that confirms it.

He lied to me. She was pregnant.

She takes my hand, her kind eyes drawing me in. 'All this time, I thought I was sparing you that news. You and Jack. I mean, it took me a while to come to terms with it. That it wasn't just Kate we lost. I wasn't that surprised she was pregnant. She was no shrinking violet – riding in cars with boys down in Sydney. I often didn't see her for days. It was always a worry of mine. I wanted her on the pill, but Brian wouldn't have it. Said it would *condone* it.'

I am astounded. She had this double life. Her condition. The prescriptions. I assumed Jack was her first. Was it all imagined, my closeness with her?

Jess pauses in thought. 'You don't know how long I wondered if she knew, if that was the trigger. I mean, they said it was only two months along. I thought she would have *said* if she did.' Her face is pained.

Now I've offended her. I feel as if I've stolen something from her, a privilege. 'She only just took a test. I'm sure it would have been you she told if she'd been home. But she was glowing with happiness about it.' I tell Jess how luminous she was, excited by the news. 'Jack denies it. Said she made it up.'

'Jack? You still have contact?'

Only every day. 'He's back in Brisbane,' is all I can manage to admit to.

She nods, deep in thought again. Her face hardens. 'Well, I can understand him being dubious. She wasn't well, Frankie. She wasn't herself, towards the end. Her behaviour was very erratic. It was part of her condition. She once told her hockey coach she had three months to live. They started a fundraiser for her.' Her face relaxes at the ridiculousness of it, but a shudder rips through me when I realise she may have been right. 'But I know she loved you. Sure, she loved Jack, but it was you who lit her up inside.' She squeezes my hand and my throat swells. 'Don't be angry with her for what she did. She felt she had no other option.'

I take a moment, walk to the window, my hand to my mouth. I realise I am angry. At her, at him. I lied for him. He swore they never had sex. I started a war with my mother that still sets off tremors between us. I stood by him. Believed him.

'The coroner did say one thing.' She holds her delicate fingers to her lips once more. A hush seems to envelop the room. I can hear the wood floors expand in the heat. 'The reports said that Kate had been *intimate* with someone that night, before she jumped.'

I'm already wounded, but her words hit me like a brick. *Intimate?* As in *screwed?*

Her eyes close, confirming it for me.

So dumping Kate wasn't the only thing Jack did that night.

I feel like I've been stabbed in the heart. My mother was right. I had brushed it off as gossip, propaganda on her part. To think I moved out because of her mistrust. Jack was right. It moulded my life, that night at the beach.

My thoughts race. 'Was it *forced?*' I start to blink fast, as if I am trying to erase the images of all the possibilities flicking through my mind.

She shakes her head, steadies her trembling hand on the table. 'No. But I still struggled with it. I mean, she was no virgin, obviously, could be quite promiscuous. She may well have initiated it – and, well, he was a teenage boy, after all. Even the pregnancy, it was foolish, but these things happen. I've come to terms with that. But I wondered over the years, how it all played out. What state she was in, alone with Jack? If something triggered her actions? Could it have been delayed, prevented even?' Her tears flow once more.

I feel sick. Why did Jack suggest I meet with her? Surely he knew the parents would have been told this sordid detail. The pregnancy. His dirty deed.

She gushes. She is caving in like a sand dune in a king-tide. I had seen it in clients. It's time to leave. Hell, *I* need to leave.

I sit with her a moment till she composes herself.

I help clear the plates, offer my thanks. I reassure her that she should call if she ever needs anything. I say a final goodbye standing on her front porch. My sobs push free and escape as I fold my arms around her frail body.

It's like hugging a skeleton. I'm afraid she'll break if I hold her too long.

实

I wake the next morning aching with loneliness. How fickle am I? I'm fine with the fact that my best friend jumped off a cliff, killing herself and her unborn child, but not that Jack screwed her first? What is wrong with me? I am sick of the pair of them. Angry at Kate for her double life, her lies. Angry at Jack. It's doing my head in. It isn't just that he had sex with her. It's that he lied about it, said he could barely be around her by that time, that they fought, that he told Kate it was over, that was it. No last shag in the dunes.

Was he trying to spare my feelings by keeping this from me? Preserve his reputation? Or is it none of my business? I've had it with trying to understand him. And when he was so adamant I shouldn't have lied for him, he was lying to me.

I never admitted it, but Jack has always been the bar for me. The standard guys need to attain to earn my trust. I rarely hooked up, but I'd witnessed a series of girls fill the crook in his arm. But somehow after what went down at the beach, I was never certain what to think. Suddenly he was no longer the subconscious bar. The image I had of Jack – one of integrity, honesty – it all seemed unobtainable. By anyone.

Maybe that knowledge had scarred me more than Kate leaving me. The idea that even good people have fatal flaws. That men are like fruit and all go bad eventually.

To add to my despair, it is a double late shift tonight; all the crazies come out at night. I think twice about boiling the kettle for tea as it will wake Jack hibernating in the man-cave out back. He must have come home late and retreated to his territory.

Too late. I hear Jack approach the back door. He knocks. I stand totally still, as if he is a T-Rex, and he won't detect me unless I move.

'Francesca. I know you're in there.'

Shit. I can see his shadow through the blinds. Can he see me?

'You okay?'

Silence.

'You avoiding me?'

Yes.

'What have I done now?' I hear him say.

I know who you've done. That's the problem. If I just shut it, he will go away.

As I hear him step away, the guilt surpasses my fear of facing him, and I open the door.

'I'm here,' I say to him.

'You all right?'

'Fine. Just psyching myself up for a double shift.' I stand, half hidden behind the open back door, preventing him from feeling welcome to wander in.

'Didn't you hear me after work last night? I knocked.' All confidence of the other night is gone. He seems as timid as a mouse.

'Must have crashed, sorry.'

Jack bites his lip, his eyes drop low.

'How are you? Have you heard from Oli?' My throat tightens.

He shakes his head and looks away. Still too raw. 'I ordered a test kit though – you can get anything online.'

I twist inside, thinking of my selfishness, ignoring his real dilemma, too caught up in teenage angst, jealousy for a girl who's been dead for years. But it's the lies that keep me distant, keep my eyes from meeting his.

'Okay, so, what, you'll be home at the usual – nine-thirty-ish? I could steal the dregs from the restaurant, bring you something after?' he asks.

'It might be a busy one, so not sure when I'll get home,' I lie.

His eyes sink to the floor again. He fidgets with a loose nail on the door strip with his fingers. The silence is excruciating. I hate being cagey with him, and wish I had gone with plan A – total avoidance.

He finally speaks. 'What is it, Fray? Is it cause of the other night? You know I wanted –'

'No.' God no. I knew nothing could happen then with the day he'd had.

'So, what then?' he asks, a hint of frustration in his deep voice. 'You're having second thoughts. Has it got anything to do with the guy I saw leave the other morning?'

'What guy?' I say. 'Believe me, there is no guy.'

'You didn't have the dude in the Hilux sneak out your back door on Tuesday morning?' he asks. I can tell he is trying to use his nice voice, but it's husky round the edges. Then it hits me. The Bathrooms Plus quote. First thing, before work on Tuesday. He thinks he has some competition.

This makes me happy with myself, but doesn't change my view on him. 'What's it to you, Jack?' I say as I mount my high horse. 'You think cause we had a thing starting here all other males need to sign in with you first?'

His eyes crinkle. *'Had?'*

317

A pit forms in my gut. I feel like a bitch. But who he is, is cloudy now.

He made a dead girl out to be a liar to cover his own dirty deeds.

I can see his nostrils flare. He hesitates, weaves his fingers through his hair then puts his hands on his hips. He stands over me like a fierce protector. 'I just didn't think letting some random stay over was your style.'

'Well, perhaps we don't know each other as well as you think,' I say, staring him down.

He looks at me, puzzled, infuriated.

'And I thought you had some class.'

'I could say the same about you.'

I slam the door, the windows shake and I pace back and forth in my once crooked kitchen that is now perfect. I watch him hop the fence, too lazy to walk to his gate in the rain. Then he is out of sight.

But not out of mind.

实

All day at work, all night, he is all I can think of. His jealousy – over nothing. How close we came, but how far away he feels now. But mostly, my thoughts are of Kate. My plan to exorcise her from my life has backfired. I hypothesise how Kate's fate may have changed if he had kept it in his pants. It made her death clearer – she committed suicide, but the news seems to have muddied Jack's role in it. Again. Surely it had to be his – even if she cheated with someone else two months before, how does that explain that she had sex the night she died?

There is only one explanation. He's played me.

I wonder if his act, his pleas to not lie for him back there, were all part of a master plan to secure his rocky future, avoid an arrest, but somehow my heart doesn't believe it.

I thought it was genuine surprise that rocked his face when I told him I knew about the baby that night. It was all an act. He knew. He must have known. It explains everything – how freaked he was when he returned, how distant. He was in shock.

So why all the lies? Knocking up your teenage girlfriend isn't noble, but it's not a crime. Is he simply ashamed to admit he took advantage of Kate, right before she died? And how the hell has he been able to move on from it? Knowing what he did. Has he no conscience?

And at the heart of it all, I thought he wanted me.

As I put on a smile, speak professionally to my co-workers and trudge through the cases, I realise I have to confront him. I need to cut the passive-aggressive bullshit and simply talk to him.

I fumble my way through the last of my shift, compiling my notes to pass on to the next person to follow up ongoing cases, and head home.

The automatic glass doors open as I approach the pedestrian bridge to the multi-level car park, and I'm hit with an invigorating gush of cold wet breeze. It's still raining, but I embrace the fresh air. As I approach my car, I see the headlights are on, but dim. I have left them on all day from the rainy trip in. The starter motor turns, but the battery isn't coming to the party.

A horrible fucking end to a horrible fucking week.

Waiting for the RACQ will take over an hour on a rainy night. Ben is hours away, Meg can't leave the kids . . . A cab would work, but leave me carless tomorrow, not to mention with a horrendous parking fee.

Jack.

I need to air everything anyway. Perhaps if I call now, I will catch him as he leaves the restaurant for home. It isn't far from his work – he can jump-start me.

If he is talking to me, that is.

To my surprise, he answers his phone. He's just leaving work. He is curt, but shows restraint in making no reference to our earlier fight, and tells me he is only ten minutes away.

'Lock your doors,' he says, before hanging up.

Level 3 of the parking station is almost deserted. Visiting hours are long gone, and most staff have passes to access other floors. I can hear the rain pelt down; the wind blows gusts of it through the open sections, dousing the concrete. I wait in my car, trying to pre-empt the best way to delineate the complex ball of questions rattling around my head. It's like I am about to detonate a bomb.

Jack's orange Subaru pulls up in the empty bay adjacent to my old sedan. Our eyes meet through double rain-chipped glass. His have lost the fire of our earlier encounter, but not the directness.

'Thank you,' I mouth to him, as he sits motionless in his car. He looks different, his hair flat with rain. Work-mode Jack – in black pants and a white shirt. He rolls up his sleeves to reveal his taut arms.

He steps out, pops the boot, and gets the cables connected to his car battery.

'How did you iron that shirt? Isn't the power still off at your house?' I ask.

'Yeah, and my neighbour was being a cow, so there was

no asking her for help.' He sends me a cold stare. 'So I used one of my stash at work.'

He opens my driver's-side door. I smell the rain in his hair. It drips on my leg. He lowers his arm between my knees to the bonnet release.

He looks up at me. I hope my gasp for breath is not audible.

'How can you drive with so many shoes under your feet?' He flicks the rain from his hair in my face. A smile flashes across his lips.

'Gross!' I say, as I wipe the wetness from my cheeks. This is why we had never got it together, Jack and me. He's never serious for more than eight seconds. He finally finds the lever, and gets up.

He leans in the window. 'Don't worry, little lady, Iyll fix yuuur wagon.'

Why could I not stay angry with this man?

'I hope you were actually on your way home,' I say.

'I'm the boss. Good excuse to leave. Left Blair with the lockup. I call it "delegation for development purposes".'

With our batteries connected, he leans in, turns on the ignition and my car purrs.

'Don't stall it, or stop for petrol on the way home; let it run,' he says, dropping his bonnet shut with a clank.

He sits down in my passenger seat while we let the engine charge a little, in case I snuff it before it recharges.

'So was this just a ploy to get me to park with you? You want to thank me personally?' Jack says, and I ignore him.

'I wasn't sure you'd even answer your phone.'

'I was surprised you didn't call your dirty-stop-out man. The ute guy from the other morning. Was it that Merc guy in his second car?'

Seamus in a ute? Never. They don't even have heated seats. I'm unable to contain a snort-laugh. 'It was a contractor from Bathrooms Plus. Don't think they've expanded into roadside assistance yet.'

I see the smirk form on his lips before he covers it with his hand during a discrete nose scratch.

'There's no one but you, Jack.'

His face relaxes. 'So why the cold shoulder? If there's no one else sniffing around.'

I breathe in. Here goes. 'You were right. What you said to me, about getting over things. I went to see Kate's mum . . .'

He sits back in the seat, his eyes narrow. 'Jess?' He looks out to the grey concrete walls, the rain speckling the black sky in the dark squares between each pillar. 'Good.' He taps his knee with his fingers. I want to grab them and hold them on me. 'How did it go? How is she?'

I tell him about the other attempts, the manic depression, that it was largely out of our hands. That it was an obvious suicide – from what she said, a long time coming.

He looks downtrodden, spent. 'I'm not that surprised.' He rakes his fingers through his wet hair. 'But in a way, it's comforting.'

'*Comforting?* What, that our friend was desperately sad half her life?'

'That she had suicidal tendencies before I met her. That I may have been the trigger, but she was . . . predisposed.'

I bite my lip. It sounds cold, but I can allow him that. 'And she *was* pregnant.'

He double-takes. 'Wait, what?'

I realise I've just told him that his unborn child was hurled over a cliff to his/her death, and all I am thinking is *I told you so*. He stares blankly out the windscreen, deep in thought. 'But . . .'

'Cut the shit, Jack. I know you were having sex.'

He thumps the dash. 'Not this bullshit again. We weren't screwing, so I figured she was making it up. Forgive me for wanting to think she hadn't been doing someone else behind my back.'

'Jack, Jess told me what the coroner found. She had sex, right before she died. The report said so.'

His eyes are wide, alert. 'Like, forced? Someone attacked her? But I thought you said it was clearly suicide?'

I try to calm myself, let the truth be told. I soften my voice like I am speaking to a child. 'Jack, it's okay if you did. She was your girlfriend. You didn't owe me anything. If you think it would've hurt my feelings . . .'

'What, you think *I* raped her?' His eyes are dark, piercing.

'No. It wasn't even forced,' I mutter.

His eyes flick back and forth, as he taps the arm rest with frustration.

'Are you fucking serious? You think I banged her *before* I dumped her and sent her off to kill herself? Is this before or after we fought about our unborn child? Or I get it, I hurled them both over the cliff – solve all my problems, right?'

My eyes slam closed. He is right. Did I actually think he could do such a thing? My head is as cloudy as the night sky.

'Seriously? No wonder you've been so pissed – finally contemplating giving me a shot then finding out I am obviously a fucking arsehole who has just been fooling you the past thirty years.' He exhales loudly, puts his hand to his mouth. 'I didn't touch her!' He chops the air with the heel of his hand on each word.

'But you must have!' I can handle that, but not the lies. 'She was your girlfriend. She was beautiful. It is not surprising that you had sex. Just tell me the truth!'

His eyes narrow as they search mine. 'You think this is about that? I'm lying to, what, spare your feelings?'

The lump in my throat swells. 'I thought . . .' I try, but I can't say the words, can't ask him how he felt. Not now, not before.

'I thought it was me you wanted.'

'I did . . . I do! You have no idea what you do to me! But it's not about that, is it, Fray? You know how I feel. But do you really think that because I wanted you that night, I'd be ashamed to say I shagged her? Or is it something else you think I did?'

I feel the tears well, and I am embarrassed by everything, but I can't give up now. I look over to him, his hair damp with rain, his brow tense as he fidgets with the air vents. 'What else have you been checking up on me about, making you doubt me? Did the assault thing get dragged up too? Search your computer system at work or something?' He shoots me a cagey glance. Ever since Sara mentioned it that night it had gnawed at me.

'Assault?' I play dumb. See what he has to say.

His face hardens. 'I hurt a woman.'

Even though I know this, I still baulk at the image. His dad's deep voice bellows in my head – *Never hit a lass, son.* And I thought he never would.

'I was eighteen. It was at work, at a pub. The chick had just glassed someone. Slashed her friend across the face with a broken bottle. She was about to hurt someone else so I grabbed her to contain her. She struggled and she hit her head on the barstool on the way down.' He is unable to hide the emotion in his voice. The shame.

So that explains it.

'I haven't been checking up on you. It's not about me thinking you hurt anyone.'

'Is that why you stayed away from me? A niggling doubt, all this time?'

His eyes well with rage and tears.

'No, Jack, I never thought that. I just thought it was her you wanted. Not me. I just think you're ashamed to admit what you did with Kate before she ran off.'

'You're as bad as Sara! Except from you it's fucking worse!' He yanks the door open, leaps out to the night air, paces across the parking space.

I open my door and follow, feeling cold and lonely. I walk over to him, touch his arm, which he flicks away, kicking the tyre on his car with his shoe.

'I can't explain it,' he shouts. His eyes have lost all warmth. 'I know it makes me look like a fucking liar, like the whole thing was bogus, but it's the truth.' He gets in his car. 'If you don't believe me, then you can just fuck off too!'

And he leaves me, looking through a foggy rain-chipped windscreen, in a cloud of doubt. And I'm seventeen all over again.

CHAPTER 28
Unravelling

I listen to the rain ping on the tin roof of my car, lost. My thoughts hum as my engine charges. I've had this feeling, ever since before Sara left, ever since the night I saved her from her burning house. That the fire has somehow blown away all the hairballs from the dusty corners, whisked them into full view, for all to see. To see, and to clear away. And this is just another dirty hairball to deal with.

I kick a random shoe back under the seat, and notice the hessian bag in the centre console. With the overload of info spinning in my head last night, I'd forgotten about the necklace Kate's mum gave me. I loop my finger under the knotted fishing line spiking out of the pouch. The shells chink as I lift them out.

Fishing line.

I put the gearstick in reverse, exit the deserted car park and start driving towards the Ipswich motorway in the pelting rain. I can't stop or my battery won't start me again and I'll be stranded with no fall-back. I drive for two hours with just one question egging me forward.

When I arrive in Toowoomba, sit through the thousand red lights to my brother's unit, his new roommate Boon answers the door. He glances at my wrinkled work clothes, my mascara-streaked face. I probably look like I've been mugged. The last time I turned up here was over a year ago, after Chapter 1 of *Seamus and the Skank*.

Ben wanders out with his t-shirt inside out, scratching his balls, boxers threadbare at the crotch.

'Ben.' I give him a half-hearted hug, eager to get to the point of my visit.

'What *the*? What's happened?' Ben looks bemused. 'Is it Dad's heart again?'

I shake my head. 'Dad's fine. I need you to help me work something out.'

'You want *me* to help *you*?' He turns his head, strokes his chin and arches one eyebrow.

'I'm serious.'

He plonks on the threadbare lounge and a spring twangs.

I sit beside my brother. 'Tell me what you know about the fisherman.'

'What fisherman?'

'The one at Double Island Point. The one I think murdered Kate.'

He stares at me as if I've finally gone mad. 'You mean Old Nick? The crab-pot Nazi?'

'Wasn't he the same guy you and Dad would see up there when we were kids?'

'So Dad reckoned at the time but, Frank, what are you on about? I mean, murdered? They found Kate. She drowned.

You gotta get over that shit. I knew Jack's reappearing act would bring all this up again.' He slaps his palms on his thighs and stands.

'I saw Kate's mum. She didn't drown. She snapped her neck. She could have been pushed – murdered.'

His face drains of colour. 'But they said she drowned, in the papers.' He starts pacing.

'She gave me this.' I put the necklace on the table and he raises his hands as if it were a rattlesnake.

'What the . . .?'

'They found it with her clothes, and there's only two places she could have got the line for it. You or that fisherman.'

I tell Ben about how Kate fell, her mental history, the other attempts. Each detail seems to chip away at him like an asteroid under fire on Atari. He looks sullen, withdrawn.

'The report said she did it the night she died, but Jack denies it. I accused him of . . .' I suck back a sob.

'Wait – how could they know that shit? Wasn't she, like, in the water for a week?' He shakes his head. When I look at him again, he has grown pale.

'It gets worse, Ben, she –'

'Woah. Wait. You got it wrong, Frank. About Jack.' He bites his lip and looks away. 'It wasn't him.'

'I know. I know *now*. It was the fisherman. It makes perfect sense.' As if a vent has blown the smoke from my mind, everything is crystal clear. 'The necklace – it was just a bundle of shells when she walked off with Jack. I'd forgotten all this but when I saw the necklace I remember her asking if there was any line back at camp. I was joking that the fisherman had a thing for her and she should try him.' A twang of sorrow engulfs me. Was this my fault after all, but for reasons I'd never imagined? 'I think he killed her, Ben. I think she found that dodgy old man, he had his way with her, and threw her off the cliff just to make it look like she drowned. We need to tell them all, Ben. First I need to apologise to Jack and we need to tell the cops and –'

My words are rushed, my thoughts frantic, but I feel an overwhelming sense of calm wash over me. It all makes sense. My best friend didn't kill herself. Jack didn't lie to me.

'Frankie, slow down! That guy, he was old as shit a decade ago. He'll be long gone by now. You gotta calm down! This all should have stayed in the past where it belongs!'

'No.' I shake my head. 'Jess needs to know the truth. She thinks her daughter killed herself. She's had to live with that. You should have heard her – it's like she spent Kate's life almost waiting for it to happen. Makes me wonder what the cops might have found if she hadn't been so convinced.'

'And what, you think dragging this back through the courts will help her?' He cuts the air with the heel of his hand. 'Leave it, Frankie!'

I look at my brother, as if I'm seeing him for the first time.

I stare at the necklace on the table. He turns his head away, puts his hand to his mouth.

I feel my hands cover my mouth. 'It was you.' I step backwards. 'You saw her after she ran from Jack. You had line in your tackle-box. You were the last to see her . . .'

He is still facing the wall. There is no sound, but I see his shoulders shake.

'I did everything to save her.' He turns to me; his eyes are livid. 'I tried everything – but she was lost to me.' He steps towards me, and I back away. His voice is pleading as he grabs my hands, as if that will make me understand.

He turns, crouches, head in hands, sobbing wildly. 'You don't know how many times I have tried to tell you this.'

A stolen breath calms me enough to work through the details. 'So you . . . you saw her after she walked off with Jack?'

He calms down marginally, and sinks into the couch again, as if readying himself to tell a tale, like a criminal admitting a confession. 'I was up the estuary, ran outta bait. I went back to my stuff to get my lures – heard her fighting with Jack up the beach. Something about her voice made me stick around. She seemed out of it. Real fucked up, you know how she got? The hyena laugh, the hysterical talking stuff?'

I can't believe what I'm hearing. All this time, all my nights wondering, and he was selfishly harbouring this knowledge. But I couldn't dwell on it. I am busy trying to rewrite the storyboard in my mind with these extra scenes in play.

'So you hear them fighting . . .'

His hands tremble. 'She ran away from him, screaming *get away from me, you never loved me*, all that. Jack was running after her, pleading with her to come back, that it wasn't safe to wander off on her own.'

'Then what?' I ask. This much seems as I'd imagined it had panned out.

'She stopped, let him catch up. I saw him grab her, try to calm her down. They sat for a bit – I watched from behind the dune. I wanted to check she was okay.'

'Like any good stalker would,' I mumble.

He ignores me and continues.

'Kate was all over him.'

My heart lurches at the thought – did Jack shag her after all?

331

'They had sex?'

'No, that's just it. He wasn't into it at all, kept pushing her away.'

'And Kate – what?'

'She went nuts again. Grabbed his neck, slapped him around, screaming abuse at him. Told him to go, just go.' He stops, as if he is reliving it all, like I'm sure he has done a thousand times in his head, sharing it with no one until now. 'Jack told her he was going for a leak, let her calm down – went over and took a slash on the dune, came back a minute later and she'd taken off. He ran down to the water, looked around, no sign of her on the beach either way. He panicked. He went up chest-deep thinking she had gone in swimming, couldn't see her anywhere.'

'Where was she?' My head is aching from all this.

'She was with me. When he went for a leak, she ran a few hundred metres then hid in the dune. I was right there watching. Told me to shut up, let him go, not tell him where she was. She needed space from him.'

'So you did?'

'So I did,' he says. 'I was infatuated with her. I would have cut off my left nut if she'd asked.'

This is no surprise. 'Then what?' I ask.

'We just talked. She told me everything, about Jack rejecting her. I calmed her down. She showed me the shells, asked for some line. She threaded them on, talking about you, about how she wished she were more like you.'

My throat swells. 'That still doesn't explain how . . .' I couldn't let that distract me from the end of this tale.

'She jumped me, she was all over me,' Ben says.

'She what, kissed you?'

'*And* some. She grabbed me, all for it.'

'And you let her? In the state she was in?' I look at him, disgusted by the male of my species.

'For a bit, yeah.'

I push him. 'You're sick.'

'C'mon, Frankie. It was my fucking fantasy. I was hardly going to not let her . . . Plus I figured Jack's the prick – dumping her arse when she's unstable, leaving her alone out there. Thought he was better than that. She was crushed. She loved him, man.'

I just shake my head. But part of me is somehow more at ease, as if what he is saying is authentic now. Credible.

'But, okay, I have some scruples. After a bit, I stopped her. It was too weird, her face was all slobbery and wet with tears, and I just couldn't get into it. I put the brakes on, told her to wait. Which set her off, a rejection all over again.'

'So, you what, calmed her down again by *having sex*?'

His head stoops over between his hands. 'She snapped, went out of her distraught mode, started talking all sexy. Asking me to do her, right then, right now. That she had to feel loved after he rejected her.'

Part of me feels disgust, the other part sympathy for his dilemma. 'So you just did what she asked.'

He stares blindly at the wall, his lip quivers.

'It wasn't the first time.'

My eyes are wide. 'You'd slept with her before?'

He keeps his head down, fails to look me in the eye, but his silence is my answer.

The baby was his. She'd cheated on Jack with my stupid brother. Repeatedly.

'When?' My head fills with rage. 'She was my best friend, you freak! She was with Jack!'

'You don't get it. She was after *me*. For months before. The last time was after your graduation. She knocked on my door in the middle of the night, her hair all curly, with panda eyes, telling me how Jack didn't love her.'

After she caught him dancing with me.

'That was you? You took her to Mount Coot tha? With the blanket under the stars?'

He shakes his head. 'Nah. I said I'd drive her home and . . . we did it in the back seat.'

My heart collapses. She had been rewriting her life, substituting characters, patching over the bits she wished were different. Making it seem special. Did that equate to being crazy? Or creatively optimistic? Was it wrong to love that part of her? Ben swallows hard. 'Once she came over and –'

'Stop! I don't want to hear it! Just tell me what happened that night.'

He exhales and wanders towards the couch. I thought of what he had lived with, all this time, but can't manage a shred of sympathy. 'After . . .' He sucks his bottom lip in. His chin dimples in the middle. 'She went into meltdown mode, screaming and shit. Saying it wasn't what she wanted, she wanted Jack, to get off her. Said she couldn't have a kid that was sick like her. That I was mad too. That the kid was mine. I mean, it was only a few weeks before and we did it *twice*, I figured it was crap, all bullshit. I tried to comfort her, talk to her, but she went all psycho, called me a rapist, flicked sand in my face and piss bolted. It was all bullshit, right? The kid thing? She didn't say anything to you, right?'

I thought about not telling him. But I did it anyway. Enough lies.

'It was no story, Ben. She was pregnant.'

'How d'ya know? I mean, well, she said that, but she didn't look it.' He scratches his head, paces like a caged lion in the cluttered lounge.

'The coroner confirmed it. Her mum told me.'

He lets out a yelp, like a dog with its tail jammed.

'You saying there was a kid? For real?' He leaps on the couch, draws his knees to his chest and rocks back and forth. His eyes fill with tears, but I have no sympathy for him now.

I realise now the reason Kate never told Jack about the baby on the beach that night. Why she didn't use it to keep him. It would only have been admitting to her infidelity. Jack knew the baby couldn't possibly be his. Was she trying to change that fact, that night on the beach?

I let him savour the news, but I'm impatient. I need to hear it all. It still didn't tell the whole story. I approach him on the couch, rest my fingers on his shoulder. 'Jess said she fell – it must have been from the headland. Focus, Ben, how does she get all the way to the point? Did you go to the lighthouse?'

He is silent, seems to be gathering his thoughts, composing himself. He stretches his face with his fingers, rubs his eyes dry.

'You said she started yelling, threw sand at you. Did you run after her?'

He glares at me, and a flash of the anger from before returns.

'I tried to get the fucking sand out of my eyes for starters, can't see shit. When I could finally focus, she was gone. Not a trace.'

'What about her shirt? The shirt we found. She ran off in her bikini?'

'I don't think she was in a state to give a rat's arse. She wanted away from me.'

'Okay, and that's it? You can't see her so you go back to your fishing?'

'No, that's only the start of it.' His eyes look fierce, full of fury.

'Ben, what are you saying?' My lungs fill with fear. 'What did you *do*?'

'She was accusing me of . . . forcing her. I panicked! Thought she'd go crying to you, telling you I'd raped her!' He turns away. 'I saw her shadow climbing the rocks at the point. She got up to the track, and started running, looking back, trying to keep ahead of me.'

'You chased her?'

'For ages – all the way up the point. I was wrecked, but I caught up. I grabbed her. She was hysterical. The moon went behind a cloud so it was pitch black, but I could see her tears all shiny on her face. I tried to talk sense into her, to not tell you what we did. She tried to pull her wrist free, called me a sex-crazed looney. I said . . .' His attention drifts, his eyes glaze over. He comes to, his chin dimpled. 'I said, you're the looney, you,' his face contorts, he lets out a sob, 'you fucking mad cow.' His eyes shut. 'It was so dark, the moon was behind a cloud or something, she was trying to pull away, but I was scared she'd tell you I made her do it. She wanted it. You have to believe me!'

I try to slow my rapid breaths. Every cell of my body wants to recoil from him. I hang my head forward, and wet drips from my eyes. He withdraws from me, curled up like a bud.

'Ben?'

The rocking abates. 'It was dark. We didn't realise we were right on the edge. I was grabbing her, she wrenched her wrist free, lost her balance and she slipped!' he declares, with sudden clarity. 'I heard her hit shrubs, ledges, but I couldn't see! It was just all ocean! And she was just gone!'

My jaw drops.

'I panicked, ran down to the rocks, stupidly thinking maybe she just hid, or she might have landed on a grassy ledge, just below the peak, that she'd survived. Then I saw her floating in the breakers below. This flash of white in the black sea.'

I feel the air being sucked from my lungs. The imagery shocks me like nothing I had imagined in all the night terrors. This is real.

'So, what, you were fighting on a ledge? She fell? She didn't even mean it?'

'It was an accident, Frankie, I swear!'

My mind seems to flip inside my head.

'You tried to get to her?' I ask, pleading for the right answer from him, dreading the wrong one.

'Of course I fucking tried!' he yells, curling up from his ball-like posture, like a rattlesnake about to hiss. 'I raced down to the beach, swam out for what seemed like hours, almost touched her – twice! She was right there! But it was so rough. The waves were loud, but I felt like I could *hear* her. I tried to tack back on an angle, only to find myself pulled further away.' And once again, the bravado, the anger, turns to shame and tears. He curls up over himself again, sobbing like a child. And I comfort him like a parent, the tears rolling on my cheeks, creeping down my neck as he cries in my arms. 'She was like a rag doll, being thrashed around. Then the white flashes stopped. She was gone. I could see you all like ants on the beach, running everywhere. When she was already gone.'

I think back to the night on my porch, when my mother told me that her body had washed up several kilometres away. I think of my brother, alone, weeping in his room, holding his tightly held secret inside.

'You never told anyone?'

He shakes his head.

'It was an accident, Frankie. You gotta believe me. She slipped!'

'You lied to the police? Told them nothing of it?' I ask. It suddenly made my omission, that she was pregnant, pale in comparison.

'They never asked,' he says, his eyes wide. 'I sat around, waiting – saw them talk to you and the guys, but they never asked me shit.' Ben, forgotten again.

I hold my miserable brother, as he lets the rage and guilt that has festered in him all these years spill over. And then it stops. As if he has purged it all, and finally felt the relief of the admission.

'Are you going to the cops? They'll lock me up, Frankie.'

I can't think about that right now. 'Is that the only reason you're telling me this? To save yourself?'

'You know the truth. You know Jack wasn't involved. They never even did it! Don't you see, Frankie? You can be together now. Isn't that enough?'

My brother, he has always seen the world in black and white: if you love someone, you be with them. It's that simple.

Ben scrubs his face with his hands. 'It was me that made her feel so . . . unhinged. It was me she was trying to escape. Do you know what that's like? Thinking I was the one responsible?'

Yeah, I kinda do.

He is still inconsolable, yet his misery seems to be laced with something else. Relief? I feel claustrophobic around him and have to leave. It is nearly daybreak now. He is still apologising as I get in my car to go. But sorry for what? Keeping this knowledge from me? Leading her to her death? Knocking her up, then depriving her of the last thread of confidence? Maybe all of it, maybe none of it. I don't care.

I am relieved when my car starts. The breaking sun peaks through the gaps in the Great Dividing Range as I take my necklace and my answers, and find my way back to the highway. As I reach Mount Coot tha I'm part furious, part empathetic. I alternate between both extremes. The poor bastard – living with it. The image of her, the knowledge, all alone. That he lost two people that night. Yet I'm angry. All the uncertainty, particularly in the days that followed – the peak of it. To think he could have saved us all the emotional turmoil, not to mention the practical – all the searches, the media plays. When he sat mute, knowing exactly where she was, letting our mother blame Jack. I cringe at his words to her. *Fucking mad cow.* It makes me sick. I stop on the emergency lane and spew in the gutter. Acid ponds in my mouth.

I think of the secrets he held so tightly all this time. The misery I felt those months after she died. All the while, he sat in his room, playing that 'Teenage Dirtbag' song on repeat, strumming his guitar, fucking up the same note over and over, for days, knowing exactly where she was.

Not saying a word.

实

The birds call and dogs sniff tree trunks on their morning walks as I arrive home to 83A Lovedale Road. I race out the back, eager to see Jack; to touch him, explain, tell him I'm sorry, make things right.

I don't have to wait long. His beautiful broad shoulders are slumped over a campfire in his yard. I want to run to him, but realise he is probably still shitty as hell.

'What rock did you crawl out of?' He sniffs, his eyes avoiding mine. 'Didn't you check your phone? I was worried.' He shakes his head. 'Thought you'd stalled it somewhere and had to hitchhike with a psychopath.'

'Sorry. I drove up to see Ben. Needed a bit of breathing space.'

He raises one eyebrow. 'So you visit a pot-head?'

I ease my backside into the empty froggy chair, hoping it is stronger than it looks. My fingers find Jack's thigh. He looks down at my hand, and up to meet my gaze. I see the muscles relax in his face.

'So, did you clear your head?' Jack asks. He puts down the tin of beans he was eating, the metal lid curled over the top. His eyes want answers.

'Well?'

'I'm sorry, Jack. I was wrong. About everything.' He looks at me with those big shale eyes, and I see relief. 'Ben told me he was the one who was with Kate. Not just that night either, so I'm guessing the baby was his.' Jack's head turns with a start to look at me. 'He said she wanted it, that she felt rejected when you didn't . . .'

Jack's face flushes with colour, his lips narrow.

'He was with her at the end.'

'As in, he actually *saw* her jump?' His head lurches back. 'Do you believe him? I mean, was he off his face?'

'She slipped.'

He looks deep in thought as I give a blow-by-blow of what Ben said happened, that her fear of him chased her to the point, that they tussled, that she skidded out from his grasp. That her life did not end by her choosing.

Jack sits motionless, his face in his hands, before suddenly jerking back to life once more. 'You don't think he pushed her? I mean, I can't imagine a kid was something he wanted at what, nineteen. Pretty convenient for him.' There's an edge to his voice.

I feel ashamed that I had wondered the same, that even for a second I considered that my own brother could have killed Kate. 'Ben can be an emotional basket case, but he's no murderer. I don't think he truly believed she was pregnant. When I confirmed it just now he was gutted.'

'He coulda just spent the last decade or so convincing himself of that, I mean, shouldn't we tell the cops? Jess has a right to know.'

'I'm not sure, Jack. It won't change things. He has tormented himself enough without dragging all this up again. There'd be no evidence at the scene, it would be likely to be just called accidental, and what will that achieve?'

I had kept quiet to protect Jack, knowing in my soul he had done no wrong. Couldn't I do the same for my brother? I thought of Jess, and wondered if it would be cruel to tell her, or cruel not to. 'You're right about Jess though. I feel as though she deserves to know her daughter didn't end her own life.' I wonder if she'll understand, or if that will bring more turmoil to our lives, opening old wounds. 'Jack, she told me Kate was adopted. That Kate's birth mum suffered from mental illness and ended her own life. She was convinced Kate would do the same. Makes me wonder how much that impacted her.'

Jack shakes his head. 'Still not right, Jess not knowing what Ben told you. I mean, why's he blabbing all this now?' He shakes his head.

'I think it had eaten away at him. Plus . . .'

His eyes are downcast, as he bites the corner of his lip. 'What?'

'He wants me to be happy. He wants me to move on.' My eyes tell him how I want to move on. He curls his hands around mine, and kisses it.

'I actually feel for the guy. Going through that. No wonder he is such a fuckup.'

'He's just on a different path,' I say.

'He was the smartest of all of us — and he threw it all away. Now I can see why. Living with this shit eating away at you. You Hudson kids are all basket cases. What do I keep telling ya? About your insides? They gotta match your outsides.'

Jack touches his fingers to my chin. 'At least it's over now, Fray. I was sure she committed suicide, the way she was at the end, even though I hated thinking of her wanting that. I know how it feels to want to escape it all, so at least we know now that she didn't choose it. At least now we can move past it.'

I hug him; the familiar smell of him calms me and I'm seventeen again, in that cloak room, in that first moment I knew I wanted him, and not just for Monopoly marathons. 'What do you mean – that you've felt like that?' I realise there's a huge part of his life I know nothing of.

Jack is quiet for a moment.

'I was pretty low when we first moved to Townsville after school. Spent a couple of years in hospitality, which is basically a life of working and drinking or both at once. Had my share of falling asleep drunk in the park, being woken up the next day by the automatic sprinklers. I couldn't shake the guilt. And the only thing I wanted I didn't deserve. It was like being kept from you was my punishment.'

'Survivor's guilt.'

He looks at me, his eyes full of emotion as we sit in silence and I yearn to uncover the chapters of his life that one night stole from me.

CHAPTER 29
Closing Time

I catch a bit of sleep and go to work in a daze. As I enjoy a break between cases, my boss skips over to tell me I have a visitor at reception. I see Jack's scruffy head hovering near the front desk. I grab my bag, and, ignoring her interrogative questions, tell her simply, 'I'm going to lunch.'

He is leaning shyly on the pole, a *Thomas the Tank Engine* lunchbox in his hands. He looks ruffled, his hair wet at the edges as if he just came from the shower, and there is a spring in his step that I haven't seen since the Oli news.

'Hey,' I say.

'I know you're busy but figured you had to eat,' he says as I guide him through the maze on my floor, away from prying eyes. I'm surprised he found me at all. 'Plus, I have some news.'

I put my hand on his arm. 'The paternity test? She let you?'

'Yeah, she was good about it actually. Guilt is a great motivator. Only took three days to get the results.' He looks straight at me. 'He's mine, Fray. No doubt. The tests confirmed it.'

I hug him, rubbing his back with my open palm. 'That's so great, Jack,' I whisper into his damp hair. I'm surprised to discover I'm genuinely happy for him, seeing how lost Jack was without such an integral role in his life – being a dad. His face softens, his eyes shine, not unlike an expectant father, excited about an impending birth of a much loved, anticipated child. 'They didn't even have to take his blood – just a swab test was enough.'

On the short walk to the riverbank, Jack speaks excitedly about the trip he's planned to Townsville next week, and that Sara had agreed to work out custodial arrangements. I wonder if that means Jack will return to Townsville too, and how I fit into the puzzle of co-parenting.

We sit on the riverbank, as he unwraps the most lavish lunch I've seen assembled from a kid's lunchbox. 'You bought me sushi?'

'Made it,' he says. I forgot this is the new Jack. 'And blueberry friands.'

'Friands? Aren't you allowed to call them muffins when you are a chef?' I ask. 'Do you have an actual chef's hat too?'

'No. They're for pussies. Just like insurance.'

I roll my eyes. 'Didn't you say you made a great Moussaka? Is that your signature dish, Mr Masterchef?'

He pauses, then smiles. 'Come to the restaurant tonight. I will cook something for you.'

I smile. 'What's wrong with my kitchen? It's recently refurbished, you know.'

'Yeah, about that, I guess I was a bit eager-to-impress, taking over your house without talking to you,' he smirks, 'but you still only have one saucepan, so you'll have to come into The Pig.'

'Do you think it's wise for me to turn up there – so early after . . .'

'Believe me, the staff will be cheering from the galleys – sick to death of my moaning about everything else. The movers got her shit today, the inspector finally allowed access to the house, so her fifty pairs of shoes are all boxed up for Townsville.'

So she really is gone. At least I know when I feel her eyes on me, they're imaginary. 'You must miss something about her though. It's always mixed feelings, after a break-up.'

'Crystal clear for me,' he says. 'It's always so quiet though, without Oli.' His Adam's apple jumps as he swallows. 'Keep expecting him to run over to my knees, stick his jam-covered hands all over my work pants. I used to get up him for that, but now I wish he was here to mess 'em up.'

'It must be difficult, Jack. I know how you were with him. But you see him next week, right? You know he's yours now. And if she's willing to start talking visitation already, that's a good sign.' He looks over at the river, throws a muffin crust to the magpie circling us.

I put my arm around him, as we sit in silence. I want to make out like teenagers at the bus stop, but something stops me. Nerves?

My beeper goes off.

'Meet me at work? Six? I will actually cook this time,' he says, as he walks me back to my office. 'I'll get someone to do the front.'

'Will it be like a date?' I ask, giddy. 'Because I have nothing to wear.'

'Then wear nothing,' he smiles.

实

As the sun retreats in the sky and the shadows grow long on the lawn, the nerves, the apprehension of where the night will lead Jack and me, begin. I change three times at home, before nervously meeting him at his restaurant, dressed in a black halter top with a low back and short skirt. I return to Duck Duck Pig with a different view on life and Jack, but the eclectic style of the place still impresses me. The rustic bird cages hanging from the ceiling, the London phone booth in the corner.

Yet my dalliance in the restaurant is short-lived, as a waiter leads me to the fire escape and closes the door behind him. I clutch my purse tightly. I'm on a rooftop. Have we opened the wrong door? Then I see Jack. He is waiting with a smile. I feel like I'm on some reality TV show, and they've just revealed my prize.

A camping lantern is shoved in the centre of a table fashioned from an old packing box and two empty beer kegs. A panoramic view of the Brisbane skyline distracts me from him, but in a moment my eyes click with his once more. His iPhone is plugged into a portable speaker on the ledge. Powderfinger lyrics twang through the plastic domes, warming my soul.

Jack has made scallops on garlic mash with a saffron sauce, followed by a divinely crunchy pork-belly with asparagus and fennel. 'You said you had nothing to wear,' he smiles, brushing the flesh of his palm down my bare back. 'I like.' I blush like a schoolgirl.

As we finish our meal, the small talk turns to reminiscing.

'It's weird, thinking back,' Jack starts, taking my hand as we sit at the makeshift table. 'The pieces of you I have kept in my head from when we were kids.' He smiles and his face lights up. He looks radiant, handsome. 'The peeks over the seat when you used to change in the back on the way home from T-ball.' He draws invisible circles on my arm with his pointer finger. 'Putting sunscreen on your shoulders, hoping you didn't see I had a hard-on.'

I lean over and poke him in the ribs.

'You know what I used to like best though?'

'You are going to tell me anyway . . .'

'When I'd be playing Atari with Ben and you would scurry from the shower to your room in nothing but a towel – those little towels. You always had the front pulled up so high – to cover all this.' He gestures to my boobs. 'Which meant that most of your back was exposed.'

I can't believe he remembers these details, all this time. Like he is giving me a commentary on my own life, from a different camera angle.

'You have such a long slender back, and it was shiny and wet.' He feathers the side of his hand down the length of it. 'I thought you were so elegant. That you were always too good for the likes of me, but that doesn't scare me anymore. Besides, I did give you a decade or so to find someone better, and all you came up with was that pretty-looking Merc-driving lawyer.' He winks.

I shake my head. 'I always thought you were too cool for the likes of me,' I say, sliding my finger down the bridge of his nose.

'I think class trumps cool,' his eyebrows jump, 'and you always had that in spades.'

We look out to the river, the lights dancing on its mirror surface, the cool breeze cutting the humid heat. Jack's distinct grey eyes are warm, his shoulder rubs against mine and I think, this is what they call happiness.

实

Between the main and dessert, Jack ducks back and forth, attending to the usual issues – an absent waiter or lack of a certain ingredient on the menu – making the evening a little disjointed. At one stage a possum scurries across the ledge, at another, he has the dish boy visit to keep me company with terrible knock-knock jokes, in an attempt to reduce his guilt for his comings and goings. I feel like an extra in a scene from *Fawlty Towers*, waiting for the rat to crawl out from a crate. I'm just about to find him to thank him and head home, when he appears again, ready to go, kissing my cheek as I grab my bag.

It is unspoken, the fact that he is going home with me. We walk to the car in complete silence. The nerves set in. I should have had more wine.

The tension between us in the car is bittersweet. I start to dread – but hope – for the red lights – as he turns to me at each stop, shoots me a heated stare, a kiss. His hand wanders up from my knee to my inner thigh.

'I stopped in on Jess on the way home from work. I was sick of the lies. I told her everything. About Ben, all of it.'

'On your own?' Jack frowns.

'You're forgetting I do this shit for a living.'

'Yeah, but not when you're personally involved. How'd she take it? Did you warn Ben?'

'She was shocked for a long time, then angry, then, I honestly think she was relieved. It's hard to know how she'll process it all in time, but I doubt she'll push it further. I'm glad I told her. I think I needed it swept away for good.'

'I wasn't trying to say you couldn't manage it on your own. It's amazing, what you do, how much your job helps people.'

'I know.' As the words leave my lips I realise, I *have* succeeded in helping to fix some of the fractured lives in this world, including my own. I squeeze his hand over the centre console. 'But I'm thinking of quitting my job,' I say. 'I think I want to teach.'

He raises his eyebrows. His face softens and he smiles. 'Yeah? You'd be great at it. You know what else? I'm thinking of demolishing the rest of my house, and taking out that ugly fence while I'm at it. When Oli comes to stay for holidays he can use the block as a cricket pitch. Think Bear will like the extra space?'

'Yeah.' I smile, my heart warming. 'Not sure Sara will like that idea though.'

'Why? She took the house, I'll keep the land. Fair division of property. Maybe we can fix up your place instead.' He arches one eyebrow. 'With your permission this time of course.'

I roll my eyes and smile.

We pull up, walk hand in hand to my little cottage – the place that started it all. His breath is hot on my neck, his arms around my waist as I struggle with the key.

I think back to the first time I walked this cobbled front path – like a leaf floating on a breeze – and how different I feel now. My house appears much the same – only a little better cosmetically – a great kitchen, a coat of paint. But the foundations are strong now. The rotted stumps replaced by solid concrete – a firm base on which to grow.

A lot like me.

I think of how easily this could have passed us by. That chance brought us together. Just like the breeze that blew me to this house. I'd spent most of adult life trying to control things, feeling responsible for Kate's death. But now I know serendipity took Kate from me, just like it brought Jack back. Both events shaped my life but were completely outside my control.

'Come with me.' He takes my hand as we approach the front door and leads me out the side. I am baffled, but curious to see what he's up to. My anxiousness causes me to imagine he's suddenly changed his mind about me, about all of this. A ball of dread bounces in my stomach.

He walks me down the stairs, and leads me out to the side yard. To the scene that was the start of us, mark two. That day when we were painting, and I gave him the three-second stare. I had left the rest of that wall naked after that. It reminded me too much of him, of that moment that we crossed a line. I had feared, and hoped, that line would be hurdled again one day. And here we are.

We stand in the easement in the ink-black night air. 'Close your eyes and don't open them till I say,' he orders like a headmaster, and spins me round.

'Okay . . .' Has he finished the wall for me? Is that the surprise?

I hear him run inside, bang about, and return a couple of minutes later. I am dying to peek.

'Okay. You can open them,' he says, breathless.

The first thing I notice is the floodlight. It is shining down on the side wall of my house. The trestles that were stacked up last time I checked are now assembled.

Then I see it.

It has been slapped on in thick blue paint over my sanded bare weatherboards.

I love you, Fray.

He sees a smile work its way through my shock. Jack picks me up, spinning me round till I'm dizzy.

'It's always been you, Fray,' he whispers into my hair.

My eyes dare a fleeting look into his. I am too overcome with joy to look for long. I lace my fingers around his neck. His hands pull me so close I can hardly breathe. His lips meet mine. All I can hear is the inhaling breaths, all I can feel is a crushing urge to know every new part of him. As the heat from him ripples through me, I feel an overwhelming sense that we are a team now. Jack and me against the world once more.

I gently pull away, exhale, and try to breathe, to still my pulse. As his forehead rests on mine, a smile sneaks on his lips. I glance over at the painted message. I look back to him, his pupils wide with happiness, and feel a surge of relief, that finally we are in sync.

I realise we are under floodlights, and we walk inside.

I feel an overwhelming lightness. Like my life can start now. Everything is in place.

I stand in the kitchen, wondering how to broach the next step, when Jack gestures to the shower. 'Give me five . . . don't go anywhere,' he winks.

I hear his work shoes being removed, the shower run. I use this time to freshen up, nervously flicking through my underwear drawer in a panic, clawing to the back, to the least used fancy stuff.

And I wait. My mind races, as my heart grows loud in my chest.

Then I hear the door creak open, see his shadow on the wall, hear his steps towards the bed.

I hold my breath, close my eyes as he slips into the sheets beside me. Just the sight of him makes me tingle. He is damp and warm.

'I just left a clueless fifteen-year-old in charge of my restaurant to go home with you, so don't even think of being asleep,' he whispers in my ear. He smells of soap, his breath sending quivers down my arm. 'You okay?' he asks. I can see his outline in the darkness, the shimmer of his eyes gazing at me.

I nod, overcome with shyness.

Jack is hesitant at first, then kisses me. The warmth of his lips washes over me, but my mind can't rest. All I keep thinking is – Jack is kissing me! Flashes of him zoom past in my head; Jack pulling faces on the window of our back seat, running naked in our sprinkler with his undies on his head, his hair combed sideways like an altar boy on the first day of school. A laugh escapes my lips.

'Something funny?' he asks. 'You're gonna give me the yips – I'm already feeling the pressure here.'

'Sorry. Nope,' I say, resuming my position. I try to relax, yet as I attempt to sink into it, the build-up to this moment, the tension of the months that led him back to me, mixing with the childhood memories – all just seem overwhelming, and I explode in laughter again.

Jack pulls away, lying his head back flat on the pillow beside me. He stares up at the ceiling, his forearm over his eyes 'Are you quite right?' The exasperation leaks out from the sides.

This is unforgivable – I have to restrain myself! I try thinking of road kill – anything to make the bubbles of laughter subside.

'I am sorry!' I repeat. 'I want this. I do! It's just surreal – I mean, *Jack Shaw is kissing me!*' I say in disbelief, as I feel the surge of laughter rise through me. I see the hurt on his face and shove it back. 'It's just dreamlike, being with you, like this, I mean, when we were kids you were like —'

'Nuh-uh. Don't start with the brother shit!' he says sternly. He sits up, grazing the touch lamp on the bedside table. Its light fills the room. I can see the emotion in his face now, his eyes filled with frustration and steely determination. 'Is that really how you see me? Right now? We're fucked if you do, Fray. Because I sure as hell don't think of you like that.'

I can feel the depth of his humiliation, and sense I need an equally powerful counter-move to redeem myself, and the night.

I slink over to his side of the bed, where his back leans on my bedhead. My bare thighs straddle him, my legs around his waist, my eyes locked on his.

'No, Jack. I don't see you like that. Perhaps I never have.'

I muster my courage. My fingers curl around the buttons securing my black bustier. I start with the top two, spilling out as I unbutton each one, all with my eyes never leaving his. My legs circumnavigate his waist, my heels dig into the small of his back.

I go on, slowly unfastening each button. Yet before my fingers can journey down to my navel, Jack takes one hand on each side, and rips the remainder free. He slides the straps off my shoulders, as he buries his face into all of me. In an instant, his lips cover my nipple, his hands plunge my breasts together. Jack's face dives deeper, as he drowns in the waves of my chest.

There is no laughter now.

We can finish what we started.

In a fumble of limbs, he has rolled me down, as the weight of him sucks the air from my lungs, his shoulders overbearing. He slips his underwear to his feet expertly with the hook of a single toe, then guides mine over my thighs, my knees, my ankles. My hands search all of him, the ripples of his chest, the softness of his inner thigh.

Until there is no space, nothing between us but heat.

No excuses. No guilt. No Kate.

Just us.

实

In the stolen hour between midnight and dawn, I watch him sleep with a love not unlike that of a child with a cherished new toy. I am filled with the hope for a lifetime of nights like this, yet also saddened that the journey to them had been stolen so many years before. But I am grateful for even just this perfect moment.

As I trace the folds of his ear with my fingertip, unable to restrain myself from him any longer, he stirs as I had secretly hoped. His arms find a tighter grip on me, as we lie wrapped in a tangle of limbs and twisted linen. I modestly pull the sheet over me, and tuck a strand of hair behind my ear as he surveys me from this new perspective.

I wedge my neck under his shoulder, resting my head on his chest. I wonder how I would have reacted, back then, to the knowledge I would one day be with Jack. That half my life later, we would be hit with this perfect blend of friendship and lust. I thought of all the movies I had sat through in my teens, glancing to the next row of seats at Jack tongue-kissing the latest in a line of blondes. And here I was, sporting a beard rash from my own session with Jack Shaw.

The sleeping giant awakes and nuzzles into me.

'Good morning.' I say, trying to contain a smile.

He looks straight into my eyes and I hold his gaze. 'You know what I'm gonna do to you first, Fray?'

I am half turned on, half running scared.

'What's that?' I whisper.

A slow grin creeps across his lips. 'I'm gonna teach you how to cook.'

Acknowledgements

They say it takes a village to raise a child, and I think the same can be said for writing a book.

Firstly, thank you, the reader (you must have made it to the end if you are reading this!) for helping Frankie and Jack's story be heard. I wrote *Losing Kate* because I enjoy writing. It is just a bonus to have others connect with my imaginary friends.

Thank you to the fabulous team at Random House Australia (and to Lex Hirst and Beverley Cousins particularly) for taking a chance on a slush-pile unknown, and fulfilling my lifelong dream in the process. I feel privileged to have shared this fantastic journey with you.

To my ever-patient husband Jamie for believing in me; for pretending to listen to my incessant plot rehashes; for taking the reins with our boys when I couldn't, and for the gift of one pink laptop that showed me you believed I could.

To my BFF Leanne Keane, for her incurable selflessness and friendship (and subtly waving the Queensland Writers Centre pamphlet under my nose). That was the step that made me think seriously about writing.

To the fabulous Helen Dunham Enisuoh, for seeing the writer in me since we were 12.

To Sophie Smith, for keeping me sane as we share stories on raising boys (and unknowingly feeding me plot ideas).

To the fabulous Lily Malone (RWA critical partner) and Sandy Curtis (QWC mentor) for their expert advice and encouragement.

To my wider circle of friends, my brother Brendan (who gets the most-excited-to-hear-my-book-deal-news award) and the rest of my ever-growing supportive family.

To my own sticky brood of boys, Finn, Nate and Josh, (the original Small, Medium and Large) for their endless spirit – I love you to the moon and back.

Last but not least, I thank my wonderful parents, Jean and Ray, for their unwavering support, instilling my love of words and belief in myself. All that I am is because of you.